Praise for *Dark Wi...*

Recipient of **2017 BUY IT N(...**
Orange County Chapter Roma...

"*Dark Wine at Midnight* is an innovative paranormal adventure that is dangerous, sexy, and gripping! Readers will be clamoring for more!"
~*InD'tale Magazine*

"*Dark Wine at Midnight* is overwhelmingly seductive with an aura of mystery and suspense. Enticing and surreptitious, [it] leaves readers completely speechless at the twists and turns Barwin takes us on this urban fantasy journey... For those who really enjoy romantic novels with a mix of sultry, seductive scenes—you really should read this. For those who don't, I would still give it a chance! Mystery, thriller, action...these all await for your entertainment in Barwin's *Dark Wine at Midnight*!"
~*Bookmark Your Thoughts Book Review Blog*

"A smoldering Paranormal Romance... Steadfastly smart and literate with a finely crafted narrative and captivatingly paced, Barwin is a confident author who instinctively understands what fans of the genre demand and she gives it to them in spades."
~*BookViral Book Reviews*

"*Dark Wine at Midnight* fulfilled all my hopes for a story that would keep me engaged, and it did that with aplomb and sparkles. Barwin is a talented writer who tops out on all the markers that identify really good writing."
~*Sharon Bonin-Pratt's Ink Flare*

Praise for *Dark Wine at Sunrise*

Awarded **2018 BEST TITLE** by Orange County Chapter
Romance Writers of America

Recipient of a **Crowned Heart** from *InD'tale Magazine*

2019 RONE Award Nominee for Paranormal (Long Format)

"A paranormal romance worthy of the genre. Sensual, sophisticated and sinfully addictive!"
~*InD'tale Magazine*

"An intoxicating novel, packed full of thrills and spills. I loved it!"

~*A Wishing Shelf Book Review*

"A clever and addictive Paranormal Romance. Barwin has delivered a novel with...action, intrigue and romantic tension...a genuine page-turner and hard to put down. *Dark Wine at Sunrise* is recommended without reservation."

~*BookViral Book Reviews*

"Breathtakingly seductive and intensely nerve-wracking, *Dark Wine at Sunrise* is a tremendous addition to the Hill Vampire series."

~*Bookmark Your Thoughts Book Review*

"You'd better get comfy because you won't want to stop once you begin reading Jenna Barwin's *Dark Wine at Sunrise*. Barwin writes with passion and a masterful hand at physical and visual description. She manages a complex plot, believable characters (of all ilk), and credible political underpinnings, creating intrigue within the story. Her world-building is exotic, the personalities are larger than life, but the experiences are grounded in the common human endeavors we all recognize. We want to be seen for who we are, we want fair opportunities, we want to be loved."

~*Sharon Bonin-Pratt's Ink Flare*

Praise for *Dark Wine at Dusk*

Recipient of a **Crowned Heart** from *InD'tale Magazine*

2020 RONE Award Nominee for Paranormal (Long Format)

"A gripping paranormal romance that will leave readers aching for more. Passionate, breathtaking and beautifully written."

~*InD'tale Magazine*

"The chemistry between Henry and Cerissa will keep you turning the page. Powerfully written and totally unputdownable!"

~*A Wishing Shelf Book Review*

"If you enjoyed the first two books in this series, you're going to love this one… *Dark Wine at Dusk* picks up with the continuing mysterious murders of the residents of Sierra Escondida. [Cerissa's and Henry's] passionate romance alights everywhere throughout his mansion. One of the most inventive love romps I've ever read is the hide-and-seek game they play in his vineyard…I won't tell more as story spoilers are not in my toolbox, but the tension and shock of the mounting climax will keep you riveted."

~Sharon Bonin-Pratt's Ink Flare

Praise for *Dark Wine at Death*

Recipient of a **Crowned Heart** from *InD'tale Magazine*

Awarded the **Crème de la Cover** by *InD'tale Magazine*

2021 RONE Award Nominee for Paranormal (Long Format)

5 Stars! "To say that Jenna Barwin has knocked it out of the park with this novel is an understatement. Tempting, spellbinding and absolutely enchanting!"

~*InD'tale Magazine*

5 Stars! "If you enjoy sexy vampire thrillers, the sort of story that keeps you guessing, a story populated with well-constructed characters, then this is for you. The best word to describe this book—and all of the books in the set is—SIZZLING!"

~*A Wishing Shelf Book Review*

Praise for *Dark Wine at the Circus*

"Meet your new guilty pleasure. Deliciously entrancing from start to finish."

~*InD'tale Magazine*

"Sultry, romantic, and always with a strong element of danger, this is a gripping installment in this series of paranormal romance novels. [*Dark Wine at the Circus*] is cleverly plotted, well-written, and is spot on in terms of balancing character development and strong pacing. Highly recommended."

~*A Wishing Shelf Book Review*

"*Dark Wine at the Circus* pumped my heart with its old-fashioned death-defying thrills and its contemporary social conscience about animals forced to perform.

~ *Sharon Bonin-Pratt's Ink Flare*

Praise for *Dark Wine at Disaster*

"Engaging and addicting, *Dark Wine at Disaster* is an entertaining addition to the Hill Vampire series!"

~*InD'tale Magazine*

"A character-led, vampire saga with a cleverly crafted and compelling plot. [It has] plenty of danger and a good dollop of sexually-charged romance."

~*A Wishing Shelf Book Review*

"Much anticipated, *Dark Wine at Disaster* hooked me from the first page, plunging deep into a legendary culture struggling to survive at the edge of peril. Order dinner delivery - you won't have time to cook."

~ *Sharon Bonin-Pratt's Ink Flare*

Also by Jenna Barwin

The Hill Vampire Series

Dark Wine at the Grave (Book 7)

Dark Wine at Disaster (Book 6)

Dark Wine at the Circus (Book 5)

Dark Wine at Death (Book 4)

Dark Wine at Dusk (Book 3)

Dark Wine at Sunrise (Book 2)

Dark Wine at Midnight (Book 1)

DARK WINE AT DISASTER

A Hill Vampire Novel
Book 6

Jenna Barwin

Hidden Depths Publishing

Dark Wine at Disaster by Jenna Barwin
Copyright © 2021 Jenna Barwin. All rights reserved.

This book or any portion of it may not be reproduced in any form or by any means, or used in any manner whatsoever, without the express written permission of the publisher or author except for the use of brief quotations in a book review.

This is a work of fiction. Names, characters, businesses, public entities, products, places, events and incidents are either the products of the author's imagination or used in a fictitious manner. Any resemblance to actual persons, living or dead, businesses, public entities, locales, or actual events is purely coincidental. Any trademarks, service marks, product names, or named features are assumed to be the property of their respective owners, and are used only for reference. Opinions of the characters are not necessarily those of the author.

Printed in the United States of America
First printing & ebook edition, 2021

Hidden Depths Publishing
Dana Point, California
www.hiddendepthspublishing.com

Cover design: Covers by Christian (Christian Bentulan)
Images used under license from Shutterstock.com and Depositphotos.com
Cover art is for illustrative purposes only and any person depicted in the cover is a model.

Interior Design by Author E.M.S.

Editing team: Katrina Diaz-Arnold, Refine Editing, LLC; Trenda K. Lundin, It's Your Story Content Editing; Arran McNicol, Editing 720.

Library of Congress Control Number: 2021918527

ISBN 978-1-952755-06-4

1) Paranormal Romance 2) Urban Fantasy Romance 3) Vampire Romance 4) Vampire Mystery 5) Vampire Suspense 6) Paranormal Romantic Suspense 7) Romantic Fantasy

Version 1.0

Join Jenna Barwin's VIP Readers

Want to know about new releases, and receive special announcements, exclusive excerpts, and other FREE fun stuff? Join Jenna's VIP Readers and receive Jenna Barwin's newsletter by subscribing online at: https://jennabarwin.com/jenna-barwins-newsletter

You can also find Jenna Barwin at:

Facebook: https://www.facebook.com/jennabarwin/

Instagram: JennaBarwin https://www.instagram.com/jennabarwin/

BookBub: https://www.bookbub.com/profile/jenna-barwin

Email: https://jennabarwin.com/contact

DARK WINE AT DISASTER

Chapter 1
Celebrations

VASQUEZ MÜLLER WINERY—SATURDAY, TWO WEEKS AFTER THE CIRCUS LEFT TOWN

A vampire, his black hair streaked with cherry-red dye, stepped up to the microphone. "Please join me in welcoming for their first dance: Señor Enrique Vasquez and Dr. Cerissa Patel."

Cerissa's pulse jolted into overdrive. The master of ceremonies' announcement made her engagement feel tangible—the one-year clock was now ticking and there was no turning back.

Excitement shot through her, and in her rush to get to the dance floor, she tripped over her own feet.

Henry gracefully caught her around the waist before she could fall onto the elegant rose-patterned carpet. Glancing over her shoulder, she exchanged smiles with him, the grin stretching her face. His bourbon-brown eyes flashed in response. She regained her footing and walked by his side to the dance floor as the crowd applauded.

The long, slinky dress she'd chosen for the engagement party—with matching high-heeled sandals—meant eager steps risked a full face plant. The stretch satin fabric was a soft ecru, the color of her feathers when in Lux form, and the dress hugged her curves.

For the wedding, she'd wear traditional attire from her birthplace, the dress she'd fantasized about since she was a small girl: a red sari with gold trim.

So for tonight's party, she chose a white dress, a nod to the more traditional color worn by brides in America. She wanted to make her fiancé, Henry—*err*, Enrique—happy.

Henry Bautista had asked her to marry him, but his younger alter ego, Enrique Vasquez, would marry her. Every fifty years or so, vampires had to switch out identities to maintain the masquerade of being mortal. The transition to his new identity had barely begun, and she worked hard to remember the change, occasionally forgetting to call him by his new name.

Practically speaking, it meant when they were out in public among uninitiated mortals and he looked like his usual, younger self, she called him Enrique.

When his black hair was shot with gray, she called him Henry.

And when she felt tired of maintaining the illusion, he was Quique to her, and only her.

The dress she wore was one of many things they'd agreed upon as they planned the party to celebrate the start of their one-year engagement. Each of them brought a unique life experience to the relationship, and they wanted those perspectives equally represented. She suspected this was the first of many such negotiations to come as they wove their lives together.

But they didn't plan the party alone. Karen Turner, both her bestie and the winery's marketing director, took their ideas and ran with them. The event room at the Vasquez Müller Winery was beautifully decorated with white and pale pink rose garlands along the walls, complementary bouquets on the linen-covered tables, soft candlelight, and enough food to feed a small town, which only made sense, given everyone from the vampire community of Sierra Escondida was invited.

Cerissa let out an excited breath, slowing her steps. After almost tripping, her overactive brain couldn't help but ask:

What else will go wrong?

The thought clung to her like a bad omen. With everything that had happened in the past few months, she wasn't surprised the question popped into her mind.

She gave a quick shake of her head to dislodge the unwelcome thought and let the happiness of the moment wash over her.

At Henry's request, the band played a slow love song. The same song she and Henry had swayed to the very first time they danced together.

She'd put her foot down during negotiations when it came to dancing a salsa. The way Henry led, his salsa was foreplay—or outright sex. It was one thing to dance like that on a crowded club dance floor when surrounded by strangers who shielded them from view. To dance like that in front of her friends from the Hill when they were the only couple on the dance floor...she refused. She was here to celebrate their engagement, not put on a titillating show for everyone.

Besides, her dress was so tight, she'd never be able to bend in all the required ways necessary to keep up with *his* salsa.

Stopping at the center of the ballroom, she turned to face Henry. His excitement threaded through her mind, the Lux crystal in his arm conveying his emotions. He looked so handsome in a classic black tuxedo with his long hair held back with a satin ribbon, replacing the more casual leather string he usually wore. When he took her hand and slipped an arm around her, the electricity flowed sharper between them.

A brief image flashed through her mind: her angel-like wings wrapped around him. Technically, he was under her wings—her protection—because of the crystal. And since he hadn't worn the tungsten bracelet that muted the crystal's communication, she felt his emotions with full force, not the usually subdued day-to-day experience.

She loved being connected to him that deeply.

Gazing into his dark eyes, she shivered with delight. His perfect lips mouthed, "I love you," and she dipped her head, heat rising to her cheeks, as his words ignited a fire lower down.

"I love you too," she whispered back.

The slow dance was over way too fast. As agreed in advance, when the song ended, they moved from the dance floor to the head table. Henry held out her chair for her, and she gracefully slipped onto it.

Chris Atherton, the rock band's lead singer and tonight's master of ceremonies, leaned into the microphone. "And now, join me in welcoming our second engaged couple, Marcus Collings and Nicholas Martin."

Cerissa applauded enthusiastically for her friends. Seniority determined the order of the event—Marcus and Nicholas danced second because they became engaged a few weeks after she and Henry did.

The two men had decided to wear coordinating suits and reserve the tuxes for their wedding. Marcus wore a charcoal-gray two-piece, and Nicholas wore a black suit in the same cut. Each wore the same black satin necktie and white rose boutonniere. Nicholas had left his signature black-framed glasses at home, opting for contact lenses.

They danced a cha-cha that would win them first place on *Dancing with the Stars*.

Cerissa took a sip of ice water—champagne would be poured shortly—and reached for Henry's hand, a cloud of happiness enveloping her.

Sitting next to Henry's champagne glass was an iced tumbler, covered with a lid. She'd conspired with Karen, and her bestie had snuck the glass onto the table when the uninitiated waiters weren't looking.

Cerissa leaned in close. "A little dark wine for your enjoyment, courtesy Biologics Research Lab."

Her lab had provided blood from nonsentient clones for the party, drawing it after providing the clones with vodka via their feeding tubes. The pouches were labeled based on the blood alcohol content, BAC options of 0.15, 0.20, and, for those who were daring enough, 0.25.

For some reason she had yet to figure out, alcohol directly ingested by a vampire would be processed quickly and neutralized. But if it was first digested by a mortal body, the effect lasted longer.

It was the only way a vampire could get drunk—by feeding on an inebriated person.

She watched Henry unscrew the lid and take a sip of his. "That is strong."

She smirked. Knowing Karen, he had the 0.25 version. "After Marcus and Nicholas finish their dance, I can get you something weaker if you prefer."

He laughed and kissed her cheek. "No, I'll nurse this for a while."

Scattered on the table near the short centerpiece—a bouquet of pale roses in a square glass vase—lay dark chocolate hearts wrapped in pink foil. She reached for one, unfolded the bright, shiny wrapper, and nipped it into her mouth. Her tongue wrapped around the rich, sweet goodness, and she let the candy melt slowly as she watched the party progress.

On the dance floor, Nicholas glowed, and his blunt-cut chin-length hair framed his square jaw with umber-colored strands. Marcus had his slightly longer dishwater-blonde hair combed back, his mustache fashionably trimmed, and his pale blue eyes focused solely on his mate. After a rocky period in their relationship, Cerissa was relieved to see the men happy together.

When they finished their dance, Marcus and Nicholas joined the head table, and Chris announced that the buffet line and dance floor were both open.

Cerissa got halfway through a plate of appetizers when the younger mates dragged her and Nicholas to their feet. The band started a techno synth song, and everyone danced together in groups of fives and sixes, each bouncing in their own freestyle moves.

The Hill tradition was that anyone could dance with anyone else at the engagement party. At the wedding reception, the married couple were restricted to dancing only with one another.

Vampires wrote the book on being possessive.

When the song changed to a slower dance, Cerissa gestured to Henry to join her—and then she noticed Ari making a beeline for Nicholas. Out of the corner of her eye, she saw Marcus stiffen and then rise to his feet at the head table.

Whatever Ari had in mind wouldn't end well. *He* might think it harmless, but Ari had no filter, and after Ari's affair with Marcus, she simply didn't trust him to behave.

Cerissa rushed to intercept him as fast as her clicking heels and restrictive dress would allow, determined to head off her cousin before he reached Nicholas.

But Gaea was faster.

The brown-haired beauty rivaled Mae West for glamour and style, yet her demeanor could cause an army general to cower. Gaea strode across the dance floor and stopped Ari in his tracks. "Young man, you have been neglectful. You promised me a dance."

Ari blushed, the first time Cerissa had ever seen him do that. "I was just on my way to congratulate—"

"On the dance floor?"

"I was going to ask—"

"No, you were not." Gaea stuck her hands to her ample hips. "If you want to dance, I'm you're only option."

"But—"

"Those are the rules tonight, dear boy."

Marcus came to a halt at Gaea's words. He had made his way to the dance floor and, from the way he glared, was intent on confronting Ari. Henry smoothly moved in to invite Marcus to dance. There was a brief pause as they resolved who would lead before the two men settled into a slow foxtrot.

Having stopped a few feet from Nicholas, Cerissa stepped into his arms without missing a beat, falling into the rhythm of the song, while keeping an eye on the interaction between Ari and Gaea. No one observing them would guess that a disaster had just been avoided.

"I'm sorry about that," she whispered. "But we couldn't leave Ari off the guest list."

Nicholas gave a relaxed shrug. "I know, I know. I saw his name on one of the invitations. He's your family. I didn't say anything."

"Please forget him and enjoy the night."

Nicholas sighed heavily. "Count on it."

Cerissa had sat Ari at the singles table between Gaea and Father Matt. The last thing she needed was her cousin messing up the party by saying something well-meaning but inappropriate, so she'd tasked Gaea with keeping him under control.

Having a duty to perform seemed to pull Gaea out of her funk. The vampire matron had blamed herself for Yacov's death ever since she learned her ex-boyfriend, Dylan, had delivered the poison that killed the revered vampire. Henry had tried, but no amount of talking could convince Gaea it wasn't her fault.

Keeping an eye on Ari had seemed to spark something in Gaea. The idea of stopping a mortal from misbehaving had been an effective tonic.

It didn't take a psychologist to figure it out.

"Well?" Gaea asked, standing on the dance floor and waiting for Ari to make up his mind.

Ari bowed and then opened his arms to the voluptuous vampire. "I'm all yours, lovely lady."

Cerissa rolled her eyes. The council had granted a blanket dispensation for tonight—any hookups at the engagement party wouldn't violate the "no dating" rule, the rule that prohibited vampires from dating unmated mortals within the Hill's walls. She wasn't sure she wanted Ari hooking up with Gaea, but if Ari was able to break through Gaea's isolation and self-loathing, she'd cheer him on.

"May I cut in?" Henry asked.

Cerissa gave Nicholas a cheek kiss, and then stepped into Henry's arms.

"Relax," Henry whispered into her ear, as they fell into a slow, steady rhythm.

She tried. Like she did with the chocolate heart, she wanted to savor the evening, letting all the fun and joy melt inside her, until the sweet goodness filled her up.

But even with Ari's attempt to stir up mischief thwarted, the question once again rose its thorny head: *What will go wrong next?*

Chapter 2

Never Off-Duty

Vasquez Müller Winery—Moments later

Tigisi "Tig" Anderson, the chief of police for Sierra Escondida, rarely let her hair down in public. To be an effective leader, she maintained a no-nonsense image as a stern commander who took bullshit from no one. She fostered that persona for two reasons: to ensure the town council didn't interfere with how she ran her department, and so that SEPD officers followed her orders to the letter—or faced her wrath.

In her mind, being silly wasn't allowed unless she was home alone with her mortal mate. Jayden Johnson served as an excellent second-in-command on the police force, but in private, he was funny as hell and made it his goal in life to make her smile.

At his request, she danced with him. She liked swaying to slow music in his arms. But her favorites were the line dances. They reminded her of her life among the Maasai, in Kenya, Africa, where she'd spent the first thirty-plus years of her mortal life. Women of her tribe would dance together, jumping in place, in circles. It was their way.

That was over four hundred years ago.

The country-music line dances of today caught the flavor of the Maasai dances, if not the form.

She twined her fingers around Jayden's hand as they strolled back to their table, the high heels feeling strange to walk in. She rarely wore them, much preferring her tactical boots. She leaned over to him and said, "They opened the buffet. Why don't you go ahead now before the line gets too long? We can dance later."

He pulled out her chair, and once she was seated and scooted up to the table, he kissed her. "All right, beautiful. I'll see you in a few minutes."

She stayed at the round table, alone, as most everyone was either dancing or dishing up food. Even off-duty, she couldn't stop herself from constantly scanning the room, and so far, the most threatening thing to happen was when her computer consultant nearly approached one of the engaged mates.

She hadn't intervened because that wasn't her job. If Ari wanted to make a fool of himself, let him. Fortunately, Gaea had neatly solved the problem.

A few minutes later, Jayden placed a tall glass in front of her. It contained red liquid and a celery stick.

"What's this?"

Jayden set his overbrimming plate at his place and relaxed into his seat. "A Bloody Mary. BAC of 0.15, so not too bad."

Indeed, the weakest of the three blends. Cerissa had tipped her off, which was why Tig had insisted that attendees either use a limo service or ride the party bus. There would be no drunk driving on the Hill.

Gaea's strange boarder, Seaton, had been roped into being the bus driver. He had no interest in parties, alcohol, or sex. His only loves were blood and video games.

Tig *tsked* to herself. His maker had no business turning him when she did—Jane was much too young. A fact made obvious when she abandoned him on the Hill's doorstep three years ago after the change left the twenty-six-year-old Seaton indifferent to her sexual advances. The council did the right thing, hunting down Jane and staking her for the unsanctioned turn. Her homestead on the Hill was now being held for Seaton.

Except something was deeply wrong with him.

It took fast talking on Gaea's part to keep the council from destroying the newly made vampire, along with Jane.

Gaea's heart had always been too big for her own good.

But even with her adoption of Seaton, Gaea wasn't having much luck socializing him. And they all knew she'd been trying.

Tig raised her tall glass and swirled it. "Ice cubes? Really?"

"It wouldn't look right to Henry's employees if the drink didn't have ice."

The winery provided servers for the wine bar and dinner buffet, but they didn't work the private room, where both spiked blood and pot were available.

She raised the glass and took a sip. "What—"

"I had them add another shot of vodka, for flavor. Drink up."

Jayden probably wanted her loosened up for more dancing...or other things. She smiled into the drink, taking a healthy gulp.

The blood did go down smoothly. Much better than bagged blood. Cerissa's product was going to be a hit once the young scientist's production facility was built. According to what Nicholas had told her, the biotech campus would fill the vacant sixty acres in the town's business district.

She took another taste. "Not bad."

Jayden smirked in response and took another bite of prime rib—almost as bloody as her drink.

Tig slowly sipped at her glass, her hand on Jayden's leg while he ate. She watched the other dancers come to a pause on the dance floor as the last song finished, then she heard a strange melody start and cocked her head.

A polka?

Jayden picked up the cloth napkin and wiped his mouth. "Take another deep drink and get ready to dance."

Partiers moved onto the floor in multiple lines. Jayden dropped the napkin, grabbed her hand, and pulled her to her feet. She was slightly taller than him, but he was much more muscular than she'd ever be.

She liked him that way.

As he brought her to her feet, she swayed slightly.

Oh yeah, the alcohol is working.

He led her to the dance floor. The mortals seemed to know what was coming. Some of their vampire mates did too.

Even the engaged couples had rushed onto the dance floor. Well, almost. It looked like Cerissa had to drag Henry to his feet to get him to join the dance.

That alone should have warned Tig.

"Just follow what I do," Jayden said, still holding her arm. "It's the Chicken Dance."

Her confusion cleared and Tig rolled her eyes. She'd seen this before, although she'd never participated in the past.

Flapping her arms like a chicken? Yeah, that was dignified.

At least she had enough alcohol in her to make her care less about her public image.

Chapter 3
The Key

Vasquez Müller Winery—Around the Same Time

Bruce watched all the rich assholes party themselves stupid. They even had a private room that no employees were allowed in. He knew because he'd already tried. The guard at the door wouldn't budge and waved him away, but the distinctive smell of weed couldn't be hidden. Bruce almost got a contact high from the plume that followed an old guy out.

Yeah, he could see why staff wasn't allowed in. You didn't want your servers getting high and sloppy with this clientele.

Back at the wine bar, he opened another bottle of Cabernet. Only one more left—the supply was starting to get low.

Jeez, this crowd can drink.

He filled another glass for a woman in a low-cut dress.

Eyes on her eyes, dude, not on her tits.

They'd reminded him about that. Multiple times.

No fun. Not that he usually had any fun at work.

Some of the bartenders were good at making conversation, talking up the guests, hoping for more tips. Bruce didn't have the patience for that nonsense.

Thankfully, this was a "tip-free" event—the host was taking care of the tips—so Bruce's lack of skill in that area cost him nothing for once.

And it being a Saturday night, the winery paid time and a half.

Not bad, really. But man, was he bored.

He had tried to get into college—everyone said that was fun—but his grades were shit. Even the community college waitlisted him; they were crammed with kids who had better grades than him, too.

Not many good jobs for guys who didn't have a college degree, unless you were good with your hands, building things and fixing stuff, which he wasn't. He only got this job because he was over twenty-one and had work experience as a coffee barista.

Yeah, he'd heard the stories about the owners. Self-made men. No college education.

Bullshit.

Those two—Henry Bautista and Rolf Müller—had *inherited* the winery from some relatives. And one of the stars of this party was Bautista's nephew, who would inherit, probably sooner rather than later, if the rumors could be believed. Seemed now that Bautista's nephew was getting married and settling down, the uncle was ready to dump the load and take off to see the world.

If only Bruce had some rich-fuck relative who'd die and leave him a million.

He'd use the money to get into video game creation. He'd always loved the games. He thought he could write a better one than anything out there, but you needed cold, hard cash to get started.

And for that, he had a plan.

Since he didn't have some stupid relative about to leave him a fortune, he had to provide for himself. He'd seen enough movies. He had an idea. It couldn't be that hard to pull off.

Besides, these rich fucks wouldn't miss the money.

The manager walked up to him. "How are we doing?"

"Ah, yeah, the Cab is getting low. Do we have any more of the 2016?"

Suri reached for her key ring, which hung from a belt loop on her pants, brushing her black suit jacket out of the way to get it. "I'll check storage. Our supply is getting low for that year."

"The way they're drinking here, what we have on the floor will last another half-hour at most. You could probably substitute something cheaper and they'd never notice."

"Henry wouldn't like that. These are his guests." She rotated the key ring, slipping her hand through the four-inch opening, to wear it as a bracelet.

Bruce was real familiar with the keys on that ring.

"Let me check the supply," Suri said. "Then I'll find out what Henry wants to do."

"Sure. I'm not going anywhere," he said with a laugh.

Chapter 4

True Love

VASQUEZ MÜLLER WINERY—LATER THAT NIGHT

Cerissa inhaled deeply as Henry led her outdoors. The early fall day had started warm but turned nippy when the sun set. A light breeze brought the sweet, earthy scent of the Hill's vineyards with it. She slipped off her high-heeled sandals and hooked her fingers around the straps to carry them, strolling barefoot on the flagstone walkway. The cool stone felt good on her aching feet.

After the master of ceremonies announced Henry and Cerissa's departure—the party would continue as long as their guests wanted to dance—Henry had told her he had a surprise for her and beckoned her to follow him.

Even if his words hadn't been slightly slurred and his sexy Castilian accent exaggerated, his gait would have given away his inebriated condition.

She was feeling the effects of the champagne herself, but her Lux metabolism burned through it almost as quickly as a vampire did. Still, she was relaxed and happy, and leaned her head against Henry's shoulder, letting the joy seep into her bones.

"Oh," he said, and stopped. "Do you mind waiting while I go back in and speak to Suri?"

"Now?" She swung around to face him, twirling her arm gracefully and coming to a halt in front of him as if they were still dancing, except she overshot by a step or two. "Can't winery business wait until tomorrow? Please?"

"I'm sorry. Suri has been asking for Henry all evening. I've put her off by saying he's around. But I really should see what she wants."

"All right." Cerissa flounced onto a nearby bench and took another deep inhale. The night air was so invigorating. "I'll wait right here."

"Thank you, *mi amor*."

"*Da nada*, Quique."

With a snap of his fingers, he aged himself, his black hair now shot through with gray, so he looked like a man in his mid-fifties.

He didn't need to snap his fingers to transform, but the lingering effect of his time performing in the circus had him adding dramatic flourishes whenever he got the chance.

She giggled. "So dashing. I'd forgotten that to talk with Suri as Henry, you have to become Henry for the rest of the night."

It sounded silly even as she said it. Vampires could age themselves, but until they fell into their day sleep, couldn't return to their younger appearance. She giggled again, covering her mouth with her hand.

He didn't exactly look pleased.

"I'm not laughing at you," she said. "I'm laughing—"

"Because you are more than a bit tipsy. I will be back shortly."

Henry left his jacket on the bench next to Cerissa, untied his bow tie, pocketed the scrap of cloth, and removed the satin ribbon from his hair, replacing it with the leather string he normally wore. It would be strange for Enrique's uncle to wear the same outfit as him, and he'd planned ahead, stashing the leather string in his pocket.

Entering the side door, it didn't take long to find an employee who knew where Suri was. They directed him to the kitchen. He slipped along the back of the ballroom to reach it.

With a glance to the party, he saw Marcus and Nicholas still dancing up a storm.

Henry shook his head. Shortly after the two men got engaged and the circus had left town, Marcus came to Henry's home for a private talk. They'd sat down across from each other in the drawing room.

"What may I help you with?" Henry had asked.

Marcus took a big breath before starting. "You realize that I've told Nicholas everything about Oscar."

"Good."

"You can no longer use the threat of telling Nicholas about Oscar as a means to control me, so nothing stops me from pursuing my concerns about Cerissa."

Henry sat forward, ready to let harsh words flow from his lips. No one would hurt Cerissa. Not even a close friend.

"Wait." Marcus held up his hand. "Something about Cerissa *is* different. I know, and I won't listen to any denials. But if you don't want to tell me, I'm not going to press the issue. She isn't a threat to the Hill, or you wouldn't be marrying her. I understand that. I trust you. We're friends, and I don't want to destroy what I value."

Henry let out a sigh of relief. "Thank you, Marcus."

"But if you ever want to tell me, I can't say I'm not curious…"

"There is nothing worth telling."

They'd shaken on it, discussed the engagement party, and let the rest of it go. Everything was now proceeding swimmingly. Nothing stood in the way of Henry's happiness with Cerissa.

He turned away from the dance floor and pushed on the swinging door to the kitchen.

"Henry, there you are." Suri dried her hands on a paper towel. "I was beginning to wonder what happened to you. It was a lovely party. Your nephew is very fortunate."

"Indeed. At some point we will sit down and discuss the transition. He will be taking over my half of the business while I travel."

"If anyone has earned some free time, it's you." Suri bit her lip. "Please don't take this the wrong way, but I was a bit surprised. I thought Cerissa was your girlfriend."

"A mistake many people have made—not to worry. She was staying with me while waiting for my nephew to join her. Was there anything else you need?"

"No, I took care of it. The servers had started to run out of the Cabernet that Cerissa and Nicholas specified, so I substituted a different vintage of the same varietal."

"An excellent decision. If that is all, I will say good night."

Minutes later, Henry returned to where he'd left Cerissa and offered his hand.

The soft white dress she wore accented her nutmeg-brown skin tones, her emerald eyes shining under the breezeway lights as she looked up at him. Her molasses-colored hair, so dark it bordered on black, was piled high in an incredible updo, studded with pearls.

So beautiful.

He snaked an arm around her waist as she rose to her feet, the light scent of Chanel No. 5 rising from her bare shoulders. They strolled under the grape arbor covering the flagstone walkway. The path connected the public side of the winery to the private.

When they reached the winery's main building—where the wines were fermented and aged—he led her to a room he'd never brought her to before. She glanced at him, the question in her eyes.

He swung open the door and inclined his head. "My private tasting room."

The look of surprise on her face was worth it. A fire in the fireplace and a bottle of Moscato chilling on ice set the scene, just as he'd planned it.

He strode over to the wine bar, and she followed. "I thought you might prefer a dessert wine rather than more champagne. You could try one of our late-harvest Moscatos—it's lighter, less alcohol."

She smiled at him. "That sounds nice, thank you."

She glanced around while he poured for her. Behind the wine bar, glasses hung on racks, different sizes and shapes for tasting the different kinds of wines. A large couch and comfortable overstuffed chairs, upholstered in dark leather, occupied the center of the room by the fireplace.

The room was designed for wine tasting and socializing and reflected Henry's tastes, with beautiful hardwood paneling, heavy drapes, expensive artwork, and a polished granite countertop covering the wine bar.

The bag she'd packed at his suggestion sat against the wall. Surprised to see it there, she dropped her high-heeled sandals next to it and enjoyed the feel of her feet sinking into the plush scarlet carpet. Were they going to a hotel later? That had been her guess when he refused to tell her the plan for the night.

Henry adjusted the dimmer switch a little, so the room was softly washed with light, and brought her the Moscato. She took a taste—the pale wine was sweet, with sparse bubbles. Not a true sparkling wine, it was nevertheless refreshing after all the champagne.

Henry's winery sat outside the Hill's wall in the public portion of Sierra Escondida, with a small vineyard cultivated behind the buildings. She wandered over to the open curtains to look out the glass patio door, which led to a veranda overlooking the vineyard, lit by scattered floodlights. The rows of vines covered the gently rolling foothill and ran right up to a tall, white-painted block wall jutting up from the landscape. The wall separated the private homes of Hill vampires from the outside world.

Visually, the vineyard appeared to continue beyond the wall. In reality, they were separate vineyards. In the distance, she could see the home she and Henry shared, with more vines tracing the slope beyond their house.

He drew the curtains closed. "For privacy. Join me."

He led the way over to the fireplace, all seriousness in his dark eyes, and she followed. He took her glass and set it on the mantel.

Wrapping his arms around her, he held her against his chest and whispered in her ear, "*Mi amor*, you have made me very happy."

"As you have me." She squeezed him tightly. "I love you, Henry."

"And I love you." He leaned back to brush her hair out of her face—some tendrils had fallen loose from her updo. "You have given me my engagement present"—she had given him a custom case to hold the whip he'd used in the tiger act when Circus Garza was in town—"and I wanted to be alone with you to give you yours."

Smirking at his phrasing, she pictured his naked body as the gift. But he probably had something more traditional in mind.

He reached for a flat, ten-inch-long box covered in gold foil paper from where it rested on the fireplace mantel and presented the gift to her with a flourish.

She eagerly tore off the wrapping to reveal a velvet case and flipped up the hinged lid. Inside was an elegant pearl necklace with a ruby centerpiece, surrounded in diamonds. Three strands of pearls, larger to smaller, swooped from the back latch to join at the center ruby, a single pearl drop hanging from the ruby.

"Oh, Henry, it's gorgeous."

Chapter 5

Bits and Bites

The Owner's Room—Moments Later

Henry's stomach fluttered. Did she really like the necklace? He had been so nervous about the gift. "I know it is more a Western tradition to wear pearls with your wedding dress, but I thought these would look elegant with the red sari you have planned."

He hoped pearls didn't violate some rule in Hindu culture. He'd tried researching it and couldn't find anything to prohibit pearls, although gold was more customary.

She set the velvet case on the mantel. "Help me put them on."

"You're sure? You like it?"

"I love it."

She presented her back to him, and he unfastened the clasp to the necklace she wore: diamonds inset in gold forming an outlined heart. Gaea had loaned her the charming, old-fashioned necklace.

He dropped the heart-shaped necklace in Cerissa's open hand, and she laid the heart inside the velvet box. "For safekeeping," she said.

Picking up the pearl and ruby necklace, she stood in front of the mirror over the fireplace, holding the pearl strands for him to take. He latched them around her bare neck. Enticed by the gentle curve and pulsing vein, he let his fingers linger on her soft skin.

She touched the ruby as she looked in the mirror. "It's elegant. It'll be perfect with my sari."

When they were discussing plans for the party, she'd told him that the Lux, in the name of blending in, adopted wedding traditions from the community where they wed, or alternatively, from their birthplace culture. She'd laughed and shared her real thoughts about the latter, seeing it as an excuse for indulging the imprint early childhood had on each of them.

His own early childhood had certainly imprinted him—that he couldn't deny—and the mark it left fed his desire to shower his fiancée with exquisite jewels like the one resting above her breasts.

He picked up the wineglass and toasted her. "To my beautiful bride-to-be."

He took a small sip, the sweet wine pleasant, then handed the glass back to her, and she drank. The necklace looked so perfect around her neck as her throat moved with each swallow.

"Thank you, Henry." She returned to the mirror and continued to admire the necklace. "You didn't have to do this."

"I wanted to."

Her grin was like the curve of a quarter moon, lighting her face with its glow. "I'm so happy. Those words seem inadequate to describe my joy—"

"I know, *mi amor*. I can feel what you are feeling."

"It's nice to be connected through the crystal, isn't it?"

"Indeed." He raised his eyebrows. "In which case, you know what else I'm feeling."

Surely the crystal made her aware of the desire growing in him. During the party, her joy had been a constant pleasant current under his skin, magnifying his own. Now, his erection responded strongly to the featherlike touches of *her* excitement, sent his way by the crystal.

And he could feel her respond to his arousal with her own heat.

She took another sip of wine and smiled coyly at him before setting the glass down on the fireplace mantel again.

Henry swept her into his arms and kissed her deeply. When the kiss ended, he pressed his lips to her neck, little kisses that drew goosebumps from her skin.

"Señor Vasquez, if I didn't know better, I would say you were trying to seduce me right here."

"And what if I was, future Señora Patel-Vasquez?" he replied, without stopping his kisses.

She looked around the room. "This is very romantic, but aren't you afraid someone might walk in?"

"No one will disturb us. This is my private tasting room. I have reserved it for the night, and with what I have in mind, the room is aptly named."

He licked his lips and took a deep inhale of her skin, smelling her blood and feeling his fangs extend again, the gland in the roof of his mouth tingling as fang serum engorged it.

She held on to him tightly. "Are we to make love on the floor?"

"The couch folds out into a bed."

"Well, before we go any further, I have a surprise for you, although not in the same category as this one," she said, touching the ruby again. "I just need my bag."

"There is a bathroom through that door." Henry motioned to the partially closed door.

"Perfect. I'll be right back, if you'll prepare the bed?"

"Of course, *cariña*," he replied, letting her go and giving her a little bow.

• • •

With a smile, she grabbed the bag and went into the bathroom. She freshened up, brushed her teeth, and removed the pearl-studded pins from her updo, unwinding the braid and running her fingers through to loosen the waves. She then slipped into a negligee. It was made of soft white lace, clung to her figure, and left nothing to the imagination.

As she changed, she kept looking at the necklace in the bathroom mirror, letting her fingers trail over the fine pearls.

So beautiful. He has exquisite taste.

She decided to leave it on, but her contact lenses had to go. The Lux technology embedded in the lenses recorded video of the entire evening and fulfilled her duty to observe the Hill community. But now? No way would she record their intimate time together. The Lux Protectors had no right to see that.

She steeled herself for what came next. Ejecting the contacts always caused a slight *zzzt* vibration as the tentacles detached from her optic nerve, and she shivered uncomfortably as the feeling zapped her eyes.

After dropping them into a case, she used her hypo to inject a stabilizer that would keep her from morphing to her native Lux form when Henry bit her.

Because biting was definitely on the itinerary for tonight.

Finally ready, she strolled out of the bathroom and struck a pose, one designed to send him into overdrive.

Stripped down to his silk boxer shorts, she enjoyed the view as he bent over to fold out the bed. When he straightened up and his eyes met hers, his reaction was instant and obvious. His pupils expanded, and he *whooshed* over to join her, taking her into his arms.

She could feel his need pressing against her through the thin fabric.

"I take it you like my outfit," she said.

He didn't answer. Instead, he began kissing along her jawline, sending exquisite shivers across her skin, tempting her to stay put, but the desire for her efforts to be fully appreciated eclipsed the sexy tingles.

She wiggled out of his arms and walked to the fireplace, letting him get a good look at the back view: her shapely derrière outlined by the tight lace negligee. With a little shake of her hips, she picked up her wineglass and turned around, striking another pose, a profile with her hand on her hip.

This time, he must have recognized that she enjoyed modeling for him, because he stayed in place and watched from across the room.

But as patient as he appeared on the outside, his urgent desire for her thrummed through the crystal and flowed like electricity to her center. The warmth of his love, the fevered excitement emanating from him, made her nipples tighten and took her breath away.

Her eyes met his, and then she dropped her gaze lower to his naked chest. She wanted to run her fingers over his firm pecs and pinch his cut glutes. The thought propelled her into motion. She sauntered to the foldout bed to pull back the covers.

She took another sip from her wineglass, licked her lips seductively, and placed the glass on the end table.

Stretching out on the bed, she asked, "Are you going to join me, Quique?"

"Of course. I was just enjoying the show."

The comment sent a zing of heat through her, followed closely by the crystal communicating a burst of his own intense desire.

He unfastened his crucifix and dropped it next to her glass, and the chain *clinked* as it fell. He crawled into bed and slipped his arms around her.

After untying his ponytail, she tossed aside the leather string. His long jet-black hair—now streaked with silver—flowed around his shoulders. She loved the way his hair looked when he wore it loose, although the strands occasionally brushed her face, tickling her nose when he hovered over her.

"BF or FF?" she asked, as he began kissing her neck again. It was their code—would he bite before or during lovemaking?

"I plan on taking my time."

He piled the pillows behind her, helping her lean up against them. After slipping off his boxers, he knelt between her legs and gently worked one of the straps of the negligee off her shoulder until both were far enough down that he could lower the bodice, the lace scraping over her dark brown nipples deliciously.

She moaned when he took the first one into his mouth, and liquid heat pooled deep within her. He looked up, making eye contact with her, his gaze never leaving, as he sucked and licked. The black pupils of his dark eyes were still expanded, and they almost wiped out his irises.

The feeling of exposure was so intense that she closed hers. He changed nipples, and she sighed in both pleasure and relief.

When she felt him move to the side, she opened her eyes. He propped himself up on his forearms, and she watched him slowly lower the negligee until it was at her hips. His lips lingered on her belly as he leaned over her, sending pleasant shivers through her.

The evening felt like one long tease to her. Eager to move things along, she lifted her hips, and he caught the hint, sliding the negligee the rest of the way before tossing it to the floor.

Which left him with his face very near her hip. He kissed the skin there, and she spread her legs further apart, making room for him.

He worked his way inward, trailing more kisses, and finally licked that spot that drove her wild.

"Oh yes," she moaned.

His chuckle vibrated the sensitive skin of her inner thigh, and she let out another gasp of pleasure when he began using his tongue to maximum advantage.

God, how she loved him, needed him, wanted him—along with all the pleasure he brought her. His tongue licked and his mouth sucked, alternating until the buzzing warmth between her legs was ready to explode.

"Oh, Henry, yes."

One more lick, and the explosion washed over her like a wave dragging her out to sea and then bringing her back to his arms. She rode the wave, his tongue chasing the spasms, drawing out as many as he could.

He gave her almost no time to recover. "Up on your knees."

She looked at him through blurry eyes. "Up?"

"And turn around."

Ah, he wanted to take her from behind. After a recent misunderstanding, they'd decided to take turns deciding what they'd do in bed—subject to veto. She suspected Henry had maneuvered things so tonight would be his choice. He liked to mix things up, and she was more than happy to go along.

She languidly rolled over and pulled herself up, using the couch's back for leverage, and slid the pillows out of the way. She rested her stomach on the cool leather, her forearms supporting her on the top edge. Adjusting her knees on the bed, she arched her back.

The movement woke her up, pulled her from that relaxed state she'd entered.

His fingers trailed down her back, massaging as they traveled, until they reached her bottom, which he kneaded gently.

The bed moved when he knelt behind her and his erection pushed between her legs. She spread her legs to give him more access and eased up higher on the couch, arching her back further. She was so wet for him. His hands left her bottom, and she felt him guide into her, slowly, the other hand lifting her hip. He grunted a manly sound of pleasure once he was deeply seated.

She tightened around his erection, loving the fullness of taking him inside her, of feeling him pulse in response.

His arms slipped around her like a serpentine bracelet. One crossed her belly to reach up and squeeze a nipple on the opposite side, while the other arm angled down to rub her clit, his muscular chest pressed against her back.

The pleasure began to build again. She moaned as he thrust into her, touching her in all the right places.

His breathy pants near her ear increased, letting her know the pleasure was nearing the peak for him.

She exposed her neck, laying her head to one side, submissive and sensuous at the same time.

"Oh, *mi amor*," he moaned, his breath warm on her neck, the anticipation of what came next tightening her core once again.

Henry licked the vein that lay exposed, the salty taste of Cerissa's skin teasing him. The velvety feel of her skin under his tongue only enticed him further, and he rose to gently plunge his fangs through that tight barrier.

A hot sensation buzzed across the roof of his mouth as fang serum shot into her vein. He kept his fingers fluttering across her clit until, moments later, she cried out her orgasm.

He took deep pulls on her neck, his own climax building to a crescendo.

The taste of her was indescribable. She was sweet in a way that clone blood could never match. And it wasn't just the sugar from the chocolate fudge cake she'd eaten for dessert that made her taste the way she did. Her flavor was so special, so uniquely her. It was only with a great deal of willpower that he didn't drink his fill.

When the final burst of heat shot through his groin, he released her neck.

"Aah," he exhaled, his mouth wide open, her blood dripping from his fangs onto her shoulder.

Slowly coming back from the whiteout of incredible pleasure, he leaned forward and licked the scarlet drops off her shoulder, hating himself for being messy. Then he nuzzled her, his nose deep into her hair, his arms holding her.

He sighed, slipping out and turning her toward him. She glowed, a light sheen of sweat and bliss that ran from her neck down between her breasts, two ripe orbs made just for his lips. With a satisfied sigh, he pulled her with him under the sheets.

She had full hips, and he rested one hand on the opposite one, as she used his chest for a pillow, and drew little circles with her fingers. The sensations she evoked began to stir him again.

Dios, he loved her. In all his life, he'd never been so happy.

Chapter 6
Secrets

Vasquez Müller Winery—Sunday

The next morning, Cerissa rolled out of bed, not sure whether to strip the sheets or not. Knowing Henry, he had probably arranged to have the room cleaned later. With a satisfied sigh, she postponed the decision and headed to the shower, where she almost blasted herself with cold water before she got the temperature adjusted properly.

Should I drive back home or go out for breakfast?

A leisurely breakfast out, reading the Sunday newspaper, sounded divine. She could then return to the Hill to work in her basement lab.

But she felt uncomfortable leaving Henry alone here for the day. She vaguely remembered when he left at dawn. He murmured something about a secret room before disappearing.

Even as she showered, she could feel his presence nearby, but she didn't know precisely where he was. Should she stay and guard him? But that seemed equally silly. Henry had been taking care of himself for two hundred years. He didn't need her to watch over him like a mother hen.

It still seemed unreal to her. She'd never expected to get married this young. The Lux usually waited until they could have children to marry, because of the life span differences between Lux and humans. Maybe in a hundred years, when she became fertile, but to do so now broke with Lux traditions, and she was incredibly happy to break with them.

Once she finished showering, Cerissa changed into blue jeans and a t-shirt and started tidying the room. Then she saw the note that Henry left, tacked to the door so she wouldn't miss it.

My dearest fiancée, the note began in his elegant nineteenth-century script. *I was so glad we could celebrate our engagement last night. My only regret is that I could not wake up beside you this morning to take you to breakfast. I have made arrangements for you to dine at the winery tasting room. They will prepare whatever you desire. I will see you tonight at home.*

A knock at the door surprised her. Henry's note hadn't told her to expect anyone. No peephole. She reached for the doorknob.

VASQUEZ MÜLLER WINERY—FIVE MINUTES EARLIER

Bruce had changed shifts with one of the other winery employees. Even though he had worked late at the party, he wanted to be the one to clean out the owner's tasting room. The owner was rich—and eccentric—and Bruce had his fingers crossed that whatever he'd caught on video would prompt the owner to pay beaucoup bucks to get it back.

The keys were waiting for him. The manager had left them with his supervisor. When he volunteered to do cleanup, the idiot looked relieved. It saved his supervisor from having to assign the job to the unwilling. Usually, no one wanted to clean up after these rich assholes.

Bruce knocked on the door. No answer. He tried the door handle. Locked. Had Henry Bautista locked up after leaving last night?

Bruce started to unlock the door and was surprised when a woman opened it. "Oh, I'm sorry," he said. "I was here to clean, but I can come back."

Grabbing the keys from the door, he quickly turned away so she wouldn't see his face.

"That's all right," she said. "I'm leaving for breakfast soon. Come back in ten minutes and I'll be gone for at least an hour."

"Yes, ma'am," he replied, already walking away.

Was that Enrique's fiancée?

What was she doing here?

Well, he'd find out soon enough when he returned.

Finished packing, Cerissa returned the pearls to their case with a little laugh. She'd fallen asleep with them on, and they had left an impression in her skin where she'd lain against Henry.

She smiled to herself. Would she always feel this happy?

She left the door to the room unlocked—Henry's employee would be back to clean shortly—and headed out to toss her bag into the Malibu. She and Henry had taken separate cars. When she closed the car's trunk, her stomach growled, demanding breakfast.

Waffles? Eggs benedict?

She went looking for the tasting room. A young woman greeted her at the door. "Hi. I'm Megan. We don't open to the public until noon, so you have the place to yourself." She gestured to the empty room. "But it's such a nice Sunday morning, might I suggest you sit on the patio?"

"What a great idea. Please lead the way."

The patio faced the vineyard, which looked incredible in the morning light. "What a view!"

The waitress smiled, handing Cerissa a small menu and a newspaper. "Coffee? A mimosa?"

"Both, please."

Maybe she should spend a leisurely morning here and ignore work for the day. Later, she could call Karen to see if she wanted to go shopping and gossip about the party—if her bestie wasn't too hungover. Karen always had the latest and greatest dirt, but she was probably still asleep.

Cerissa touched her neck, missing the weight of the pearls against her skin. That was another reason to call Karen. She eagerly wanted to show off her new necklace to her bestie.

Bruce waited around the corner until the fiancée—Cerissa, he remembered—was gone. He'd never done anything like this before, but he'd seen the opportunity to make some easy money when Henry reserved the owner's room for the entire night. It was one thing to reserve the room for a few hours, but reserving it for an overnight stay? That suggested something juicy might happen that Bruce could catch on video.

He locked the door from the inside and walked over to the bookcase, fishing out the slender fiber-cam from the hole he'd drilled. The digital recorder was taped to the back of the bookcase. He removed it and packed away the device—he would look at the video later.

Now, all he had to do was clean the room and get out of there before anyone caught him with the camera. He changed the sheets on the bed and collapsed the mattress frame, folding it back into a couch, and returned the seat cushions. He then wiped down the wine bar and washed the wineglass. The bathroom had hardly been used. He made quick work of cleaning it.

Finished, he grabbed the bag of cleaning supplies with the camcorder hidden inside and locked the door behind him. He stopped at his car to stash his stuff, returning to the supply closet to put away the cleaning supplies and then to the laundry room to drop off the dirty sheets and towels.

He straightened his white shirt and untucked his tie, which he'd stuffed between shirt buttons to keep it from getting wet as he cleaned. Now, for another boring day of drudgery working the wine-tasting room.

Sunday was a busy day for both tourists and locals. They liked to hang out in the courtyard garden surrounding the tasting room and drink themselves stupid. The fiancée still sat on the patio eating breakfast, so he hung back and let Megan serve her.

Later that day, Bruce clocked out, eager to see what was on the video. When he got home to his crappy one-bedroom apartment near downtown Mordida, he grabbed a beer from the refrigerator and sat down at his laptop. It didn't take long to transfer the video file.

He twisted off the bottle cap and took a swig, waiting for the video to start. He almost snorted out his beer when he realized what was happening on the screen.

His boss, Henry Bautista, right down to the long hair streaked with gray, had escorted Enrique Vasquez's fiancée into the owner's room and proceeded to screw her on the foldout bed.

What the hell was Bautista thinking, fucking his nephew's fiancée at their freaking engagement party?

What a stupid, rich asshole.

As Bruce sat there watching the two go at it on video, his own dick grew hard, and he thought about jerking off. But then he reached the end of their fuck session and his eyes widened.

He bit her.

The asshole sucked up her blood and everything, even licked it off her shoulder. How sick.

The guy really was a perv.

I suppose when you're that rich, you can get a girl to do anything.

Bruce's asking price just skyrocketed. Henry Bautista would pay a fuck-ton of money to keep that nastiness off the internet—and to keep his nephew from finding out.

Though, if the nephew wanted to inherit, he'd probably have to let it go no matter how pissed he was.

And where *was* the nephew, anyway? How did he not notice his fiancée missing that night?

Maybe the two dudes were sharing the girl.

Ew.

Toward the end of the video, as sunrise approached, Bautista climbed out of bed and opened a hidden panel by the fireplace that revealed a lever. He pulled the lever, and one of the walls opened slightly. Stepping through the opening, he closed it shut behind him.

Would the real fiancé appear for sloppy seconds? If he did, Bruce would double the ask.

He kept watching the video. Enrique didn't show up. Now Bruce was curious. Where did Bautista go? And why?

Bruce would have to go back another time to find out. Not today, though. It would raise too many questions if he returned to work too soon.

He'd wait until his next shift tomorrow afternoon and then go exploring. The whole thing stunk of scandal, like the articles in those tabloids his mother devoured. He wouldn't get a second chance at the money. Better to know the whole story before he wrote his demand note. What he found out might justify more cha-ching for the video.

Because if those tabloids had taught him anything, there was money to made from people who hid secrets.

Chapter 7

Surprise, Surprise!

SIERRA ESCONDIDA—THE SAME DAY

After a fun day shopping with Karen, Cerissa said goodbye and returned home. The sun had set, so she arrived at Rancho Bautista shortly after Henry did. They were supposed to meet with Gaea at eight o'clock to discuss the mortal rights subcommittee, and they rushed to get ready.

Half an hour later, standing at the front door of Gaea's Mediterranean-style mansion with its smooth chocolate-brown stucco and elegant scrolled ironwork balconies, Cerissa squeezed Henry's hand and then rang the doorbell.

They waited a few minutes, but there was no answer. Cerissa looked up into Henry's eyes, the question in hers.

It had been Gaea's idea to meet the night after the party. Why wasn't she answering the door?

Had they read the message wrong?

Cerissa took out her phone and opened Gaea's email. The message clearly said tonight at eight.

"Try the doorbell again," Henry said.

She pressed the old-fashioned doorbell in the shape of a Celtic knot. The multi-tone chime sounded.

Muffled by the door, she heard Gaea say, "Yes, yes. I'm coming."

Moments later, the door opened. Gaea stood there, a silk robe wrapped around her, citrine flowers on an azure background, the bathrobe slightly askew, and her hair looking like she'd just come through a wind tunnel.

Cerissa suppressed the gasp that almost escaped her mouth. She'd lived with Gaea when she first arrived on the Hill and had never seen Gaea look so disheveled before.

"If this is a bad time, we can reschedule," Cerissa said.

"Oh my word, child, did I make a mistake?" Gaea's gaze flitted from Cerissa to Henry. "I thought our meeting was tomorrow night."

Henry waved his hand. "We can come back tomorrow night if that would be more convenient for you."

"No, that won't do. It's my mistake—no reason for you to make a second trip. You're here now." Gaea glanced over her shoulder. "Our discussion won't take long, will it?"

Cerissa caught Henry's eye and shrugged. He echoed the motion, but said, "It shouldn't."

"Then come in, please do. I don't know where my head's been." Gaea led the way. "We can talk in here."

The cozy parlor was reminiscent of a Victorian-era sitting room. The furniture was all antiques from the 1800s, including Cerissa's favorite, the heavy wood-framed platform rocker with violet crushed-velvet cushions.

Gaea sat with a sigh on a tapestry chair and tightened the belt on her robe, then ran her fingers through her long, light brown hair to brush the wayward strands back. She usually wore it in an updo, either a French twist or a chignon, but now it floated down to her shoulders in scraggly waves.

Cerissa still couldn't believe Gaea was entertaining them looking the way she did. It was just so out of character.

But then, maybe it wasn't. Was this a symptom of depression? A side effect of her isolation?

Cerissa held out the small box containing the necklace she'd borrowed. "Thank you so much for the loan. It looked perfect with my dress."

"You're welcome, child. Now, what did you want to ask me?"

Henry took Cerissa's hand. "We discussed it with the council, and we think you would be a good addition to the mortal rights subcommittee."

Gaea's hazel eyes grew big, and she shook her head. "No, absolutely not. I can't take Yacov's place. That—that would just be wrong."

How to convince her? "I understand why you feel that way," Cerissa said. "But you have the status of being the oldest vampire in the community. Only the founders have been on the Hill longer than you have. And the consensus appears to be that only one founder should be on the subcommittee, so it just makes sense that you, as the oldest non-founder, fill the open slot."

Gaea sighed. "But it's my fault Yacov died."

Henry reached out and took Gaea's hand with both of his. "I must disagree. Any fault lands squarely on Dylan's shoulders, and only his. With every mortal we bring here, we take the same risk. None of us can control what another person does."

The only control vampires had over a bitten mortal were the power to wipe their memories, the power to compel the mortal's return, and the power to stop them from speaking about vampires to uninitiated mortals. Those powers did not include stopping mortals from committing evil acts.

"I've spoken with Shayna," Cerissa said. Yacov's widow would remain a part of the community for at least a year. "She doesn't blame you. You'd be doing her a big favor if you didn't blame yourself."

Tears formed in Gaea's eyes. "Child, I don't see how she can feel that way."

"Because she knows you. We all do."

Henry patted Gaea's hand. "I have nothing but respect for you. But it's not my forgiveness or Shayna's forgiveness that you need. You need to forgive yourself."

When he said that, the tears rolled down Gaea's cheeks, and she used the back of her free hand to wipe at them. "I don't know what to say, dears."

Cerissa smiled at her, an encouraging smile, and offered a tissue from her purse. "Say you'll be on the subcommittee."

"I don't know…"

"Think about it." Cerissa stood to wrap her arms around Gaea. "Please. We need you to help—"

"Hey, sweet cheeks. When ya coming back to bed?"

Cerissa pulled back, startled to hear Ari's voice.

Gaea gasped. "Just a moment, please." She scurried out to the hallway. "I told you to stay upstairs."

"So? Who said I was any good at taking orders?"

"Go upstairs or I'll take a hairbrush to your backside, I swear I will."

"Now you're singing my song."

"Get back to bed. Now."

Gaea returned to them, blushing a surprising amount of red for a vampire. "I'm so sorry about that. He followed me home, and I decided to keep him for a while." She paused, a finger tapping her chin dimple. "You don't mind, do you?"

GAEA'S DRIVEWAY—FIVE MINUTES LATER

The moment Henry closed the door to the Viper, Cerissa started laughing. It started as a light giggle and, as he drove past Gaea's vineyard onto Robles Road, soon ramped up to outrageous guffaws.

He glanced over from the driver's seat, concerned. "Cerissa, are you all right?"

She shook her head and breathlessly said, "I'll be okay. Give me a minute."

The laughter returned.

Now he wasn't sure what to do. Gaea had shooed them out with a promise to consider working on the subcommittee. And then Cerissa started acting, well, strange.

"Cerissa…"

Slowly the laughter died out. "I can't help picturing Gaea with a hairbrush and Ari being on the receiving end." She blotted at her eyes with a tissue. "I know Ari was flirting with her at the party, but I didn't think it'd actually happen. I would have bet that the only person Ari wouldn't succeed at bedding was Gaea—and you, of course."

Henry turned up the curving driveway leading to Rancho Bautista del Murciélago, the name he gave their home in the late 1800s. "Why?"

"Gaea is one sharp cookie. I figured she'd see right through him."

He had to agree. The two seemed like an odd couple. "Maybe whatever he has to offer, she may need right now."

"Yes, like a target for her hairbrush." Cerissa giggled. "I'd nearly pay to see that."

"Indeed." Henry parked in the garage. "Speaking of paying for things"—he reached into his back pocket and unfolded his wallet—"I was so distracted last night by your loveliness I forgot to give you these."

She furrowed her brow. "Credit cards?"

"Remember after the initiation ceremony? I mentioned all of the ways in which mortals are taken care of financially?"

"The social security contribution, the gold, the trust fund, stuff like that?"

"Exactly." He held out the cards to her, pleading with his eyes for her to take them. "I have had credit cards on my accounts issued in your name. You should use these for everything."

She dropped her hands into her lap. "That isn't necessary. I can take care of my own expenses."

"I know you can." He didn't want to offend her, but this was his obligation under the Covenant. Not to mention, it made him feel, well, *manly* to provide for her. "But would you do me the honor of accepting these regardless?"

"Quique, really, I have my own money. And, in fact, I should start contributing to our joint household expenses."

He waved his hand. "That isn't necessary. And it would make me happy if you would take these cards and use them."

"It's not fair to put it that way."

"Please?" He reached for her wrist, gently pried open her closed fingers, and laid the cards on her palm. "Now that you are living with me, I must file quarterly reports to show that I'm providing for your support. This is one of the safeguards we instituted to protect the mortals who are brought here. I have nothing to report for you other than room and board. That is not acceptable."

She stared into his pleading eyes, stunned by the vampires and their paternalistic system. At one level, she understood some of it—without safeguards, a vampire could hold a mortal captive on the Hill and abuse them, and no one would ever know. But this was over the top. "You have more to report than room and board. You've spent money on me. We go out to dinner, the movies, the trip to Santa Barbara, that sort of thing."

"Perhaps. But I should also be paying for your clothes and whatever else you need."

She could tell he took this seriously, so she didn't answer flippantly, much as she would have liked to. "I understand you see this as a problem. I'm trying to see it from your point of view. But the last time someone supported me in that way, I was a child. I am not a child anymore. This isn't right."

"Please don't misconstrue our tradition." He wrapped his hands around hers. "I do not view you as a child. You are my equal. You cannot imagine how important that is to me, to be with someone who is my equal."

Henry paused and took a deep breath.

Oh no. What else is coming?

He didn't need oxygen to survive, but without air, he couldn't speak, and such a deep breath signaled he had a lot more to say.

"Our system is not set up with someone like you in mind," he continued, releasing her hand, "someone who has money they earned before coming to the Hill. Our mates become part of the economic structure we have—like Karen, who works for the winery. Many of the mortals work in whatever business their vampire runs, and are paid, either above or below the table, depending upon the arrangement they have. Or they work for the town, or for another vampire's business. But in any case, it is still the vampire's responsibility to prove that their mate has sufficient income from work on the Hill to cover their expenses or the vampire has to pay for those directly. While you are Leopold's envoy, my understanding is that you have been paid in shares of the business you formed with him. You have no active income, so it is best if I pay for your living expenses."

"And who sees these reports?"

"Just the council."

"So Rolf will know how much you spend on me."

"I assume so."

"You know so." She looked at the cards like they were something repulsive. "This wouldn't be some sort of competition to show who spends the most on their mate?"

Henry narrowed his eyes at her. "This is not a competition. I have set your credit limit much lower than what Rolf gives Karen, so no, there is no attempt here to compete with Rolf."

Something about that bothered her. Why did it matter that Rolf spent more on Karen than Henry had offered her? But then, Karen had an addiction to designer clothes.

No, that wasn't it. After accusing him of making it a competition, she felt chagrined to realize her first impulse had been to do the same.

"Fine," Cerissa said, folding her fingers around the cards, then slipping them into her purse. "This really isn't necessary, but if it will make you happy, I'll use the credit cards."

"Thank you, *mi amor*."

She waited for him to open her car door for her. Another old-fashioned gesture he'd asked her to accept, to which she had acquiesced. How many more such requests would there be now that they were engaged?

He used his phone app to close the garage door behind them, and then she took his hand as they strolled past the driveway fountain headed to the front porch.

"Are you going to return to your work?" he asked, unlocking the front door and opening it for her.

"I have to finish reviewing the building plans for the new lab. I have them spread out all over the dining room table."

The council meeting to approve the project was only weeks away, and the reminder kick-started a buzz of nervous excitement through her.

"Very well," he said, giving a slight bow then closing the front door behind them. "I have some work to do at my desk. What do you say to putting a cap on it? Two hours, and then do something together?"

"You have yourself a deal. As long as it has nothing to do with a hairbrush," she said with a smile.

Chapter 8

Shaken, Not Stirred

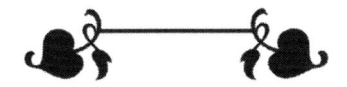

HENRY'S HOME OFFICE—ONE HOUR LATER

A low rumble caught Henry's attention. He cocked his head, listening as the resonant roar of a distant train headed toward him. Then he shot to his feet. His house was nowhere near any train tracks—he immediately knew what was happening.

From the fear that blasted through the crystal, his mate must have heard the noise too.

"Cerissa!" he called out, bolting from his home office and *whooshing* downstairs and across the foyer. When he'd last seen her, she was headed to the dining room to work.

The rumbling increased, the floor vibrating along with the sound.

"Henry, what is that?" she yelled over the noise.

He rushed to her side as the whole house began to rattle around them.

"We must get away from the windows. Hurry, crawl under the table."

Arched picture windows ran the length of the room. She rose from her chair but didn't move. Confusion filled her eyes.

The noise grew louder, like a freight train was barreling down on them, and the floor shook, rolling in a north-south direction.

With supernatural speed, he moved the chairs away, then pulled her under the large mahogany table with him.

"Henry, what—" She fell silent as he laid her down facing the floor and straddled her, positioning his body as a shield above her, bracing himself on his elbows and wrapping his hands over her head to protect her in case glass started flying.

The rolling became more violent, and then, without warning, she morphed. He was now huddled over a blonde *puma*.

"It will be all right, *cariña*."

She let out a deep-throated meow-like scream and struggled against him to get free.

"No, Cerissa, stay down." He had both arms wrapped around her and wrestled to hold her in place.

As the frequency of the rolling waves grew faster, things began to fall. He could tell by the sound when the mirror over the fireplace crashed onto the hardwood floor. Crystal vases, picture frames, and other *objets d'art* joined the mirror. So far, no sound of broken wood or window glass. He'd been through enough earthquakes before to discern the difference.

Apparently, Cerissa hadn't. The cat trembled in his arms.

The earthquake lasted at least three minutes—three very long minutes. Cerissa never stopped meowing. To her credit, she didn't scratch to get him to release her, although the claws of both front paws were dug deep into the dining room carpet as she tried to pull away.

When the shaking stopped, he kept one arm hooked around her and stroked her coarse fur with the other, trying to comfort her. Since he smelled no blood, he concluded she hadn't been hit by flying glass.

"It is all right, *mi amor*. We are all right, and from the sound of it, the house will be fine too. Just a few broken things. Nothing to worry about."

Then Cerissa started using her teeth and claws to push and pull at her clothes.

Hmm. If she wasn't ready to morph back, he might as well help her off with them. He unzipped her dress, and she wiggled out of it. Her bra and panties took a little more work to remove from the cat's body.

"Stay here," he said. "I don't want you cutting your paws on the glass." He crawled out from under the table, and despite his instructions, she followed. "It was just an earthquake. This house is built to withstand them. We will be fine."

He knew he was rambling nervously, filling the air with the sound of his voice. Through the crystal, Cerissa's initial panic and fear had battered him. But once she transformed, her panic calmed somewhat.

Still, the *puma*'s emotions urged him to flee, and her desire to escape the building threatened to overcome his common sense, so he tamped down the crystal's connection.

Better. Now I can think more clearly.

He stood, and she almost tripped him, trying to wedge herself between his legs.

He patted her head. "Stay here while I inspect the house."

She let out a very long and pitiful meow. He knelt to pet and soothe her, but she sat up on her haunches and clung to him with two paws, like she was trying to climb onto his shoulders.

"Cerissa, stop that and look at me." He pushed her back down to the floor and tried to lift her furry white chin. It was immovable. "Cerissa, we are going to be fine. Perhaps we should stay right here for a little while longer. There may be aftershocks."

Once the words were out, he realized that wasn't the most soothing thing he could have said, and in less than a minute, an aftershock rolled through.

He grabbed her by the scruff of her neck and dove back under the table, huddling over her.

The aftershock wasn't as strong as the first earthquake, which was a good sign. But then the lights went out. He hoped it was a central problem and not specific to the house. It would likely get fixed faster with less expense to him if the problem belonged to the electric company.

He wasn't sure what to do next. If he lived alone, he would inspect the house and check out the extent of the damage. In particular, he wanted to make sure the automatic gas shut-off valve had worked. But Cerissa wasn't reacting well to the situation. He hadn't expected this from her. She usually had courage under fire.

"Cerissa," he said, "I need to inspect the house. Please stay right here and I'll be back for you."

As he moved off her to slide out from under the table, she grabbed his shirt with her teeth.

He sighed. "Fine. You may come with me, but watch where you step."

She released him, and he scooted out from under the table. He took a step and stumbled.

She'd rushed between his legs again, almost tripping him.

"Cerissa, heel."

She looked up at him from where she stood between his legs, her big amber eyes plaintive, and meowed that deep growl again.

"Do you want me to carry you?"

She rubbed her forehead against him but slinked to the side.

He figured that would have to do and walked them around the debris.

One small cabinet had overturned and there were broken pottery shards on the foyer floor they had to avoid, but they made it to the hallway unharmed.

In the kitchen, the cupboards were open and shattered dishware covered the floor and counters. Busted food containers spilled flour and sugar across the tiled floor. Fortunately, the refrigerator was a built-in, so it hadn't tipped over. The doors of the refrigerator were open, however, and perishable food and bags of blood had toppled out.

"Stay here," he said. Wearing leather-soled shoes, his feet were protected. He did his best to put away what he could and close the refrigerator door. Even without electricity, the refrigerator would keep its contents cold for a while, but he'd turn on the backup power soon.

She lifted a tentative paw, as if she wanted to follow him.

He surveyed the room for where she might safely go. The artwork at the far end hadn't jumped off the wall, so the kitchen table was clear of debris. He lifted her awkwardly, giving a little bounce to get her more firmly seated in his arms. She screamed her protest in his ear while he carried her to the kitchen tabletop, not stopping her meowing until all four paws were firmly planted.

He then went looking for his emergency kit and a flashlight in the pantry. He had excellent night vision, but a flashlight would be helpful if he had to do any emergency repairs.

Without warning, she leapt to a clear spot, scrambled to the basement stairs, and scratched at the door.

"We will check your lab later. You cannot just bolt downstairs. There may be glass everywhere, and you will need protective gear to deal with it. We must check the gas and power first, and the exterior. Stay here and I will carry you outside in a moment. The lab can wait."

He lifted the emergency kit—a very large plastic container he'd prepared, which included the emergency medicines and equipment Cerissa had provided—and lugged it past the glass. He came back for the *puma* and carried her to the front door, setting her back down and scooping up the emergency kit. He then led the way outside. Cerissa could see in the dark as well if not better than he could, but she stayed glued to his side.

He placed the earthquake kit in the driveway, a distance from the house. If another aftershock hit, he didn't want loose roof tiles flying down and hitting her. He clicked on the flashlight. "Stay here."

She didn't listen, immediately following him. He sighed and continued forward.

He started with the utilities. The automatic shut-off for the natural gas had worked. Good. Once he confirmed that no pipes were broken, he could reset it and turn the gas back on, but not before.

He checked the electrical panel next, to see if any breakers had tripped. None had, so the problem was on the electric company's end. He had a gasoline-powered emergency generator but wasn't ready to start it yet.

Instead, he flipped the inverter switch to run off battery power stored from the solar panels behind the pool house. The batteries only powered essential items, such as the refrigerator, alarm system, HVAC, and a charging station for phones and laptops.

He shined the flashlight on the corners of the house, and they seemed square. The house hadn't moved off its foundation. That was a relief.

The patio, however, was a mess. Half the water from the pool had slopped out over the edge, flooding the patio and into the pool house. The water remaining in the pool still rocked back and forth in gentle waves.

Inside the pool house, Henry shook his head at the sopping-wet rug, the water wicking up the furniture and bedspread. The damage caused by the overflow would take some time to clean up. But there was nothing to be done about it tonight, except to turn off the electricity. If the power came back on, he didn't want electrical appliances shorting out because of the water.

He switched off the subpanel breaker, then returned to the main house to check the chimney. A few top bricks appeared to have shaken loose, but the rest of the structure looked solid. Even the tiled roof looked in good shape.

As Cerissa followed him, her fear continued to leak through the crystal, and he redoubled his effort to shut down their connection. He couldn't let her distract him.

Now what to do? It would be dawn in about ten hours, and he didn't want to leave Cerissa alone to deal with the mess. It wasn't safe for her to sleep inside until the aftershocks stopped and they knew the true extent of the damage.

Besides, since his place was secure, he had duties to perform under the community's emergency response plan.

He took out his phone and tried to call Rolf. The phone didn't work. Either a lack of electrical power to the local cell tower or the antennas had been knocked down.

Time to go.

He and Rolf had agreed in advance that Rolf's house would be base camp during this kind of emergency, since he had a larger lawn area.

"Cerissa, I want you to wait by the emergency kit. I'm going to grab our go-bags, and our laptop computers, and then we are driving over to Rolf's."

She loped back to the front of the house and sat on top of the plastic box. She looked so strange, perched there with her wristwatch around the cat's forearm—her dewclaw kept the band from sliding off—and her engagement ring peeking through her furry paw.

Convinced she'd stay in place, he went back inside. There was not as much broken glass upstairs. She wasn't one for knickknacks, and the two pictures in her bedroom had managed to stay on the walls. The bathroom was wrecked—cosmetics and hair care products had fallen out of the medicine cabinet and off the shelves, plastic bottles rolling across the floor everywhere. He took a moment to upright the liquids so they wouldn't leak and leave a mess.

Her prepacked bag was in her closet, and her laptop on the small desk. He left both on the upstairs landing and went to his closet to get his bag.

He managed to carry everything in one trip, and even remembered to grab her purse and the clothes she left behind in the dining room. As he got to the front door, another aftershock hit. She jumped off the plastic box.

"Cerissa, stop!" he yelled, frantically motioning. "Stay back."

Chapter 9

Here, Kitty

RANCHO BAUTISTA DEL MURCIÉLAGO—MOMENTS LATER

Red roof tiles rattled and slid off the eaves, landing with a crash. Cerissa jumped off the plastic box and sank to the ground, covering her head with both paws and growling at the moving earth. It took all her willpower not to bolt into the nearby woodlands.

The shaking grew worse and panic crawled through her veins as memories from her childhood flooded her mind.

Walls falling. Ceilings collapsing. Fires starting. People screaming. Dead bodies in the street. Terrible foul smells.

She squeezed her eyes shut, trying to block the disorienting images and scents, her brain unable to process them in cougar form.

Destruction. Destruction everywhere.

Destruction she couldn't escape. The helplessness had terrified her.

She was only three years old at the time and had been locked in her human form by the Lux, so she couldn't morph into a creature more likely to survive the quake.

But she did survive that night. What grieved her, though, was that over a thousand people in her hometown of Surat didn't make it to morning.

Tonight's violent shaking threw her right back into the sensory memories from her childhood. She could smell the smoke from the house fires, the caustic scent of burning flesh, and pungent, sulfurous odors rising from the cracks in the earth.

Morphing helped calm her. As a cougar, she could outrun the quake's danger zone, escape from the collapsing walls, and leap to safety.

Henry hadn't understood her decision to morph. He hadn't understood that holding her down only made the experience worse.

And she couldn't understand why he hadn't turned into a bat or a wolf. He would have been much safer in either of the two forms he could adopt.

When the aftershock stopped, she uncovered her head, opened her eyes, and, with a sniff at the air, searched for Henry. He stood in the doorway, looking up at the eaves as if waiting for something else to fall. When the tiles remained on the roof, he locked the front door and carried their belongings with him.

She meowed at him. *Hurry! Before another aftershock strikes!*

"We will take your car," he said, walking by her. "It has more room for the luggage, and I want to bring a sleeping bag for you. You and Karen will probably sleep outdoors this morning, just to be on the safe side."

He opened the garage door using the manual release.

She eyed the garage skeptically. Going inside another structure didn't seem like a good idea.

He opened the car door. "Come on," he called.

She didn't. She sat waiting for him to back the car out.

In addition to the sleeping bag, he took two cases of blood out of the extra supplies she had stored there and put them in the trunk. None of the boxes had fallen over—a minor miracle.

He strode from the garage to grab the emergency kit waiting on the driveway next to her, but she refused to follow him when he called to her. Once everything was in the car, he stood by the passenger door.

She didn't move.

He gestured to her.

Well, he wasn't getting the message. She didn't want to be inside the garage if she could help it.

"Come on. We need to leave for Rolf's."

No choice.

She rushed into the garage and jumped onto the seat.

He knelt by her, stroking her until she purred. Except she'd be happier if they left. *Right now.*

"Are you sure you don't want to change back? I have your dress here."

He started to reach for it, and she stopped him, latching on to his arm with her teeth.

He got the message and scratched around her ears, her nose sniffing along his wrist, the smell of his cologne distracting her.

"Very well," he said.

She let him put the seatbelt around her. Anything to get them out of the garage.

Henry rarely drove the Malibu hybrid—it was Cerissa's car, and when they took it, she drove.

Strange, not to be at the wheel of the Viper.

The steep driveway curved past a sloping incline on the right. They were lucky no boulders had been knocked loose and fallen from the ridge above them. The contractor who last fixed the slope had done a decent job.

On the other side, a gentler hill ran up to the house. Rows of grapevines covered the area where a lawn would normally be grown.

Once on Robles Road, he watched for downed power lines and other objects that might be lying on the asphalt. The streetlights were off, making the stars in the night sky appear more intense. The long shadows cast by the dark vineyards and an unnerving silence made everything seem eerier. The Hill was never this quiet in the early evening hours.

He thought back to other earthquakes. Collapsed bridges and overpasses were a major hazard for unsuspecting drivers right after a major shaker, and he muttered a brief prayer of thanks that no such structures existed between his house and Rolf's.

Cerissa had quit meowing as well, her large amber eyes focused on the road, her anxiety lessening and no longer screaming at him through the crystal.

When they arrived at Rolf and Karen's house, the two were outside. Rolf was working on pitching a large olive-colored tent. With his military background, it wasn't surprising he'd already set up an organized campsite.

Henry closed the door to the Malibu, and Karen greeted him with a hug.

"Are you all right?" he asked her.

"We're fine. I have a few small cuts from flying glass, but nothing that won't heal. Is Cerissa okay?"

He glanced at the passenger seat, where Cerissa remained as a *puma*. "I think the earthquake scared her."

Karen went over to her and eyed the cat through the car's window. "How nervous is she at the moment?"

"Better than earlier. When I did something she didn't like, she gripped my arm with her teeth or pushed me with her paw, but she is still herself—no bites or scratches. Petting seems to comfort her, as well."

"Got it." Karen opened the door and squatted down to be on eye level with the cat, scratching her back until she purred loudly, closing those big amber eyes. "Hey, girlfriend. Rough night?"

Seeing Cerissa was in good hands, he joined Rolf in setting up the main tent, holding the tent upright as Rolf pounded in each stake with one swift whack of his hammer. The women would need a place to sleep, although he noticed that Rolf had also set up two smaller pop-up tents quite a distance from each other, one on each side of the main tent.

Rolf read the unasked query in Henry's expression. "For privacy."

Henry understood immediately. This may be the arrangement for more than a few nights, and Rolf had no intention of taking a vow of celibacy during this time.

While the women would sleep in the main tent, he and Rolf would be in the bomb shelter during the day. Rolf had built it during the Cold War scare in the 1950s, and it could withstand anything, including a major earthquake.

It was fortunate they had the option. Otherwise, they'd likely have to burrow into the dirt, given that the houses weren't safe until the initial aftershocks were over and they'd fully assessed any structural damage. That wasn't Henry's favorite way to sleep during the day, particularly when there might not be running water to clean up with the next evening.

"So how is your house?" Rolf asked.

"The foundation appears structurally sound. It will take a while to sweep up the glass and return books to shelves, but the damage is not bad. The pool house, however, was flooded. It's going to need water remediation."

He already estimated it would cost between twenty and fifty thousand dollars to repair the wet walls and replace the furnishings.

"And you?" Henry asked.

"About the same."

"Is the power off here too?"

Rolf bent over to hammer in the last stake and then straightened, stretching his back. "After the second aftershock, our lights went out. From what I can tell, it's not on my end."

"And the horses?"

Rolf snorted a laugh. "Karen checked them the minute we were outside. They were a bit hyper, but she calmed them down. They'll be fine."

"And Mort and Sang?" Henry looked around. "Where are they?"

"In the dog run. I'll release them later."

"It sounds like we both weathered this one pretty well."

"*Ja, ja.* But we won't know how much for sure until we can inspect the winery for damage. Have you tried listening for news reports yet?"

"Nothing but static on the car radio." Henry had tried tuning in the local stations on the drive over. Cerissa didn't have satellite radio. "Do you plan on setting up the ham radio?"

Rolf had his amateur radio license, as did Henry. Many of the vampires who lived on the Hill kept amateur radios for use in emergencies. Back in the day, before cell phones, he'd actively encouraged it within the community. They had call letters starting with the standard West Coast designation, followed by letters abbreviating "Sierra Escondida" and ending with the initial of the owner's first name. The vineyards were spread out over the grape-growing valley, each vineyard averaging around fifty acres, and the radios helped when regular communication networks failed.

Henry stood there a moment, scanning the community. Rolf's house was built on the crest of one of the rolling hills, surrounded as it was by large mountains to the south and north. The parallel mountain ranges ran for thirty miles to the west before angling to merge together, forming a point. The wall to the east completed the triangle, protecting them from intrusions by the mortal world.

Lights were completely off throughout the Hill—every house was pitch-black. On a normal night, the hillsides were spotted with glowing homes and floodlights.

The houses now looked lifeless, their lights snuffed out, reinforcing the strangeness of the situation.

"I've started the generator and have the radio hooked up," Rolf said. "TV will take longer. I need to rewire the satellite dish to give us a feed out here. The video feed to the pool area developed a wiring problem after the last World Series party, and I haven't fixed it yet."

"How did Karen handle the earthquake?"

"Didn't even faze her—aside from her sounding like a drill sergeant," he said with another snorted laugh. "We were in bed and she used her foot to kick my ass out, yelling, 'Move, move, move.' Apparently, supernatural speed wasn't fast enough for her."

Henry laughed at that.

"Anyway, since there was nowhere to shelter, I pulled her into the hallway. Her room is dangerous during an earthquake."

"Dangerous?"

Rolf shook his head in disgust. "She has too much stuff on the shelves overhead—I've told her that before. As it was, we were pelted by falling stuffed animals and superhero action figures. Why Karen likes those things, I will never understand."

Not the first time Rolf had complained about Karen's toy collection.

Rolf flicked his fingers toward the car. "What's wrong with Cerissa?"

"It was her first earthquake, I think. She does not seem to be dealing with it well. Perhaps Karen will be able to reassure her."

"That *thing* afraid? Now I've heard everything."

Henry rolled his eyes. "Please do not refer to her as a 'thing'—she is my mate."

Cerissa had not only saved Karen's life but was providing Rolf with adrenaline-enhanced blood on a regular basis. Despite Rolf's acceptance of her, his private potshots continued, more a commentary on Rolf's personality than a reflection of his true feelings about Cerissa.

"Fine," Rolf grumbled. "But explain why she didn't just flash the two of you to somewhere safe?"

"Rolf, she— This is not the time to talk about it. We should focus on the task at hand. What else needs to be done?"

Before Rolf could answer, the radio lit up and the speaker started squawking. "All-hands announcement. Report your status. Over."

Rolf loped over to the base station and keyed the microphone. "K-six-S-E-T, K-six-S-E-R. Tig, this is Rolf. We're fine. No power. Henry and Cerissa are with us and okay. Over."

"Do you have your list? Over."

"Ten-four. I have seven homes to contact on La Flor Street. Now that Henry is here, we're going to head out. I'll leave Karen on base radio and take my handheld. Over."

"Good. No one from your assigned area has made contact with us yet. Tell Cerissa to bring her medical bag. I have Dr. Clarke working with another team. Over."

"Ah, well—"

"Is there a problem with Cerissa? Was she hurt? You said they were okay. Over."

"No, I think she's in shock. First earthquake." Rolf shrugged, making eye contact with Henry. "If she's up to it, we'll bring her. Over."

"Ten-four. K-six-S-E-T."

"K-six-S-E-R."

Rolf hooked the microphone back on the side of the transmitter. "We need to get going. Can you ask your mate to get her *sheiße* together?"

Karen had managed to coax Cerissa out of the car, and they padded over. Henry knelt in front of the cat. "We need to go check on other community members, make sure they are all right. We'd like you to go with us for medical support. Can you morph back and get dressed? I'll put your bag in the big tent."

She made a rumbling sound, a cross between a growl and a purr. He wasn't sure how to translate that.

"If you're not up to it, you may stay behind with Karen."

Then he felt Cerissa's response through the crystal. Her anxiety was replaced with a sense of obligation, of doing the right thing. The feeling calmed her fear.

He carried her travel bag to the large tent, and Cerissa slunk in after him. He exited and zipped the flap to give her privacy.

A minute or two later, she emerged in mortal form, wearing blue jeans and a t-shirt, and pulled her long hair back in a ponytail. She went into his arms, burying her face against his shoulder. He hugged her to him and kissed the top of her head. "Was this your first earthquake?"

"No. As a child, I was in a terrible one."

Ah. Now he understood. "Another powerful one?"

"Yes, but can we talk about it later when we're alone?"

"Of course. I'm just glad you are feeling better. I was beginning to become concerned."

"I'll be all right now." She hugged him tighter. "I'm sorry I, ah, you know, wasn't much help earlier."

"You must take care of yourself, *mi amor*. It is important." He held her and stroked her hair. As much as they needed to leave right away, he refused to rush her. "If you are feeling better, Rolf and I should start checking on our neighbors. Others may not have fared as well."

"Okay." She grabbed her medical kit and put it in Rolf's SUV. "I'd rather be of help than to sit here and wait for the ground to shake again."

"Very well, if you're certain you are all right." He paused. "You won't morph again?"

"I won't. I took some stabilizer to help." She smirked at him. "Although it might be fun. I'd love to see Rolf explain to Tig why he has a cougar in his car."

Chapter 10
Don't Let Go

MORDIDA TROPICAL APARTMENTS—THIRTY MINUTES EARLIER

"What the f—" Bruce started before he recognized the odd rumble and slight shaking that marked the beginnings of an earthquake.

He stayed planted on his couch, his game controller in hand, waiting to see if it would end. He was winning the battle on *Call to Action*. He refused to abandon the game because of a little rumble—he'd lived in California all his life, and shakers happened all the time.

Except this one didn't stop.

Instead, the shaking ramped up, becoming more violent. His kitchen cupboards opened, and cans fell onto the floor with a loud *thump-thump-thump*.

Then the TV started to rock on its stand.

"No!"

He jumped to his feet, dodged around the coffee table, and staggered across the room, fighting to keep his balance.

Damn, I should have mounted it to the wall with a good bracket.

He'd spent a fortune on the large TV—at least, a fortune for his budget. He grabbed a hold of the nearby windowsill to steady himself and gripped the top of the television with the other hand.

The shaking became more violent, thrusting the floor back and forth. He lost his footing and, falling backward, took the screen with him and landed on his back, his head barely missing the solid wood coffee table.

"Fuck," he said with a groan, still gripping the television, which lay balanced across his stomach and chest. His back throbbed—he must have tweaked it on impact. He suppressed an impulse to chuck the television to the side.

Priorities were priorities.

Sounds of more stuff crashing off counters made him grimace. Then his laptop slid off the coffee table, landing next to him.

Shit, shit, shit. He couldn't afford to lose that either.

The shaking finally stopped.

Bruce hurt too much to lift the television off, and instead lay there waiting for the sharp spasms in his back to ease up.

Did any of his friends have a Vicodin squirreled away? He might need one, and no way was he going to the emergency room. With a quake like that, he'd be in the waiting room all night while they took the more badly injured victims first.

Then an aftershock rolled through, and the lights went out. He lay there in the darkness. And wow, was it dark. No streetlights outside, no blue lights on his game station, nothing.

Where the hell did he leave his flashlight? He knew it was somewhere in the kitchen.

When the rumbling died down, he eased the television to the side, his back screaming with each movement, and propped the stupid thing against the console table it had originally sat on. He grabbed a couch cushion and placed it on the floor to catch the television in case it fell over again.

Only then did he feel his head throb and rubbed the spot. Checking his fingers—no blood. Ice would help.

He straightened up, and his back spasmed again, dizziness stopping him. When the stabbing pain passed, his eyes adjusted to the darkness. The moon and stars outside the window cast a tiny bit of light through the window, enough to see the room was a mess.

He returned his attention to the most important matter—the television. A spider-web crack appeared in the top corner. He ran his finger over the break. It didn't feel too bad. As soon as the power came back on, he'd check to see if it still worked. He stooped to pick up the laptop next, and his back reminded him to move more carefully. He ignored the pain and checked the laptop for damage. The screen looked okay...

Fuck! The video!

He hit the power button. Nothing.

Come on, you have to work.

How was he supposed to get his million dollars if he didn't have the video of his boss fucking that woman? Maybe the battery was dead.

He couldn't remember the last time he'd charged it.

The camera might still be okay. He tripped his way to the kitchen, dodging debris, and opened one drawer after another, trying to find that flashlight his mother had given him. Where was it?

Then he remembered. He'd put it in the drawer by his bed, right next to the lube.

He made his way to the bedroom—stubbing his toe in the process on something hard—and found the flashlight.

Sweeping the light across the room, he looked for where the camera should be on the old bookcase his mother had given him when he thought he might go to college. Everything on the shelves had fallen to the floor. He dug through the pile of stuff and threw the dirty socks and underwear to the side, until he got to the small black box.

Picking it up, he hit power and waited.

Come on, come on, come on.

Finally, the screen flashed, and he scrolled to the video and played it. The seconds waiting for it to load were the longest of his life. When the playback began, he breathed out a sigh of relief.

The video was fine.

He still had a chance at his million dollars.

He opened a drawer and placed the black box gently among his clean underwear. Aftershocks could be expected, and this would protect the camera and its precious recording.

His lower back continued to throb. He returned to the kitchen, clearing a path with his foot, and, after setting the flashlight on the counter so he could see, opened the freezer, taking out an ice pack he used when he exercised too hard, wrapping it against his lower back and fastening the Velcro closure over his stomach. He then grabbed some ice cubes, folded them in a kitchen towel, and held the makeshift ice pack to the tender spot on his head.

He started picking up the dented canned goods from the floor one-handed, which turned out to be a bad idea. Each stoop sent shooting pain down his leg.

He stopped and stood straight up, giving the muscle spasms a minute to calm down. Then it hit him.

Would he even have a job? If he had this much damage, what about the winery?

His bank account wasn't exactly flush. He had enough to pay one more month's rent and food, but then he'd be broke. And if the winery was damaged, he'd have to act soon, or Bautista wouldn't have any money to pay for the video. Or would a rich man like him have tons of cash hidden away?

He ignored the rest of the mess, eased himself onto the couch, careful not to tweak his back again, and used one of those free paper pads real estate agents left on your doorstep to write out the blackmail message. Last he checked, bitcoins were going for eleven thousand each. A hundred sounded like a nice, round number.

In the morning, he'd buy a newspaper and cut and paste the message, and have it delivered. Waiting until he learned where Bautista disappeared to in the early morning no longer made sense.

Sure, he'd still search for the hidey hole once he returned to work—but who knew when that would be? The earthquake could disrupt everything for weeks. He had to get his money now, while the getting was still good.

Hmm. How long would the post office take to deliver mail after an earthquake? Maybe he should splurge on FedEx.

The one thing he couldn't do: hand-carry it. The community where Bautista lived had a guard at the gate. No way he was sneaking past that.

No, he'd check on the fastest delivery and send it off tomorrow.

Chapter 11

To the Rescue

Rolf and Karen's home—Around the same time

Cerissa got into the back seat of Rolf's white Cadillac Escalade, and Mort and Sang jumped in to join her. The two German shepherds were always glad to see her, sniffing and nuzzling her to get some love. Even when she was in her cougar form, it never threw them—they always seemed to know it was her.

Henry loaded the large box of emergency medical supplies into the back. Rolf said goodbye to Karen, who'd happily agreed to stay by the radio. She'd be able to find out faster how her friends on the Hill were doing by remaining behind. Rolf then fastened each dog into its harness, and Cerissa buckled into the center seat between them.

With one arm around each dog, she let out a deep breath, feeling better than she had since the first earthquake. She stroked their fur and talked to them, distracted from her fears by the comfort Mort and Sang offered.

"They're guard dogs, not pets," Rolf grumbled as he drove.

Cerissa caught him watching her and the dogs in his rearview mirror, and as much as she felt like making a rude gesture, she ignored him.

Henry motioned to Rolf. "Please let her be," he said quietly. "If the dogs are keeping her calm, she will be better able to help us."

"Ach," Rolf replied. "You coddle her too much."

"Just like you do with Karen."

Cerissa smirked at their banter, the type of exchange she'd come to expect from the two men. But it was true—she truly felt calmer with the two dogs leaning against her.

The list Rolf had was for the seven homes in the valley's lowlands, located on a residential cul-de-sac. It wasn't far from the town's cultural center where the country club, police station, and town hall were located.

When they turned onto the street, Cerissa let out a gasp. Most of the homes had sustained some cosmetic damage, but one had suffered serious destruction.

She blinked, stunned by what she saw. Marcus and Nicholas's home looked like a giant had crushed the house with his fist.

***

Henry leapt from the SUV before it stopped. The brickwork that formed a façade on Marcus's two-story colonial home had collapsed, leaving the front door completely blocked. He ran around the structure, hopping the fence and looking for a way in.

Haphazard piles of brick were everywhere, blocking the other doors as well, the dusty, dry smell of old mortar accosting his nose. Rolf leapt the fence to join him.

"Hello," Henry called out. "Marcus, Nicholas—are you in there?"

Marcus leaned out a second-story window. "I need help. Nicholas is trapped."

Rolf began clearing bricks away from the back door, tossing them behind him at breakneck speed.

"Rolf, hold off on that," Henry said. "Find the gas shut-off—we need to be certain it's off." Rolf gave a brisk two-fingered salute and dashed away just as Cerissa arrived at Henry's side. "Cerissa, please wait here."

Henry extended his claws and scaled the exterior of the house, crawling over the rough plaster left behind when the bricks tumbled off. Reaching the wooden windowsill, he propelled himself through the second-story window that Marcus had leaned out of.

"He's in his room." Marcus ran down the hallway, leading the way. "I was trapped downstairs right after it happened. I only just found him. Something heavy fell on his head, he's bleeding, and was talking to me a few minutes ago, but I can't get him to respond now." Marcus rattled the doorknob. "The doorframe buckled. I can't open it."

Henry pushed his shoulder against the door. Beside him, Marcus did the same. Even with their combined strength, it wouldn't budge.

"I think there is only one way to get inside," Henry said, and hammered his fist through the door's paneling, creating a large hole.

He hesitated the barest of seconds, wondering if he should transform into a bat and fly inside. But no, that would take more time than just ripping the door apart at superspeed, and Cerissa would need access to provide emergency treatment. Using the hole as a starting point, he and Marcus alternated, tearing pieces from the door.

By the third try, he could see Nicholas's legs. The mortal was trapped on the bed under a tall bureau and not moving.

As soon as the hole was large enough, Marcus boosted himself up and over, climbing through, and Henry followed.

Marcus got on the far side of the half-fallen bureau. "Here, help me."

Together they lifted it off, bracing their arms across the drawers to keep them from sliding out and falling on Nicholas. Marcus then bit his own wrist and held the bleeding wound to his mate's open lips. Some of the blood dripped into the unconscious man's mouth, but his Adam's apple didn't bob—unless Nicholas swallowed, the blood wouldn't work.

They needed Cerissa.

Henry started making a bigger hole in the door. Before he could remove the remaining remnants, Mort and Sang leapt past him, Rolf and Cerissa behind them in the hallway.

Cerissa's gaze focused beyond him into the room. "Marcus—stop! Don't move him," she yelled. Ducking, she stepped through the large hole, carrying the smaller of her medical bags. Marcus eased the mortal back onto the bed. "Quique, please bring up the rest of the medical supplies. Rolf, can you radio for an ambulance?"

"Will he be all right?" Henry asked.

"I don't know. Please, go."

<hr />

SIERRA ESCONDIDA POLICE STATION—FIVE MINUTES EARLIER

From the crow's-nest over the police station, Tig caught the scent of burning wood before she saw the source. She swung in an arc, scanning for the source with her binoculars, and abruptly stopped when she saw the red flames lighting the night sky above Gaea's property. Her house and vineyard backed up to the higher foothills, which were covered with dense, dry brush.

If those hills caught fire, the magnitude of the disaster would be doubled.

Hell, it would be a million times worse.

Tig keyed her portable police radio. She had both a police radio and a mobile ham radio strung over her shoulder so she could talk on either system. "Dispatch, this is Chief Anderson. We have a ten-seventy-two. Flames visible from the crow's-nest. We need both fire trucks." She gave the address. "Are they available?"

A moment's pause. "Ten-four. Both are available. All crews have been called in on overtime. The fire chief is currently inspecting the business district for gas hazards. Do you want him too? Over."

"Let him complete his inspections. We don't want to fight fires on two fronts. Just get me those trucks. Out."

She climbed down the ladder, carrying the binoculars, and called out to Zeke, one of her reserve officers, who was waiting in the lobby for his assignment. "We have signs of fire at Gaea's. Take over the crow's-nest. Keep scanning for smoke or other problems. Radio me if you see anything else. Got it?"

"Yes, ma'am."

Tig handed off the binoculars and dashed deeper into the police station, grabbed the keys for the police van—it had medical supplies and various rescue tools—and ran back outside.

As she sped onto Robles Road, she hit the siren and keyed the hands-free radio. "Captain Johnson, we have signs of fire at Gaea's. I've got ladder trucks on the way. I'm headed there and will try to raise her on the ham radio frequency. I put Zeke in the crow's-nest to replace me. If we have any spare volunteers, send them to Gaea's. Over."

She waited for Jayden to answer. He was running the emergency operations center in the squad room. She could count on him to think on his feet and keep all their resources properly tasked.

"Ten-four," he said a minute later. "I just heard from Rolf and Henry. They are tied up at Marcus's. Structural failure; Nicholas has been hurt. We don't know how severely yet. I've dispatched an ambulance to pick him up."

Damn. Her stomach dropped. It would destroy Marcus if something happened to the mortal. "Keep me updated. Out."

She grabbed the ham radio. "K-six-S-E-G, K-six-S-E-T, do you read me?"

No response from Gaea. Tig pounded her hand on the steering wheel. Keeping her foot on the accelerator, she repeated the call signs, but still no response.

The closer she got, the denser the smoke became, turning from black to white at the top plume. It didn't look good.

MARCUS AND NICHOLAS'S HOME—AROUND THE SAME TIME

Cerissa rushed to Nicholas's bedside. It had taken all her willpower to force herself to enter the partially collapsed building. The urge to morph into a more agile form rode her skin, and she gritted her teeth against the feeling. The stabilizer she'd taken earlier helped, but only a little. After everything she'd gone through to remain in the community with Henry, she couldn't morph and out her Lux identity now.

She just couldn't.

She dropped her medical bag on the floor, flung it open, and took out a stethoscope and a blood pressure cuff. "Marcus, please move aside. Let me examine him."

When Marcus didn't move, she tried to shove him away from the bed.

He stayed in place, tightly holding Nicholas's hand, trying to coax him to feed, refusing to look at her, refusing to budge.

"Please, Marcus, move. I can't help him if I can't get close enough to examine him."

"My blood will cure him, if he would just wake up."

"Is he on any medications?"

"None that I know of."

As they spoke, Cerissa wedged herself closer, her hip pressing against Marcus's to create space, and started a manual examination of what she could reach, palpating Nicholas's abdomen. No swelling. She checked his extremities. Nothing appeared broken.

"What happened?"

"That chest of drawers fell on him," Marcus said, gesturing with his free hand at the tall chest angled at the side.

She stuffed the buds of the stethoscope into her ears and listened to Nicholas's heart, then his lungs. His heart was beating fast, but his breathing was steady for the moment.

"Move back," she said a little louder than she intended to. She wrested Nicholas's hand from Marcus and squeezed past his hip to wrap the blood pressure cuff on Nicholas's arm and pumped it up, then let the air slowly escape, listening through the stethoscope.

Not good. His systolic reading was high.

Henry returned carrying the larger emergency box. "Where should I put it?"

"Right over here." Cerissa pointed next to her. "Marcus, you must move. Nicholas has a bad gash on his head. Let me see what I can do."

Henry gripped Marcus's shoulder and eased him away. "Trust me. Cerissa will help him if she can."

Mort and Sang moved in to fill the space next to her and sat down. Anytime Marcus tried to move closer, they growled.

Rolf finished his radio conversation and snapped his fingers at the dogs. They didn't move. "That was Jayden. The town's paramedics are on their way. Ten minutes out if the road from town is clear of debris."

"Good," she replied.

"Just remember, they don't know what we are."

She ignored his condescending comment and scanned the room, trying to figure out what happened to Nicholas. A white marble bust of a man's head lay on the floor. She pushed it with her shoe—very heavy. When the chest of drawers tipped over, the bust must have hit Nicholas's head before rolling off the bed. It was the only object around that could have fallen on him and left behind the large gash.

The blood dripped off his scalp, forming a rusty pool on the tan pillowcase. The area around the gash was swelling, and a small amount of blood dripped from his nostrils. She pressed a gauze pad against the wound and taped it down. "He probably has a concussion—that, or the bust hit both his nose and his head. We need to get him to the local hospital."

She didn't like the signs and took his blood pressure again. The rising systolic reading was indicative of intracranial bleeding.

Rolf snapped his fingers at the dogs again and pointed to the door. "We've got spectators gathering outside. I'm going to check on the rest of the block, make sure everyone is okay." He went to grab Sang by the collar. "*Fuß!*"—heel—"*Fuß!*"

Sang growled and snapped.

Cerissa waved Rolf off. "Leave the dogs alone. You're interfering with my concentration."

"I need them to search for other victims."

Cerissa let out a huff and petted the dogs, giving each a small dose of her aura. "I'm okay. Go with him."

Mort whined and licked her arm.

"It's okay. Go."

The two dogs jetted out of the room, and after giving her a scowl, Rolf followed.

She knew she'd get an earful from Rolf later for "corrupting" his dogs. Tough.

She pulled a small suitcase from the larger kit Henry had carried up, flipped it open, removed a green canister tank, and started administering oxygen to Nicholas using a face mask. Then she took out a chemical ice pack, popped the barrier, and placed it over the gauze to slow the swelling. She didn't start an IV because of the possible brain bleed—additional fluids would make it worse.

Next, she grabbed a collar brace from the kit. "I'm putting a rigid collar on him to immobilize his neck for transport."

"Can't you wake him up?" Marcus asked.

"I can't give him a stimulant because of the head wound."

"If he could just feed, he'd be all right."

"There may be another way. When was the last time you bit him?"

Fang serum was her main concern when using vampire blood intravenously to heal a patient. "We don't want to accidentally turn him."

"Last night." Marcus glanced at his watch. "At least nineteen hours."

Nicholas's breathing was becoming more labored, despite the oxygen, another sign of internal bleeding.

Vampire blood would help—it healed the vascular system first, which only made sense. Without blood flow, it wouldn't be able to reach all parts of the body to facilitate the turn.

But she'd been down this road before. One pint was the most she could give intravenously without risk—more, and it could start the transition to vampire. It would be horrible to save his life only to have the council vote to destroy him. They strictly enforced the prohibition against creating new vampires.

And given it had been less than twenty-four hours since the last bite, reducing the amount of blood she gave him was the prudent thing to do.

Cerissa used a sixty-milliliter syringe and a special silver-plated needle to draw the blood from Marcus's arm. "Do you understand, Marcus? If we give him blood now, and he wakes up, you can't feed him more."

"I understand. Please, just help him."

When she finished drawing the first dose of Marcus's blood, she found a good vein in Nicholas's arm and slowly infused the ruby-red fluid. Once it was all in, she pumped up the blood pressure cuff again and took a reading.

Not good. She bit her lip. In theory, she could give six more doses. But no one really knew how much margin of error existed. She'd remain conservative—perhaps only four more.

She couldn't use any Lux tools even if the Protectors hadn't forbidden it. Marcus had already been suspicious of her, and she couldn't do anything to increase his suspicion. She prepared to take another blood draw. Under the circumstances, what more could she do?

CHAPTER 12
WHERE THERE'S SMOKE

GAEA'S HOME—SAME TIME

Tig parked off Robles Road so she wouldn't block the fire trucks when they arrived and *whooshed* up the long driveway leading to Gaea's house. It took her a few seconds more to reach the burning home, but this way the emergency vehicles had full access.

Smoke poured out from the back of the house. She pounded on the front door. No one answered. Still no cell phone reception. She'd tried multiple times on the radio to raise Gaea. Right now, only two people lived there. Gaea, and her guest—her adopted son, Seaton. Neither had answered.

"Gaea!" Tig shouted.

"Back here!"

Tig ran in the direction of Gaea's voice. Seaton and another man, half-dressed with his back to her, were trying to fight the fire with garden hoses. The gas line must have blown. The kitchen was totaled, and the fire was working its way deeper into the building.

Gaea aimed another hose at the garden and surrounding brush, wetting it down. "We tried to call. Oh dear, I don't know how it happened. We checked the gas main right after the quake, it looked just fine, and then, I don't know. We were upstairs. There was a loud explosion, and we barely made it out the front door."

"The fire trucks are on their way." Tig could hear the sirens and see the lights coming up Robles Road. "Is anyone else inside? Anyone hurt?"

"We're fine." Gaea glanced down at the black-smudged robe she wore. "Just a little smokey."

Tig let out a snort. "I'm going out front to guide the trucks in. I'll start watering down the vineyard on that side."

"Thank you."

Tig hoofed it back to the front, standing by the fire hydrant, which was forty feet from the structure, the minimum per code. The trucks pulled into the driveway and stopped near her.

"Hi, chief," the fire captain said. "We've got this. Is the gas off?"

"Homeowner said it was. She's around back with garden hoses."

The captain signaled one of his crew. "Check the gas main."

The man took off at a run with a wrench in hand. The rest of the firefighters began laying out hoses and connecting them to the hydrant. Seeing all the buff males, she was surprised some of the Hill vampires hadn't gone shopping closer to home for a mate. Only uninitiated mortals staffed the fire and police stations located in the business zone, making them fair game without violating the Hills's no-dating rule.

Within minutes, the hoses were charged, and the water hit the fire with a *hiss*, turning it instantly to steam.

While the firefighters knocked down the blaze, she radioed Jayden for a status report. No other problems needed her attention, so she decided to stay at Gaea's until the fire was out.

Red embers flew overhead, the sparks lighting the night sky before landing. Tig stayed at the fire captain's heels. Once he had the flames under control, she asked, "Can we direct some water on the vineyard? We can't let the sparks spread the fire to those hills."

"Yes," he said tersely, a *stay in your own lane* glance following it.

But he spoke into a radio, and two men peeled off to connect a third hose. They began sweeping water across the vineyard, which was heavy with almost-ripe fruit.

This was going to kill Gaea's harvest.

Tig thanked the captain and went looking for the vampire matron. Gaea stood at the sidelines near her backyard flower garden, flanked by Seaton, who had his face buried in a hand-held computer game, and—

What the hell is Ari doing here?

Tig raised her eyebrows at the half-dressed mortal on Gaea's other side, then shook her head.

First things first.

"Is everyone okay?" Tig asked. "Smoke inhalation? Burns? Anything?"

Ari saluted. "All good, chief."

Seaton grunted, not looking up.

Gaea shook her head, looking a little embarrassed. "Is everyone else all right?"

"Marcus's house collapsed. Nicholas was injured—not sure how bad—but Cerissa is there with him. He'll be on his way to the hospital shortly."

Gaea and Ari spoke at the same time.

"Oh dear. Marcus must be in knots," Gaea said.

"So Ciss and Henry are okay?" Ari asked.

Tig nodded to both of them but answered Ari's question. "They're fine. Like everyone else, they had some minor damage, glass breakage. No injuries."

Then she really eyed what Ari wore. Boxer shorts, white with red hearts. And it hit her.

Of course.

The council dispensation had given him carte blanche. *That* was what he was doing here.

She scrubbed her face. At least she didn't have to fire him. She'd told him the next time she caught him violating the Covenant that he'd be kicked off the Hill and not allowed back. As much as she might want to grump about it, he wasn't violating the rules—not at the moment.

She narrowed her eyes at him. "Why didn't you grab some clothes to get decent?"

"Hey, this is all I had handy when the fire started. Wore it to the party, under my suit. Never know when you're going to get lucky." He smirked in Gaea's direction.

"Ari, behave yourself," Gaea said.

"At least I had my priorities straight." Ari huffed. "I was too busy to dress—I had to get the important stuff out of her house. Gaea's desktop computer, her laptop, her e-reader, and her phone are over there." He pointed at the pile on a garden bench, far enough from the water and smoke. "She was too busy grabbing her jewelry to help with the really valuable stuff."

"Now, Ari." Gaea laid a very white hand on Ari's brown arm. "Some of those jewels are over four hundred years old. Priceless."

"Ha," he said, a deep, throaty sound. He gripped Gaea around the waist, tugging her over for a kiss. "I've got all the jewels you need right here."

Tig shook her head. At least he had the decency not to grab himself when he said it.

MARCUS AND NICHOLA'S HOME—AROUND THE SAME TIME

Nicholas's eyelids began to flutter. Cerissa placed her fingers on his wrist's pulse points.

At least, that was what she intended to do until Marcus shoved her away from the bed, taking Nicholas's hand away from her.

"How are you feeling?" Marcus asked.

"Like I've been hit by a truck." Nicholas lifted the oxygen mask and rose on his forearms. The ice pack slid off. "My head hurts."

Cerissa patted the air, gesturing for him to stay down. "Don't try to move. Keep breathing the oxygen. You have a concussion and possible spinal injury. I've immobilized your neck with a brace. There was an earthquake. We're going to get you to the hospital soon."

"Would Marcus's blood help?" Nicholas asked, still holding himself up.

"Already done. Intravenously. You can't have any more for another twenty-four hours, understand?"

"Uh, yeah."

"Now, put the oxygen mask back on and lie down."

Nicholas slowly lowered himself onto the pillow.

Squeezing around Marcus, she returned the ice pack to Nicholas's head. "If you're able to, hold this on and apply pressure."

Marcus frowned at Cerissa. "Why does he have to go to Mordida Community Hospital? Why don't you take care of him at Dr. Clarke's surgery center? You and Shayna."

Yacov's widow was a surgical nurse. They'd worked together before.

Cerissa shook her head. "He may still need a neurosurgeon. That's very specialized. Even with the earthquake, they'll fast-track head injuries. He'll get a better standard of care than we can give him. And I think Shayna is out of town."

Cerissa took Nicholas's blood pressure again, which had returned to normal. His breathing had become regular as well.

A short while later, they heard a commotion below. The paramedics had arrived.

Cerissa fished into her bag and pulled out a jar of salve. "Marcus, let me give you something for those cuts and that large abrasion before they get up here."

Marcus must have been hit by flying debris during the earthquake. A large gash crossed his face. While a vampire would heal quickly, she had something that would speed the process.

Last thing they needed was the paramedics insisting on taking him to the hospital for stitches.

Marcus looked at her as if she were crazy. "Mortal medicines don't work on vampires."

"This will." She took the salve and spread the microbeads on his cut arm. The cut immediately closed over and healed into a scab.

Marcus frowned at her. "What is that?"

She continued to apply it to his cuts, including the bad gash on his face. Now that he'd seen it work, he let her. "It's vampire blood microencapsulated in an inert suspension. It's one of the by-products of my research."

She continued to dab the salve on his wounds until all were treated. Then she used some to treat Nicholas's cuts. She figured the small amount of vampire blood in the salve wouldn't harm him.

"Do you really think I need to go to the hospital? I feel better—"

"You still need a CAT scan to be sure. Head injuries aren't to be treated lightly."

She spread a little more of the salve on Nicholas's last scrape, but she didn't treat the head wound. The doctors at the hospital would need to see that to take the injury seriously.

Marcus pointed at the medication. "Whose blood is it?"

Cerissa looked at the jar. "This one's Henry's. If you'll give me some blood samples, I'll make up one for you to keep. Nicholas can use it for cuts, abrasions, and minor burns."

She was just putting the jar away when the paramedics reached them by ladder, coming through the now-open window, the cool night air following them in. She gave a quick report. The two-man team decided to transport Nicholas to the hospital.

As the paramedics lifted him into a rescue basket, he said, "Thanks, Cerissa. I appreciate what you did for me."

"Glad to, Nicholas." She gave his ankle a friendly squeeze. "I'll be in touch tomorrow to see how you're doing."

CHAPTER 13

BAD, VERY BAD

ROBLES ROAD—FIFTEEN MINUTES LATER

Henry used the mobile radio to contact Tig while Rolf drove. "K-six-S-E-T, K-six-S-E-R. Tig, it's Henry."

"Go ahead. Report."

"La Flor Street is clear."

While Cerissa treated Nicholas, Rolf had taken a roll call of everyone else on La Flor Street to make sure no one was badly injured or trapped in one of the buildings.

"Only one person hurt," he continued. "Nicholas is being transported to the hospital with a head injury."

"Do we know the severity?" Tig asked.

"Cerissa treated Nicholas before they left, but he needs further scans and treatment." On the off chance an uninitiated mortal was monitoring the open radio frequency, Henry erred on the side of caution and didn't explain the nature of the treatment. Tig would likely get the hint. "And Luis drove Marcus to the hospital. Marcus's car is buried under rubble."

"Ten-four. We've had one fire, a few structural failures but only minor injuries."

"A fire?"

"At Gaea's. The fire department has it under control. It didn't spread."

Henry let out a sigh of relief. At this time of year, brush fires were a major threat. Like all homeowners on the Hill, he'd removed brush to meet the four-hundred-foot clearance requirement.

"The town hall survived like a champ," Tig added. "No damage there."

"That is good to hear. We are headed back to Rolf's house unless you need our help."

"Thanks, but we're good. The emergency plan rolled out without a hitch."

"Have you heard how big it was and where the epicenter was?" No one on La Flor Street could provide him with an update. They'd all been too busy responding to the immediate crisis.

"The news isn't good," Tig said. "The epicenter was in Antioch, according to the reports so far. But I haven't heard the size estimate yet."

Antioch lay to the north of them, near the Sacramento-San Joaquin River Delta.

"And we felt the quake all the way down here?" Henry couldn't believe it. "That has to be the largest one we've had in twenty years."

"Yeah. We'll see what the fallout is later. I have to get back to work. Out."

Tig wasn't exaggerating when she said the news wasn't good. The death count would be high if the earthquake caused the dams to fail in the river delta, and the resulting property damage would be devastating.

Henry laid the radio on the front console and looked over his shoulder. Mort and Sang sat on either side of Cerissa like she was their queen and they were the royal guards. She had a hand on each dog, petting it. He refrained from telling her the ramifications of Tig's report—she seemed at peace for the first time since the quake hit.

When they arrived, Karen greeted them, talking nonstop, reporting on the rest of the Hill. Marcus's house had experienced the worst direct damage, but another home had its roof collapse when an old tree, rotted with age, fell on it. The occupants escaped without injury.

No one had received news from outside the walled community, but it had only been a few hours since the quake had hit, and the power was still off to most homes.

Which reminded him. This wasn't over. "Have you counted the number of aftershocks?"

"At least five," Rolf said. "That's not a good sign."

"We need more information." Karen waved in the direction of the television. "Let's see if we can get a local channel. I have the satellite dish working."

"Really?" Rolf looked impressed and slipped his arm around her shoulders, pulling her close. "I might just keep you around."

"Hey, it's nothing that any gal couldn't do."

Not wanting to stare while Karen and Rolf kissed, Henry looked around and spotted the pool furniture. He carried the four-cushion couch over to the television so they could watch in comfort, then went back for two matching chairs. Cerissa sat down on the couch, and Mort and Sang sprawled at her feet. She stooped down to pet them and scratch their stomachs.

Rolf clicked the television remote and then scowled at her. "What have you done to my dogs?"

"Nothing. They just appreciate it when someone is nice to them."

"You are spoiling them. You'll turn them into house pets."

"Someone's grumpy." She cast a mischievous look at Henry before continuing to scratch behind Mort and Sang's ears. She looked back at the dogs and said, "Isn't he being a grump? You two wouldn't mind being pampered, now would you?"

Karen laughed. Mort sat up and put a black paw in Cerissa's lap, like he wanted to join them on the couch.

Henry set down the two chairs he carried and *tsked* at the dog. Letting the dogs on the furniture wouldn't go over well with Rolf.

"Mort, down," Henry said, shooting a disapproving look at Cerissa. The dog reluctantly returned to his post at her feet, and Henry sat down on the couch next to her. "Cerissa, do not annoy Rolf."

She gave each dog a kiss on the top of its furry head. "Fine."

He worked an arm around her shoulders, bringing her against him, and he felt her body relax into his. "I thought we were going to watch the news," he said.

Rolf had flipped through the satellite television channels, stopping on an old movie. "I'm getting there."

Karen took the seat next to Rolf, curling her legs on the couch and leaning against her mate.

"There," Rolf said, stopping on a major satellite news channel.

The on-the-scene reporter looked away from the camera, accepting a paper from someone offscreen.

"We have confirmation the earthquake was seven point eight in magnitude."

Henry whistled. A very large one, indeed.

Through the crystal he sensed Cerissa's anxiety spike, and he squeezed her, pulling her closer to him and taking her hand in his.

The reporter stood outdoors on a residential street that appeared to be at the top of a rise, flood waters engulfing lower-level homes behind her.

She was illuminated by a single light, and the paper folded on itself, fighting the wind. The bottom-screen chyron identified her as being in Hayward.

"The epicenter was just east of Antioch, along the Midland fault. As you can see behind me, reports of flooding are starting to come in all along the delta." The reporter touched her ear, as if listening to someone through an earbud. "We have unedited news chopper video."

The shot cut to an aerial view. Henry had a hard time getting much perspective from the video, as it was pitch-black except for a spotlight from the helicopter highlighting a circle of raging brown water.

"The levees have broken in spots," the reporter continued. "The dirt walls gave way within minutes of the quake. The delta river system has flooded nearby farms and homes. Efforts are being made to evacuate residents in the area."

Henry stood, releasing Cerissa's hand, and started pacing behind the couch, still watching the newscast. The water they received from the delta was critical to the life of his vineyard. "This is not good."

"Why didn't they reinforce the levees?" Cerissa asked.

Rolf snorted. "The taxpayers refused to pass the bond initiatives necessary to fix them."

"Oh yeah," Karen said, sounding angry. "And don't get me started on all the naysayers who refused to consider the two bypass tunnels that the former governor proposed. Would've rerouted the snowmelt, bypassing the levee area. Too expensive, they said. Will hurt the environment, they said. Now look at the mess we're in. The environment is screwed up and everyone will have to pay five times as much to fix the problem."

"Only scientists and farmers raised the alert," Henry added. "Their voices were not loud enough."

"Water is boring—until you don't have any." Rolf patted Karen's leg. "She's right. They should have built the tunnels when they had the chance. But they didn't."

Henry scrubbed a hand over his face as his stomach twisted into knots. "We won't know until we see the real extent of the damage, but this could have a major impact on California. And on us." He sighed. "No water—no wine."

Cerissa reached behind the couch to where he paced, grabbing his hand as he came by again. "Oh, Henry, I don't know what to say."

He shook his head. "It's hard to just stand here and watch that destruction and do nothing, to see a disaster coming our way and not have enough power to prevent it." He came back around the couch and sat next to her. "Maybe it won't be as bad as we imagine."

"Bah! Are you joking?" Rolf scoffed. "A seven point eight? In Antioch? We'll be lucky if the whole delta doesn't succumb to liquefaction."

Henry didn't explain it to Cerissa. She was a scientist, after all, and he assumed she knew that in an earthquake, water pressure increased in saturated soil, decreasing its ability to support structures. The result caused the collapse of dams, bridges, buildings…and dirt levees.

Her face fell at Rolf's words, affirming his decision to stay silent.

"And as the earthen levees fail"—Rolf gestured vehemently at the videos of the damage—"salt water mixes with fresh. All the water will be useless for agriculture or drinking."

As much as Henry knew Rolf was right, now was not the time to worry their mates. Cerissa in particular seemed anxious again from the earthquake itself, despite the brief respite cuddling the dogs had given her. "Rolf, we do not yet know the extent of the damage. Do not borrow trouble."

"I already know it will be bad. The only question is, how bad?"

After the reporter repeated the same information and video for the third time, Rolf flipped through the other news channels. They didn't have anything new to report. He turned off the TV. "Better to conserve power for now. We don't know how long we'll be using the generator."

"Well, that's my cue." Karen stood. "I'm going to bed. Good night, everyone." She kissed Rolf, and then went to the main tent to sleep.

Cerissa followed, but veered off to the car, got out her laptop, and set it up on the camp table.

Rolf walked over to her. "You have internet access?"

She shook her head, looking distressed. "I'm connected to the Enclave. Different system."

Henry leaned over her shoulder and understood immediately. She had access to instantaneous satellite photos that even the major news outlets didn't have yet. A lot of the levees had indeed failed. Flooding had been instant. Homes were wiped out. The casualty rate would be high, people drowned in their sleep, no time to escape.

Cerissa slid the computer to Rolf and showed him how to scroll through the images. She stood up and walked off toward the woods that ran between Henry and Rolf's property. Henry furrowed his brow, trying to decide what to do. She probably just needed space to process all of this—she had high empathy for any suffering—but he wasn't convinced she was thinking clearly after everything they'd been through tonight.

He followed her, as did Mort and Sang. Rolf showed some restraint for a change and kept whatever snide remark he might have been thinking to himself.

That or he was simply too fascinated by the satellite images of the destruction.

As she entered the edge of the oak woodlands, Henry caught up to her. He put his arms around her and pulled her to him. "Haven't you seen disasters like this before?"

He felt her swallow hard against his chest. "When I was a small child a large earthquake devasted Surat. Thousands upon thousands died."

Thousands. ¡Dios mío! The tragedy she must have witnessed.

The homes constructed in the early 1780s—around the time she was born—would have fared far worse than Marcus's house had and completely collapsed under those circumstances. "Was this your first earthquake since that one?"

"My first big one, yes. I've been through small ones, but none like this."

No wonder she reacted the way she did.

Henry leaned back to look in her eyes and brushed her hair away from her face where it fell out of the ponytail. "Why did you morph?"

"Why didn't you? A bat could escape easier."

"And leave you alone? No. If I had needed to in order to rescue us, I would have, but it was unnecessary. Our house is reinforced, built to withstand a quake."

"It's good to know that now. During the Surat earthquake, I was trapped in my human form, helpless. When the quake hit tonight, my instinct shouted at me to morph into a cougar for better maneuverability, and morphing creates a buffer against the fear. I don't feel things quite the same in cougar form."

He kissed her. The crystal vibrated with her continuing anxiety. "Do you need more cougar time?"

"I don't want to leave you."

"I will be fine. And you don't have to be gone long. I will still be awake when you return." He kissed her lightly and then turned to walk away. He paused, remembering something, and looked over his shoulder. "Rolf has mentioned a troublesome skunk in these woods, so if you find it, I am sure he would be happy if you disposed of it."

"I'll see if I can."

Perhaps the hunt would distract her from her anxiety, while also helping Rolf. And if she got hit by the skunk's spray, it wouldn't matter, since morphing back to mortal form would rid her of the nasty scent.

Henry grabbed Mort and Sang by the collars. The dogs tried to pull away to remain with Cerissa, and she made a shooing motion in their direction.

"*Fuß!*" he said sternly, and the two reluctantly trotted beside him back to camp. He couldn't let the dogs follow her onto the mountain. It wasn't safe for them.

Rolf looked up from the computer. "You really do coddle her, don't you?"

"I warned you before."

"I didn't call her *that thing*. But you're at the age where fang fever starts. The way you're acting with Cerissa, you're showing some of the symptoms."

Leave it to Rolf to be crude about it. Sure, two hundred years was the point where the desire to turn one's current mate could surface strongly if it hadn't before, which was why some called it mating fever instead of the cruder fang fever. "And your point?" Henry demanded.

"With her as your mate, you'll never have the opportunity to turn anyone."

"Rolf, with the current moratorium, few of us will have that option anyway. And I'm not showing fang fever symptoms."

"*Ja, ja.* Tell yourself that. Just because you're marrying that thing—"

"Rolf," Henry snapped.

Rolf rolled his eyes. "Just because you're marrying *Cerissa* doesn't mean you're exempt from the drive to reproduce. The way you baby her—"

"I'm taking care of my mate, who I love," Henry said with a growl. His irritation over Rolf's prodding grew hotter. "There is a difference, and I will thank you to keep your observations to yourself."

Chapter 14

One, Two, Three...

Rolf and Karen's home—Moments later

Cerissa moved a little further into the woods. She hadn't spent much time in the area to the west of Rolf's house, so there would be plenty of new territory to explore. After glancing back at camp to make sure Rolf wasn't watching, she stripped, hung her clothes from the branch of a tree, and morphed to cougar form.

She shook from nose to tail, flinging off the anxiety like water, then loped off into the dense woodlands. She stalked around the ancient oak trees, the thick bed of dry leaves crunching under her paws, the varied scents of other animals causing her nose to twitch back and forth.

By the time she finished her hunt, dressed, and returned to camp feeling better, Rolf was at the shortwave radio, listening intently to something. Cerissa heightened her hearing to eavesdrop—it was Tig reporting. Still nothing as bad as the delta, but property damage had turned out to be a little worse than first anticipated.

Mort and Sang lay at Rolf's feet. They raised their heads as she approached. Mort's eyebrows twitched and his dark eyes looked at her mournfully, as if he were asking for love. She stopped to reassure them both that all was well, letting a trickle of her aura quiet each dog.

Henry was working, using her laptop. After telling the dogs to go back to sleep, she walked up behind him and kissed the top of his head. She could see he was sending an email to his assistant winemaker, asking for a full report on the winery.

"I am glad to see you back," he said, turning toward her and closing the laptop. "You are looking better."

"I'm feeling better, thank you. And I took care of Rolf's skunk. Did Karen open any wine? What goes with skunk, red or white?"

She managed the question with a straight face, and Henry rolled his eyes in response.

"I don't think there is a protocol for that." He lifted a bottle from the crate containing boxed cereal and canned food. "It appears Karen opened a red. Will that please madam?"

He laid the bottle across his forearm like a waiter would. The wine was one of the more expensive ones he produced.

"*Oui, Henri,*" she said with a smile. "It will have to do, since we are 'roughing it.'" There were no wineglasses, so she held out a coffee mug while he poured. "Thank you. Not exactly how the Ritz would do it, but it will work." She took a sip. "That is good. It's been open the right amount of time."

"You should eat something." He opened the ice chest and started rooting through it.

"I'm fine." She had just devoured a skunk, so didn't that count?

"Cerissa, you've morphed twice tonight. And been through an earthquake and cared for Nicholas. You need at least a sandwich."

"Henry—"

"Some chicken salad. You'll enjoy it."

"Yes, *dear.*"

Why does he treat me like a child sometimes?

Perhaps his need to be in control was rearing its head because of the stress of tonight.

Or maybe because of my initial reaction to the quake?

Time to show him that she could take care of herself. "Please move over. I'll make my own snack."

Rolf took off his one-ear headset. "Aah, Cerissa, before I forget, give this to Karen in the morning." He handed her a piece of paper. "It's the phone number for the cleaning service. Henry tells me that his house is worse than mine, so they can start there."

"Okay. But I don't want strangers in my lab."

Henry nodded. "Perhaps you can call Luis and see if he will help you. But at least let the professional cleaning crew go downstairs and assess it first."

She shrugged. "Maybe. I want to visit Nicholas. Depending upon how long that takes, we may have to wait two days to clean the lab."

"Fine. But let the cleaning crew get started on the main house tomorrow. No offense to Rolf's fine accommodations, but I prefer not to sleep in a bomb shelter that was built at the height of the atomic weapons scare."

Rolf marched over, squaring off. "And just what is wrong with my bomb shelter?"

"It is old, musty, dusty, and filled with spiders. It has only one redeeming quality—it is lightproof."

Cerissa wrinkled her brow. It was uncharacteristic of Henry to complain. He was always so gracious. Perhaps the stress of tonight *was* getting to him.

Rolf poked at Henry's chest. "It is neither musty nor dusty. I keep it clean and aired out, just in case I need to use it. And I'll pay you a dollar for each spider you find."

"You have not refurbished it since you built it. We both know the cots are seventy-year-old army surplus."

"They made things to last back then."

"Yes, if you are satisfied with the comfort of a World War II army barracks."

"If you have a better offer, take it."

"Perhaps I should."

Yup, the stress was getting to them both.

"Does Karen have any popcorn?" Cerissa made a show of rummaging through the food supplies. "If you two are going to fight, I want popcorn. That is what they offer at boxing matches, isn't it?"

She smirked at them.

Rolf looked at Henry. "Haven't you taught her how we deal with smart-ass mortals?"

"Once or twice," Henry replied.

Both men *whooshed* to her, each grabbing one of her arms and legs. Lifting her, they carried her to the pool. Mort and Sang followed, barking.

Cerissa eyeballed where they were headed. A lot of water had slopped out of the pool during the earthquake.

"There's enough to cushion her fall," Henry said.

"Yes, but aim for the deep end. I hate cleaning blood off my pool tiles."

"Guys, I didn't mean anything by it. I take it back. I'm sor—" The last word didn't quite make it out, as she landed with a splash in the pool fully clothed. Water rushed up her nose, and when she surfaced, she coughed and sputtered.

The two men turned and walked away.

"The least you could do is bring me a towel," she yelled after them, treading water, goosebumps flowing across her skin.

Rolf turned. "There are towels in that cabinet." He pointed to a boxlike table. It served as a drink stand between two lounge chairs and had a door on the side. "Be my guest."

He gave a sarcastic flourish of his hand as he resumed striding toward camp.

Cerissa swam to the shallow end, got out, and grabbed a towel, using it to shield herself as she undressed. She then morphed. Her hair and body were instantly dry. She grabbed a second towel and wrapped it around her shoulders. She spread out her wet clothes and shoes so they would dry, and then walked barefoot to where the guys were.

"Nice trick with the hair," Rolf said.

Cerissa blew a razzberry at him and ate her snack, which Henry had covered in plastic to keep the bugs away.

Both men had decided to feed again. They were drinking from a new variety of blood pouch that she had been working on in her lab—shelf life of six months, the contents instantly heated to body temperature when the pouch was squeezed, and the packaging came with a straw wrapped in cellophane that could be punched into a circular indent in the top.

Although Henry had objected months ago to the idea of drinking blood through a child's straw, the new packaging made feeding on the go easier. Tearing the corner and trying to drink it straight from the pouch resulted in dribbles running down his chin, which her fastidious fiancé hated even more than the children's straw.

Finished with her sandwich, she washed the plate in the plastic tub, using the water jug Karen had left out to rinse it, then turned to Henry. Carefully choosing the angle so that Rolf wouldn't see, she partially unwrapped the towel to flash Henry a full-frontal view, then rewrapped the towel and started walking toward her smaller tent.

That was all the invitation Henry needed.

He finished off the pouch of blood he'd been sipping from and used Cerissa's wine to rinse his mouth.

"Rolf, I will join you in the shelter in a bit," he said before hurrying to catch up with Cerissa.

"You are a slave to your thrill hammer," Rolf called after him.

Henry crawled into the small tent after Cerissa. As he turned to zip the flaps, he replied, "Perhaps, but if one has to be a slave to something, that is not a bad choice."

CHAPTER 15

PROCLAMATION

SIERRA ESCONDIDA POLICE STATION—TWO O'CLOCK IN THE MORNING

By the time Tig returned to the police station, everyone had reported in.

She found Jayden still staffing the small emergency operations center—the EOC, in state emergency management systems lingo.

The room was crowded. Her day-shift officers, the mayor, and two vampires who served as part-time officers—Zeke and Liza, specifically—were all present. Tig immediately figured out why everyone had gathered there. The emergency generator was running, and between the television in the corner, and the reports coming in over the radio, they got the latest news without wasting fuel at their homes.

Jayden glanced up at her. "I was just getting an update from the substation. It's not looking good in Mordida."

Tig motioned for the radio microphone. They were lucky the radio towers still operated. "This is Chief Anderson. Please report."

"Lieutenant Rodriguez here, ma'am." The lieutenant didn't know the true nature of the Hill's occupants but was a damn fine officer, one Tig relied on frequently. "So far, there's been minimal damage reported in the business district. No fires. But there's been looting in Mordida. Not a lot.

We don't expect it to spill over here."

"Let's not take any chances." The last thing she wanted was looters up on the Hill—some of the permanent residents might be inclined to solve that problem using old-fashioned means. "We're calling a curfew. I'll fax the notices. Set up roadblocks at all four main entry points into Sierra Escondida's commercial district. You can use the two swat vehicles to cut off Alameda. It's a five-lane street—you'll need the vehicles for cover. How well staffed are you?"

"Everyone who was off-duty reported in shortly after it happened, all except Officer Brown. His wife was injured and he's at the hospital with her."

"Understood. Staff each barricade with two officers. Have three patrol cars work the smaller streets. Don't get trigger-happy. Business owners can come through tomorrow during the day with IDs. The rest of the officers should bunk down at the station and get some sleep—if you need more beds, see if the fire station can accommodate you. The sleepers can relieve the first shift in six hours."

"Yes, ma'am."

"If a problem develops, use pepper spray at the blockade. If the looters try to come past you, do not hurt civilians. I don't want to hear any allegations of police brutality, understand?"

"Yes ma'am. We'll get right on it. How is the Hill?"

"One fire and it's out. A few injured, one seriously enough that he was transported to the hospital. Lots of damage. I'm going to stay here and run the EOC. Either Captain Johnson or I will be available to provide direction. I'm signing off for now. Carry out your orders."

"Roger that, signing off."

Tig set down the microphone and turned from the radio equipment to look around the small, crowded EOC. Too many people to get things done efficiently. "Day shift—go home and get some sleep. Report for duty at eleven. If the sub-station needs additional relief, Jayden will dispatch you to the barricades."

"Yes, ma'am," they replied, almost in unison, and quickly left.

Her demeanor had a tendency to put the fear of God into the mortals on her staff. It worked for her.

"Captain Johnson," Tig continued, addressing Jayden. "You're going to need a few hours of sleep. Use the cot in the back room. You'll relieve me after sunrise. There's a late moonset, so I'll be able to stay at the EOC desk longer."

Just one of the reasons the squad room had no windows. She looked at the television monitor that was above Jayden's head. Video of damage at the epicenter was being broadcast. It looked terrible. "This is going to impact us for a while. But first things first."

"Chief, do you want me and Liza to go help with the barricade?" Zeke asked, breaking into her thoughts.

"Not a bad idea. But wait a moment." Tig turned to Winston Mason, the current mayor of Sierra Escondida. "Mayor, let's take care of the paperwork. I know Marcus left the forms in that file cabinet." She pointed to the cabinet behind where the mayor stood.

No one questioned why the town attorney hadn't reported for duty—he was still at the hospital with his mate.

The mayor grunted his response, brushing his eyebrows with the fingers of one hand. Tig's tired gaze followed the movement, watching the corkscrew hairs immediately pop up. His bristly eyebrows could use trimming before they spun cocoons and turned into butterflies.

He opened the top drawer and thumbed through until he found the file. He took out two forms. "What time did the earthquake hit?" the mayor asked.

Jayden looked down at the emergency log. "Nine fifty-three."

The mayor started writing on the blank lines in the resolution. "Did they figure out the epicenter of the quake?"

Zeke spoke up with the answer. "East of Antioch, according to the reports I've heard so far. They think the Midland fault let loose. But it's possible we felt it so hard down here because of a second fault. It's gonna take the white coats a while to figure it all out."

"Good enough." The mayor filled in the date, time, and nature of the emergency and signed the document. "There. You have your proclamation declaring the local emergency to protect the public's health, safety, and welfare."

"Thank you, mayor. And the curfew?" Tig asked.

"What time do you want it to begin each night?"

"Make it from eight at night until eight in the morning," Tig replied. "For the business district. It won't affect our people, so long as they stay on this side of the wall."

"Any restrictions during the daytime?" he asked.

"Only those who can prove they live on the Hill or have business in Sierra Escondida may enter during the daylight hours."

"Done. Here." He handed her both papers.

"Captain Johnson, before you go to sleep, would you please run off fifty copies of each? Zeke and Liza can take them to the blockades."

The copies would serve as official notice of the curfew for anyone who tried to come into Sierra Escondida without a legitimate reason. If they refused to leave, they'd be arrested.

She turned to Zeke and Liza. "Take a list of the current mates with you and give it to the blockade commander, so there aren't any mistakes."

"Do you want me to stay here?" the mayor asked.

"That's not necessary. Just keep your two-way radio turned on. If I need anything, I'll call you over our standard emergency frequency."

"Agreed. Good sleep." He waved as he left the EOC.

"How's your ranch?" Tig asked Zeke.

"Well, if you wanted buttermilk, I have a feeling that's all you'd get from the cows right now."

"Any damage?"

"Nah. But the cattle are pretty edgy. Lucky they didn't stampede."

She didn't want to think about that. They had been fortunate that so few people had been hurt on the Hill. "And your place, Liza?"

"I'm good, Tig. My house was rebuilt in the eighties—designed to move in an earthquake without breaking."

Jayden came back in with the copies. He handed them to Zeke.

"See y'all later," Zeke said, as he and Liza left for the blockade.

Tig leaned back in her chair. It was just her and Jayden left in the EOC. "You better go get some rest."

"Are you sure? I could run home if you need anything."

"I keep a few bags of blood in the refrigerator here. But if you could bring in the ice chest, I'd appreciate it. I threw what we had at home into it, just in case one of our residents needed some to get through the night. It's in the back of the police van."

"No problem. Anything else?"

"Not now. I'll see you in about six hours—I'll brief you then if anything happens."

Jayden walked the few steps to where she was sitting. He leaned over and kissed her. Usually, they kept a strict separation between their work and personal lives, but this was an unusual set of circumstances.

When his lips left hers, she sighed. The stress had her wound up tight, but the kiss helped.

"You're going to have your hands full tomorrow," she said. "The mates of some of our residents are going to want to get contractors started right away to get their homes cleaned up and repaired."

"I won't clear anyone to come onto the Hill who isn't vetted. I don't care how anxious our residents are."

Tig motioned at the six video monitors—all blank screens. "Putting police patrols on the wall will be our priority. What good is it to mount security cameras on the wall if the cameras aren't hooked to emergency power?" she mumbled, disgusted. "Cheap. We wouldn't have to patrol the wall now if the council hadn't been so damn cheap."

The video feed was also sent to the guard shack at the entrance to the community, but without power, the guards had nothing to monitor.

"We won't have any problems," Jayden assured her. "No one is going to get past the blockade, let alone over the wall."

Yeah, famous last words.

The last thing they needed was looters making it over and discovering the hard way what the Hill hid. Tig shook her head, the fatigue of responding to the emergency catching up with her. She sure hoped Jayden was right.

Chapter 16

Recovery

Rancho Bautista del Murciélago—The next day

Monday morning was a mad dash to get everything done. Fortunately, the cell towers were working, although intermittently. Cerissa had to call the cleaning service twice. Halfway through the first conversation, she lost the signal.

By the time eleven thirty rolled around, she had returned home, toured the damage with two cleaning crews—one for the main house, and one for the pool house—and switched to the power generator to give the crews adequate electricity and allow the solar batteries time to recharge. Since Henry was a current client, the cleaning contractors had given her call higher priority.

The basement lab had less damage than she'd expected. She locked the door, deciding to clean it herself later. With professional crews working on the rest of the house, she felt free to go visit Nicholas. Karen joined her and, during the drive, joked about having a party just to use up everything from the freezer in her garage that had defrosted. Apparently, Karen and Rolf's freezer wasn't on backup power like Henry's.

A police blockade stopped them at the border of Sierra Escondida and Mordida. The officer signaled for Cerissa to roll down the driver's window.

"There was sporadic looting last night. We're asking residents to respect the curfew and return before eight."

She took the flyer he handed her and passed it over to Karen. "We're going to the hospital to see the assistant city attorney," Cerissa said, twisting her hands on the steering wheel as her heart sped up. "Ah, Nicholas was injured last night."

Strange. She'd never been nervous before when speaking to the police. Why now?

"Just be back before the curfew starts. No one is allowed in the business district after eight p.m."

Karen leaned over and said, "We'll be back on time. Thank you, officer." To Cerissa, she added, "Let's go."

Cerissa's heartbeat returned to normal once they were away from the blockade, but getting to the hospital turned out to be a challenge. Because of the damage, some of the roads were closed. By the time they got to Nicholas's room, lunch had been brought in.

"I won't make the standard comment about hospital food." Nicholas pushed the food tray away as they settled into the guest chairs by the bed.

"Do you want us to get you a burger?" As Cerissa drove to the hospital, she'd noted that some of Mordida's fast-food restaurants were thriving—simply packed with customers. They must have had backup power.

"Would you?" he asked with a laugh. "A double-double, animal style."

She had no idea what he was talking about, but Karen's nodding said she understood.

"Done deal." Karen bounced to her feet. "There's a drive-thru right across the street. You could have cardiac bypass surgery and score your next artery-clogging meal on the way home from the hospital."

Nicholas raised an eyebrow at Karen's comment. The movement wrinkled the large white bandage taped to his temple.

"Ow," he groaned, raising his hand to rub the area around the bandages. "When you put it that way, maybe I should stick with hospital food."

"You're young enough to get away with it." Cerissa took his chart down from the holder on the wall. Apparently, Mordida hospital hadn't entered the electronic age yet. "Do you mind if I check? Make sure you have no dietary restrictions entered?"

"Go ahead."

She flipped through the pages of the chart and looked at his lab work. "You aren't on a restricted diet. Your cholesterol is fine. You can indulge on occasion, as long as you exercise regularly."

"I do cardio every day and weights three times a week."

"Well, there you have it. From your chart, it looks like you're doing fine, by the way. The neurologist is happy with the CT scan. You have a very mild concussion. That's the best news of all. Marcus's blood really made the difference."

"I'm just glad it was you and Henry who came to my rescue," Nicholas said. "I don't know if anyone else would have had the presence of mind to do what you did."

"I'm glad it all worked out." Cerissa returned the chart to its holder.

Nicholas picked up his fork and turned over what looked like a breaded chicken patty.

Karen gave the lunch tray a skeptical look. "I'll get you that burger, if you want."

"Please. I can't bring myself to take a bite of this mystery meat." He stabbed it again, and the fork slowly fell to the tray, upending the patty. "The doctor said they'd probably release me later this afternoon. I told them I could get a ride after seven, so they'll probably keep me until Marcus shows up."

"Did you know there's an eight o'clock curfew?" Karen asked.

"Crap. I figured we'd eat out. There goes that idea. I guess I can always grab more fast food on the way back. But I'll need to eat something now to hold me over until then."

"I'll be back in fifteen." Karen headed to the door and then stopped, swinging around. "I forgot to ask. You want fries with that?"

"Of course. And a chocolate shake. If I'm going to be bad, I might as well go whole hog."

"Want me to come with you?" Cerissa reached for her purse's shoulder strap, which she'd left slung over the guest chair.

Karen waved her off. "Nah, it doesn't take two of us. I'm going to walk there. I'll be right back."

After Karen had left, Nicholas picked up the TV remote. "Have you seen the news reports?"

"No. We've been so busy this morning arranging for cleanup, we haven't had time."

"It's not good."

He switched on the television, and they watched as the newscaster summed up the damage. Buildings had been destroyed in Antioch, bridges had collapsed, and levees were breached in the river delta. But they were lucky—widespread liquefaction had not occurred, so the delta hadn't undergone a complete meltdown.

The death toll had reached fifty-eight. It could climb higher, as search parties were still combing through the flooded areas. Video of collapsed buildings, as well as flooded homes and agriculture, played over and over again.

A terrible apprehension crawled down Cerissa's back and her throat tightened. Nausea hit her in a wave. She squeezed her eyes tightly closed and forced air into her lungs, thinking through the steps to ground herself.

One...breathe.

Two—she focused on her feet—*feel the solid floor.*

Three...

She hesitated, knowing the words even if she didn't believe them yet.

I—I'm safe.

She opened her eyes, took another slow breath, and repeated number three. Then once more.

The same feeling, where her heart rate accelerated and her chest became tight, had struck at least a dozen times since the first earthquake. Even though she hated the sudden panic attacks, she refused to crawl into bed and not get out, as much as she wanted to do just that. So far, she was managing to pull herself out of them before they became too strong.

"Cerissa, are you all right?"

"I'm—I'm just a bit overwhelmed by it all."

"We don't have to watch the news." Nicholas muted the audio. "I'm worried myself. There's going to be water shortages for quite a long time.

We've already been in drought conditions for years. This is just going to make it worse."

Cerissa shook her head. "I don't know how the vineyards are going to stay in business."

"Oh, I know the answer to that. Mordida isn't going to like it, but Henry and Rolf will take care of their own. They're on the board of directors for the Sierra Escondida Water Company. The board will cancel the contract, terminating Mordida's right to draw from the Hill's aquifer."

Henry had never mentioned the water company before. "I don't understand."

"You know that all the land on the Hill is owned by a trust."

"Henry mentioned it was designed that way so no mortal could ever buy or inherit the homes there."

"That's right. Well, the trust formed SEWC to manage the underground water rights that run with the land. In exchange for those rights, SEWC manages the aquifer and provides water to the entire Hill, even those properties that aren't directly over the aquifer. The Hill hasn't needed all the water they could draw, so the board sold that excess water to Mordida. The Hill also gets water from Northern California—"

"Wait. Why would we buy water from NorCal, and then sell our water to Mordida?"

"It's just the way water works. If the Hill stopped taking their share, they'd lose it over time. So they've kept drawing on it and they can't resell it to Mordida—a quirk in the law makes that disfavored. So SEWC sells water from the aquifer. If we stop getting NorCal water, we aren't going to be in a position to sell any water to Mordida."

Cerissa's head spun from the information. "This disaster is going to be with us for years."

"Too true. Every grower in the San Joaquin Valley knew it was only a matter of time before the big one hit and the delta collapsed. But no one would listen to them."

"I'm back," Karen announced, as if the smell of fried food hadn't already heralded her arrival. She set out the burger, fries, and shake for Nicholas on the hospital tray table. "I got you something too, Cerissa. We're overdue for lunch; we might as well eat with Nicholas."

Cerissa accepted the grilled chicken sandwich and tried to get her mind off the disaster as they ate and talked. Nicholas left the television on, but with the sound off. Every now and again she would glance up at it before quickly looking away.

An hour later, they said their goodbyes. Nicholas was tired and wanted to grab a nap. Before they left, Cerissa offered Nicholas the use of their guest room. She expected the cleaning service to finish and her home to be livable again by the time the hospital released him.

He wasn't sure what arrangements Marcus had made, but said he'd call later with their answer.

On the way home, Karen suggested they stop at the winery to get an early assessment of the damage. "I've been afraid to call Suri, but Rolf wanted me to go by. Do you mind?"

"Of course not. Henry will probably want the same report."

Cerissa felt strange walking the flagstone pathways under the grapevine lattice. Less than seventy-two hours ago, they'd all been here celebrating her engagement.

Superficial cracks had developed on the building's smooth stucco finish—or had they always been there, and she was just now noticing them?

Karen led the way to the manager's office. "Hi, Suri—you know Enrique's fiancée Cerissa, right?"

"Yes, from the party. Welcome, please, have a seat. What may I help you with?"

Suri looked remarkably together under the circumstances, in casual pants and a knit tunic jacket over a gauze blouse. Her short black hair accented her dangling earrings, and she toyed with one, rotating it. Cerissa had considered cutting her own hair but could never bring herself to do it. Henry adored her long waves.

After a few minutes exchanging information on how their homes had fared, Karen shifted her feet. "I hate to ask, but do you have a damage report yet?"

Suri grimaced. "Well, the good news first. We didn't lose any bottled wine."

"And the bad news?"

"We were about to bottle the Cabernet Sauvignon casks from two years ago. They'd been blended into the bottling tanks. We lost twenty-five percent when a tank tipped and leaked, and another fifteen percent from barrels that fell over and cracked."

"Forty percent gone?" Karen plopped onto the guest chair. "Oh, crap. What are we going to do?"

Suri shook her head. "I don't know. We need to find some other way to replace the income."

Cerissa's throat tightened. How was the winery going to survive the loss?

She had no idea what Henry's finances looked like. She'd assumed he was rich from the investments he'd made over the years and his lifestyle. But losing forty percent of one of his bestselling wines on top of an impending water shortage that could affect future growth?

She knew how much Henry enjoyed being a vintner. He took pride in his skill at blending high-quality wines. Would the loss kill his winery business?

Her heart broke a little at the thought.

Chapter 17
Sleeping Arrangements

Rolf and Karen's home—An hour later

After their visit to the winery, they returned to Rolf's place. Cerissa walked over to the makeshift camp to wait for sunset. Thanks to an early moonrise, Henry was already awake, and she could feel his frustration at being trapped in the small bunker, waiting for night to arrive. Mort and Sang came running from the vineyard to greet her and Karen.

"Are you okay alone? I'm going inside. I desperately need a sponge bath." Karen sighed heavily. "The one thing I hate about roughing it is the lack of running water."

The Hill's water hadn't been cleared as safe yet. Pipes might have been broken by the earthquake, causing bacteria to enter the clean water. So it had to be boiled before they could drink it or wash with it.

"Go ahead. I'll be fine."

"If you want, go take Candy for a ride. I'll bring the dogs inside with me," Karen said, grabbing two gallons of boiled water and heading for the back door to the kitchen.

"Thanks." Cerissa loved that horse. She'd been riding Candy when she was first introduced to Henry, and the memory made her smile.

In the feed closet she found carrots for all the horses, who were milling about in the corral. As soon as she arrived at the fence, they trotted over. She fed them, taking a moment to greet each one, but lingered with Candy.

The beautiful chestnut mare with a white blaze on her forehead nickered her welcome but took the carrot, crunching it down quickly.

"Would you like to go for a ride?" Cerissa asked her.

Running her hand across the mare's forehead, she sensed the answer was "no." The earthquake had made Candy uneasy, and the mare didn't want to leave the safety of the corral.

"Some other time, then."

Another soft nicker in answer, then Candy nudged her.

"What, you want another carrot? Greedy, aren't you?" Cerissa walked over to the bin and brought back another carrot for each of the horses.

After saying goodbye to them, Cerissa returned to the outdoor campsite. A glass of wine sounded good—something to take the edge off her unease—and she found the same bottle from last night.

Once poured, she took the mug with her, leaned up against a large elm tree near the bomb shelter, and sipped her drink, eager for the comfort of being close to Henry.

The wine didn't sit well. All she could think about was when the next aftershock would hit and how much worse it would make the situation at the winery.

The water issues, along with the damage at the winery, would take their toll on Henry. How could she help him shoulder these burdens? Falling in love had created a protectiveness she'd never experienced before.

As the sun started to set, she walked the short distance to where the bomb shelter entrance was hidden.

Her phone buzzed. *How are you feeling?* Henry texted.

She texted back: *Looking forward to seeing you.*

Where are you?

Right outside your door.

A series of emojis appeared: a face blowing a kiss, Dracula with fangs, a big purple eggplant, and a red heart.

"Henry!" she exclaimed. She hadn't realized he'd become a fan of emojis. And if she translated that correctly, he hoped biting and sex were on the menu.

We'll see, she texted back.

He was the first to emerge minutes after dusk fell. He had already shaved and combed his raven-black hair into a neat ponytail. Since Rolf was the younger vampire, he woke later and was probably still getting ready.

Cerissa went into Henry's arms and gave him a big hug, her wine mug pressed against his back.

He leaned into her hair, and she could feel the deep breath he took. When his tongue lightly stroked the vein in her neck, she pulled back. "Hey!"

His eyes took on a sultry look. "Can I help it if you are so tempting?"

She glanced around. Karen was still in the house. "I guess not."

"But I should feed—or I'll make you my meal."

"Over there," she said, pointing at the makeshift kitchen.

She waited until he finished his first pouch. After what she had to tell him, he might need a second. With a shot of vodka.

She sat across from him at the camp table and explained the news from the day. "I'm sorry, and I should probably let Karen tell you, but the winery lost almost half of the Cabernet production that was being bottled."

"I am sorrier for those people who lost their lives, *mi amor*. Do not worry about me. The winery will be fine."

Would it? She suspected he was glossing over the situation to protect her. That, or the reality wouldn't sink in until he saw the damage for himself.

Watching Henry feed reminded her that she hadn't eaten anything since the grilled chicken sandwich six hours ago. She looked in the ice chest and found eggs, cheese, and sausage, enough to make an omelet.

"Oh," she said, as she worked. "I forgot to mention. The doctor is releasing Nicholas this evening as soon as Marcus can pick him up. Our house has been cleaned, so I told him that he and Marcus could stay with us."

Henry smiled at her. "Thank you. I'm glad you did. But let me call Marcus to repeat the offer."

She felt taken aback. Why wasn't her invitation good enough? They'd been over this before. When it came to their home, she didn't have to ask his permission.

He held up a hand as if seeking her patience. He must have read her reaction through the crystal. "Some of us are touchy about who we share crypts with. I'll make sure Marcus understands he's welcome."

Okay, that was fair. Still, it bothered her.

She ate at the camp table as Henry made the call to Marcus. Although she heard only one side—she didn't enhance her hearing to eavesdrop on what Marcus said—she could tell the two were exchanging information about the disaster.

After a few minutes, Henry put the call on speaker. "We were fortunate," he said. "The cleaning crew has already been through our house to clear out the broken glass and other hazards. As Cerissa told Nicholas, you are welcome at our place."

"Thank you. We accept. I'll call Gaea and let her know we've been able to make other arrangements. One of our households was going to move into Kim Han's old house. She and Seaton can have it for now. There is another small home available, but it needs cleaning and the utilities turned on before we can move in."

"As long as you are talking with her, ask her to come over to my place around ten. We need to hold a meeting of the SEWC's board of directors."

"Hmm," Marcus murmured. "Under state law, we'd normally have to post a twenty-four-hour notice before holding the meeting. But under the circumstances, we qualify for the emergency meeting exception. Would you swing by town hall and post the notice on the door?"

"Consider it done," Henry said.

"And the website—we need to post there too. You can log in at the police station; they have power and internet access."

Cerissa nodded to let Henry know she didn't mind the detour to the town center.

"I'll take care of it," Henry said. "I'm at Rolf's house, so I'll notify him, and then I'll call Zeke and Winston."

Once he hung up, she asked, "Since Zeke is involved, would you prefer it if I stayed here with Karen?"

The cowboy had tried to seduce her when he thought Henry was dead. After everything that had happened, she didn't want Henry's jealousy to relapse and add to their stress.

"No." He reached across the table to stroke her jaw. "I think that would send the wrong message. You should not have to leave your home because of Zeke's presence."

"Thank you. I would prefer to be near you. The earthquake has left me feeling…uneasy." She moved from where she'd been eating and sat down on his lap, leaning up against him to nuzzle his neck.

The door to the bomb shelter closed loudly and Rolf strode toward them. "Are you two always like this? Rutting in public?"

Before Cerissa could respond, Henry touched a finger across her lips as if to say, "Let it go." "Rolf, you need to feed."

"I know what I need, and I don't need you telling me what I need."

Henry whispered in her ear, "He wakes up this way. Once he's fed, he'll be in a better mood."

She furrowed her brow. She still hadn't gotten to the bottom of Rolf's need for adrenaline-enhanced blood. Was waking up grouchy a symptom of the problem?

Karen came walking out of the house toward the camp. Freshly washed and in clean clothes, her mood was light enough to lift them all out of their funk. Rolf drank down his first pouch of blood for the evening and motioned for Karen to come to him. She did, and despite his earlier criticism of PDAs, gave Karen a deep kiss.

When the two finished kissing, Henry said, "Rolf, the SEWC board is calling an emergency meeting. My house, at ten. We thank you for your hospitality of last night, but Cerissa and I will need to get back there to prepare things for the meeting. Before we go, I'll help you take down the tents."

"Don't worry about the tents. I'll take care of it later." Rolf waved him off and then shot Karen a lusty look. "Why don't you two go and make whatever arrangements are needed now?"

"My bags are already in the car," Cerissa said to Henry.

Sleeping in the tent was fine for one night, but she really preferred her own bed. And it looked like Karen could use some private time with her mate.

"Then we shall take our leave." Henry smirked at Rolf, and as Cerissa walked by his side to the car, he whispered in her ear, "Apparently, I'm not the only one enslaved to my thrill hammer."

Chapter 18
Redux

Rancho Bautista del Murciélago—Ten minutes later

Cerissa rolled her go-bag across the threshold, relieved to be home. The cleaning crew had done a great job. They'd disposed of all the shattered glass and stacked the broken picture frames against one wall.

"We can hold the meeting in the dining room." Henry closed the front door behind her, carrying his bag and the emergency box. "Do you mind?"

"Not at all. I'll clear my building plans off the table."

"Thank you. I'm going to turn on the gas so we can cook."

Both the stove and oven used natural gas. "Cook?"

"Yes, you should eat."

"I had an omelet at Rolf's. I'm fine."

"That is not enough."

She opened her mouth to argue but realized he was right. "Are you sure it's safe to turn on the gas?"

"I received a text. The lines have been tested, and based on the pressure, there are no leaks between the main line and our house." On the way in, he'd turned off the portable power generator. "We are back on battery backup power, so only the kitchen lights work. We need to conserve the generator's gasoline to make it last—no telling how long utility power will be out. You will find camping lanterns in the storage area next to the pantry."

She found two battery-powered lanterns and went to the dining room. While she could adjust her eyes to see in the dark, Nicholas wouldn't be able to, and she wanted to be prepared for his arrival.

The cleaning crew had rolled up her architectural plans and neatly stacked the paperwork she'd left behind. She picked up the rolls, moved the plans to the long buffet cabinet opposite the windows, and started thinking about her development project. Would the council delay the approval hearing because of the earthquake?

She didn't want to ask Henry—he was already too stressed with everything else. But Nicholas might know. She'd ask him later.

When she finished organizing everything, she followed her nose to the delicious smells coming from the kitchen, leaving the lanterns in the foyer but carrying an envelope she'd found.

She held it up to show him. "Henry, the cleaning crew left this for you."

"Please leave it on the island counter. I'll open it later. It's probably the invoice for today's work." Henry then gestured toward the refrigerator with the fork he held, sizzling coming from the fry pan on the stove. "There was a nice filet mignon, so I'm making it in a cognac peppercorn sauce. How does that sound?"

"Wonderful. I'll make pasta to go with it."

While a baked potato struck her as the standard side dish for a steak, the battery backup system didn't power the microwave oven—which drew too much current—so cooking pasta on the stovetop was faster than baking a potato. She could toss it in butter and herbs.

As she stepped toward the pantry to find the dry pasta, a distant rumble began. She immediately dove under the kitchen table. Visions of the ceiling collapsing—the way it had when she was a child—filled her mind.

"Damn it!" she yelled, huddling with her arms tightly hugging her knees. The kitchen lights flickered but stayed on. "Why can't the ground stop shaking?"

Henry crawled in close, putting his arms around her. "This is normal. Aftershocks happen. The fault is releasing stress, and at less intense pressures. That's good news."

Something fell with a crash, and she jumped, hitting her head on the underside of the table. "Ow."

"Are you all right?"

She rubbed her scalp. "I will be, but the steak won't."

The sauté pan with the steak on board had jolted off the stove and rattled onto the floor, continuing to bounce until the tremors died away.

She waited for Henry to crawl out first. He offered his hand to help her up.

"You're sure it's safe?" She eyed his hand like it was a cobra and considered staying right where she was.

"You will be fine. Come."

She took his hand and reluctantly emerged from under the table.

"And there are two more steaks," he continued, "so the meal can be redone."

Maybe the menu should be changed. The quake had stirred up some of her early childhood beliefs she was forever fighting to shake. In her distress, she couldn't help wondering if cooking beef brought bad karma in the form of an aftershock.

But they had limited fresh meat—the Hill's delivery service normally brought groceries today, and that hadn't happened—so she told herself to drop it and kept her thoughts to herself.

Henry cleaned up the mess on the floor and then started the second steak on the back burner this time. With any luck the ground would stop shaking long enough for him to finish cooking it, but if another tremor hit, at least the skillet would have to travel a further distance to fall off again.

At the same time, he started a large pan of water for pasta and another to boil for cleanup. Bottled water was reserved for drinking.

She took a plate out of the cupboard. "Ah, I ordered new dishes today, to replace the broken ones." She held out her phone so he could see the design. "I hope that's okay. I used the department store credit card you gave me."

He finished turning the steak and gestured with the oversized fork to the plate on the counter. "You could not get replacements to match these?"

"The pattern was discontinued. So I picked out something new in your color scheme."

"Thank you." His voice carried a note of reluctance.

"You don't like it? I can cancel the order."

"They are a more modern design than I would normally choose, but we are a couple now, so you should have a say. Everything else, I picked out. It's only fair."

She kissed him. This whole couple thing was still new territory for her, and she appreciated his willingness to cede some ground to her. He tended to control everything without realizing it.

When the doorbell rang, she left Henry in the kitchen and went to answer it. Nicholas entered first, carrying a small suitcase, followed by Marcus. Marcus must have been able to salvage clothes and eyeglasses from the wrecked house for Nicholas.

The large white bandage on Nicholas's head had been replaced with a smaller flesh-tone one covering the gash. The doctor who sutured him had shaved his hairline on one side. Balancing the haphazard cut was going to be challenging for Nicholas's stylist, but other than that, he looked okay.

Cerissa welcomed them and gave Nicholas a gentle hug. "I'm so glad to see you doing well."

"It's good to be out of the hospital. Any longer and I would have caved and eaten their food for dinner."

"I'm glad you were spared. Did you get takeout on the way home? Henry is cooking, and we can put another steak on for you, if you haven't already eaten."

"Steak sounds great. There wasn't the time to grab anything and make it back before the curfew."

Marcus carried a large document box. "Henry's in the kitchen?" he asked.

"Yes. I'll help Nicholas up to his room with his bag"—she reached for the bag, taking it from Nicholas's hands—"if you want to tell Henry to put on the second steak."

Marcus scowled at her. "Where will the board be meeting?"

"In the dining room."

Marcus headed there with the box.

She grabbed one of the battery-powered lanterns from the foyer table and led Nicholas up the staircase, his bag in her other hand. "Marcus doesn't seem to be in a good mood."

"Our house will have to be rebuilt from the ground up. It's off the foundation. Both cars are totaled. He had to rent a compact car, as it's all the rental company had available. He's unhappy about it. That, and he lost one of his favorite Warhol paintings. One of the rarer ones."

"I'm sorry to hear that." Cerissa walked into the guest bedroom and laid his bag on the bed. "The bathroom is through that door," she said, pointing to it. "Let me know if you need any help with unpacking, or if you need any toiletries. Henry must have a disposable razor in his travel kit if you need one."

Nicholas rubbed the stubble on his chin and then adjusted his black-framed glasses. "Thanks, but we should probably go downstairs and eat. The board members will start arriving soon."

"Oh"—she held out a hand, stopping him—"before I forget. Do you think the council will postpone the hearing on my project? You know, because of the earthquake?"

Nicholas looked thoughtful. "The hearing's scheduled for what, three weeks away?"

"Almost four."

"Unlikely they'll delay it. The public notices have already been mailed. The paperwork is in order. This really should be a no-brainer for the council."

"That's a relief. Leopold has been pushing me to get the project approved."

Nicholas patted her back. "I'm sure it will work out."

Cerissa led the way downstairs carrying the lantern. Just two nights ago, she and Nicholas were celebrating their respective engagements. Things had happened much too quickly for her thoughts to keep up with them.

Despite Nicholas's reassurance about the project, a frisson ran down her back, and the same unwelcome question from the party popped into her mind.

What will go wrong next?

Chapter 19
Fighting Back

RANCHO BAUTISTA DEL MURCIÉLAGO—TEN MINUTES LATER

After cooking a steak for Nicholas, Henry excused himself and headed to the dining room, his hand looped through the handles of two battery-powered camp lanterns, a mug in the other hand.

On arrival, he offered the mug of clone blood to Marcus. "For you."

"Thank you." Marcus looked up from the box of files he'd been searching through. "It's fortunate town hall fared better than my house. I was able to find these files right away."

"Excellent." Henry picked up the file containing the agreement between SEWC and the Mordida Water Company and skimmed through the pages. "Here, it is as I remembered it. We may cancel their allotment with thirty days' written notice. They must stop drawing water within sixty days of the notice."

When the contract was signed, MWC installed their own pump station. Legally, Henry couldn't break in and turn off their pumps. And even if he did, it wouldn't solve anything. MWC would just turn the pumps back on.

"Yes," Marcus said with a nod, "but they'll try to negotiate retention of some portion of the allotment. This should give us plenty of time to convince them that our board won't agree."

The doorbell rang. Henry would much rather shovel out the cages of his six circus tigers than bang the gavel for this group. But he'd made the commitment, so he brought one of the lanterns with him to light the foyer for the mortals who were attending and answered the door. He directed the first arrivals—Rolf and Karen—to go into the dining room.

The mayor was close behind them, parking in the circular driveway by the fountain.

While Henry, Rolf, and Gaea represented the interests of those residents who grew grapes, the mayor didn't make his living from the land and represented the second group on the Hill, those who lived on much smaller residential parcels—most of them only a quarter acre. Then there was Zeke, who had been elected to the board by those who raised livestock and grew other crops. Their water usage was different from the vintners.

After the mayor was directed to the dining room, Gaea arrived next, and Henry welcomed her with a hug. "I was sorry to hear about the fire. How are you feeling?"

"The kitchen is a total loss," Gaea said with a flip of her wrist. "Fortunately, the second story didn't extend above it. While inconvenient, I've decided not to move out during reconstruction." She patted his back. "Now don't look so stressed—I'll be fine."

Henry nodded. "I'm glad to hear no one was hurt in the fire."

"And how did Cerissa weather the quake?"

"Her first one." They'd decided on continuing this cover story, since Rolf told Tig the same thing. Cerissa's invented background hadn't included a previous stay in earthquake country. "This is new territory for her."

"Well, Señor Bautista—I mean, Señor Vasquez"—his new identity—"I expect you to take good care of her through it all."

"Of course," Henry said with a bow. He'd learned to be tolerant of Gaea's overprotectiveness of his mate. Cerissa had stayed at her house when she first arrived on the Hill and was initially under the older vampire's care.

Gaea looked around. "Is that whelp of mine here yet?"

"Winston is in the dining room. We're meeting there. Marcus will take you."

From the heavy thud of Western boots on the porch, the next set of footsteps had to be Zeke's. Henry frowned. Despite what he'd told Cerissa, welcoming Zeke into their home annoyed him.

Muzzling his resentment, Henry put on his business face. "Good evening. Please come in."

"Thanks, don't mind if I do." Zeke took off his black cowboy hat and dropped it on the entryway table without asking. "Is everyone here? The stable out front seems a mite crowded."

He hooked a thumb toward all the cars parked in Henry's driveway.

"Yes, they are all here." Henry gestured to the dining room, and then changed his mind, resting a hand on Zeke's shoulder to stop him. "But I am glad we have a moment alone. I didn't get a chance to thank you for your help capturing Yacov's killer."

"Don't mention it." Zeke swept his fingers through his hair, brushing out the kink caused by wearing a hat. "You can't imagine how surprised this cowboy was to find you'd risen from the grave again. But I'm glad to see it."

"Thank you. I know we have had our differences over Cerissa. Now that she and I are engaged, I am hopeful we may set those past conflicts aside and do what is best for the community."

"That's all I care about. Besides, we're all good, you and me. And when you get right down to it, I'm happier being a bachelor."

Yes, Henry had heard the rumors about Zeke and the circus aerialist, a quick fling that ended when the circus left town—the type of relationship Zeke appeared to prefer. But words were cheap, and he'd keep an eye on the cowboy's behavior around Cerissa.

Henry motioned toward the dining room door. "You should go in and join the others."

Zeke passed Marcus, who returned to the foyer. "Where's Nicholas? We'll need him."

"Right here," Nicholas said, as he and Cerissa joined them, carrying another lantern.

"How are you feeling?" Marcus took Nicholas's arm and guided him to the dining room.

"I'm fine for now. I'll stay as long as I'm feeling strong."

"Good. I value your legal insight."

Henry closed the front door and locked it before escorting Cerissa into the dining room. He carried the foyer lantern to the main table, and she placed her lantern on the side buffet.

"Well, now that the last of us are here," the mayor said, "let's get started." Winston had served as mayor for close to fifty years and had a habit of moving the agenda along, trying to assert dominance any chance he got.

However, Henry—not Winston—was chair of the SEWC's board. It was one of the few community titles he'd retained when he decided to cut back on his civic activities and focus on building the winery into a larger business venture. Water was just too integral a part of how he made money to relinquish the reins. Sometimes, he had to remind the mayor of that fact.

Henry took his seat at the head of the table and tapped the gavel once to get everyone to stop talking. "We have called this meeting because of the impending water crisis. With the levees damaged, we anticipate that water from Northern California may be unavailable for the indefinite future."

"My thoughts exactly, Henry," Gaea said.

The mayor *harrumphed*. "You don't think we'll be able to negotiate to keep some of our allotment that flowed through the delta?"

Nicholas caught Henry's eyes, and Henry nodded. He trusted the mortal.

"Mayor," Nicholas began, "we don't think it's going to be a matter of negotiation. I've been watching the news reports all day. There will be no water flowing from NorCal, not until there is a workaround."

Zeke cut in as soon as Nicholas paused. "Sounds like water conservation is going to be the watchword of the day."

"Precisely," Henry said. "We should consider instituting rationing on the Hill and encourage smart water management techniques. I've tested out the latest remote sensor program. Using the software interface, I'm able to see how much fluid flows in each plant's veins from my computer and make adjustments to the irrigation system to compensate."

Rolf nodded his agreement. "Mayor, we may need the council to offer financial incentives to get vineyard owners to switch to water-efficient techniques for watering their vines."

"Well, we'll have to see." Winston looked less than pleased. "The town's reserves are in good shape thanks to my fiscal management, although most of those funds are already allocated to other planned projects."

Henry didn't correct him, but it was Councilwoman Carolyn's financial insight that had the town on the right fiscal path—not the mayor's. She was an independent certified financial planner—emphasis on independent.

"Ach," Rolf scoffed. "This is much more important to the survival of our community. We can postpone the park landscape project, and use the money to offer loans to community members at a very low interest rate to pay for water-efficient irrigation—"

"Now, Rolf, you know as well as I do that the landscape project itself is necessary to cut back the town's water usage. Drought-tolerant plants are going to replace—"

"Then postpone the library expansion. Or the community center—we have over two million in that fund, and we're more than ten years out for the rebuild."

"Now you're robbing Peter to pay Paul."

"No, I'm making priority policy decisions. Something we should all be capable of doing. Besides, by the time we need the money, the loans should be repaid."

Henry couldn't let this get contentious, as much as he agreed with Rolf. "I suggest we pass a motion to ask the town council to institute the program, and how it is done can be debated by them at a later time."

The mayor puckered his mouth like he'd sucked on an unripe grape. "Perhaps you are right. I so move."

The motion passed unanimously. "Good." Henry made a note of it on his copy of the agenda. "Our next order of business is a motion to cancel the allotment of water granted the Mordida Water Company from our underground aquifer and authorize Rolf and I to do what is necessary to bring about a just resolution of the matter."

"They're going to scream like stuck pigs when they get that notice," Zeke said.

"And we anticipate that they may take legal action." Marcus tugged at his mustache, pausing for a moment. "While our first step is to cancel the allotment, if we put conservation measures in place, we might be able to give back some of the allotment. But we should allow Henry and Rolf to guide those negotiations and decide what is fair under the circumstances."

The mayor cleared his throat. "I don't know, Marcus. This is something the full board should keep a close eye on. I don't think two of our members should control the whole negotiation process."

"Winston," Gaea said, "I think Rolf and Henry will have our best interests at heart."

"But Gaea—"

"'But Gaea' my tired ass. Winston, I'm grateful you're willing to do the day-to-day work of running this community, but sometimes you have to let go of the reins and let someone else drive the horses. You can't always be in charge."

"Well—well—" Winston sputtered.

Marcus jumped in. "I think Gaea means that you have many important duties to attend to, mayor. Now is the time for you to focus on your duties as mayor of the *entire* community, not just this one problem. It would be best if we formed an ad hoc committee of less than a majority of this board, convened for the sole purpose of negotiating with Mordida. Sometimes these things can be resolved faster if we don't have to hold public meetings."

The group fell silent as everyone looked to Winston.

"Your point is well taken, Marcus," Winston replied, looking mollified.

"Good. Do we have a motion?"

"I so move," Zeke said.

Henry kept his surprise from showing. Perhaps Zeke had meant what he said when they were in the foyer.

Gaea raised a finger. "I second it."

"Hearing no objection"—Henry paused, waiting for someone to disagree—"the motion is passed unanimously. Marcus, please draft the letter tonight, so that I may sign it and we can get the notice delivered to MWC tomorrow."

Marcus nodded. "Consider it done."

"Thank you." Henry turned to Gaea. "The next agenda item is a status report on water quality."

Gaea cleared her throat. "I've spoken with the chief engineer. He tells me that they should be able to give us an all-clear by tomorrow. They've tested most of the Hill and haven't found any contamination in the water lines, but he wants to make sure."

"Yay!" Karen said.

Henry tapped his gavel once, more from being startled than any belief that order was needed, and Rolf rolled his eyes as the rest of the board snickered at Karen's enthusiasm.

Henry waited for the laughter to die down. "That is good news."

Gaea fluttered her fingers, signaling she had more to report. "The maintenance crew has been working around the clock since the quake. I think they deserve some sort of reward for their sacrifice."

Rolf frowned. "Overtime pay isn't enough?"

"Gaea makes a good point." The mayor steepled his fingers together. "They reported to work even though they would rather have been home, taking care of their families. I'd recommend a bonus, rather than a pay raise."

Rolf pursed his lips, anger in his eyes. "It's a waste of our money."

Marcus ignored the exchange. "Henry, if you'll allow me to take care of how we accomplish that, we should be able to give them a bonus of sorts and stay on the right side of the law. We'll call it hazard pay."

"Do we have a motion?" Henry asked.

"I so move," Winston responded.

"Second," Gaea called out.

"Do I need to take a roll call vote, or is it passed unanimously?" Henry asked the group.

Rolf scanned the board members, looking for support for his position. "This is not a time to spend money unnecessarily. I vote no."

"Anyone else? Very good. Let the minutes show four in favor and one against. Is there any other business before the board?"

"There is one other thing," Rolf said. "We may have to institute rationing. I'm not suggesting we make that decision tonight. I hope that the carrot—financial incentives to switch to more efficient watering techniques—will be enough. But if it isn't, we need to spread the word that the board will consider rationing and fines for those who exceed their ration. Agreed?"

"Let the record show that there is agreement with that path. Now, if there is nothing more"—Henry paused, glancing around the table—"then we are adjourned."

He picked up his gavel and brought it down.

20

MORE BAD NEWS

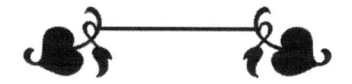

RANCHO BAUTISTA DEL MURCIÉLAGO—MOMENTS LATER

Henry carried one of the three camp lanterns from the dining room, leaving Marcus and Nicholas with sufficient light to work on the letter, and followed everyone else out, except for Rolf and Karen, who remained behind. The meeting had gone better than he had hoped.

Zeke and the mayor left quickly.

Cerissa joined him to see Gaea to the door. "I'll call you soon, and we can get together," Cerissa said.

Gaea smiled at her. "Of course, child. I was thinking of putting together a canasta tournament. Just the ladies. Think you're up for it?"

"I think I'll be able to hold my own. I beat Henry the last time we played."

"Do tell." Gaea's eyebrows rose almost to her hairline. "The great Henry beaten at cards by his mortal mate? Whatever is this world coming to?"

Henry squeezed Cerissa's hand. "You'll have to ask her what she was wearing when she won. I don't think it was a fair game."

A furious blush colored Cerissa's cheeks.

He chuckled. They'd been lounging in bed. She had been wearing a lacy bra and panties set, but that wasn't truly why she beat him. After all, he liked to think he'd been just as distracting in silk boxer shorts.

"I don't need to ask her." Gaea laughed with him. "Her blush reveals all. Good night, Cerissa." Gaea gave her a hug. "I'll see you soon. Good sleep, Henry."

"Good sleep, Gaea." Henry closed the front door behind her and led the way back to the dining room, Cerissa trailing him.

He found Rolf making suggestions for the letter to MWC, and the normally even-tempered Marcus was ready to explode.

"Rolf," Henry said, drawing everyone's attention away from the impending battle. "I want to talk with you about reallocating some of the winery's capital improvements on our work plan. Would you mind joining me in the drawing room?"

"Sure. Marcus and Nicholas can take care of this." Rolf rose to his feet.

Henry nodded in Karen's direction. "Please join us. We may be able to use the situation to our advantage in marketing our wines. Scarcity may allow us to raise prices higher for the impacted vintage."

Cerissa touched his arm. "Henry, I'm going to stay here and show Marcus how to access the printer."

Her printer sat on the buffet table, and he'd plugged it into a portable power supply earlier, anticipating the need. It was fortunate after all that she was using the dining room as a makeshift office, though he really should clear out one of the upstairs storage rooms and convert the space to a real office for her.

"Thank you, *cariña*. Karen, Rolf—let us adjourn."

Henry carried one lantern into the drawing room so Karen could see and pulled his favorite chair over to face his friends, who took seats on the rustic leather couch. "Where do you want to start?"

Rolf steepled his fingers. "The loss of almost forty percent of the two-year-old Cabernet is going to hurt our bottom line. I think we should consider a staff reduction."

"A layoff? Really, Rolf, it is premature—"

"Do you have the money to keep payroll going on half the profit? *Scheiß*, I don't have those kinds of reserves, not for long."

"We shouldn't rush into it. With a shortage, Karen may be able to use that in her marketing material to justify a price increase."

"You'll have to double the price to make up for losing half the sales."

"Not quite. We have to double the net, not the full sales price."

"Ach. Don't quibble. That wine won't sell at that price. Right, Karen?" Rolf turned to her.

"Nuh uh." She wagged her finger at them. "Don't put me in the middle of this. You two set the price; I market it. We've always done it that way. I'm not going to be responsible if it fails."

"Then we could use the reserve fund to make it through next year," Rolf said.

Henry scrubbed a hand over his face. "You mean the money we set aside for the bottling room upgrades?"

"*Ja, ja.*"

"If only we'd made those improvements before the earthquake," Henry said.

"Don't whine to me. I wanted to make the expenditure last year, but no, you liked bottling wines the old-fashioned way."

Yes, he did. But clearly, the old-fashioned way had cost them dearly. And his personal cash flow wasn't good right now. Too much tied up in real estate and other non-liquid assets. If they needed a cash infusion, how would he get the money?

"This is only the start of our conversation." Henry stood, gesturing toward the door. He couldn't take any more of Rolf's irascible nature tonight, not with the stress they were all under. "We will discuss this further tomorrow after I inspect the loss and know our precise situation."

"Fine." Rolf stood. "But we can't support employees sitting around with nothing to do. A decision will have to be made soon."

After Rolf and Karen left, Henry returned to the kitchen to open the envelope the cleaning crew had left. The bill for today's work wasn't bad, but the estimate for water remediation in the pool house was fifty-six thousand dollars. It included removing drywall, using fans to dry the room, and then replacing the drywall and carpet.

He scrubbed a hand over his face. His homeowner's earthquake insurance was unlikely to cover it—the policy deductible was high. He really had no choice but to pay out of his own pocket to have the work done. With a resigned sigh, he checked the time.

His assistant winemaker, William, had agreed to meet with him, despite the late hour. Henry powered down two pouches of clone blood and aged himself until gray streaked his hair and tiny wrinkles formed on his face. William only knew him as Henry Bautista.

He stopped in the dining room to sign the letter Marcus had prepared and let Cerissa know he'd be gone for a while, then headed for the Viper.

The blockade wasn't a problem. Technically, he was out after curfew, but the guards at the Hill's gate knew him, and his winery was nearer to the Hill's wall than the blockade, so he didn't have to deal with the substation police.

He found William waiting for him in the bottling warehouse. Scanning for damage, Henry glanced around the industrial-style room—two stories high and half the size of a soccer field. The insulated concrete walls were unfinished, and large dome lights hung from the open ceiling. The dome lights were off due to the power failure. The harsh glow of the emergency lights cast long shadows over the bottling equipment.

On Friday, the day before the engagement party, he and William had spent most of the night siphoning aged wine barrels into enormous stainless-steel tanks from which the wine would be bottled, blending barrels together to even out the balance of flavors—oak, tannins, and acidity—in order to ensure the final product was up to their standards.

Twenty barrels of their two-year-old Cabernet had been used to fill the tanks. Once bottled, the wine would age for another year at least before being sold.

The tanks sat on large wooden open-frame platforms, so a forklift's tongs could slide between a platform's frame and individually raise the tanks to gravity fill the bottle feeder. The tongs of one of the forklifts had been slid into a tank's platform and left locked in a slightly raised position when they finished for the night.

"The tank wasn't more than six inches off the ground," William said, as they toured the bottling room using a couple of powerful flashlights to supplement the emergency lighting. "Just enough to slide and tip, hitting the wall. It broke the testing spout"—which looked like a hose bib and was affixed about a foot from the bottom of the tank—"and the wine bled out all over the floor."

Henry shook his head. The concrete floor was stained solid purple by the grapes, but at least the day crew had sopped up the ruined wine and dried the floor.

"I know you like to mix in smaller batches," William continued, "but we really should overhaul our process and move to larger fixed tanks and use pumps rather than gravity feeders."

William had mentioned this before. As much as Henry embraced changes in technology, he preferred his old-fashioned approach to wine blending and bottling. His insistence had cost them dearly. "And the barrels themselves? We still have one hundred and twenty left?"

"Almost half of those were damaged. Let's go to the cellar so you can see."

"Is the basement structurally sound?" Henry asked.

"It looks safe to go down there, but some large cracks have developed in the southern and northern walls, and the floor. I have a structural engineer scheduled for tomorrow to inspect."

Henry clenched his teeth. More expense. Would insurance cover the damage? Unless the whole building collapsed, it was rare to meet the deductible in an earthquake.

And that was assuming the insurance company didn't go insolvent. Homeowners could get coverage through the state's special program—he had. But the winery had to buy from a specialty company that only wrote earthquake insurance. If the insurer went insolvent in the "big one," there wouldn't be enough money to go around.

From what he'd heard so far, this quake was the "big one" that could send the specialty companies running to bankruptcy court.

He accompanied William downstairs to the staging area in the cool underground cellar where the barrels aged. Henry walked briskly to the alcove nearest the service elevator.

While they'd taken steps to strap the barrels still aging in place to prevent those from being tossed to the ground during an earthquake, once the barrels were removed from the main part of the cellar and stacked in the staging area alcove for transport upstairs, nothing kept them from falling and smashing into each other.

Timing. Had the quake hit last week, they would have survived with minimal losses of wine.

"The quake banged the loose barrels against each other. Some cracked and leaked." William indicated what looked like a discard pile. "We finished sorting through them this afternoon to see which were still intact."

"Thank you for doing that." Henry shook his head. He stared at the evidence. Hearing about the loss was one thing, but seeing it in person drove home the reality. Between the bottling room and the casks, they'd lost the equivalent of almost four hundred cases of wine.

"When do you want to blend another tank?" Henry asked. "We cannot allow too much time to pass."

William signaled his agreement. "We'll finish cleaning up the bottling area first. Fortunately, the glass bottles were still in their shipping cases, so we didn't lose them."

"Excellent. How soon can you get them unloaded to be washed?"

"With the aftershocks we've been having, I don't want to unpack the bottles yet."

Henry nodded. It was sound logic. "You mentioned structural cracks—"

"Over here."

William pointed to where the ceiling met the vertical wall on the cellar's south side. Henry moved closer to inspect it and his stomach churned. Large fissures had opened there—very large.

William had downplayed the size when he called them cracks. Henry's hand went to his crucifix, twisting the chain that hung around his neck as he examined the fissures in the wall and ceiling.

"This is why I want the engineer's clearance before we start operating heavy equipment above this ceiling," William added.

Henry hated the delay, but William was right. The bottling room was directly above them, and they had no choice. Safety came first. "Agreed. We wait. Email me when you get the report." Henry's phone rang. "If you'll excuse me."

He answered once he was far enough away that William wouldn't hear. "Hello, Anne-Louise."

"Enrique, I've been trying to call you for two nights now."

He growled. To his ears, it was more of an accusation than a statement of concern. "We had an earthquake. The phones have been out."

"That's no excuse. You should have found some way to get word to me. We've been watching the news out here. How is everyone on the Hill?"

"We are fine. No deaths. Marcus's house is a total loss, and Nicholas was hurt, but he is recovering. And there was one fire—Gaea Greenleaf lost her kitchen."

"The San Francisco community didn't do as well, from what we hear."

"Then you know far more than I do. I've been too busy dealing with the aftermath and have not been in contact with them."

"I could not imagine why you hadn't called. I was thinking of coming to visit again."

So soon? She was on the Hill only three weeks ago to see him perform in the circus. "This would not be a good time. Travel in some areas is restricted, and there was damage to the main freeway. Everyone is still coping with the disaster."

"How is Cerissa doing?"

"She is fine. A little shaken up, but fine." It never stopped surprising him how Anne-Louise had seemed to bond with Cerissa. Surprising him even further, Cerissa had made clear his maker and ex-lover wasn't invited to the engagement party, and Anne-Louise hadn't taken offense.

"Have her call me when she gets a chance. I want to talk with her about my house. I have another idea for the moon room."

At Cerissa's suggestion, he was building a small residence on his property where Anne-Louise could stay when she visited—one not connected underground to his main home, like the pool house was.

He'd just lost hundreds of thousands of dollars in the quake. He had no money to waste, especially on his maker's whims. "Anne-Louise, I am not going to spend another dime on architectural plans, only to have you change your mind again. No more ideas. No more revisions."

"You wouldn't have that money if it weren't for me, Enrique Bautista Vasquez. If I hadn't turned you, you would be dust by now."

"And my life would be more peaceful than it is."

A loud *beruck* emitted from the phone. Anne-Louise's dismissive scoff set his teeth on edge.

"You have always been ungrateful and spiteful," she snapped. "Money and business are all you've ever cared about."

Opening his first business—and learning how to make money lawfully—had allowed him to end their relationship. "You just resent it because it meant my freedom from *you*."

"Why, you *salaud*! *Connard*! *Rat-meunier*!" she began, ticking off a list of invectives in French.

Bastard and asshole were bad enough, but he bristled at "rat-sucker," which implied the insanity that came from feeding on animals.

"Then it is fortunate for you that I am in California and you are in New York. I suggest you stay there."

He stabbed the button to disconnect the call and took a deep breath. He had more important things to deal with than his maker's unreasonable demands.

But where was he going to get the money to deal with *all* of them?

Chapter 21
Death's Window

Gaea's house—Shortly before the board meeting ended

Seaton heard the tinkle of breaking glass and smelled the enticing scent. Mortal. Male. One who didn't belong there. He sniffed again—fresh blood was in the air. He followed his nose down the pitch-black hallway. The power was still out, and they hadn't yet bothered to dig the battery-powered lights out of Gaea's emergency supplies in the garage.

It didn't matter to him that the house was dark. He could see well enough without any artificial light. He crept with supernatural stealth down the long hallway until he was at the entrance of the parlor and leaned in enough to see a man climbing through the window.

One who wasn't a vampire's pet. Easy enough to tell—no scent marker from repeated bites.

Free for the taking.

The sweet smell of blood was more powerful here. The man must have cut himself on window glass. Seaton smiled a twisted smile.

He *whooshed* to the center of the room and then stood very still. No reason to attack quickly. Like a snake toying with a field mouse, he locked eyes with the intruder.

The man froze.

Slowly, Seaton stalked toward his victim, the anticipation building in him. He reached out and pulled off the ski mask that covered the man's face. It was pale white with fear. Seaton grabbed the man's hair and yanked his head to one side, almost snapping the spine. Only then did he plunge his fangs into his victim's neck.

The taste was exquisite. He took long pulls, feeling the rich fluid flood him with power. The man's heart fought him, fought to keep pumping, but as he drank his fill, the heart could take no more and gave way with a *pop*.

Much as a mortal would suck on a straw until every last drop was slurped out of a glass, Seaton sucked his victim dry until the veins flattened.

When he could get no more satisfaction from the limp body, he let it drop to the floor. He languidly walked over to a nearby chair and fell into it. He felt relaxed and powerful. Flushed. The warmth of the blood chased the chill from his bones. But he didn't have the sexual response that he knew most vampires experienced with feeding.

His maker had been too young to turn him. It had left him different.

No one had to tell him.

He just didn't connect with mortals. He didn't want the kind of relationship that he saw others on the Hill pursue. He only wanted to use mortals the way a mortal would use a cow. Enjoy a fine meal and discard the parts of the carcass that were inedible.

And what a fine meal they offered.

He was still rocking in the velvet chair when Gaea came home. She must have sensed his presence in the parlor and went to see why he was in there. With her nose aimed high, she sniffed at the fresh blood in the air.

"Where do we put this kind of trash?" Seaton asked her. His mother had taught him a guest should clean up after himself.

"Oh, Seaton," Gaea said with a sigh. She went over to the dead man and touched his wrist.

Why did she bother? Her vampire senses should have told her he'd been drained and had no heartbeat.

"My dear, this is not good. We'll have to call Tig."

"Really?" Seaton asked, confused as to why the chief would need to be involved. Did they always contact her for cleanup?

"Yes." He could hear both the disappointment and anxiety in her voice.

Was he in trouble? It didn't make sense to him. "But I found the guy breaking into your house. He didn't belong here."

"I know, dear. But you really mustn't kill unless it's *absolutely necessary*," she scolded him. "We've talked about this before. The council will not be pleased. You should have held him until help arrived."

Seaton thought it was more fuss than one mortal was worth. "He wasn't one of the pets kept here on the Hill. Why wasn't he fair game?"

"Because no hunting is allowed within a hundred miles, and then, never kill them. You'll have mortals coming after us with torches and pitchforks if you do. Oh dear, whatever are we going to do?" She balanced a finger on her lower lip. He knew the look. She was trying to figure out what to do next. "Well, we can't cry over spilled blood, now can we? You stay here. I'm going to call Tig."

Seaton hadn't planned on going anywhere. It felt good to just sit there, rock, and watch the dead mortal. Yes, he preferred it when they were dead. Something about the dead felt reassuring to him. Almost as good as the peace that washed over him when he played video games. Almost.

CHAPTER 22
DOUBLE TROUBLE

GAEA'S HOUSE—FIFTEEN MINUTES LATER

Tig shook her head when she looked at the body. She'd known it was going to be an uphill battle when Gaea obtained a visitor's permit for Seaton.

Jane, you irresponsible bitch.

Seaton's maker had screwed them all over with her carelessness. It was that European bitch's disregard for responsibility that dumped the problem on them. They'd all known then that something was wrong with him.

And now this.

Jayden had already worked a full day, so Tig hadn't disturbed his sleep to ask him to assist. On the way to Gaea's house, she'd called her reservists, and Zeke had been available. He'd just arrived home from some meeting at Henry's and rendezvoused with her at Gaea's.

Now he knelt by the body, searching for the perp's ID.

"What happened?" Tig finally asked, and rubbed her nose, the smokey smell left over from the fire bothering her sensitive nose.

Gaea's shoulders sagged. "I was at the SEWC board meeting—Henry held it at his house. This man tried to break in while I was gone. You can see the broken window."

"Where's Ari?"

"He went home."

"Florida?"

"He said something about an apartment in Mordida."

Good. That meant he was nearby if she needed her computer consultant. Tig looked at the window. The glass had fallen inside. It was definitely broken from the outside.

She stuck her head through the window's opening. The garden hose box had been moved so it was under the window. The dead man must have thought the half-burned house was abandoned for the night. A small tarp had been thrown over the window frame to protect the burglar from broken glass as he crawled in.

Damn. Looters had made it over the wall, despite the patrols. Tig stood in front of the young vampire. "Seaton, what happened?"

He sat there looking at her as if she were some freak and continued to lethargically rock himself. "Why waste breath on a mortal's death?" Another back-and-forth motion. "I don't understand you people."

Tig gave him a hard stare.

Finally, he gestured at the glass. "I heard the window break."

"Go on."

"He cut himself. Fresh blood. He didn't belong to anyone on the Hill." Seaton cocked his head to the side and looked at her quizzically. "Can I go back to my video game now? I have a charged brick that will last the night."

Tig didn't answer him. The swearwords on the tip of her tongue weren't appropriate when on the job. Instead, she turned to Zeke. "Any ID on the body?"

"Yup." Zeke held up an open leather wallet. "He lives in Mordida. Ethan Tash."

"We'll bag the wallet and the body, and take him to Dr. Clarke's morgue. It will be up to the council to decide what to do."

Dr. Clarke doubled as the town's coroner. If they decided to release the body, his report would cover for them on the cause of death.

"Council?" Zeke shoved his cowboy hat back and nodded in Seaton's direction. "But California follows the Castle Rule. He gets the benefit of the doubt."

"You're seriously going to argue that Seaton reasonably feared imminent death or great bodily harm? A vampire versus a mortal?"

"Hey, chief, it's your call, but iffn' it was me, well, I'd cut him some slack. How was Seaton supposed to know whether the man was armed with silver or a stake? Just 'cause the dead guy was mortal doesn't mean the vampire always wins. Kim Han learnt that the hard way."

"There's the law, and then there's doing what's right. Seaton wasn't in any real danger. The man wasn't even carrying a weapon."

"But even Seaton ain't got no x-ray vision. No way from lookin' could he tell if the thief was packin'."

She was trying to impress on Seaton that going for the throat wasn't always necessary. She didn't need Zeke's attitude undermining her. It was bad enough her reservist was less civilized than most vampires, hunting whenever a legal opportunity presented itself. She didn't need more vampires with his frame of mind.

"Zeke—"

"Whatever you say, ma'am." Zeke looked away. "I'll go get a body bag from the van. Be right back."

"Bring the camera, too. We'll need photos of the crime scene. I'll start logging the report."

"There was a second one, you know." Seaton gave a nonchalant wave toward the window.

It took a moment for Seaton's comment to sink in. When it did, Tig's anger spiked hot. "Why didn't you tell me that before?"

"You didn't ask. It ran off when it saw me drain this one."

Saw him.

Crap.

Tig turned to Zeke. "How good are you at tracking?"

"You know better than to ask that, ma'am."

She did. "Go hunt for the second person. Now."

Zeke's smile reached his eyes. "My pleasure, ma'am."

"But I want them alive. Understand?"

Zeke tipped his hat as he moved quickly to Gaea's front door. "Yes, ma'am. He might be shy a pint if I need the bite to control him, but he'll be alive."

23

THE HUNT

GAEA'S HOUSE—MOMENTS LATER

Zeke sniffed the night air outside Gaea's window. Unlike some of the younger vampires, he still knew how to hunt. His trips to South America made sure of that.

He scanned the area, looking for telltale signs. The night breeze brought a scent with it—mortal, sweaty, and so scared that the intoxicating adrenaline made his fangs run out. Then he spotted grape leaves bent out of place and footprints in the irrigation ditch.

Ah ha. So the varmint had gone through Gaea's vineyard. He tossed his cowboy hat into the cab of his Ford truck so he wouldn't lose it, swept his fingers through his hair, and took off at a run between the rows of grapevines, a swift shadow in the night. But running at supernatural speed blurred his vision, so he stopped his *whoosh* at the end of one row, pausing to get his bearings. The footprints continued in the dry grass leading to the oak woodlands that dipped into a rough ravine. The steep, rocky slopes wouldn't be easy for a mortal.

But for him? It was a stroll in the park.

Extending his claws, he silently scrambled down the ravine to the dry riverbed below. Come winter, the water would be waist high and running fast. The thief was damn lucky fall rains hadn't kicked in yet.

The scent continued northeast toward Robles Road. In the distance, a light bobbed around. Probably a flashlight. It traveled down the center of the flat, sandy bottom where the gray stones were less concentrated.

Zeke climbed back to higher ground. Paralleling his prey, he overtook the light and caught sight of a mortal scrambling along the rocky riverbed. This was too easy. There had to be a way to have some fun with the thief.

He continued to follow from above. They were almost at Robles Road. Not that the mortal could make an easy exit from there, but he wouldn't be surprised if Tig sent out an alert for the nearest police car to patrol the area. She couldn't let this one escape, and it wasn't like the chief not to have a backup plan.

No way am I letting anyone else get him.

This varmint was his prey, and only his.

Zeke sped ahead. He crossed the road, went back down into the ravine, picked up a few dry riverbed stones, and entered the culvert that ran under the road. The corrugated metal tunnel was tall enough that he could slink through it and not be seen.

The mortal approached the tunnel from the other side, stopping every few feet to whip the flashlight behind him, only to resume stumbling over the round rocks. In the dark culvert, Zeke flattened his body against the cold metal wall, making himself almost invisible.

The next time the mortal pointed the flashlight away from the tunnel, Zeke tossed one of the rocks to the left, so it landed behind him. The man spun around, shining his flashlight in the direction of the rock. Zeke sent the next one sailing to land between the culvert and the man. At the *thunk* of the rock hitting hard dirt, the man swung the flashlight around again, this time looking up at the road overhead.

Zeke could smell his panic in the air. But he could smell something else, too, something distracting. He narrowed his eyes, ignoring the scent. He had to focus on capturing his prey—then he'd figure it out.

He sent another rock sailing, this one to the right, once again landing behind the intruder with a *thunk*. The man took off running deeper into the culvert and straight at Zeke.

"Whoa, there, pardner." Zeke caught the man, swinging him around, and stripped off the guy's ski mask. "Let's see what we have here." Zeke held the captive at arm's length. "Well, well, missy."

A girl. So that was the scent that'd been bothering him.

But hadn't Seaton said there was a second *man*? Zeke ran Seaton's words through his mind.

No, he'd said *it*.

Seaton was a strange one, that was for sure.

"Let me go," the thief said, struggling to free herself.

Her flashlight pointed up in his face and blinded him for a second.

"Now hold still, missy. Nothin' else for you to do now. How many others were with you? Is there a third?"

"Like I'd tell you."

He smiled at her. She froze when she saw the fangs. Then she started struggling more violently.

"Damn. You are a cute one. Ow," he yelled, as she bit down on his arm. Zeke wrenched free of her teeth, grabbed her hair, and pinned her against the wall of the culvert. "I'm the one who does the biting around here."

The woman continued to fight against him. Enough fooling around. What was it his mama used to say?

Don't play with your food.

He stared into the eyes of his captive, mesmerizing her until she stopped moving. He then sank his teeth into her neck.

The rush of fear in her blood hit his taste buds. What a wonderful, tart taste. He didn't have the problem some people did, but he appreciated the occasional adrenaline-spiked blood hit from a real victim.

Stopping at one pint—just like he promised Tig—he let go and picked up the still-dazed mortal.

Damn. He fought against the urge to take the filly to bed now. No matter what his dick wanted, he knew better than to take advantage of a mesmerized victim. The chief was all about consent. And he'd been on the receiving end of unwelcome advances before—his maker had used him vilely—and he had no interest in perpetrating that on someone else. So as much as he might be turned on by the bite, he wouldn't act on it.

He walked out of the culvert, carrying the mortal, and got back on the road. He phoned Tig, who met him with the van.

"There," he said, as he dumped the thief into Tig's back seat. "This one's all yours."

Tig sniffed at the air, then gave him the stink eye so hard he could almost smell it.

"No, I didn't do what you're thinkin'," Zeke said, somewhat irritated. "I'm not a rapist. Had a good feed, that's all."

He didn't enjoy having to specify that. She should know by now that he abided that line.

Tig's look eased up, and then she nodded. "All right, Zeke. Thanks for bringing her in."

"You're mighty welcome," he said, not able to keep the sarcasm from coming through. Then he thought better of it. "And chief? You're gonna need me to wipe her memory. I've got a good foothold, since I fed on her and all."

"We'll see. First I want to find out where the breach in security is—how they got over the wall." She looked at him expectantly.

"I wouldn't know, ma'am. She refused to answer any questions when I caught her."

"Okay. I'll call you when I need your assistance."

"And if you decide to get rid of her, I'd like first dibs."

He'd never turned down a good meal. Waste not, want not, as his mama would say.

Tig gave him a look that said his comment wasn't welcome. "No one's getting rid of anyone."

"Well then, ma'am, I'll just mosey on back to Gaea's and get my truck."

"Do you want a lift?"

"Naw, I'm good walkin'. But I'll be over at Jose's Cantina later. Feel like playing a few hands of poker." He rubbed his hands together. "Feelin' flush, you might say."

Chapter 24
Interrogation

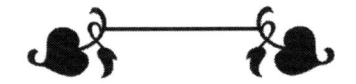

ROBLES ROAD—MOMENTS LATER

Tig put the van in gear and drove to the police station. She phoned Liza. "Are you available now? I'd rather have you as the witness, since Zeke bit the culprit to make them compliant."

"Sure." A pause. "I'll be at the station in ten minutes."

"Thanks."

After meeting in the parking lot with Dr. Clarke to transfer Ethan's body to his care, Tig escorted the would-be thief inside the station to the interview room. White female, mid-twenties if she guessed right, bleach-blonde hair. No ID in her pocket.

What was she doing breaking and entering on the Hill?

Tig sat the woman into a chair, where she docilely settled.

Hmm. The perp would need food and water when she came out of the haze. And a painkiller. She was going to have a headache from blood loss.

Zeke could be a greedy pig at times.

Tig walked back to the break room and rummaged through the refrigerator. Jayden kept meat and bread at the station for making sandwiches on the go. She sniffed—still fresh. That would have to do. She grabbed a carton of chocolate milk, and it completed the meal for her suspect. Tomorrow night she'd have to replace Jayden's stash. For now, she took the food back into the interview room and waited.

It didn't take long for the woman to rouse. "Where am I?" Blondie asked.

"Eat first," Tig ordered her. She went through the first-aid kit, found some acetaminophen tablets, and put them on the plate next to the sandwich. "For your headache."

"How do you know I have a headache?"

"Experience."

Blondie picked up the tablets and washed them down with the chocolate milk. "My neck hurts. What happened? Was I in a car accident? I don't remember."

"Don't try to think about it right now. Instead, we're going to talk about how you got up here."

"Why should I talk to you?"

"I'm chief of police." Tig took out her badge and identification to show the woman.

"Shit."

"Your friend was caught breaking into one of the homes up here. You ran off. Want to explain yourself?"

"Look, okay, yeah, but—I mean—" She stopped again, rubbing at her temples. "I'll talk to you. But can I eat first?"

Liza wasn't here yet anyway. "Go ahead."

The woman took a bite of the sandwich and scrunched up her nose. "This is just bread and ham. No mayo, no mustard. Didn't they teach you how to make a sandwich in cop school?"

Tig ignored the comment and watched as the suspect ate. When Liza opened the door and stuck her head in to say she'd observe through the one-way glass, Tig thanked her.

Setting her phone on the table, Tig put it into record mode. "Now, what's your name?"

"Rita," Blondie mumbled around her sandwich. "Rita Rodgers."

Tig leaned over to a computer terminal near her and typed in the name. "Address?"

Rita gave an address for an apartment in Mordida, and Tig added it to the search.

Rita's DMV record popped up. So she was only nineteen. No priors. No wants or warrants.

"How did you get over the wall?"

"That was easy. We watched your patrols. Like clockwork. We had a good twenty minutes to scale the wall."

Damn. I should have given more explicit instructions to the evening patrol officers.

"How did you know the cameras weren't working?"

"City power is still off—though you got lights." Rita gestured at the ceiling. "Did the power come back on?"

"No, we have a generator. Again, how did you know the cameras weren't working? They could have been on battery power."

Rita took another bite of her sandwich and shook her head. "The cameras were dead, ya know? The lens didn't light up when we waved at them."

Damn cheap council.

"Why did you pick that particular house? It's pretty far up the Hill. Why not one closer?"

"Ethan knew that the woman who owned it wouldn't be home tonight. At least, that's what he told me," Rita said, finishing the last of the simple sandwich.

"That would be Ethan Tash?"

"Yeah. Where is he?"

"He's in custody." Resting in the morgue was the same as being in custody, Tig reasoned. "Why did you target Gaea's house?"

"Ethan knew Dylan, from school, before Dylan went to prison."

Oh crap. Gaea was not going to be happy about that. "Go on."

"Dylan had told Ethan that the woman he lived with had a ton of jewelry that she kept in her house. Dylan had told him which room it was in and how to get at it. Wasn't in a safe or anything. We read about the fire in the local newspaper. We figured we'd get in and out quickly."

"Why did you need the jewelry?" The thought "to buy drugs" followed, but Tig didn't voice it.

"We needed money for school. Tuition was raised again, and we were both going to have to drop out." She took a big gulp of the chocolate milk. "I'm an accounting major. We couldn't make enough money working part-time to pay for the next semester and couldn't qualify for more student loans. If I worked full-time, I'd have to quit school."

Tig shook her head. She'd read about problems like that. "Was anyone else working with you?"

"No. It was just us."

"Neither of you told anyone about your plan?"

"No. Why would we?"

"If no one else was helping you, how did you know Gaea wasn't going to be home?"

"The website. After the earthquake, we kept watching it. We knew this was the break we needed. Gaea was supposed to be at the board meeting—we saw the notice on the SEWC website. And Dylan never mentioned anything about another man living there." Rita took another slug of chocolate milk. "Gaea sure did move fast to replace Dylan."

Tig growled.

"Hey, no disrespect meant. We just didn't expect the man who attacked Ethan. When we saw the burned-out kitchen, we figured she was sleeping somewhere else and wouldn't return. Piece of cake."

How could smart kids be so stupid? "Are you lovers with Ethan?"

"No, just friends."

"Who would miss him if he were gone?"

"That's a strange question."

"Just answer it."

"Ah, he has family in Carlyle. He hangs with a study group at college. But he doesn't have a girlfriend or anything."

"Do you have a boyfriend?"

"No."

"Family in town?"

"My family's from Carlyle too."

Tig leaned back in her chair. A decision had to be made about Rita's future, and it had to be made quickly. They had a night or two at most. Tig turned to the computer and emailed the mayor and the vice mayor.

Knowing those two, she'd bet money the girl wouldn't receive any mercy. Rita would be transferred to the Mordida County jail by dawn—that was, if they let her live. But whether it was jail or death, well, that was a bet Tig refused to take.

CHAPTER 25
FUN AND GAMES

RANCHO BAUTISTA DEL MURCIÉLAGO—THAT SAME NIGHT

"You're home," Cerissa said, as she walked into the game room to find the big-screen monitor lit and a game controller in Henry's hands. The electricity had come back on while he was away. In his absence, she had followed the instructions he'd left her and flipped the inverter switch to the off position, which rerouted the system to put them back on utility power.

He was sitting on the couch, playing an interactive video game. She could tell by the fact he wore a headset over his gray-streaked hair.

"Come here." He tilted his head in the direction of the television screen, and his fingers continued to fly over the controller.

He looked okay now, but she'd gotten a definite spike through the crystal. Something had upset him—greatly. They already knew about what happened to the Cabernet production. Did something else occur?

She eased onto the sofa. "How was your inspection of the winery?"

He shook his head. "Not worth talking about."

Uh oh. That didn't sound good. "I'm here when you want to discuss it."

"Nothing to worry you about." He leaned over and kissed her, before returning to the game.

"Well, I'm done with work, and I was thinking of going to bed." Usually, the thought of joining her in bed got his attention. But he continued to focus on the video game as he worked the other controller. She stood. Perhaps it was best to let him unwind this way. "Go ahead and play and I'll see you tomorrow night."

"Don't leave. I have something I want to show you." He hooked an arm around her waist and pulled her onto his lap.

She focused on the screen. "You're playing the vampire game, aren't you?"

"Yes." He continued to work the controller, both of his arms encircling her. "Pick up the other controller."

"Why? Do you and Rolf need to build your scores on an inexperienced player?"

The last time she and Karen played as mortals in the game, Rolf's and Henry's vampire avatars had quickly killed them both. She hadn't tried playing the game again after that.

Henry moved the microphone out of the way, probably so Rolf wouldn't hear what he said next. "Do you trust me?"

"Of course."

"Then pick up the controller."

She sighed. "You'll have to let me go. I can't reach it." He removed one arm from around her, and she slid off his lap and onto the couch. Grabbing the spare controller, she slipped on the headset.

"All right. Now what?"

He leaned over and pressed two buttons on the controller she held. A new female character appeared on screen. She moved the joystick, trying to remember which buttons made what body part move. But something didn't look right with her character.

Why didn't the avatar have the weapons usually given a novice vampire hunter? "Where are my crossbow and garlic spray?"

"Look closer."

She did. "My character has fangs!"

"Welcome to the tribe, Cerissa," Rolf said over the headset.

Henry gestured to the screen. "We talked and decided that since you can become vampire, you are entitled to play a vampire character. If you don't like her appearance, we can change it for you."

"No, she's fine. Thank you."

A rush of warmth ran through Cerissa, and she smiled a silly grin. Henry hadn't said anything about her ability to turn into a vampire after he found out the night they got engaged. And she'd been too nervous to ask.

This meant he accepted her.

She pressed the controller buttons, experimenting with how to move the character. The avatar had weapons on her belt that only vampires carried. She practiced picking up each one and using it.

Henry leaned over and captured her lips for a quick kiss. "Stay with us. We will protect your character. It will take a while for you to build up sufficient points to truly protect her against the more advanced mortal players."

"I really don't know what to say," Cerissa said into the microphone. "I'm touched. Thank you both."

Rolf let out a snort. "Don't get used to it. And don't think you can goof off and play video games instead of working in the lab. You need to make progress on your cloning project if you're going to support Henry when we lose the winery."

Henry put his hand over his microphone. "Do not listen to him. The winery will be fine. It is more important that you enjoy life. Work will always be there."

He put an arm around her and pulled her to him for a longer kiss. She kept one eye open, watching the screen to make sure nothing happened to her character. She felt very protective of the newborn her.

Rolf interrupted the kiss. "Quit making out with Cerissa or your character is going to get staked."

On screen, Rolf took defensive action against a hunter who had entered the graveyard where the vampires gathered.

Cerissa returned her full attention to the game and maneuvered her character to pick up the long whip from her belt. She unfurled and cracked it in the direction of the vampire hunter who'd tried to sneak up on them. The whip wound around the man's avatar, immobilizing him. She did what she'd seen Henry and Rolf do before: she pulled the whip handle toward her character without letting the whip unwind. It kept the man imprisoned, unable to fight back, as she reeled him in. Once within striking distance, her character attacked the human's neck, feeding voraciously.

Game vampires were such messy eaters. It wasn't like that in real life. She watched as points racked up on her score.

Henry patted her leg. "Nicely done."

"Exhilarating."

"Enough talk," Rolf said over the headset, sounding like his typical irritable self.

"Indeed." Henry lifted his hand from her leg and returned it to the controller. "Let us hunt."

Hunt. Could Rolf's need for the hunt be satisfied by the game?

It was worth considering—later. Right now, distractions could get her character killed.

For the most part, she stayed back and watched how the guys handled tactical situations. When they found themselves up against novice players, they let her take the lead. She was able to score a few more kills that way.

"Have you thought of a name for your character?" Henry asked. "When we sign off for the night, you will have an opportunity to enter the name."

"I don't know. Do you have any suggestions?"

"How about 'Blood Slut'?" Rolf asked over the microphone.

"Rolf..." Henry began, a warning sound in his voice. To Cerissa, he said, "Ignore his teasing. You may pick any name you want, *cariña*."

"That's it. Cariña. That's what I'll name her."

Rolf laughed. "I told you she'd pick something sappy. I win the bet."

"Bet?" she asked.

Henry smiled at her. "I will happily pay." He leaned over and lightly kissed her cheek. Into the microphone, he said, "Good sleep, Rolf. I will talk with you tomorrow."

Henry took off his headset and ended the game. He then showed Cerissa how to name and save her character. They had to switch over to the Spanish menu to get the tilde that appeared above the "n" in Cariña. He helped her operate the controller by wrapping his arms around her, placing his hands over hers, and she loved the feeling of being enfolded by him.

With her character safely recorded in the world of stored electrons, she set the game controller down.

Henry shut off the video screen and turned back to her. Gently, he brushed the back of his fingertips across her cheek. "Tell me, how does it feel to be a vampire?"

Caught off guard, she looked away, slightly embarrassed. "You mean to become...dead?"

"That is one way of looking at it."

She paused, trying to pick her words carefully. She didn't want to hurt Henry's feelings or feed into his insecurity. He spent years believing he had no soul and was damned, but learning that vampires were created by the Lux—whom he stubbornly declared were angels, rather than stranded alien astronauts—had helped flip his self-hating belief.

But how could she put it delicately?

"Morphing into one just feels…well…" Her sentence tapered into silence. Henry waited patiently, looking at her. With a sigh, she said, "It feels a little wrong."

"Wrong? Why?"

"It's like I'm killing myself. I know it's not the same thing, and I'm not *really* dying, but it feels just, well…" There was really no way of talking around this. "Unnatural."

He seductively brushed his lips against her cheek. "I see. Then you are not interested in trying it again?"

"You mean now?"

"Yes."

"What about Marcus and Nicholas?"

Henry rose from the couch and strode over to the door that connected to the hallway leading to the kitchen. "There. Locked." He returned to sit next to her. "No one will disturb us."

Cerissa eased back so she could look into his eyes. The way he looked at her, he wanted something. Something she hadn't been able to give him before. When she considered it, she was surprised he hadn't asked sooner.

She blinked rapidly to turn off her contact lenses—she had no intention of recording her first bite as a vampire—and closed her eyes to morph.

An involuntarily shiver racked through her when she finished—the chill of death. She wasn't sure she'd ever get used to it. She opened her eyes and looked at him. He tilted his head slightly, a submissive motion, offering her his neck. The vein looked so large to her, so perfect, so magnificent, so…*enticing*.

She may have had the strength of a centuries-old vampire, but she didn't have the same control. At vampire speed, she sank her fangs into his neck.

The slightly salty taste of his skin acted as a tantalizing precursor to the heavenly nectar flooding into her mouth. An exquisite buzz spread through her veins, zinging right to her clit. She sucked again, and his muscular body melted against her.

Damn. Why didn't I get undressed first?

Reaching for her blouse's collar, she ripped it down the front and shrugged it off. That was all the invitation he needed. His fingers snapped the bra cups apart, leaving the destroyed undergarment hanging from her shoulders, and his hands ran over her breasts, the nipples pebbling against his palms as she continued to feed on him.

She ran her hands over his chest and, wrapping them around the center line of his button-down shirt, yanked it apart. She vaguely heard buttons hitting the floor as he slipped out of it.

Even though she didn't need to breathe in this form, she panted between pulls on his neck. The charge from the blood and fang serum almost sent her over the edge too soon.

His hands wandered lower, finding the top button of her jeans, popping it open. With a moan, he pulled his hands away from her jeans, gripped her arms and, with a push, gently said, "Enough."

She wanted more, gods, did she want more.

But she refused to hurt him and forced herself to stop.

He immediately rose to his feet, unfastening his pants and yanking them off with his underwear. She finished unbuttoning her own jeans and kicked them away by the time he looked back to her. In one motion, she pulled him down on top of her, wrapped her legs around his, and brought him inside her with a moan.

He kissed her crimson lips, tasting his blood on them. The experience deepened his desire for her. Because of her allergy to vampire blood when she was in human form, he had never thought he would share his blood with her.

The fight with Anne-Louise had stirred something in him. He hated when his maker took his blood now, but memories of what it was like in the beginning reminded him of how exhilarating being bitten by a lover could be.

And the stress of everything made him crave it more—enough to risk Cerissa's rejection when he asked for what he desired, holding his breath, waiting for her answer.

To his amazement, she'd willingly offered it up, and he loved her all the more for her generosity.

But now it was his turn. He kissed her neck and then pierced the tender skin with his fangs as he continued to thrust inside her, trying to hit the right spots, just the way she liked it.

He felt her start to peak right away—with the blood exchange, their lovemaking had turned into a quickie, fast.

"Oh, Henry," she called out when she came, and then morphed back to human.

He kept sucking as she bucked underneath him. It was so strange, to taste her blood go from vampire to human in an instant. Both were like the finest wines to him, her vampire blood like a deep Zinfandel, her human blood like a lighter Sauvignon Blanc, and the sudden switch made him drunk on her, overpowering his senses, until he came in a blinding explosion of pleasure.

Afterward, he held her, licking her neck as she hugged him tightly.

"I'm sorry, Henry. I couldn't contain the form that long. When I came, it was… Well, I couldn't hang on to it. I'm just lucky I didn't take Lux form. Next time, I'll use the stabilizer."

He stroked her hair. "You have no reason to apologize, *mi amor*. You have no idea the gift you have given me. I never thought it would be possible to feel your lips on my neck that way. Thank you for indulging me."

"You're welcome, Quique."

And Rolf was wrong. Henry didn't have mating fever—he already had the best of both worlds: a mortal mate and a vampire one.

She smiled coyly at him. "Besides, you weren't the only one who enjoyed it. But you owe me—this was supposed to be my turn to decide. Now I get two in a row."

"Of course, *mi amor*." He gave her a luscious leer. "But then you'll just have to wait twice as long to see what I have planned next."

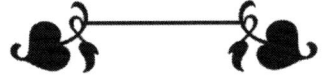

CHAPTER 26

DISCOVERY

VASQUEZ MÜLLER WINERY—THE NEXT DAY

On Tuesday, with electricity restored citywide, the winery's tasting room reopened. Bruce worked the afternoon shift. The winery was still standing, which meant he had a job for now, but the rumors about damage to the cask cellars made him wonder how long that would last.

He wiped down the oak countertop with its high-gloss finish for the umpteenth time. His back still hurt, and getting to work was a fucking pain after the earthquake. The roads were a mess. They should just close the place for a week.

Sure, billboards lined the freeway and directed tourists to the winery's tasting room. But no one was interested in wine tasting right now. All the tourists who were visiting during the big one were in a hurry to return home—no one was stopping by for a quick drink.

The low traffic made the afternoon drag by and meant tips were nonexistent.

Bummer.

He straightened the bottles and washed two dirty wineglasses, returning them to the rack.

He would have played a game on his phone, except it violated the rules. Getting fired right now was a bad idea. He needed the job—at least, he did until he had his money.

Man, he was bored. They didn't even have a television. Wasn't that un-American? What kind of bar didn't have a TV? Instead, they played that music the Boomers and Gen Xers liked. What did they call it? Yeah, smooth jazz. Gross. Made him want to gag.

But he wasn't the audience they were after. The Boomers and Gen Xers were the ones who had the money for pricey wines, and idle time to drink it. But maybe he'd have that kind of money soon.

He'd gotten the blackmail message written, his laptop recharged, the video copied to a flash drive, and the whole thing sent to Bautista's home. It hadn't been hard to find the address. Unfortunately, FedEx wasn't guaranteeing any delivery times, thanks to the earthquake, so he only paid for two-day express. Cash, of course. He wasn't stupid.

"Aren't you overdue for your break?" his supervisor said, glancing at her phone. "If you don't go now, you're not going to be back in time to relieve me. I got yelled at last time. This time I'll tell Suri it's your fault."

"Don't get all bent out of shape." Bruce couldn't swear at Megan, much as he wanted to. He'd been given more than one warning to clean up his language on the job. "Just let me get more Pinot Noir. We're out."

Bruce went into the back room and took his time returning. The door to the manager's office was open. He futzed around by the stockroom door where he could see across the hallway to where Suri sat at her desk. He'd been watching all afternoon for a chance to slip into her office, but she seemed to be glued to her chair.

Finally, he gave up and reported back in at the wine bar.

"Take the scenic route?" his supervisor asked. "Took you long enough to get two bottles."

"Here," he said, handing her the bottles. "I'm going now."

He couldn't delay his break any longer. He went through the back room, out into the hallway to the punch clock, and swiped his employee ID. He looked in Suri's office. Luck was with him. She was gone.

He tiptoed over to the key safe. The metal box was anchored to the wall by Suri's desk, and he slipped the key for the owner's tasting room off the hook. It was the same way he'd gotten the key before when he hid the camera. The key safe was always left open during business hours.

Of course, the manager had a copy on her key ring too. But it was easier to raid the key safe—just a matter of finding the manager's office empty long enough to borrow it.

When he volunteered to clean the owner's tasting room on Sunday, no one questioned why he would take the key. But now he had no excuse. He had to steal it on the sly.

With the key in his pocket, Bruce slunk through the back hallway, and after unlocking the door, he carefully closed it behind him so no one would hear the latch shut then rushed to the hidden panel.

Now, to find out where Bautista disappeared to instead of sleeping with the hot chick. It took him a few minutes to figure out how to open the compartment. Bautista's body had slightly obscured his view on the video, but since he knew the panel had to open, he kept playing with the wood frame until he found the right combination to make the damn thing pop open to reveal the lever.

He moved the lever, and the wall opened, as it had on the video.

Bruce had seen Bautista return the lever to its "closed" position and shut the panel before entering. Bruce wasn't so sure he would know how to get out, so he left the panel open and the lever up.

Using his phone as a flashlight, Bruce entered the dark passageway. It led to a door. He opened the door and was in a windowless room. The room had only one piece of furniture—a small single-wide bed. It was covered with a simple fitted sheet. No top sheet or blanket. A pillow in a matching pillowcase was at one end of the bed.

That was strange. Why would Bautista sleep in here, rather than with the hot girl?

The walls were plain concrete block, unfinished and unpainted, but another lever was on the wall—this one wasn't hidden.

If he pulled on it, what would it open?

Bruce looked up at the ceiling. Just a single light bulb protruded from the flat surface. He threw the wall switch, and it illuminated the room.

The floor was unfinished concrete, except for a metal rectangle. He grabbed the handle and pulled it back—the metal rectangle rose. Pitch-black down there. He shined the phone's flashlight into the hole. A staircase led to a level below.

Bruce checked the time. He had less than five minutes before he had to return to work.

He left the trapdoor open and walked down the staircase to an underground tunnel with a dirt floor, which led to a solid wall, with another strange handle. He pulled, and the wall scraped open slightly.

Damn. He about jumped out of his skin. He was lucky he hadn't peed himself. The noise had been so loud that he was sure someone would catch him now. He froze, waiting for the sound of footsteps.

When he heard nothing for a full thirty seconds, he peeked around the corner and realized he was looking into the cask room—the large underground storage room where wine was aged. No one was around.

He pulled the door shut and retraced his steps.

Taking the stairs two at a time, he shut the trapdoor behind him and turned out the light in the windowless room, stepped through the doorway back to the owner's room, and secured the panel shut.

He then double-timed it to the exit and cracked the door slightly, peering out. He didn't see anyone. No sound of approaching footsteps. He slipped out, closed the door, and turned the key. Locked.

He reminded himself to act cool as he walked past Suri's office. He looked in. Still empty. Another look around and he stepped inside, going straight to the key safe, and, after returning the key, rushed back to the door of her office.

And almost ran over his boss.

"Hey, I'm sorry," he said, stepping back to avoid a collision.

"Were you looking for me?" Suri asked.

"Yeah, I was. I—I wanted to see if you'd done the schedules for next week. I know it's early, but can I find out my days off?"

She walked over to her desk. Bruce followed. From the looks of it, the schedule was just about finished. "Right now, you have the weekend off."

"Thanks. That helps. Sorry to bother you."

"No bother. That's what I'm here for."

"I better get back. My break's almost over," he said as he walked out the door.

Shit. He was moving and talking fast, but he couldn't control it. Suri looked at him strangely. Had his nervousness given him away?

He didn't wait to find out. Bruce clocked in and barely got back to his station on time.

"You're late," his supervisor said, keeping her voice low so the two customers wouldn't hear. "I'm going—the counter is yours."

Bitch.

He made small talk with the two customers as they tasted wine and debated among themselves which one was better. The women were retired locals who had suffered no damage to their homes.

But Bruce's mind was elsewhere—pondering what the lightless room had meant. Why had the owner slept in that room when he had a hot girl he could sleep next to? It just didn't make sense.

As he poured another Cabernet, the ruby color of the wine reminded him of the color of blood that had covered Bautista's lips in the video.

Fangs.

Blood.

Slept in a lightless room during the day.

In a sudden flash, it all came together for him.

He smiled.

He'd never have to work another drudge job again.

27

EARLY RISER

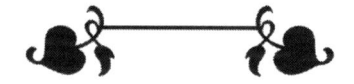

RANCHO BAUTISTA DEL MURCIÉLAGO—THAT AFTERNOON

Henry's eyes snapped open at two minutes past three in the afternoon.
Early moonrise.

Except something was wrong. He was where he was supposed to be—his basement crypt. When he had gone to sleep that morning, he had been alone, with his hands resting on his chest. Unlike mortals, he never moved when asleep.

But now, Cerissa was curled up around him, and his arm had been moved so it draped around her shoulders.

How had that happened without waking him?

"Cerissa?" he said softly. "What are you doing here?"

"You're awake? What time is it?"

"There is an early moonrise. But that does not explain what you are doing here against my wishes."

"I was tired. I thought I'd take a nap with you."

"And so you just flashed here?"

"No, I did it the old-fashioned way. I picked the lock."

"I will have to invest in a better locking mechanism. Perhaps Rolf is right, and I should install an alarm system on all the crypt doors."

"What good would that do?"

"A sleeping vampire can still attack and defend himself against an intruder. I must've been sleeping too soundly to have heard you. That is disturbing."

"It's the crystal. With the implant in your arm, you don't perceive me as a threat, so your defenses aren't triggered."

"Still, it is risky for you to be near me when I am sleeping. Something as simple as you having a nightmare could create a fear response and trigger my defenses. I have explained this to you before."

"But you wouldn't hurt me."

"I wake up starving each night. I do not like the idea of relying on my control or your technology to protect you. I prefer not to take the chance."

As he said it, the delicious scent of her warm blood caused his fangs to descend, and the taste of fang serum leaked into his mouth, amplifying his desire. He couldn't take blood from her now. The ravenous hunger would demand more than was safe.

He closed his eyes and forced the hunger from his mind.

She buried her head on his shoulder, holding tightly to him. "Please don't be angry with me, Henry. I just wanted to be near you."

He ran his hand down her back and patted her perfectly shaped bottom. "I guess it is all right this once. But I prefer you not make a habit of it."

"Yes, Quique."

Was she acknowledging the request or agreeing to it? With Cerissa, he sometimes wasn't sure. He then became aware that there was something else. She was hiding something. He could feel the disquiet emanating from her. "What really happened?"

She nuzzled tighter against him. "Sweetheart, you have trust issues."

"No, I am beginning to listen to my instincts when it comes to you. Why are you really in here with me?"

"I missed you and I was tired."

"That is not the real reason, is it, Cerissa?"

"You're not being fair."

"The truth, *cariña*."

"Ah, well, there was one small other thing."

"And that was?"

"We had another aftershock today."

He sighed. "How big was it?"

"It was big. Three point two on the Richter scale."

That was nothing compared to the first one. He understood her reaction to the big quake—her childhood experience sounded terrible—but why was she so afraid of small quakes?

"Cerissa, I still have trouble reconciling that you are brave enough to kill Dalbert but are afraid of a little tremor."

"It wasn't little. And going up against a vampire adversary is nothing. But when the whole planet shakes, what can one do to fight back?"

"Cerissa, it is not the whole planet shaking. It is just the plates in our region that moved."

He patted her back, trying to comfort her. As much as he tried to understand her fear and never wanted to see her terrified, the way she clung to him made him feel, well, manly.

He knew it was not very enlightened of him to feel that way, but somewhere in his subconscious he liked the idea that there was something she was afraid of that he was not.

"It is all right, *mi amor*. This house is built to move with the quake, remember? You are safe here."

He continued to stroke her back and felt her relax a little.

She drew circles on his chest with her fingers. "I was afraid something might happen to you."

"Even if the roof fell in, I would be fine. I could easily dig out once it was night."

"I just wanted to be sure. That's why I came in here. Once I was here, well, I felt safer in your arms. Getting your arm to move took a little work, but I finally got it draped around me."

"I understand. But if you are feeling better, I should get up and feed." He was feeling the need a little too urgently. "And you should have dinner. Have you eaten yet?"

"No. The earthquake happened at noon. I've been in here since then."

"Let me get up and shower and dress. Then I will make dinner for you and Nicholas. How does that sound?"

"That sounds nice."

"And you should be upstairs before Marcus rises. He's in the crypt across from this one."

"He may be suspicious of me, but he wouldn't hurt me."

"You are correct, he would not hurt you. But being down here would be viewed as very unusual. Mortal mates do not join their vampire when they sleep. It isn't safe or practical."

She sat up. "I don't want to embarrass you, Henry. If you want, I'll flash to the Enclave, and then back to my room, and meet you in the kitchen."

"That would be a good idea, *cariña*."

"Oh—I almost forgot, the water department engineer announced today that the tap water is safe to drink and shower in. Or should I say, it's as safe as it was before the quake. I thought you'd want to know."

"Thank you, *cariña*. And please make sure all the drapes are closed when you return."

"Count on it." She kissed him. "Ooh, that tickles."

She fingered his long beard and then winked out of sight. He was glad she was gone. As rational as he had sounded, the desire to feed on her had begun to overwhelm his sense of control.

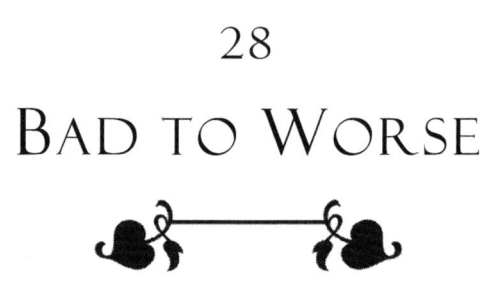

28

Bad to Worse

Rancho Bautista del Murciélago—Moments later

Henry grabbed his phone from the charging station and exited the crypt, running into Marcus, who was reading something on his phone as he walked to the staircase.

"We've already received a response from MWC," Marcus said. "I'll read it upstairs and meet you in the kitchen in twenty minutes after I shave."

"Very well."

"And the water's been cleared by our engineer."

Henry schooled his face, so he'd react like Cerissa hadn't already told him. "That is good news. Let me or Cerissa know if you need anything."

Marcus gestured his thanks, his nose aimed at his phone as he climbed the basement stairs. It had been a while since Henry had seen Marcus's bushy handlebar mustache, which his friend trimmed to a more popular style each night.

Henry used his basement bathroom to get ready. It was a long-ingrained habit to bring down clean clothes prior to sunrise, so he could get dressed as soon as he woke.

He examined his hair in the mirror, parting the strands with his fingers. As expected, the color had returned to its normal solid black, the gray vanishing when his day sleep restored him to the way he looked on the night Anne-Louise killed him, which included the heavy beard he'd worn in the early 1800s.

Once shaved, showered, and wearing the equivalent of office casual, he was ready to face the world and went upstairs to the kitchen. Cerissa and Nicholas were sitting at the kitchen table, talking.

Henry walked up behind her, and when he placed his hands on her shoulders, she started and swung around. "Oh," she cried, clutching a hand to her chest.

"I did not mean to startle you." Leaning over, he stroked her back to calm her and gave her a chaste kiss, then looked across the table. "Good afternoon, Nicholas."

"Hi, Henry. Marcus is upstairs already getting dressed."

Henry nodded, but before he could reply, Cerissa gestured to the stove. "And water is already heating."

"Thank you, *cariña*." He strode over to the burner, turned off the flame, and checked the temperature in the pan with a candy thermometer. A little too hot. He added cool water until it dropped closer to ninety-eight degrees, and then added a pouch to warm.

Although he usually tried to stretch the time between waking and feeding—to prove he was in control of his hunger—both Cerissa's visit and Nicholas's presence in the kitchen were taxing his control. He removed the pouch from the water, snipped the corner, poured the dark wine into a coffee travel mug, screwed on the lid, and took a long sip.

The beast within began to recede.

He added a little hot water from the tap to raise the pot's temperature a smidge, and then dropped in a second pouch for Marcus. Once it was warm, he poured the red liquid into a mug.

"Do you want to take this up to Marcus?" he asked Nicholas.

"Sure, Henry, thanks."

After Nicholas left, Henry peered into the refrigerator, sipping at his mug. "What do you feel like eating?"

"The service dropped off fresh groceries today. I took out all the old food that may have spoiled when the power went off, so everything you see in there is safe."

"How does Baked Fish Veracruz sound?" he asked from behind the refrigerator door. "It's early for dinner, but the fish will take a while to prepare."

"Lovely."

He took a whole cleaned red snapper out of the refrigerator, along with tomatoes, peppers, and onions. After rubbing the fish with cut lime, he seasoned the skin, stuffed the fish with sliced sauteed vegetables, then layered more on top before sliding the pan into the oven. "In thirty minutes, the fish should be done."

"Thanks," she said. "If you don't mind, I'll go downstairs to the lab. I have some work that got interrupted this afternoon."

He kissed her and then spent the time looking through his winery email. William's message about the structural engineer's visit filled him with foreboding. The written report would take days to prepare, but the initial prognosis was worse than expected.

The fish had been baking twenty minutes when Marcus stormed into the kitchen, his body language unmistakable.

Henry stopped reading William's email. "What is wrong?"

Marcus flapped a sheaf of paper in the air. "That email I got? I printed out the attachment. Twenty-five pages to tell me that the Mordida Water Company is refusing to honor the notice. They say they will continue to take the full allotment of water each month. They don't recognize the board's right to limit their take."

"What do you mean, they don't recognize our right? It's clear in the contract."

"MWC claims we've waived it, because we've never enforced it before."

Henry crossed his arms. "I never needed to enforce it before. Now I do. What kind of people do not honor the written word?"

"Modern-day mortals," Marcus spat out.

Henry felt his head begin to throb and scrubbed a hand over his face. The weather had pushed his harvest into mid-October, a few weeks away at least. Proper watering was essential to the current crop. With the partial destruction of this year's bottling production, if he lost his current crop too, they'd have to buy grapes from another provider at a time when everyone would be facing the same problem. Not to mention the structural repairs that were needed.

More likely, the winery would be financially ruined. He'd be forced to shut down.

But if they kept watering at current levels—and if Mordida kept taking their full draw—the aquifers would be reduced to dangerous levels by next spring...and then there would be no more harvests, as without water, the vines would wither and die.

He tried to keep the anguish out of his voice. "What can we do?"

"We need to demand arbitration and hire a water law attorney to represent us."

Henry nodded. For as long as they had worked together, he and Marcus had always included an arbitration clause that required the parties to submit to binding arbitration in front of an impartial umpire, rather than a trial in front of a judge in court. It also required that the hearings be held at night. A little unusual, but most people who did business with the Hill were accustomed to the nighttime clause.

"This is ludicrous." Henry slumped onto one of the kitchen island stools and rubbed his forehead with both hands. "We wrote that agreement to reserve our rights to the full use of the Hill's aquifers."

He sat there for a moment, struggling to resist defeat as a foregone conclusion. He couldn't let all these adversities drain the fight from him. He straightened up and looked Marcus in the eye. "How dare they try to steal our water."

"Don't worry." Marcus laid a reassuring hand on Henry's shoulder. "We will stop them. I'll draft the letter to demand arbitration."

"And the water lawyer? Do you need my assistance researching it tonight? I want the best. You and I both know that water law is tricky."

"No need. I know who you'll want. Christine Dunne. She's one of the top attorneys in the water field. But we need to move fast, file for a preliminary injunction right away."

Nicholas joined them and took a seat on a counter stool near Henry. "I left messages at her office and with her answering service to see if she's available tonight."

"Very well," Henry said. "Thank you both."

"We've been through worse battles." Marcus rinsed out his mug and placed it in the dishwasher. "Don't worry. We'll prevail on this one too. After Nicholas eats and once the sun sets, we'll drive to the office. I have a meeting with the mayor. Nicholas can try to set up a video call for later tonight if Ms. Dunne responds."

Cerissa entered the kitchen while Marcus was speaking and frowned at him. "Nicholas should take it easy. He's still recovering."

"Don't worry, I won't overdo it," Nicholas said from where he sat at the granite-topped island. "And it'll feel good to get out of the house. I've been lying around for two days, and I'm tired of it."

The timer *dinged*. Henry rose from his stool and, after slipping on mitts, removed the baking dish from the oven. Wonderful fragrances rose from the steam—it made him wish it tasted as good as it smelled. Unfortunately, his palate was forever ruined for anything other than blood or wine.

"Baked Fish Veracruz is ready," he said, placing the hot pan on a trivet.

Cerissa sniffed in the direction of the rising steam. "The spices smell great."

"The fish needs to cool for a few minutes, and then I'll slice it for you."

"Thank you, Quique. It's very sweet of you to cook for us."

"My pleasure, *cariña*."

Once the red snapper was sufficiently cooled, Henry plated rice for each mortal, and then cut off a piece of the snapper and laid it on the rice. Using a large spoon, he ladled the spiced broth and vegetables over the fish and rice.

Marcus looked puzzled. "You know, that smells familiar."

"That's because you have eaten it before."

"Aah, of course."

Marcus had been mortal when Henry opened his restaurant in New York during the early 1840s, making Marcus one of the few vampires to have tried the restaurant's signature dish. Henry set the full plates on the kitchen island, at the stools Nicholas and Cerissa sat at, and brought over a Sauvignon Blanc to go with it.

Nicholas took a bite of the fish. "This is wonderful. You'll have to give me the recipe."

That was not going to happen. Henry smiled politely. "I am sorry, but it is one of my most closely guarded secrets."

After dinner, Marcus and Nicholas left for their office. Cerissa stood and took the dishes to the sink. "I'll take care of the cleanup."

Henry gave a little bow and went up to his office. The anxiety over the water battle had been growing despite his effort to hide his feelings from his guests.

He eased into the executive chair at his oversized desk and swiveled to face the computer monitor on the side return. Although he trusted Marcus, Henry always did his own research.

A search of the internet for experts in water law kept turning up the same name, over and over again: Christine Dunne. A seasoned litigator and former city attorney, her credentials justified Marcus's opinion of her.

She *was* the attorney they needed.

He then started searching for information about the MWC's board of directors. They were all volunteers. The real power was the executive director for MWC, Jackson Aldridge, and MWC's attorney, Dick Peters. They had to be the two behind this grab for the Hill's water.

He remembered Jackson Aldridge from the negotiations when the agreement was signed in the late 1980s. Jackson was the executive director of MWC back then. Thirty years later, and he was still in the same position.

At the time they did the deal, Henry hadn't liked the man, but that wasn't a reason not to sign on the dotted line. Now he wished he'd listened to his gut instinct.

He kept thinking of that old saying, *I have a little list, they never will be missed.*

Except he was too civilized to use the methods popular before he was turned, when lopping off the heads of your enemies settled disputes.

But a legal fight? He wasn't looking forward to it.

Hopefully, Christine Dunne would be the sword that could end this battle. Because as much as he hated facing the truth, he knew the survival of his winery may well depend on stopping MWC from stealing their water.

Chapter 29

Consequences

TOWN HALL—A SHORT TIME LATER

Tig watched the mayor and vice mayor vie for control, as usual. Marcus had arrived just in time to referee.

The small conference room next to the town attorney's office felt crowded with the four of them. She was there mostly as an observer, waiting to carry out the decision the council's representatives would make about Rita and the dead body.

"This would be easier if Seaton hadn't killed the burglar," the mayor groused.

Tig folded her hands on the table. Observer or not, she had other duties to finish and wanted them to stay on target. "We can deal with Seaton next. Right now, I have a body to dispose of. Do we turn Ethan Tash over to his family, or cremate and bury the ashes? You also need to decide what our story will be when we turn Rita Rodgers over to the district attorney for prosecution."

Winston sat at the head of the conference room table. "Wouldn't it be easier to have Zeke finish what he started? Then we wouldn't have to tell the district attorney anything."

So much for being an observer. This was intolerable. "She's just a child, mayor. A death sentence is a bit harsh for attempted burglary."

Winston's pale complexion turned bright red as he sputtered. "That's not what I meant, and you know it. We should do what Gaea did with Dylan. Convince the mortal to sign a confession but have Zeke blur her memory so she won't clearly remember watching *how* Seaton killed Ethan Tash."

Tig narrowed her eyes. What if the new memory didn't take? Wiping a mortal's memory was one thing, but substituting a memory—a memory that would explain the knife slash they'd made across Ethan's neck after they used vampire blood to heal Seaton's bite—was riskier.

And a good defense attorney might claim duress. They'd gotten away with it in Dylan's case, but the ruse might not work a second time so soon, and a trial could trigger a second autopsy. Dr. Clarke had lied about the cause of death in his coroner's report. A real autopsy might discover the slash was made postmortem.

"We have to do what's best for the community," Marcus said. "Tig is right—we have to decide what to do with Ethan first. The two thieves may have told someone of their plans. Others may know he was involved."

Tig scoffed. "Rita said they told no one."

"But she may be lying," Marcus said. "If we don't account for Ethan's body, the investigation might lead to the Hill. Better to turn the body over, mesmerize Rita to forget completely, and send her back to school."

Rolf almost jumped out of his seat. "Not prosecute her? She should spend time in jail for what she did. Make an example of her, so others won't trespass on the Hill."

"I understand, Rolf," Marcus said. "But why send her to jail when she won't be able to remember why she was there? She is unlikely to try again without her friend. Ethan appeared to be the one who had the information and organized it. Wipe her mind of the whole thing. Leave her with no memory of being on the Hill or of Gaea's jewelry." Marcus looked thoughtful for a moment. "Besides, who would give testimony about what happened? Seaton wouldn't be able to pull it off. And we don't have a mortal who was around for the capture to testify in court during the day."

Tig nodded. "Jayden won't perjure himself."

"No one expects him to. We respect Jayden for that." Marcus tugged on his mustache. "The best plan is the one Tig mentioned from the beginning. Report the death and have Tig clear Seaton of responsibility. She has the staged photos—"

Using a kitchen knife Gaea had retrieved from the ashes of her kitchen, along with a few pints of donor blood, Tig had created a believable death scene at the expense of Gaea's carpet. Dr. Clarke's report would confirm the blood type on the rug matched Ethan's, even if it didn't.

Marcus continued, "A phone call to the district attorney should satisfy them. Seaton was within his rights."

"Marcus, we've relied on your wisdom for a long time," the mayor said. "You always seem to have a clear view of these things, so I agree. It's the best we can do."

Tig saw the anger glow in Rolf's eyes. Obviously, he was vexed that the girl would get off without punishment. And technically Rita was guilty of felony murder—Ethan's death occurred during her participation in a dangerous felony.

"Rolf," Marcus said, "look at it this way. Without witnesses, we can't make felony murder stick. All we have her on is trespassing. With her clean record, and in light of her age, a judge is likely to give her probation. She's spent two nights in our jail. She was chased and captured by Zeke—not exactly a pleasant experience for any mortal. Consider that her punishment."

"We have become much too soft on crime." Rolf slammed his fist on the table. "We should reinstitute the whipping post for these situations."

Tig cringed. She knew just how controversial *that* suggestion would be.

Marcus patted the air, asking for calm. "We agreed a long time ago to forgo those types of punishments for mortals. This is not the time to resurrect them, Rolf, not with all our mates clamoring for equal rights."

"Not my mate."

The mayor *harrumphed*. "Whipping Ms. Rodgers provides no deterrent value if the mortals in Mordida don't know about it. And there would be no way to advertise it. We should view this as the isolated situation it is—we haven't had a burglary on the Hill in two decades."

"It really is the best way to deal with Rita under the circumstances," Tig said.

Rolf looked at them angrily. "Fine. But perhaps we should have Zeke hunt her again. Leave her with a feeling of terror—she'll be afraid to return to the Hill even if she won't remember why."

Would Rolf get off vicariously on the hunt? Was that why he suggested it? So far, he'd suffered no political consequences for his hunting habit.

The mayor laughed. "Not a bad idea. We could set up seats and sell tickets to the event."

Tig thumped the table with her hand. "Absolutely not. Do you really want to see our mates protesting in front of town hall? So far, the griping about mortal rights has been steered to the subcommittee. If they start picketing council meetings, you're not going to be happy at election time. You'll be remembered as the council members who upset everyone's mates."

Rolf flicked his fingers. "Bah," he spat out. "You overestimate the reaction."

Marcus raised his palms again as if trying to calm everyone. "Look, no one is happy with the situation." He looked from the mayor to the vice mayor. "Chief, please make the necessary arrangements. You should be able to take care of the release of your prisoner tonight. The body can be delivered to Mordida tomorrow."

Tig nodded her agreement. The sign of a good compromise was that no one wanted it.

"I'll have Zeke wipe Rita's memory, and then report Ethan Tash's death, so we can put this behind us."

"Excellent." Marcus stood. "I'll bring in Seaton, so we can deal with him."

"One more thing." Tig motioned for Marcus to sit. "The two burglars were able to get over the wall because the cameras were off."

The mayor's eyes looked like the lights had come on. "The power failure?"

"Precisely. The council needs to provide funds for an emergency generator to power the cameras and the guard shack whenever there's a blackout."

"Now, Tig," the mayor said in that haughty tone he had. "We are going to have a lot of extra expenses because of the water problem—"

"And your expenses could have been a lot higher if more people had breached the wall. Captain Johnson staffed the EOC all night—staring at mostly blank security camera screens."

Rolf snarled at her. "The better question is how those two got past your officers. The blockade, the curfew—their failure is your fault."

Tig rose to her feet, her muscles tightening, preparing for the fight, and leaned on the table, staring at Rolf, who sat directly across from her. "You know as well as anyone that we don't have enough officers on staff. Under these circumstances, the police cannot provide perfect protection from someone determined to get past the lines. Those two snuck down a side street and bypassed the blockade."

Marcus's hand landed on Tig's shoulder. She whipped her head around and glared at him.

He has one second to remove that condescending appendage before I rip it off.

Marcus snatched back his hand, and his gaze cut away from hers before returning. "I'll draft a proposal to provide automatic battery backup generators for the cameras. Do you think solar might work?"

She might as well let his error go but glared at him one last time for good measure.

"Possibly," she said after a moment. The council would have a hard time saying no to backup power after what happened with the earthquake. "Ari may have an idea of what would best power them."

"Then ask him." Marcus gestured at the door. "As long as you're on your feet, would you ask Gaea to bring in Seaton?"

Seriously?

After trying to stop her from giving Rolf the beat-down he deserved, was Marcus honestly asking that of her? She wasn't the attorney's handmaiden. Besides, she really hated wasting time on matters like these in the first place. The council would make the final decision on Seaton, anyway.

"*Please*," Marcus added.

Tig glanced around the table. Most of them were looking away, hoping the tension level in the room would go back down if they ignored it. She swallowed the growl she felt and headed for the door.

Moments later, everyone shuffled seats. Seaton and Gaea took chairs opposite the mayor and vice mayor, with Marcus on the other end of the table from Tig.

"Now, Winston, I don't understand why you've summoned us in here." Gaea's fists were firmly planted on the table. "Seaton was entirely within his rights to kill the thief."

Rolf gestured in Gaea's direction. "I agree."

The mayor steepled his fingers for the umpteenth time. "Of course Seaton has rights, but he also has obligations. Like any of us, he has the obligation to avoid taking any action that would draw attention to our nature. Draining a mortal, when he could have used other, less deadly means to stop the burglar—well, he's not living up to his obligations."

Tig had to agree. Seaton wasn't automatically entitled to his maker's place on the Hill. He had four years to prove himself compatible and compliant and pay the fee to join the community.

He had enough money to buy in, since, as Jane's only child, he had inherited everything the dead vampire owned. But given his odd personality, he was unlikely to prove himself compatible or compliant. Still, Gaea insisted on trying to redeem him.

The mayor continued his speech. "If he can't adapt and fulfill his obligations, given his…uniqueness, the council may decide to put him down rather than turn him lose on unsuspecting mortals."

Marcus huffed. "If Seaton were to concede he hasn't lived up to his obligations, what remedy do you have in mind?"

"Well," the mayor said, "at this point, I don't think it is a whipping offense."

Tig raised her eyebrows, running a hand over her short afro. The mayor was willing to have Henry whipped for violating the social niceties of the Hill, but felt Seaton, who used a burglar's break-in as an excuse to fill his belly direct from the tap, was less culpable and entitled to a lesser penalty?

The inconsistency in punishments pointed to what Tig had suspected all along: politics played a bigger role in council decisions than she liked. And the mayor's ongoing resentment of Henry was on full display thanks to this inequity in penalties.

"Perhaps," Marcus began, "perhaps we should have Matt evaluate him before making a decision."

Tig sat back in her chair. *That's an interesting suggestion.*

Father Matthew Blaine was the Hill's resident Episcopal priest and a trained psychologist. He was perfectly qualified for the task.

The mayor drummed his fingers on the polished table. "Agreed. Before we put this before the whole council, we should obtain Matt's opinion. Rolf?"

"*Ja.* If it will get a decision made, I'll agree, but I really think no punishment is required here."

Gaea glanced over at Seaton. "Do you agree to meet with Father Matt and cooperate?"

"If I have to," he replied, sounding sullen. "I really don't understand. The guy wasn't one of your pets."

Gaea elbowed him. "Sit up, young man, and apologize to the councilmembers. Winston is right that you have obligations as a member of the community."

Seaton took in a deep breath and exhaled fast. "Whatever. I'm sorry."

Gaea stood. "I'll call Father Matt as soon as we're home."

Marcus looked over at Tig. "May we head to the police station now? I thought we could release your prisoner before it gets too late. Rolf and I have a videoconference call that starts in fifteen minutes."

"Sure." Tig texted Jayden to ready the prisoner, and then walked Marcus the short distance to the police station. On the way, she phoned Zeke and explained the plan. The cowboy was more than willing to jump into action.

When they reached the jail cell where the prisoner was confined, Tig opened the door. "You're free to go."

"It's about time," Rita replied, sounding annoyed. "Do I have to show up at court or whatever?"

"We aren't pressing charges," Marcus said. "But heed my warning: don't ever return to our community."

"Don't worry, I won't," Rita said. "Ah, what's going to happen to Ethan?"

"Ethan is dead," Tig replied.

Rita stood there, looking shocked.

"This way, please." Tig took Rita by the arm and led her through the small police headquarters, past the booking room, and into the outer waiting area. Then she opened the exit door, which buzzed, and motioned for Rita to leave.

Rita walked outside and froze when Zeke stepped out of the shadows.

Tig locked the door and watched unsympathetically as Rita turned around in a panic and pounded on the double-glass doors. Zeke wouldn't do more than scare her—and maybe take one more pint.

And technically, Rita *was* guilty of felony murder. Tig knew it in her bones, even if she couldn't prove Rita's guilt in a court of law. If the young woman hadn't gone along with the burglary, had discouraged it even the smallest bit, Ethan might have blown it off and lived.

With any luck, the residual fear from whatever Zeke had planned would dissuade Rita from participating in any future criminal activities. It was all Tig could hope for under the circumstances.

Chapter 30

Punishment

Sierra Escondida Police Station—Moments later

Zeke laid a hand on Rita's shoulder. The tart aroma of fear wafted off her. "Now, there's nothin' to be afraid of, missy. I'm gonna give you a ride home."

"But you—you—attacked me."

"Yup, that I did. But don't you worry none about that now. I'm just here to take you safely to your place." He gripped her arm and led her to his truck. He wouldn't take her memories away until they got to where she lived. It was cleaner that way. "Do you live with a roommate?"

"I live alone," she said, as she climbed up into the F-150 cab.

She had a cute butt. Too bad he'd promised Tig he wouldn't seduce the little thief. Given some time and charm, he knew she'd warm up to him. It could've been a nice hookup for both of them, maybe even lead to friends with benefits. But no, Tig said it was a "conflict" with his job and might spur Rita to recall what happened to Ethan.

Zeke clucked to himself in regret, got into the driver's side, and checked the message on his phone. Tig had texted him Rita's address, which he plugged into the truck's navigation while Rita sat stiffly in her seat.

"Put your seatbelt on," he said, backing out of the parking space and giving her a little side-eye.

She did as he asked but watched him like he might attack her at any minute.

Damn, if only he hadn't promised. The circus performer had whetted his appetite. He'd had a few nights of sex, and it left him wanting more.

But he'd been right when he told Henry he wanted no strings attached. Still, a regular bedmate would be nice.

He waved at the guard as he passed the Hill's gate and glanced over at Rita. She sat there stiff as a board.

The problem was that he had to be careful picking up women in Mordida or the other neighboring towns. Word would get around that he was a player, which wasn't a bad thing, but he had to age himself each year, which was a pain in the ass.

And finding women who didn't live nearby was another problem. If they were tied to their careers, they wouldn't want to move to Mordida. There'd be no regularity.

And he had no desire to have someone move into his house on the Hill—it defeated his bachelor lifestyle.

But this all meant he went through dry spells.

"So, missy," he said when they stopped at a red light.

She about jumped out of her skin. "Y—yes?"

"You have a boyfriend?" The last thing he wanted was to have her boyfriend waiting at the door for her. Then he'd have to mesmerize them both.

"Why'd you want to know that?"

"No particular reason. Just making small talk."

She looked at him like he was lying and crossed her arms. "The answer is no. And the light's green."

"Don't worry." He took his foot off the brake. "We'll get you home soon enough."

Well, one good thing about his promise was that it looked like it would take more than a fair bit of charm to reverse her wariness, and he didn't have much interest in that level of effort. Truthfully, he wasn't really that interested in someone as young as her, anyway. He was so tired of young women like Rita, like the circus performer. It took forever to coax them into his bed. They were so focused on commitment, marriage, and babies—and their reputation.

A woman in her forties was a better choice for him than someone like Rita. Usually, they had their baby-making out of the way by then, and if they were career-oriented, they may be up for some fun without the ties of marriage. And they knew what they liked in bed. No guessing, no games.

But the young 'un is right here.

Except he had almost nothin' to talk about with a filly Rita's age, he reminded himself again. And talkin' was nice alongside the bedding. The music young 'uns listened to was hideous, too. Even today's country music wasn't what he liked. And square dance? Not a single gal he'd dated in the past ten years knew how to square-dance. What was more, the young 'uns didn't pay much attention to current events, except the ones who majored in political science, and they were rather vocal about it. He got tired of them quickly.

"Turn here," she said.

"The navigator says to wait."

"It'll put you on the wrong side of the street. Trust me."

"Whatever you say, missy." He made the turn. In a few blocks, he pulled over at the curb she pointed to. He put the truck into park and started to get out.

"Where are you going?" she asked, her voice shaking.

"Gonna walk you to the door, make sure you get in okay."

"I'm okay on my own. I'd rather—"

"No arguin'. Let's go."

He followed Rita up the path, through the front door of the apartment complex, and down the beige hall to a brown door just like all the other brown doors they'd passed. "This is me. You can leave now."

"I know for a fact this ain't the right one. You're in apartment 110, not 105. You don't got to be afraid of me. I'm a police officer."

She eyeballed his clothes. "No, you aren't."

"I'm in plain clothes tonight."

"Sure you are," she scoffed, and walked to the next door, stuck the key in, and turned the knob.

He didn't give her a chance. Reaching beyond her, he pushed the door open and followed her in, then shut the door behind himself. He glanced around at the pitifully furnished studio apartment.

Fear filled her eyes. Yup, this was going to taste real good. He didn't give her a chance to fight and *whooshed* to her, biting her neck in one smooth move. As the fang serum hit her bloodstream, she relaxed into his arms, and he felt the buzz of her adrenaline-spiked blood fill him.

After a pint—maybe a little more—he stepped back and looked in her eyes. He wiped her memory of going to Sierra Escondida and of vampires. Then he gave her a new one of meeting a guy and having an alcohol-fueled fling to explain her missing time. A new memory wouldn't always stick, especially if she fought it, but having a hole in her memory might make her question the gap. Sometimes a new memory was enough to stop that from happening.

Finished, he helped her sit down on the couch still mesmerized.

Tig had told him Rita's story about not having enough money for tuition. Feeling sorry for her, he opened his wallet and counted out all he had on him, leaving the wad on the kitchen table under the saltshaker. Eight hundred dollars was his walking-around money.

He hoped it was enough to keep her in school one more semester.

Chapter 31

Fighting Fires

Henry's Home Office—That Same Night

Minutes before the videoconference was scheduled to start, Henry drank an extra pouch of dark wine and aged himself.

Nicholas was up to date on all the tech Marcus never used and had sent out invitations via email to join the videoconference with the water attorney. *Gracias a Dios* they had Nicholas as their assistant town attorney.

Henry ran his finger across his crucifix, feeling the ridges under his shirt, calming his nerves. It was only Tuesday, two nights after the quake, and ever since it hit, he'd spent his hours awake running from one crisis to another, trying to put out the fires.

He sat down at his computer and clicked the link. When he activated his camera, Nicholas and Marcus were already logged in, and then Rolf's image popped up on the screen. An unfamiliar woman joined them shortly.

"This is Christine Dunne," Marcus said, "Christine, this is Henry Bautista and Rolf Müller. Both board members."

"It's a pleasure to meet you," Christine said.

"We are glad you could work us into your schedule on such short notice, Ms. Dunne." Henry clicked his mouse to expand her image and looked closely at her.

Christine Dunne was a handsome older woman, probably in her late fifties or early sixties. She had the confidence of someone who was used to winning. It made her seem more attractive.

"Please call me Christine." On screen, her image was highlighted when she spoke. "I was quite intrigued by your situation. So, you're the one who signed the contract in 1987?"

"Yes," Henry said.

"You were over eighteen at the time?"

Henry scrunched his eyebrows. Why did she ask that? "I was definitely over eighteen, I can assure you." He quickly did the math. "I was twenty-one, having recently inherited from my uncle."

He had purposely assumed a new identity when they started negotiating the contract. It worked to their advantage. If he had changed identities after signing a major contract, the old "him" might have been dead and unable to help enforce the terms.

Christine smiled reassuringly. "I wanted to confirm, because a contract signed by a person under eighteen might be defective." She looked offscreen for a moment. "I've read the contract and the other documents Marcus emailed me. Why don't you tell me what happened when you negotiated this agreement with the Mordida Water Company?"

"It is simple. We had an excess of water and Mordida wanted to purchase it. We granted them a certain number of acre feet per year. Each year, we could cancel or reduce their allotment with written notice. We have given timely notice and they have said they will not honor it. If we have to, we will go to arbitration."

"Arbitration? You think they will agree to arbitration?" she asked.

"The contract calls for arbitration," Henry replied. "All our contracts do."

"This one doesn't." She held up the photocopy of the contract. MWC had included a copy with its letter.

"What?" Henry almost yelled as fear raced through him. He focused on Marcus's image. "No arbitration clause?"

Marcus moved offscreen and came back with a copy, flipping through the contract. "It has to be here somewhere. I know I, er, my predecessor put it in here."

Henry couldn't contain his panic. This was the worst news possible—Marcus had changed identities since the contract had been negotiated and would be unable to reassure Christine.

"The version we signed had the clause," Henry explained rapidly. "I signed the original and three copies. Inked signatures. The originals were not faxed—they were mailed to MWC for their signatures. We received the signed original and one signed copy back. They kept the other two signed copies. I don't understand. How could this happen?"

"I'll go through my files," Marcus said. "I'm sure I have in storage a copy of what was mailed to them. I didn't throw out anything I received from my predecessor. I'll get to the bottom of this."

"I also may have the signed carbon copy in my files," Henry said. "The document MWC sent is only a copy of a copy of what they signed and sent to us."

Christine cocked her head, raising an eyebrow. "Usually it's the attorneys who care whether we are in court or in front of a private arbitrator. Why is it so important to you?"

Henry paused for a moment. He was so upset by the discovery that he wasn't thinking straight. "I'm sure Marcus can explain why."

"I'm sure he can. But you were clearly upset by this. If I'm going to be your attorney, you need to trust me. Why is it so important to *you* to avoid court?"

Henry's mind suddenly blanked. He'd answered this question hundreds of times before, but in that moment, all he could think about was how they might lose their water—and their vineyards. "Normally, we have a clause in all our business contracts that require private arbitration of any disputes."

"You've already said that. Why do *you* want to stay out of court?"

"Ah, trials are held during the day. Our clause specifies that the arbitration hearings must be held in Mordida, at night."

"At night? That's a bit unusual."

"I do not go out in the day."

Christine's brow furrowed immediately. "You don't—"

"I—I have a skin ailment that does not do well when exposed to the sun. I have adjusted my sleeping hours accordingly, and I am not available during the day."

"I see. Well, I've dealt with stranger things in my long career. You'll just have to readjust your sleeping hours if we have to go to court. I assume if you cover up completely, the sun won't be a problem. But in all probability, we'll be able to reach a settlement without having to go into court. There's no need to worry about—"

"You do not understand," Henry interrupted her, frustration and rage creating a sudden, sharp hunger for blood despite all the extra dark wine he'd drunk. "I cannot go out in the daylight at all. It is not an option. The absence of the arbitration clause that I *know* we included in the original contract must be our first priority. We will have no bargaining power if we have to go to court. Nothing else matters as much as that."

She looked at him like he had a mental illness, rather than a physical one. "All right. Marcus and I will work on it. For now, don't worry. You have Christine Dunne fighting for you, and I don't lose. We'll find a way to take care of this."

"That's right," Marcus said. "No need to get upset now, Henry. We'll get it fixed."

"You better," he snarled. Being civilized, playing by mortal rules, had gotten him nowhere. Perhaps he owed the MWC officials a personal visit.

"Let me talk with Henry and Rolf," Marcus said, "and then I'll call you back, Christine, and we can continue working."

Christine nodded. "Henry, Rolf, it was good to meet you. I look forward to working with you in the months ahead."

Once Christine signed off from the videoconference, Henry glanced at Rolf, then Marcus. "This was a bad way to start out with her. I know I am partly responsible for that—I highlighted my abhorrence of daylight too strongly. If she comes here to work with us, she'll notice other inconsistencies and figure out what we are." Henry took a deep breath, knowing there was only one option. "We cannot hire her. I don't care if she's the best. We'll have to start over with someone else."

CHAPTER 32

NOBODY'S FOOL

MARCUS'S OFFICE—MOMENTS LATER

Marcus tried not to roll his eyes at the camera. "Henry, don't worry. If she becomes suspicious, she won't be the first outside counsel I've had to put the bite on to maintain control. It's one way to keep the billable hours reasonable," he said with a laugh.

"I am tired of being civilized and giving mortals all the advantages. Mark my words. We may have to level the playing field by taking things into our hands."

What was it with Henry? This was so unlike him. He was being overly emotional about the arbitration clause. Of course they'd figure out a way to win without violence.

"It will work out, Henry. Trust me. Christine is who we need."

"I don't know."

"Look, we won't end up in court. I'm sure it was just a scrivener's error that is easily corrected."

After confirming that Henry and Rolf agreed with hiring Christine—despite Henry's drama over the decision—Marcus bade them good night and initiated a videoconference with just himself, Nicholas, and Christine. "I checked our offsite document log, and I'm going to have to get the negotiation history out of storage," he told her. "It won't be available to you until Wednesday afternoon."

"That's fine. It's too late for me to rearrange my schedule for tomorrow. But I can be in Sierra Escondida by Thursday. Should I work at your office or rent an office in Mordida?"

"You can work at town hall. Nicholas will meet you there in the morning to let you in. We have a guest office for just these circumstances."

"Good, that will hold down costs." She sat back and tapped her pen on her lips. "Henry's reaction was rather extreme. I've heard of skin ailments that can't stand daylight, but under the Americans with Disabilities Act, courts will make accommodations and allow them to cover up completely, even their faces, and draw the blinds, though most courtrooms these days are windowless." She furrowed her brow, shaking her head. "I feel there's more to this."

"I believe his skin ailment—"

"Marcus, I know this is early in our relationship, but you'll have to learn to trust me, and quickly. No skin ailment should garner such an intense reaction. Does Henry have a criminal history? Something that makes it difficult for him to testify in court—other than his skin ailment?"

"Absolutely not."

"Not that you know of, at least." She paused. "Well, he better come clean with us, and soon. I mean, I understand his skin ailment is difficult to deal with—he's probably been teased about being a vampire and is sensitive about not being taken seriously. But it's not a reason to completely refuse to go to court if the judge accommodates him—and they should."

Marcus cringed at the v-word, but quickly agreed and ended the videoconference. His comment to Henry had been prescient.

"Christine is too smart," Marcus said to Nicholas, who sat in the guest chair on the other side of the desk, having used his own phone to join the conference. "If she puts in much time on the Hill, she'll figure things out. But with the proper precautions, she can be controlled."

Nicholas narrowed his eyes. "Precautions?"

"Just as I told Henry, I may have to bite and compel her, so she can't speak to the uninitiated about what she sees on the Hill."

"Now wait a minute. You were serious about that? I thought you were just mollifying Henry. I don't agree to that, Marcus."

On the sliding scale of sexuality, Marcus had never experimented with women, nor had he any interest in them as lovers. Christine truly presented no threat to his mate. How could he convince Nicholas this situation was different from the affair he had with Ari? He was only just beginning to rebuild Nicholas's trust in him.

Marcus reached for his mate's hand. "The threat posed by Ari will not be in play with Christine. I have zero interest in women."

"But with fang serum—"

"Even with that. I've fed on women before, and the temptation to make it anything more than a meal has never occurred."

"I want to talk with Father Matt first."

Marcus nodded. He was learning to live with the aftermath of his infidelity and understood why this was a sensitive topic for his mate. "Our next session is tomorrow night. We can discuss it then."

"All right, but if I agree, I want to be in the room when you bite her." Nicholas shook a finger at Marcus. "Fool me once, shame on you. Fool me twice, I have no one to blame but myself—and that's not happening."

CHAPTER 33

A RELUCTANT PATIENT

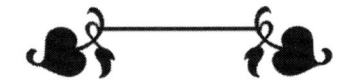

THE HILL CHAPEL—THE SAME NIGHT

Cerissa raced out of the house with her medical bag in hand, leaving Henry to his videoconference.

Father Matt had phoned her, telling her about the situation with Seaton and asking for her medical expertise on Seaton's behalf. What she knew about vampire medical conditions you could put in a thimble. But she had to admit that her curiosity was piqued.

She'd known Seaton from her time boarding at Gaea's house and thought of him as a bit strange. Gaea had warned her about being alone around him.

His maker had been turned in Europe in the 1990s. At the time, the European communities hadn't yet banned the creation of new vampires.

Cerissa had assumed his maker, being a young vampire, didn't have enough power to create him. But she never expected his odd behavior might be characterized as a *medical* problem.

When Cerissa arrived at the Hill Chapel, she tapped on Matt's office door. He opened it a moment later. "Hi, Matt," she said.

"Please come in."

Cerissa entered the homey, comfortable office. Shelves stuffed to the brim with books ran along one wall, and a brightly colored mandala—in reds, oranges, and yellows—hung on the opposite wall. The mandala reminded her of the sort of artwork that had decorated her childhood home in India.

Seaton sat on Matt's couch with his shoulders hunched. His eyes followed her as she walked over to him, her medical bag in one hand. "Hello, Seaton."

He grunted at her. Except for the disagreeable disposition, the red-headed Seaton could pass for a twenty-something Rupert Grint, with his red hair, round face, and blue eyes.

She glanced at Matt and waited for direction. "Before you arrived," he said, "I was explaining to Seaton why I asked you here. He understands that you're a doctor and a researcher."

"I'm happy to help if I can." She placed her bag on the coffee table in front of her.

Matt turned back to the young vampire. "We might as well get started. How are you feeling, Seaton?"

"I don't understand why everyone is so concerned." Seaton directed his comment at Matt like Cerissa wasn't even in the room. "I don't like to play with my food the way you do. So what?"

Matt looked at Cerissa. "Seaton doesn't understand why the rest of us enjoy sexual relationships with mortals."

"Well, let's see if there's a medical explanation for his situation."

"Where do you want to start?" Matt asked.

"Tonight, I'm just going to take a few samples to test." Cerissa opened her medical bag and extracted the implements she needed. "I see that you have two glasses ready."

"Yes."

"I'd like to start with a blood draw. I'm going to demonstrate on you, so Seaton will know what to expect."

"I know what a blood draw is," Seaton said, sounding irritated. "I haven't been vampire that long."

"Of course," Cerissa agreed. "But I'm still going to demonstrate on Matt so there are no surprises."

She was collecting as many samples as she could get, so she could run comparisons. She showed them the silver-coated collector needle, then explained how the silver wouldn't burn them but would prevent their skin from adhering and make it easier to remove the needle.

"Matt, do you know what blood type you were when you were human?"

"B positive," he replied. "Why?"

"So far, all vampires I've tested were O negative blood type—the universal donor. I think something happens at the DNA level when a vampire is turned that alters their blood type." She tied the rubber strip above the bend in Matt's elbow and had him make a fist.

"Really?" Matt responded. "I didn't think that was possible, to alter someone's blood type."

She already knew the Lux-like morphing strand encased the human DNA and was responsible for transforming a mortal to vampire, but she couldn't share that level of detail. "My guess is that whatever happens when you're turned, it's at a genetic level."

She gently inserted the needle and then pressed the collection tube into the chamber. Blood flowed into the clear tube. She watched his face closely to make sure he was all right. The process didn't seem to bother him.

"How are you doing?"

"Fine. No problem. I can tell it's made of silver, but it's not painful. Very easy."

She made eye contact with Matt and smiled, acknowledging his attempt to reassure Seaton about the process.

She filled five collection tubes and then withdrew the needle. Matt did the same thing she'd seen Henry and Rolf do when she took blood from them: he declined the cotton ball and licked the site instead.

Two glasses of blood sat on the coffee table. She picked up one and handed it to Matt. The idea was to get his fangs to deploy. In a resting state, vampire fangs lay along the roof of the mouth, similar to snake fangs. "All right, drink up."

Matt took the tumbler and quickly downed it. "What's next?" he lisped a little through his fangs.

"Bite down on this." She offered him a glass jar with a dark gray rubber membrane stretched over it. A rubber band held the membrane in place.

He bit, and a golden liquid rolled down the side of the glass and filled about a quarter inch at the bottom of the small jar.

She held out her hand for it. "That's good."

Matt carefully disengaged his fangs from the rubber membrane with a slight *pop* and raised the jar to examine it. "Curious. I really had no idea what the fluid looked like."

"The gland in the roof of your mouth produces the serum." She took the jar from him and screwed on a lid. "The gland is crisscrossed by the muscles that cause your fangs to extend. Now it's Seaton's turn." She turned to the young vampire. "Are you all right with what you've seen?"

He didn't answer her. Instead, he looked at Matt when he spoke. "I don't like having her here. I want to get this over with."

"It won't take that long, Seaton," Matt said. "Cerissa is going to come close to you to take the blood sample. Do not attack her."

"I know she's Henry's pet. Off-limits."

"Yes, off-limits."

Seaton finally looked at her, now staring intently. His gaze was like a predator's: unwavering and emotionless. She should be afraid, but she wasn't. Even if he attacked, Matt was a good forty years older than Seaton and much stronger because of it. Not that she couldn't defend herself, but it was best not to display her true strength if she could avoid it.

She sat down on the couch next to the patient as he continued to watch her. After drawing his blood, she labeled the test tubes so she wouldn't get them confused with Matt's.

"Okay, drink your drink," she said, handing him the other tumbler filled with blood.

Seaton never took his eyes off her as he drank.

"That should be enough." Cerissa handed him an empty jar with a membrane stretched over the top. "I need you to do the same thing Matt did. Bite into the membrane and pull it slightly forward, as if you've bit into someone."

Seaton took the jar from her. Rather viciously, he bit into the rubber membrane, making large holes, ripping the rubber. Cerissa watched, scrunching her brow. No liquid appeared in the glass.

Something was wrong. "Let me try," she offered, taking the glass from him. "Now don't bite me."

Seaton continued to stare at her, power in his gaze.

She ignored it. "Seaton, are you listening?"

"I'm listening."

"I'm going to hold the jar." She rotated it, so the virgin section faced Seaton. "I want you to bite into it slowly. Don't rip it, just let your fangs sink in. I'm going to apply a gentle pressure. Do you understand?"

"I'm not stupid, you know. I'm just not interested in a relationship with my food."

"Are you attracted to other vampires?" she asked.

"No."

She looked over at Matt. "Has he discussed his sexual preferences with you?"

"Hey, I'm in the room."

Cerissa felt heat rise to her face. Just because he'd ignored her presence, didn't mean she should give him the same treatment—she was more professional than that.

"I'm sorry, I shouldn't have asked Matt."

He nodded once. "I was straight as a mortal. But since that bitch killed me, nothing, you know? Not interested at all."

Cerissa made a mental note of that. "Okay. Let's try again, all right?"

Seaton shrugged, so she held up the jar. He bit into the membrane, and she gently pulled without ripping the rubber. Nothing appeared at the bottom of the clear jar.

She dislodged his fangs from the rubber and sat back. "Strange." She reached into her bag and pulled out a nitrile glove. "Seaton, I'd like to examine your fangs. Will you permit that?"

His eyes narrowed. "You want to put your hand in my mouth? You do know what I am, don't you?"

"Yes, I do. You're not the first vampire I've examined this way. But you have to promise not to bite."

He stared at her intently. "You aren't afraid."

"Why should I be?"

Matt interrupted them. "Seaton, are you trying to mesmerize Dr. Patel?"

"Yes. That's what we do."

"Here on the Hill, it's not what we do. It's not considered polite. Please stop."

"She's prey. Why should I care if she's offended?"

"Seaton, let's discuss this after Dr. Patel leaves. For now, can you restrain yourself long enough to allow her to examine your fangs?"

"Yeah." Seaton sounded like an unhappy teenager instead of the twenty-something he was when he was turned.

Cerissa placed a hand under his chin, and he jerked away. "Hold still, please." She repositioned her hand. "Now open. Wider, please. That's good. Now keep your jaws open."

She ran her finger around the roof of his mouth and felt the gland.

Something about it seemed smaller, less prominent, than with Henry's gland. She slid her finger down the back of the fang, carefully avoiding the tip. She didn't feel the grooved opening that should be there.

She withdrew her finger and took a dental mirror out of her medical bag. "If you'll hold still for just a moment longer, I'm almost through."

"Uh huh," Seaton mumbled, his mouth still open.

She placed the mirror behind his fangs. Solid. No opening. She withdrew the instrument, and he closed his mouth. "Interesting. You don't appear to produce the serum that other vampires produce. Your fangs are solid—no opening in the back through which the fluid flows into the bite."

"Really?" Matt looked incredulous. "I've never heard of that before."

"It may be related to the problem." She looked back at Seaton. "Your bite doesn't impart any sexual stimulation to the recipient or to you. It can't without the serum. It may be why you don't bond with mortals."

She glanced at the collection jar, at the rubber dam shredded where Seaton first bit. Without the blood thinner in fang serum, clotting would make feeding more difficult—was that the reason why he ripped the membrane when he bit?

"May I see?" Matt asked, interrupting her thoughts.

She handed the mirror to him. "Seaton, do you mind if Matt looks?"

"What the fuck?" Seaton screwed up his face in distaste. "You two are real geeks."

"But you'll let him look?"

"Whatever."

Matt moved closer. "Okay, open, please." Matt moved the mirror around. "Amazing. You'll have to discuss it with Dr. Clarke."

Yeah, although she disliked Dr. Clarke, he knew more about vampire physiology than she did. "There may be something else Seaton is missing that explains why he doesn't bond with mortals. I'll have to think about it. We may need a biochemical solution rather than a psychological one."

"Good. We can look at it from both fronts."

Cerissa returned to the coffee table where she had placed her medical bag. She stripped off the glove and put the mirror away to be cleaned later. "One other thing. I may want Dr. Clarke to take x-rays, if Seaton is willing. I'd like to see if the serum channel is blocked. Perhaps we could drill a small pinhole—"

Seaton suddenly stood up and approached Cerissa.

She turned to face him. "Sit down."

He continued to advance.

Adrenaline quickened her heartbeat, and she morphed her blood—if he bit her now, he'd find himself with a mouthful of the sulfur compounds garlic imparted to blood.

"Sit down or you won't like the consequences," she said.

Seaton stopped. He looked startled. Slowly his face took on a look of confusion. "Something is different about you."

"I'm bonded to Henry now. When I was rooming at Gaea's, I wasn't yet."

"No, that's not it. I don't know why I didn't see it before. You're like us."

Now it was Cerissa's turn to be startled. "I'm not vampire."

"No, no you aren't." Seaton took another step closer, peering in her face as if seeing her for the first time, and sniffed in her direction.

Matt was out of his chair in a flash, putting himself between Cerissa and the younger vampire. "Seaton, back off."

"I'm not going to hurt her. She wouldn't taste good." Abruptly he turned around and plopped back on the couch.

How had Seaton detected the before-and-after difference in her blood if Matt hadn't? Was his sense of smell more acute than Matt's?

Cerissa grabbed her medical bag, morphed her blood back to normal, and walked to the door. Better to leave quickly rather than risk Seaton detecting other ways she was different. "Matt, may I speak to you outside?" she asked.

"Certainly. Seaton, I'll return in a few moments. Please remain here." Matt followed her and closed the door. "I'm sorry about that, Cerissa."

"No problem," she said, feeling a little shaky.

"Thank you for understanding. He doesn't understand the effect he has on others. I hope my work with him can change that."

"Me too. Have you ever seen anyone like him before?"

"No. I've heard that children of young vampires can have dementia or turn out antisocial. Seaton is more along the antisocial continuum. There have been more severe cases than Seaton's in the literature, but no mention of this aspect."

"Literature?"

"Case histories have been published in *Living from Dusk to Dawn*."

"What is that?"

"An online magazine for vampires. Registered members have access. Topics range from practical advice on living in modern times to highly technical medical articles on our physiology."

Seriously? Why had no one mentioned this resource to her before this? Henry had to know about it, didn't he? Something may have been written up on vampires with Rolf's condition—vampires who needed adrenaline-enhanced blood to remain stable. Those archives could be a huge boon to her research.

"Is there any way I can get access? I've been doing some research in another area, and it might help if I read what others have published on the matter."

Matt looked thoughtful. "I'll have to arrange special permission. Mortals aren't usually allowed to view those files. It takes five vampires vouching for the person to get them login access."

"I think we can find five members of the community who will vouch for me. I'm assuming my mate doesn't qualify—he wouldn't be objective."

Matt laughed. "You guessed correctly."

"But Tig would back me. As would Gaea. Maybe Liza or the mayor...even Dr. Clarke found my assistance helpful when we saved Marcus from silver poisoning."

"All right, I'll get your application started."

"Thanks, that will help."

"For now, I'm going to keep working with Seaton," Matt said. Cerissa started to object, but Matt cut her off. "Yes, I understand there may be a physiological component, but that doesn't mean he can't learn socialization skills to help him fit in better with the community."

"I hope you're right. I wouldn't want to see him banned."

"Banning is the least of his worries," Matt said, his eyes sad. "I'm afraid it's more severe than that. If he doesn't show improvement soon, the council may have no choice but to destroy him."

34

MORTALS: 1 – VAMPIRES: 0

TOWN HALL CONFERENCE ROOM—LATER THAT NIGHT

Henry grumbled to himself. Attending two public service meetings in one night was interfering with his winery duties.

He backed the Viper out of the garage. As he drove to the town hall complex, the videoconference with Christine replayed in his mind.

Really, it was unconscionable that the MWC contract didn't match the one he had signed. The whole situation made him want to storm into MWC's headquarters and bite that *pendejo* who refused to honor the contract. Henry clenched his jaw, knowing he couldn't express his anger that way.

And now he had to spend precious time chairing the mortal rights subcommittee meeting. He should have postponed the twice-monthly meeting. Too much was happening to maintain his normal commitments.

The winery desperately required his attention. He wanted to go over the budget tonight to see where cuts could be made without a layoff. The ruined wine would hurt their cash flow by next October. After spending a year in the bottle, the Cabernet would go on sale in the fourth quarter, at which point they'd really feel the loss. But if he could figure a way to compensate by cutting expenses now, they'd make it through.

As he strode past the other committee members where they lingered talking in the hallway, he curtly said, "Hello," and went inside the conference room, taking the chair at the head of the table—the chair Yacov used to occupy during their subcommittee meetings.

His throat tightened at the thought of his lost friend.

He swallowed past the grief as the other members entered the room. "If you could please take your seats, we'll get started."

Nicholas took a seat to Henry's left, and Haley Spears grabbed the chair next to Nicholas. Haley had been leading the charge for mortal rights, organizing the mortals behind her platform. With Haley across from Gaea, it gave the appearance of the mortals against the vampires.

Henry sighed. Maybe next time he'd reserve a smaller meeting room with a round table. King Arthur had it right. A round table would create a feeling of equality.

"I want to welcome Gaea to our subcommittee," Henry said, after everyone had sat down.

Gaea had been a sort of ombudsman for Hill mortals prior to the formation of the committee—someone they could approach confidentially if they ran into problems with their vampire. She had served them well in that role, which explained the mortals' enthusiasm for her appointment.

"We appreciate her willingness to serve on such short notice," Henry continued, "considering everything that has happened."

Gaea smiled genteelly and swept her hand, indicating the other committee members. "You've all done marvelous work so far."

The night after the earthquake, the town clerk delivered the minutes and work binder to her. That had not given Gaea much time—only a night, really—to review the material. Still, Henry shouldn't have been surprised to learn she'd read through the binder so quickly. Gaea never did things in half measures.

"Gaea, do you have any initial thoughts to share?" Henry asked.

"Yes, I do…the proposal on filling the available vampire slots." She tapped a finger in her chin dimple as she paused, a habit he'd seen many times. "Frankly, I think the number should be split fifty-fifty, right down the middle. Half of the fourteen would come from mortal mates we agree to turn. The other half from unaffiliated vampires who need a home."

Haley flopped back in her chair and huffed. "That doesn't work for us. Close to fifty mortals live on the Hill. Seven won't even make a dent in the list of those who want to be turned."

"Because you want to be turned, my dear?"

"I didn't say that."

"But it's what you're thinking. Your chance goes way down."

"As does everyone else's."

Henry held up his hand. "We have worked hard to keep these meetings from becoming contentious. Let's step back a moment."

Nicholas nodded. "From what I understand, Cerissa plans to provide clone blood for the communities, with the Hill getting the first production because she's building the lab here—and New York receiving the second, right?"

"That's correct." Henry cocked an eyebrow. As assistant town attorney, Nicholas had reviewed Cerissa's project application, which explained why he knew the distribution plan. "Because Cerissa's sponsor is the chief executive officer for the New York Collective, they get second priority after the Hill." But Henry couldn't figure out why Cerissa's project made a difference to their discussion. "What is your point, Nicholas?"

"Aren't we about to be in a position to open more homesteads for the unaffiliated? We have enough land and resources, particularly if unaffiliated vampires who join our community bring non-farming skills to the table. Why not expand our numbers and give them an opportunity to buy in?"

Henry tapped his fingers on the walnut table. Expanding the Hill's numbers wasn't his favorite idea. Right now, they were small enough to control the problems that arose in any group. "With the water restrictions that are likely to occur—"

"There are ways around that. Require them to have xeriscape with no outdoor watering. No private swimming pools. They can use the country club pool. No bathtubs—showers only with low-flow showerheads. Restrictions on the amount of water they can use each month, and instead of fining overuse, cut them off from further water until the next month."

"I'm not sure we can legally do that."

"Sure we can. This is an emergency water situation brought on by the levee collapses. We'll have no problem putting those restrictions in place for as long as the problem continues."

Gaea pursed her lips. "Let me see if I understand. You're proposing that all fourteen spots be filled with mortal mates who want to be turned? And that we *also* build new homes for unaffiliated vampires and expand our numbers?"

"Yes." Haley flicked her blonde hair over her shoulder. "And that new vampire—what's her name—"

"Anna Balmer."

"Yeah, her." Haley nodded. "She shouldn't get one of the fourteen spots."

Henry furrowed his brow. "But she helped us catch Oscar. Tig promised—"

Nicholas jumped in. "Tig promised to recommend her for a home. She has. The council is considering it, but for now, Anna has a month-to-month license to remain on the Hill, just like Seaton. The consensus is that the council wants to protect her—make sure no one tries to take retribution against her for helping us—but they want to make sure she finds her feet and fits in."

"Well, my dears, what about essential skill sets?" Gaea asked. "With all the mortals complaining about Dr. Clarke's bedside manner—"

Haley snorted. "You mean his lack of a bedside manner. I'm tired of going to a veterinarian who treats me like an animal. There are mortals who delay getting medical care because they can't stand Dr. Clarke."

Henry nodded, knowing Haley spoke the truth. Gaea had previously shared with him the various complaints about the doctor.

"Yes, yes, that," Gaea said. "We may want to recruit mortals who are trained physicians. If they fit in, we could turn them..."

Haley frowned. "And what if they take your offer and then move? One of our spots would be used up with no benefit to the mortals here."

Henry raised his hand for silence. "There may be a way. If the people with those skill sets are turned by someone who is not their mate, the maker would have more control over calling them back to the community. Mates may be unwilling to force someone they love. We can tell those with desirable skills that they must serve the community for a time—twenty years, let's say. Then they should be free to go as they please."

Nicholas looked perplexed. "Are you suggesting an indentured servant class? I couldn't support that. Never."

"Indebtedness, yes, but not a servant. The details could be worked out. The cost of buying into the Hill is significant. If we considered that a loan, and forgave a portion of the loan each year..."

Nicholas frowned. "And how does that differ from an indentured servant?"

"Well, is it any different from student loans? Those loans must be paid back..."

"Nuh uh," Haley said, shaking her head. "Don't even go there. My generation is sick of carrying that load. A college-educated public, well, it serves businesses at all levels. University should be free."

"Now, now," Gaea said. "We can't solve every problem. But turning someone is a unique boon. If it's being done to fill a need in the community, why shouldn't they pay us back if they leave prematurely?"

"Jayden raised this with me after the whole mess with Oscar." Nicholas spun his pen over his yellow legal pad as he spoke. "Oscar was able to screw with the heads of the unaffiliated because membership in treaty communities is based on wealth. It's created a vampire underclass. We have to think of how to even things out so they don't feel so disenfranchised."

"What do you suggest?" Henry asked.

Nicholas looked thoughtful. "We've never been able to meet our RHNA numbers. The state has been threatening to penalize us for the failure."

Gaea's eyes widened. "Our what?"

"Regional Housing Needs Allocation—the acronym is pronounced REE-na. The state imposes it on each city. It's a requirement to zone for low-income housing. This may be one way to do it."

Gaea let out a short laugh. "My head is spinning. Are you serious?"

"Yes, I am. I'm not sure we want apartments on the Hill. With the trust owning all the land, we're not structured to be active landlords. We're better off staying with our current single-family residence model, where the lessee is responsible for maintaining the building."

Henry felt a frantic loss of control invade his chest. "But I'm not sure we want low-income community members. They bring problems with them. We want people who are like us."

Nicholas *tsked*. "Henry, I never thought you'd be a NIMBY. You've worked so hard to make sure our community is multicultural."

Henry started to bristle when Gaea asked, "NIMBY?"

"Not in my back yard," Nicholas said.

Henry shook his head. "I don't want us to lose our way of life."

"And that's the problem." Nicholas looked calm but serious. "Our way of life has become strictly about who has wealth. Stagnant. We need to change how we think about who can live on the Hill."

Henry crossed his arms. "Even now, it's not strictly about money. We look at other factors—"

"But if they don't have sufficient money to buy in, you never get to those other factors. What if we flipped the analysis? Grade applications on those other factors first. Then look at financial factors. Isn't that what you did for Father Matt?"

Henry started to object, but instead let the room fall silent. He waited for them to start again. This battle was not as urgent to him, after all. Even if all fourteen slots were reserved for mates, for making new vampires, he'd never turn anyone. He'd never have a child. He'd never know the bond that Gaea had with her progeny.

¡El diablo! Where did those thoughts come from?

Was Rolf right? *Did* he have fang fever after all? He couldn't call it mating fever, because he was already mated to Cerissa.

Or was he beginning to realize that his marriage to Cerissa meant no vampire children for him ever, and that sacrifice was harder than he originally believed?

The idea of sharing his blood with someone other than Cerissa—aside from an emergency to heal a friend—felt unfaithful somehow. So he'd decided to forgo having children himself. And he hadn't discussed his decision with Cerissa because it was all theoretical, anyway, a pipe dream. Why raise a potentially contentious topic with her? There were not enough deaths creating openings on the Hill to even consider siring a child.

Until now...

Gaea's nose tip lifted an inch higher, and her eyes took on an *I'm older, I know what's best* look. "But the real limit has been the amount of blood Olivia can deliver."

When blood bank discards first became available, the council awarded Olivia the exclusive franchise to collect and distribute the blood to Hill vampires. However, the quantity—and quality—of discarded blood continued to be limited.

"And Cerissa's clones solve that problem," Nicholas said.

"Not for a few years, at least." Henry couldn't speak for Cerissa on this—still, he knew her rough timeline. "The council needs to approve her project plans so she can start construction. And with the earthquake and the water shortage—I don't see how she can get it built and in operation by next year."

Nicholas smirked. "Now you're the one who sounds mortal. You usually think so long term."

Henry glared at Nicholas, anger flaring in his chest at being challenged again. "Explain yourself...please."

"By the time we can build new homes, say another cul-de-sac like Marcus and I live on, Cerissa should have finished construction and started the production phase of her project. This subcommittee is trying to make a long-term plan that works. There are still more than four years left before the treaty imposes severe penalties"—a euphemism if Henry ever heard one, given that the penalty was death—"on unaffiliated vampires. So we have time to build housing, meet the blood needs, and expand membership by at least ten vampires, without causing a blood shortage."

Henry nodded, his temper cooling down. Nicholas made sense. "I will want to check with Cerissa to confirm your expectations are realistic under the changed circumstances."

"Sure," Nicolas replied, "but we need to move on this soon. Mortal mates are getting restless. They feel that the whole Oscar thing threw off the focus on their rights. They aren't willing to wait—they aren't getting any younger, so the time pressures are building."

Henry frowned. "But I thought we wanted to have a full package—all the Covenant and policy amendments together so the council adopted them all at once."

"Things changed." Nicolas gave a shrug that reminded Henry of Marcus.

Will I adopt Cerissa's mannerisms over time? It had never occurred to him before.

"In part," Nicolas continued, "things changed due to the situation Oscar created. Some of those issues are now more urgent than others. Before the council starts using up the fourteen slots, we need a plan in place."

Haley looked over at Nicholas. "But I thought the idea of allowing dating on the Hill had become more urgent, now that Shayna is single."

Henry answered before Nicholas could. "She must wait a year before dating, based on her religious beliefs. So while we should not delay, she has time."

"Then what about Ari and Gaea?" Haley asked. "Everyone knows what happened after the party."

Gaea *harrumphed*. "Not that it's any of your business, young lady, but I have permission from the council to continue to see Ari."

Haley smirked. "Noted. Circling back, then, I'm concerned about this idea of essential skills. Why can't existing vampires be retrained in the areas we need?"

Nicholas laughed. "The best night school for attorneys is in Southern California. It would be hard for someone on the Hill to go at night without leaving the community. And medical doctors are even harder to train at night. Dr. Clarke got lucky that one of the best veterinarian schools in California was in Mordida, and through a generous donation to the school, they arranged night classes and allowed him to complete his internship at night."

"What about computer skills?" Haley asked. "Seaton seriously needs a profession. He loves computer games. Is there any chance Ari would train him on computers? Could he take a night class at the local college?"

Gaea shook her head. "Not until we can solve his problem with seeing mortals as only dinner."

Henry focused on Nicholas. If anyone qualified in both categories—a critical role and a mortal mate—Nicholas was it. "What about you? Are you interested in one of the essential skill slots?"

"Not at this time. If we're able to add another attorney to the community in the short term, it wouldn't be me. Marcus wants to be able to take time off to travel. Right now, he can't. He feels tied to the Hill like it's a boat anchor." Nicholas stopped, looking embarrassed, as if he realized he'd revealed too much personal information.

Henry had no idea Marcus felt that way. He understood the restlessness that came from spending over a century in one place. He'd dealt with it by getting his pilot's license and traveling—along with the occasional adventure, such as performing in the circus.

"Ah, um..." Nicholas said, his cheeks reddening, his hands fluttering. "Please keep this confidential. But if we could locate another attorney who is suitable for the Hill, I think Marcus would jump at the chance to see them turned."

Henry swallowed hard. Did Marcus really want to leave? They'd been friends for decades, yet Marcus hadn't mentioned a word to him.

No, he couldn't let that happen. There had been too much loss already. He'd never support turning another attorney if it meant saying farewell to his friend. Never.

Chapter 35

Figures Don't Lie

Vasquez Müller Winery—Thirty Minutes Later

Henry flipped the light switch in his winery office, grateful to be finished with the subcommittee meeting. Now, he could finally focus on his own business affairs.

He strode to his desk. Someone had straightened up after the earthquake, except they put everything in the wrong place. He moved the award his Cabernet had won at the last wine expo from the desktop's right corner to the left, and slid the brass paperweight to the center. Touching the memento sent a fleeting wave of warm nostalgia through him. Méi had designed the engraved metal grape leaf to celebrate the Hill's hundredth year.

He looked over at the bookcase behind his executive chair. The shelves must have been emptied entirely by the shaking, given how haphazardly the books had been returned, but their reorganization would have to wait.

Years ago, when he first made Rolf a partner in the winery, Henry had decided they would share an office rather than sacrifice space needed for wine production. The office décor had been a compromise. Rolf wanted modern and Henry preferred traditional.

They let the interior designer decide how to implement their preferences. A creative use of brushed nickel lamps, dark blue wallpaper in a modern design, matching hardwood desks instead of the smoked glass Rolf wanted, and abstract *objets d'art* scattered around created a room in disharmony with itself and reflected Henry's current mood.

Although if he were completely honest, the room didn't bother him this much on other occasions. Clearly, the earthquake had left him easily irritated by the slightest dissonance. Just as he bristled too easily at Nicholas's comments during the meeting.

He rifled through the bookcase and located the annual budget binder. He could have studied the PDF at home on his computer, but he preferred a printed document for this kind of thinking. He saw things differently when he could touch the paper. He never understood why.

Earlier, he'd blocked the crystal so Cerissa wouldn't know how upset he was over the MWC contract. For now, he decided to keep the block in place. Going over the budget wasn't likely to improve his mood.

He took a pad of lined yellow paper out of the desk drawer and uncapped his fountain pen. As he worked through the fiscal year budget, he made a list of cost-cutting measures in bright indigo ink.

First, they could hand-pick the grapes themselves. Moving at supernatural speed, it wouldn't take long—in the early days, they'd gathered the harvest themselves, and could again.

For a moment, he pondered what would happen to the migrant workers they usually hired to pick the grapes. Hopefully, they had other work lined up.

Second, he would have to talk with Suri about whether they could economize by reducing the hours of the wine bar, and whether any of the waitstaff were performing poorly.

Third, they could increase special event pricing by ten percent for the next high season. They frequently had to turn away people in the spring through August. It was time to test a price increase.

He leaned back in his chair, lifting the pad to stare at his handwritten notes. Short term, they could make those three changes. The real issue was long term. Was it worth pouring more money into a business that would ultimately fail due to the water shortage?

He closed the budget and dropped the pad back on his desk. He'd been a vintner for over a hundred and thirty years—with a brief intermission during Prohibition, when he switched to making wine for sacramental use, among other things.

Creating fine wines was part of his persona, a part he couldn't imagine giving up. He had to figure out how to squeeze more cash out of his personal accounts to help the winery survive through the lull.

He phoned Ken Mitchell, who'd been his personnel accountant for the past ten years, and explained the situation. "What can I do?"

"Well, start by cutting back where you can," Ken said. "Twenty thousand dollars for a custom-made suit is a bit much."

"It was—" Henry paused, not wanting to explain it was bulletproof and he needed it because Oscar had tried to assassinate him. "Understood. Anything else?"

"Over a million dollars to support a bunch of tigers for life?"

"Ah, that was really a business expense for the circus."

"Yeah, and not even counting that, your circus continues to operate at a loss. You can't afford to keep making up the difference."

"That's non-negotiable. I promised. The next five years, they need my support."

"Hmm. Let's see, then…your jewelry expenses have been over the top. You spent five hundred thousand for a diamond last month. I'm assuming that's an investment. Perhaps you should sell it now to free up more cash."

"I cannot. It is sitting in the engagement ring my fiancée wears."

"Oh boy. I see. Then that would explain the fifty-thousand-dollar jeweler's bill for this month."

"Yes, for the setting and her wedding necklace."

"Do you anticipate any other expenses like those?"

"The wedding bands will be less expensive." He didn't care whether he wore a fancy ring.

"And the engagement party—did you invite any business guests?"

"A few—"

"Give me the number, and I'll come up with a pro rata deduction for the expense."

"Anything else?" Henry asked.

"I assume there is a wedding planned?"

Not just a wedding. Other parties and celebrations, at a time when all the spare cash he had needed to go to the winery. "We will try to keep those expenses on the lower side."

"Perhaps you could do a small, at-home wedding. You have a nice house and yard—plenty of room for an intimate celebration—"

"I will have to speak with my fiancée."

"At least you've reeled in your sports betting."

Indeed. And his bookie was feeling the loss. But since mating Cerissa, he hadn't had much time to study the teams and place bets, *gracias a Dios*. "Anything else?"

"The bottom line, Henry—your immediate cash flow is not good. Can you sell any investments to free up cash?"

Henry had considered the question already. When real estate prices dipped a few months ago, he'd bought another apartment building in New York, and at the time it made the purchase a steal. He couldn't resist the opportunity.

Then the market continued to go down, and the four million he invested was wiped out in the drop, which should have been all right, as he planned to hold the building for the long term. Prices would rise again…

But that was his weakness—a bargain. It was one of the reasons he was in the winery business. He'd bought out another winery that went bankrupt in the late 1880s, grabbing their barrels and bottling equipment at a steal.

"This is not a good time to sell," Henry finally said. "Some of my real estate holdings would sell at a loss, so there would be no cash gain. Same with my stock portfolio."

He didn't have to explain that to Ken. Anyone who managed money knew stocks had taken a recent tumble, thanks to the earthquake pushing down an already bear market. Now was not the time to sell anything.

"I know, but you're going to have to do something if you need more cash for the winery."

"I understand."

"You have a number of properties that are fully paid for—sell them or take a loan against them."

"I live off those rents. If I take a loan, how will I make the payments? If I sell, what will see me though the next year?"

His accountant paused for the moment. "Henry, you've always been conservative with how you spent your money and managed your business interests, aside from your sports betting. In the past six months, you've been on a spending spree the likes of which I've never seen you on before. I know you have personal reasons for your increased expenditures, but I wouldn't think to this degree. Is something wrong?"

"No," Henry replied quickly.

The question hit too close to home. Something *was* wrong. Fang fever? Or was it the turbulence of the disasters that befell them, from the VDM's attacks all the way to this week's earthquake? Was he spending to compensate, to feel in control?

"I'll be in touch when I have a solution," Henry said, then clicked off the phone and buried his face in his hands.

Yes, since he met Cerissa six months ago, he'd been spending a lot more than he usually did. His marriage to Cerissa was his first and—he prayed—his only marriage. He wanted the wedding and reception to be something they could look back on with joy over the years.

And he'd just asked her to let him pay for her expenses. How would she feel if he suddenly had to reduce her monthly spending…and cut back on the wedding they were planning?

She would probably welcome the opportunity to hand back the credit cards. She didn't want him to support her from the start.

No. He refused. How could he expect his fiancée to shoulder the load with him and still be a man?

As soon as he finished forming the question, the phrase *toxic masculinity* shot to the surface of his mind.

He'd already struggled with the decision to accept another man's child as his own, and in the process, wrestled the toxic masculinity demon to the ground. He didn't have to give Cerissa children to be a man, and he could be an adoptive father to hers.

But money—money wasn't the same thing, was it? Was his desire to support Cerissa another side of the toxic masculinity he'd been raised with? Or was it just their way on the Hill?

The whole train of thought left him unsettled.

He'd say nothing to her, not yet. This was his problem to work out. Somehow, he'd come up with a solution on his own. Because dumping this on Cerissa felt completely wrong. If anyone could solve it, he could. He just had to.

Chapter 36
Tectonic Stress

Rancho Bautista del Murciélago—Around the same time

When Cerissa arrived home, she went straight to her basement lab. She wanted to refrigerate the samples as quickly as possible. She didn't know how long fang serum would survive outside of a vampire. She unpacked it and looked at the yellow liquid through the clear glass.

"Cerissa?" Henry asked, standing at the door.

She jumped and clutched the jar to her chest. "Don't sneak up on me like that!" She breathlessly ran the words together. "Not when I'm working."

"I am sorry. I move quietly without thinking. Years of habit, I suppose."

"I know. But as acute as my hearing is, it doesn't always pick up your movement when I'm distracted."

She looked away. There was more to it than that. She didn't want to admit the earthquake still had her unnerved. The slightest rumble sent her jumping out of her skin.

To avoid meeting his gaze, she set the jars on the lab bench and busied herself gathering the containers holding the blood samples, then paused, cocking her head to one side. There was another reason she hadn't detected his presence. "Why are you blocking the crystal?"

"I didn't want to disturb you with, ah, the water problem. I've been on a bit of a roller coaster."

"What happened?"

He ran a hand over his face. "Among other things, apparently there is a problem with the contract." He explained the details. "I may have to testify during the daytime, which is impossible."

"What if you covered up all over? Would that help?"

"If any sunlight filtered through my clothes, I'd burn, roasting alive. But the main problem is staying awake."

"Hmm. Maybe I could work on creating a blood-based stimulant, along with a topical to protect your skin."

She had a lot on her to-do list, including the research she had to do to solve Seaton's and Rolf's medical problems, but neither of those was urgent. No one expected her to figure them out overnight. Henry's issue was far more pressing.

"Let me put these away," she said, opening the lab refrigerator and placing the blood samples upright in a tube tray, "and then I can join you and we can talk about it."

"What do you have there?"

"These?" She held up the jars holding the yellow liquid. "Fang serum."

She placed the jars in the refrigerator and closed the door.

"Why do you have that?"

She didn't like keeping secrets from him, but she really had no ethical choice. "Ah, I can't tell you. Doctor-patient privilege."

"I see. I will wait for you in the drawing room." He strode to the door, then stopped and turned to face her. "Perhaps we could enjoy an evening swim. The pool has been refilled and tested."

If there was going to be a water shortage, why did he waste water filling the pool? Or did it have to stay filled to keep the pool in good condition? She bit her lip, then decided not to say anything and trust that he knew what he was doing.

"Quique, before you go, may I ask for a favor?"

"Of course, *mi amor*."

"You shouldn't agree until you hear what it is."

"And yet I already have." The corners of his lips twitched up. "What is it?"

"May I have another sample of fang serum from you?"

"Does it have something to do with your patient?"

"I want another sample, for comparison."

"Very well. Now?"

"Yes, please." She began looking through the cupboard above her lab bench. Things were messy, but they had been messy before the earthquake.

She didn't really like taking time out to clean and organize—too many other projects needed her attention. So it took her a few minutes before she found another sample jar that was sterile. She unscrewed the cap and pulled a rubber dam across it.

He leaned against the doorframe. "If you would clean your lab, you would be able to find things quicker and easier."

Grrr. Mr. Neat Freak needed to learn when to keep his mouth shut. "And if you didn't come in here, you wouldn't be tempted to nag me."

The hurt on his face made her regret her words. Before she could take them back, he turned to leave. "I did not know my presence was not welcome."

"Henry, please don't go. I'm sorry. I want you to stay. It's just that you promised to let this be my space. That I didn't have to keep it as neat as the rest of the house."

He turned back to her and bowed slightly. "My apologies. You are right. I did promise that."

She walked up to him and slipped her arms around his waist. "Quique, please don't be angry with me."

"I am not angry." He hugged her close to him, then leaned back to meet her eyes. "I promise, I will not criticize your lab. I will not even joke that, from the way things look, you have yet to clean up from the earthquake," he said with a wan smile.

She smiled back. "It was a lot worse after the quake. But I'm fine with the way it is now."

"All right. Now how do you plan on obtaining this sample you asked for?"

She broke from their embrace and walked over to the cupboard again.

"Here." She handed him a pouch of blood in a self-heating cover. "Bon appétit."

He shrugged. He was hoping she might have a slightly different inducement in mind—her own sweet blood. But then, he'd likely shoot his load in her vein, and she'd never get her sample.

He drank down what she offered and smiled at her. She started to hold up the collection jar for him but suddenly stopped.

A small drop of the fluid dripped from one fang, and he caught it with his tongue.

Staring at his mouth, she asked, "Is that normal?"

"Yes. When I drink blood, I can feel the pressure build. If it is not released, some of the fluid does drip out."

"Interesting." She held up the jar. "Here, bite through the rubber."

He bit, giving her a seductive look in the process. He was feeling aroused by her presence—and the fang serum. He pushed the subcommittee and other problems from his mind.

Grab the moment.

When the gland in the roof of his mouth felt completely drained, he lowered the jar and handed it to her.

She held the glass up to the light. "About one milliliter, the same amount I got from Matt, give or take a little. The same clear yellowish color."

He didn't say anything over the fact she'd just let slip who one of the other samples was from.

She took off the rubber dam and sniffed the contents of the jar. "Odorless."

He waited while she screwed on the cap and labeled it, then eyeballed her gorgeous bottom as she leaned over to place the container in the lab refrigerator.

Yes, he had ways to distract himself from all his other worries.

He walked to her and pulled her into his arms again. "Now that I have provided my assistance, what is my reward?"

"The knowledge that you're helping a fellow vampire isn't enough?"

"No." He kissed her forehead…her cheek…her chin…then her luscious lower lip.

She kissed him back. "And do I have to guess what you want for your reward?"

"Suggestions are always welcome."

"Hey, it's my turn to choose, remember?" Her brow furrowed. "And what about the pool? You went to all that trouble to get it ready—aren't we going for a swim?"

"Marcus and Nicholas have moved out—their temporary home was ready this morning." He smirked at her, sweeping her into his arms and carrying her up the basement stairs. "With the house all to ourselves, we can do both. But it is your choice. What will it be?"

Chapter 37
Revelations

Rancho Bautista del Murciélago—Wednesday, the next day

When Henry woke in the late afternoon, his first thought turned to the pool play he and Cerissa had enjoyed last night, which managed to infuse fun into an evening that had pulled him from one troubling problem to another with no resolution.

Relaxed and rested, he felt ready to focus solely on winery matters tonight. It helped, too, that the face-to-face meeting with Christine Dunne wouldn't happen until tomorrow night, so he had the next twelve hours to conduct winery business uninterrupted. He rolled off the cot, grabbed his phone, and headed to the basement bathroom to shower and shave.

According to the text Cerissa sent him, she'd spent the afternoon at the Lux Enclave in her lab, working on his daytime problem, but promised to join him for dinner. She'd worded the text carefully so if Marcus or someone else read it when he did, they wouldn't know the "bat cave" meant the Lux headquarters.

Last night, after swimming—and other things—they'd discussed her ideas for dealing with his daytime problem. At the time, he expressed his appreciation for her help but warned her not to get her hopes up.

He finished getting ready, and she arrived home at seven.

After eating together, he gave her a lingering kiss before she flashed back to the Enclave to continue her work for the evening.

Now he had business to attend. The structural engineer's report on the earthquake damage to the winery hadn't landed in his email inbox yet. He was anxious to get it dealt with, but nothing waited for him.

He went upstairs to his home office and looked through the physical mail waiting on the desk. Cerissa had deposited it there for him earlier in the day.

An express FedEx envelope with no return address was on top. Could it be the engineer's report? He was expecting a PDF by email, but perhaps the delivery plan had changed during the day.

He ripped the strip off the top to open the package. Inside was an unlabeled flash drive, and a letter. The letter was amateurish.

If you do not want this on the web, pay one hundred bitcoins.

Whoever wrote it had cut letters out of a newspaper and glued them onto the page.

He laughed to himself. He knew of a current scam going around that involved messages claiming to have hacked the recipient's email account and demanding an outrageous ransom in bitcoins. The scammers hadn't realized that a hundred bitcoins were currently valued at around three and a half million dollars, thanks to the earthquake driving up prices.

Prior to that, the cryptocurrency had been trading at around ten thousand per bitcoin. He had considered adding some to his portfolio, but the price continually fluctuated. He hadn't liked the uncertainty created by amateur speculators who drove the wild price swings. They created false value when they bought based on emotion. Now he wished he'd purchased some given how the earthquake had inflated the trading price.

He smirked at the letter. The bottom line was no one had that kind of money lying around to pay a ransom. This was likely nothing more than a scam.

He looked at the flash drive again, pursing his lips, and considered whether to toss the whole thing in the trash.

But the physical nature of the demand stopped him. The blackmailer had gone to the trouble of sending hard media by FedEx—not an inexpensive method—to Henry personally at his home address. Most of these scam artists used email and relied on mass distribution to find someone who might pay. And it wasn't as if he'd never been blackmailed before in his long life.

Checking it out was the wise move.

But he didn't want to plug the flash drive into his computer—the memory device might contain a virus, after all, someone's idea of a cruel joke, or, alternatively, a real ransomware attack. He grabbed an old laptop from storage, one that wasn't connected to the internet, set it on his desk, and inserted the drive.

When the video started, he stared at it, frozen, not able to think through what he was seeing.

The owner's tasting room. Cerissa, propped against the pillows fully naked. Him spreading her legs to go down on her. The profile shot made certain that the viewer saw them both clearly—from the way his tongue lavished her to the ecstasy on her face, it was there in perfect clarity.

And not just him as Enrique. Henry—his older alter ego—had made love to her that night. If this was released, it would devastate Cerissa. The embarrassment, the stares from those he worked with who didn't know what he was—they'd assume she had cheated on her fiancé on the night of her engagement party.

Then a sense of foreboding crept over him. He hit fast-forward, carefully watching the video.

No. It can't be true.

The blackmailer had caught the bite on video.

His heart grew tight as despair crushed him, and he clamped down to block the crystal.

The council would blame him if the video got released. The vampire was always held liable for this kind of exposure—and he was a founder. There were those who were jealous of him—including the mayor—who wouldn't hesitate to use this to reinstate the whipping post penalty or kick him out of the community altogether.

He scrubbed his forehead. He was supposed to know better. He was supposed to evaluate the risks.

A roar of rage erupted from him. Thankfully, Cerissa wasn't home. He didn't want her knowing about the video. Not yet.

How would she react once she saw it?

Her—naked—for the world to see?

At times, Cerissa seemed shy around sex. She didn't want anyone else seeing them in *flagrante delicto*. The one time she drew a line in the sand with the Lux Protectors involved her special contact lenses that recorded everything she saw. She insisted on the right to turn them off, refusing to record when he made love to her.

This video—the exposure would mortify her. If he felt violated, she would feel it times ten. Hell, times a hundred.

No.

He picked up the phone and thought of calling Marcus, but the town attorney wasn't the right person to call under the circumstances—he might feel obliged to report it to the council.

When Rolf answered, Henry said, "I need your help."

"What is it?"

"Meet me at the winery. At the owner's tasting room. Do not say anything to Karen. If Cerissa asks, I will tell her we had winery business to discuss."

"I'll see you there in fifteen minutes."

Henry arrived first and connected the laptop to play through the large-screen television hanging on the wall. Waiting for Rolf to show up, he paced the length of the room.

He stopped when the door opened. "Join me." He sat down on the couch and pressed play. "This flash drive arrived in the mail today."

Rolf took a seat and silently watched the video as Henry and Cerissa entered the room, as Cerissa sipped a dessert wine, as Henry gave her the pearls, as Cerissa appeared in the lace negligee. Henry stopped the video before it got to the more revealing parts.

"Nice tits," Rolf finally said.

Henry turned and bared his fangs at Rolf. He was already furious enough without Rolf's flippant comment.

"Bah, I didn't mean any offense. She does have nice tits."

"I did not ask you here to critique her as if you were watching a porn video." Henry tapped the mouse a couple of times and began playing again at the relevant point.

"You're not half bad yourself," Rolf said. Henry's naked backside was captured in profile. "But there is a reason straight men prefer videos of two women having sex." He crossed his arms and shrugged. "They don't have to compete with the man in the movie."

"Rolf, I did not ask you here for your cultural insights, either."

"You're the one showing me a sex video of you and Cerissa."

"It is *this* part that is important. See?"

When the bite began, Rolf's demeanor turned from joking to serious, but he gave a dismissive wave. "Anyone seeing this would not know what is happening. They would think you were kissing her neck. They can only see the back of your head here."

Henry didn't reply. He knew what was coming, and his fingers rubbed the crucifix he wore under his shirt. When the on-screen Henry released Cerissa's neck, he raised his head and cried out in pleasure, fangs prominent and blood dripping down the side of his mouth. To his mortification, he'd bitten her on the side the camera was positioned to capture. The marks on Cerissa's neck—clearly visible in the video—would leave no doubt in anyone's mind what they were seeing.

"This is not good," Rolf finally said.

Henry stopped the video and handed Rolf the note.

Rolf focused on it, then looked up and laughed. "What's a bitcoin valued at now?"

"Thirty-five thousand dollars at my last check."

"Three and a half million dollars? Are they crazy?"

"Look at that"—Henry pointed at the freeze frame of his fangs—"and tell me if they are the crazy ones."

"All right." Rolf sat there, looking deep in thought. "It's technically not a violation of the Covenant. While such 'activities' are forbidden in Mordida, this area is still part of Sierra Escondida."

"You're arguing I didn't violate the Covenant by biting my mate. But selecting this location for my *activities* showed poor judgment. There is a catchall in the Covenant that would penalize this, based on the outcome."

Rolf shook his head. "I think we can keep this from being reported to the town council, since arguably no violation of the Covenant has occurred, *in my opinion*," Rolf said, sounding like his vice mayor persona. "Do not contradict me, and we should be fine. But we need to call Tig and let her investigate it."

"Whoever did this had access to the room to plant the camera. From the angle of the view, it is my guess the camera was on that bookshelf." Henry got up and strode over to it. He started to move things to see if the camera was still there.

"Don't touch it!" Rolf shouted, *whooshing* at supernatural speed to grab Henry's arm. "If there are fingerprints, you don't want to smudge them. You're clearly not thinking straight."

"Perhaps not."

Rolf leaned toward the bookshelf. "I can't see anything. The camera is probably gone. Did you notice anything out of the ordinary that night?"

"Aside from having other things on my mind, no, I didn't. If the camera is small enough, though, it might still be hidden."

"Ach, let's get Tig and Jayden over here right now. Let them hunt for the camera's location and dust the room for fingerprints. We don't have to show them the video, but we should give them the note and tell them in general terms what's on the video." Rolf sounded confident. More confident than Henry felt. "We don't tell them about the bite, for now."

Henry considered the suggestion, and his pulse rate calmed for the first time since watching the video. "That sounds reasonable."

"All we need to do is find out who did this. Then we get the video back and mesmerize the blackmailer to make them forget what they saw. Even if they have other copies of it, they won't remember where those copies are. I think that's the best we can do under the circumstances."

The anger, the rage, the sense of violation ratcheted higher as his fear subsided. Henry clenched his fists. "I would prefer to break the blackmailer's neck, but that is not an honorable solution."

And then it hit him.

What might *Cerissa* do to the blackmailer when she learned of this violation?

He couldn't confidently predict her response anymore when it came to expressing rage—he'd never have predicted she'd kill Dalbert, the vampire who had bribed Dylan to kill Yacov, and yet she did.

Madre de Dios, he couldn't tell her about the video. No matter what he'd promised in the past about being honest with her. He just couldn't. He had to protect her from herself.

Chapter 38
Under Pressure

SIERRA ESCONDIDA BUSINESS DISTRICT—FIFTEEN MINUTES LATER

Tig stopped the police van outside the restaurant where Jayden had grabbed dinner. She waited a minute, then the door opened, and he rushed out to meet her at the curb, stuffing a credit card into his wallet as he jogged her way.

Rolf's phone call about the blackmail scheme had put them both into high gear. Whatever the blackmailer had on Henry might also threaten the Hill.

First the earthquake, then the burglary, and now this.

When it rains, it pours. The saying was as true in California as it was in her Kenyan birthplace.

Once Jayden shut the van's door, she stepped on the gas, anxious to begin the investigation before things spun out of control.

When they arrived at the winery, Rolf gave them a rundown on what happened. Henry just stood there, his face shut down, his arms crossed, and his body so twisted with anger that she could see the cords in his neck.

Rolf started to hand her the letter, and she stopped him. Jayden opened the crime scene kit he carried and took out a pair of tweezers, handing them off to her. She used the tweezers to pick up the letter and read the cobbled-together text. "Who has touched it?"

"Just Rolf and I," Henry replied.

"Good. I have your fingerprints on file. Neither of your mates touched it?"

Henry shook his head. "Neither Cerissa nor Karen are aware of it. We would like to keep it that way. I do not want Cerissa to know about this. The video is very, ah, *explicit.*"

"We understand." Tig slipped the letter into a large transparent bag without folding it. "Discretion in these kinds of investigations is important. May we see the video?"

"I would prefer not to show it." Henry's jaw clenched, the muscle bulging like he was cracking nuts with his molars. "We spent the night here"—he gestured at the couch—"celebrating our engagement. The bed folds out. Cerissa slept here, while I slept in the wine cellar using a small private room Rolf and I built for that purpose."

So he had sex with his fiancée. Big deal. This culture was so uptight about sex. In that way, she felt lucky to have been raised by the Maasai into adulthood.

Nonetheless, no one liked having their privacy violated—that she understood. At least he was fortunate in one respect so far: if this had been a revenge video, it would already be online.

"How does the recording begin?" she asked.

"It starts when we enter the room."

"You are fully clothed?"

"Yes."

"Then let me see that part. I want to see the camera angle."

"We already know where the camera was hidden." Rolf walked to the bookcase. "Over here. We haven't touched the shelf."

"Just the same, if we could see the first couple of minutes, it would tell us where to look for fingerprints."

Jayden walked over to Henry and laid a hand on his shoulder. "We're going to need the flash drive at some point," Jayden said. "We may be able to tell something from an examination of the computer file. The blackmailer—if he or she was stupid—may have left metadata embedded in the file that identifies them by name."

Uncertainty filled Henry's eyes. "How could that be?"

"Some workplaces format flash drives with a business name for tracking purposes." Jayden gestured at the rectangular drive sticking out of the laptop. "If the blackmailer took the drive from their workplace, the metadata might tell us who they are, or at least where to look."

Jayden's knowledge about computer forensics exceeded Tig's, and she was relieved he'd approached Henry about this.

"With home computers, people will often use their first name as their username, too," Jayden continued. "So their user subdirectory may begin with their first name."

Henry still looked skeptical. "Who will do the computer analysis?"

Tig frowned at the question. Henry had to know Cerissa's cousin would be assigned to do the analysis. "Marcus has cleared Ari to do forensic computer work for us."

"No. It cannot be Ari." Henry backed up, folding the laptop and hugging it to his body. "I do not want Cerissa knowing anything about it. It would be too…embarrassing for her."

Tig understood how Henry felt. Even with her permissive attitudes around sex, she wouldn't want Jayden's family to see a video of her and Jayden in bed.

"I know someone we can use," Jayden said. "Very discreet—they work for the Mordida crime lab."

"The flash drive will not leave my possession." Henry shook his head, still hugging the laptop tightly. "And I will be there when any tests are run. No copy will be made."

What was Henry trying to hide? Was something on the video other than vanilla sex?

For now, she didn't need the answer, just the storage device. "How does this sound? After we fingerprint the flash drive, I'll put it in an evidence envelope, and you'll initial the outside. The envelope will only be reopened in your presence. But we need to store it in the police locker to preserve the chain of evidence."

He nodded very slowly. "I will consider that."

"Now, if we could see the first few minutes of the video."

Henry relented and played the opening sequence. He stopped it before Cerissa came out of the bathroom.

"That's enough for now," Jayden said. "And congratulations again on your engagement."

"Thank you. But even that moment of celebration has been violated. If I find out who did this, I swear on my mother's honor, I'll drain them."

Rolf punched Henry's arm affectionately. "Changed your mind about the 'honorable way' already?"

Henry growled in his partner's direction.

"Founder," Tig interrupted them. "Please, do not make that kind of threat. We will find the perp and bring him or her to justice. Promise me you won't take matters into your own hands."

Henry frowned. "For the moment."

Jayden returned to his crime scene kit and pulled on nitrile gloves. Best to get this done quickly, before Henry raised more objections. "You're right about one thing. That bookcase was probably the location of the camera."

The video was made with a typical spy cam, the type sold at those security stores that offered nanny cams and the like. The compression quality was high grade.

He took out a jar of magnetic powder. "The camera lens was good enough that you can clearly see faces. So it wasn't cheap. My guess—the blackmailer retrieved it already. He or she wouldn't abandon a pricey item like that."

Jayden used a magnetic applicator to pick up the fine black granules and then gently trailed the powder across the shelf and other contents. In this way, no bristles touched the surface, reducing the chance of damaging the fingerprints.

Everyone stood around watching him work, like an ant under a microscope. It didn't bother him—he was used to it. He photographed and then transferred the prints to preserve them.

He frowned as he studied the angles. Which shelf did they stash the camera on? Using tongs, he moved the artificial flowers to one side, searching for the camera. Just as he suspected, nothing.

Then he saw it. A pinhole drilled in the back of the bookcase, toward the top of the shelf where fresh sawdust lay. He swept it into a bag and labeled it. Then he again dusted for prints. He found more and lifted them. He estimated where someone might grab the bookcase to move it and dusted the end. An excellent set of prints appeared—all five fingers.

"We're in luck," he said as he collected them, and then, using a portable scanner, started a search of the police databases to see if they belonged to someone with an arrest history.

While the search ran, he moved the bookcase. More sawdust on the floor and a sticky residue on the back of the bookshelf.

"This is the shelf the camera had been on, probably a fiber-cam and microphone threaded through the artificial flowers. See this hole?"

He pointed it out as the others looked over his shoulder. Having three vampires in close proximity to him reminded him just how strange his life had become.

"The camera was fed through here, and the recorder attached to the back of the bookshelf with duct tape. See the residue? I have some good prints. We can compare them to what was on the letter. And keep in mind, whoever you hired to clean in here could have touched the end of the bookshelf, so the fingerprints won't be definitive."

The scanner dinged, and Jayden read the results. "No match. The perp isn't in police databases."

"Do you fingerprint your employees?" Tig asked.

Henry and Rolf looked at each other, and then Rolf answered, "No, we do not violate their civil liberties that way."

"It was worth the question. We'll have to do this the hard way."

"And what would that be?" Henry asked.

"We'll need a good pretense to question your employees."

Jayden had an idea and gestured at the patio doors. "What with the earthquake and all, we could claim someone broke in here."

Tig shook her head. "I don't want to alert whoever did it that we're focused on this room."

"Okay." Jayden paused to label the card he'd transferred the fingerprints to, noting their original location. Then he glanced at Tig. "Well, we could put someone in undercover to collect fingerprint samples."

Rolf brushed his long bangs back and furrowed his brow. "How does that work?"

When Tig nodded at him, Jayden explained. "We bring someone in who no one knows. You say they are a new employee. Or maybe a consultant, hired to improve the winery."

They'd done it before under different circumstances. Jayden himself had played the undercover role the last time they used the ruse, but the winery staff might recognize him from the party.

"The undercover officer is introduced as a consultant and talks with everyone who works for you," Jayden continued. "He'll interview each employee about how the winery might be improved. In the process, each one will be offered a soda, or water glass—some smooth, clean surface that will be pretreated to pick up fingerprints. We'll collect them that way. After each interview, the undercover agent will bag and label the object. That's it."

Henry looked pensive. "We will have to explain this to our manager. We do not want her thinking she is doing a bad job. She is too valuable to us."

Tig held up her hand. "You can't tell her the truth. Everyone who had access to this room is a suspect, and she can't be ruled out. So tell her what you like, but not the true reason."

"I can handle it, Henry." Rolf gave Henry's back a pat. "Suri trusts me."

"Who will you get to do this undercover work?" Henry asked.

"I have in mind a classmate from the police academy," Jayden said as he began packing his kit. He had everything from the room he needed for now.

Before leaving, he kneeled to check the doorknob. No sign of damage. But this kind of lock could easily be opened using a lock-bumping key. "You need a better locking mechanism," he said as he returned to his feet. "A burglar with the right tools could break in without leaving any evidence. Does your manager keep a list of who had access?"

Rolf frowned. "I doubt it. But wouldn't asking put too much attention on this room?"

"True. If the blackmailer is one of your employees, we don't want them to rabbit."

"Let's try the subtle approach first," Tig said.

Jayden nodded. "My friend is working in the San Francisco crime lab, but I think he'd be able to get a leave of absence for a few days if the chief called his supervisor and explained the situation."

"Of course, we will find a way to cover his salary and any expenses," Henry said, his shoulders slumped, his eyes looking resigned. "No need to have the extra expense appear on Tig's reports to the council."

Jayden understood Henry's concern. If the town council saw the extra expense, they might question Tig about the investigation. And then Cerissa might hear about it.

This had to be eating him up alive.

"Don't worry." Rolf gripped Henry's shoulder. "We'll cover the costs."

Jayden gave his most reassuring smile. "Then we better get to work."

Chapter 39

Searching

The Lux Enclave—The same night

Cerissa placed a sample of Matt's fang serum into the analyzer. She set the machine for "human/vampire." The analyzer was programmed with all known medical knowledge on both variants, and she pressed the key series to start the analysis.

Morphing into her native form made it easier to operate the Enclave's lab equipment, which was designed for her six-fingered hand. The sixth finger—a second thumb, really—emerged from the side of her wrist. She missed having the extra appendage when she took human form.

A white sarong wrapped under her large, angel-like wings and served as a lab coat. She had tied back her pale, straight hair to keep the fine strands from falling into her face.

Morphing and working from the Lux Enclave seemed to calm the anxiety chasing her. Henry didn't want her seeking comfort in his arms during the day whenever one of those blasted aftershocks hit. By staying busy and away from the Hill, she kept her mind off the tremors.

Besides, he had too much on his plate right now to spend much time comforting her even at night. If anything, she should be providing *him* as much support as she could.

While the test ran, she opened her laptop computer—one compatible with human computer systems and connected to the internet. She started to research sun protection in scientific journals. Halfway through the articles, she received an email notification. She opened it and smiled to herself. Matt had already arranged access to the research database maintained by *Living from Dusk to Dawn*.

She entered the login and password he provided and began exploring the site. It didn't take her long to skim through most of the scientific research that was posted.

She snorted when she came across an article Dr. Clarke had submitted. He had written up the use of dialysis that saved Marcus from silver poisoning. He even took all the credit.

Asshole.

But Leopold, her sponsor, left a comment attributing the breakthrough to Cerissa, and an online battle between the two followed.

Cerissa shook her head, smirking at the screen. Not much different from the human world, then.

She continued scrolling through the index. No research on fang serum. It was an entirely unexplored field. There were quite a few articles on abnormal vampires, though. With a wave, she sent the articles to her reading tablet. She would study them for ways to help Seaton.

Most of the other research focused on cures for silver and garlic exposure, and there were even quite a few articles on sun exposure. She downloaded those.

She quickly read one article. It mentioned that bewitched stones were reputed to allow a vampire to stay awake and go out into the sun. The writer had collected stories but never seen such a stone. Cerissa downloaded that article as well, although she thought that bewitched stones would be a dead end.

Even more interesting was a history of vampires that included a report on the mother of vampires.

Could this possibly be the first vampire turned by the Lux prototype?

Cerissa transferred that article as well. She would read it when she had free time. Right now, she had too much to do.

When the machine testing the fang serum *dinged*, she stepped over to see the displayed results and swiped at the air above the machine, sending the data to her Lux computer, and, using her neural link, ran a comparison, displaying the breakdown in the air above her desk.

Father Matt's sample was identical to Henry's and Rolf's. Nothing new there.

The serum's liquid was what would remain if you removed all the white cells, red cells, and clotting factors from blood, which wasn't surprising. Floating in the yellow liquid were five unique compounds: a sexual stimulant, an anti-clotting agent, a marking agent that warned off other vampires, a psychoactive substance that probably accounted for a vampire's limited mind-control abilities, and, last but by no means least, the Lux morphing hormone.

How she wished she had the original vampire genome. Was fang serum an evolutionary quirk, or did the first vampire created by the Lux have it?

Over twenty-six hundred years ago, the prototype had been allowed to roam in a suburb of Mesopotamia. It turned a mortal before it was destroyed, and the Lux had left the mortal for dead, not understanding at the time what had occurred. Only later did her predecessors learn the deceased mortal had risen.

Cerissa didn't know how analyzing the original vampire genome would help Seaton exactly, but sometimes the discovery of something you weren't looking for was the breakthrough you needed. Take warfarin—it started out as an ingredient in rat poison and became a life-saving blood thinner.

She made a few notes in her journal for follow up later and went to the refrigerator to retrieve a sample of Seaton's blood for testing when her phone rang.

"Hi, Karen," she answered. The phone automatically translated the Lux language—which was sung—into English.

"What happened tonight?"

"Can you be more specific?"

"Henry called and then Rolf flew out of here like a bat out of hell."

Cerissa laughed at Karen's pointed simile. "Henry texted me that he had a personnel matter at the winery and would be gone for a while."

"Bullshit. They leave that stuff to Suri. Unless the problem was Suri, and I know they are happy with her work. She's doing a great job running the day-to-day operations of the winery. Especially after the earthquake."

"Maybe there was structural damage that they only just discovered. Henry has been hesitant to discuss the damage with me. He's afraid it'll upset me."

Her heart warmed as the words left her mouth. It was considerate of him, really, not to say anything, considering how much the earthquake had upset her.

"Then why didn't Rolf explain it to me? I'm involved up to my eyeballs in marketing the winery. If there was a big problem, he'd tell me. No, I think those two are hiding something."

"Perhaps. But if they are, they might have a good reason for it."

"Not even a little curious?" Karen asked her.

"Well, yes, now that you raise it. But if I ask him about it, it'll sound like I don't trust him. He said it was a personnel matter. Let's leave it at that."

"I may ask Rolf."

"Okay, up to you. But Karen, I'm at the Enclave lab right now. Can we talk more later?"

"Sure thing. Bye."

Cerissa clicked off the call and began analyzing Seaton's blood. The first test results were no surprise. His blood type was O negative, just like all the other vampires she had tested.

She put a sample into the DNA analyzer.

Once finished, Seaton's DNA results were startling. She had mapped the vampire genome but had only tested a limited number of blood samples so far. From what she could tell, there were certain markers that seemed to run consistent from maker to offspring. She had enough DNA samples—some coming from Oscar and his dead offspring—that had allowed her to trace the pattern.

But something about Seaton's results were off. The allele of one of the genes was drastically different. She hesitated to call it mutated, not knowing what normal—or original—really looked like.

She made notes into her laptop. It was possible that the modified allele controlled whether fang serum was produced. Had it mutated because his maker was so young, or had he inherited it that way?

Cerissa wasn't sure whether a cure could be implemented at a genetic level, but it might help to know what caused it. She sent off an email to Matt, asking if he knew anything about Seaton's maker that would help.

Because with Jane dead, Cerissa couldn't run a comparison of maker to offspring.

Wait. I'm missing something.

Fang serum was needed for the turn. Jane couldn't have made Seaton if she didn't produce fang serum. QED: Seaton's lack of fang serum had to be a mutation.

Unless there was another way to make vampires that she didn't know about.

Damn, if only I had a sample from the Lux prototype.

After completing her notes on Seaton's DNA, she switched gears to work on Henry's problem. Could she find a stimulant that kept him from falling to sleep at sunrise? Before medications would work on a vampire, they had to be processed through a human body, just like alcohol did. She'd made a painkiller that way.

So she researched stimulants, found the strongest amphetamine with long-lasting effects, and went to the clone room, where rows of blood clones lay connected to feeding machines, chose one, and peeled back the catheter embedded in the clone's chest to inject the medication.

The clones she'd created were genetically modified to remove the sentient portions of their brains, so essentially, the clones were organic machines that produced human blood. She didn't have any hesitancy experimenting on them for that reason—they weren't alive.

Her theory: if she injected a stimulant into a clone's bloodstream, and allowed its body time to process the medication, then the stimulant should work on Henry when he drank their blood. She took out an empty collection bag, and hooked the blood removal catheter to the bag, but kept the valve turned off for the moment.

An alarm sounded, and she jumped. *Damn it.* She hated how the earthquake had left her with a heightened startle reflex, even in Lux form.

The alarm continued beeping—the clone had gone into cardiac arrest. Cerissa pressed an emergency call button, summoning the *karibu* who assisted in her lab. Together, they performed CPR.

Twenty minutes later, the clone's heart gave out completely.

She dismissed her assistants and began the process to drain the blood from the dead clone.

As she made notes in her journal, it struck her. The clones received no exercise and had been engineered to produce blood, which was why their hearts weren't robust enough to withstand a strong stimulant.

Hopefully, the blood she drained from this one would keep Henry awake during the day. She had no intention of sacrificing another clone. She needed all the prototypes she had to keep Henry, Rolf, and Leopold well fed. Losing even one meant they'd have to rotate donor blood into their feeding schedule, the taste of which left much to be desired.

And it would take months to grow a replacement. The clones were a precious resource she couldn't afford to waste.

Once she finished collecting the blood, she collapsed onto a nearby chair. A tear rolled down her cheek and she angrily wiped it away.

The loss of one clone wasn't really such a big deal, and being Lux usually gave her space, kept her distant from the anxieties that plagued humans. So why was she crying now? Those feelings shouldn't have been able to sneak in so easily to overwhelm her. She shook her head violently. It just didn't make sense.

Chapter 40

Freeloader

Mordida Tropical Apartments—That night

"Yeah, yeah, I'm coming," Bruce mumbled, heading for the door to his apartment.

The wine bar had closed at seven—no reason to keep it open late on a Wednesday, thanks to the earthquake—and he'd barely been home long enough to take a piss. Then someone pounded on his door, and he'd groaned. All he wanted to do was nuke a frozen burrito and scarf it down.

Bruce opened the door and, without being invited, Tyler came striding in.

The dude looked a bit like the actor who played Kelso from *That '70s Show* reruns. "I got your text. So, what's happening?"

"Ya couldn't text back?" Bruce asked, and closed the door behind him.

"I saw your car. You wanna go shoot some pool?"

Tyler went straight to the refrigerator and helped himself to a cold beer. Again without being invited. Dude was presumptuous. But might as well tell him.

"I'm gonna be rich."

Tyler snorted. "What, are they handing out money for playing video games?"

"Don't be an ass. Remember that camera equipment I bought?"

"Yeah, the spy stuff?"

"Yup. I hid it in this rich guy's private room at the winery, and I caught him on video screwing this girl. And damn, is he twisted. A real pervert." Bruce elbowed Tyler aside and grabbed himself a beer too.

"Bro, let's see it."

"Don't you want to know how much money I'm asking for?"

"Okay, how much?"

"A hundred bitcoins."

"That's not much."

Yeah, Tyler *was* a moron. "You think a cool three and a half million isn't much?"

"Seriously?"

"Really, dude. Don't you keep up? Bitcoins are going for thirty-five thousand apiece now."

When he'd written the note, bitcoins were closer to eleven thousand each. By the time the letter got delivered, the price had skyrocketed, making him one lucky dude.

"You're nuts." Tyler flopped onto the couch and stuck his hand in the potato chip bag lying on the banged-up coffee table, which was a hand-me-down from Grandma. "Who would pay that kind of money for a sex video?"

"Wait until you see it." Bruce started the video on his laptop, then plopped his butt down on the overstuffed recliner and grabbed the chip bag before Tyler ate the whole thing.

A few minutes into the video, Tyler said, "She's hot. How come all the chicks like that go for rich guys?"

"Yeah, but get this—that chick— Well, the old dude is fucking his nephew's fiancée."

"No shit?"

"Just keep watching."

They did. When the old man released the girl's neck, Tyler put his hands over his eyes. "Yuck, that's gross. How can you watch that?"

"Yeah, it is pretty gross. But that's what's gonna make me rich. A sick fuck like that will probably pay any amount to keep this off the internet."

"Screw that. You should put it up on one of those porn pay-per-views. I bet there are other sick pervs who'd pay to see it."

"Wish I'd thought of that sooner." Bruce pushed back on the recliner—another hand-me-down from Grandma—and it went *caa-chunk* as he stretched out. "I'll put it on pay-per-view if the guy doesn't give me the money. But ya know, I think he'll pay."

"Because he's boning the hot girl?"

"More than that. Something bugged me about the blood thing. I've been researching it. I think the guy's a vampire."

"Dude, whatever you're smokin', can I have some too?"

Bruce wadded up and threw the empty chip bag at Tyler. "No, for real. Look, he drinks blood. He's got fangs—did you see those pointed things dripping blood? And he sleeps during the day."

"How do you know that?"

"Just before sunrise, he went to this secret room. No windows. He didn't come back out until after the sun went down."

Bruce had seen Bautista leave on Sunday after it was dark out. His boss's distinctive Viper had been in the parking lot all day.

"Seriously?"

"After I saw the video, I went back and found the room. I tell ya, he's either a vamp or one of those crazy wannabes."

"Who is he? I mean—what makes him so rich?"

"He's one of the co-owners of the winery I work for. His name's Henry Bautista."

"Weird. That name sounds familiar."

"He's, like, this rich playboy who lives in that private community behind the walls—you know, Sierra Escondida."

"No, that's not where I've heard the name."

Tyler screwed up his face like he was thinking. Which had to be a painful event for his friend. Dude was as stupid as the day was long.

"I got it." Tyler snapped his fingers. "It was my uncle who mentioned that name. He was goin' on about something the other day at my parents' house. He was really pissed about somethin'."

"Well, it's Henry who's probably pissed by now. I sent him a copy and a note demanding the bitcoins. Now I have to figure out how to do the swap."

"The swap?"

Bruce scratched his head. "Yeah, where I get the money and give him the only copy of the video."

"You haven't figured that out yet?" Tyler asked.

"No. That's the hard part."

"Got anything else to eat?" Tyler rolled off the couch and headed to the kitchen, carrying the wadded chip bag, and tossed it into the trash like a basketball player at the free throw line. "Three points!"

"Yeah, in your dreams."

"For real, though, ya got something for this winner to eat or what?"

Bruce pushed hard on the footrest, and the lounger folded with a *clunk*. He moved over to the kitchen's breakfast counter. "I got a couple of burritos in the freezer—nuke both, will ya? We'll each have one."

Tyler started the frozen burritos and then leaned his forearms on the breakfast bar, facing Bruce, looking eager. "Ya know, you can't do it in person. That's where the person always gets nailed. I've seen it in the movies before. You need a Swiss bank account. He transfers the money to you, and then you send him the camera disc. I could help."

But Bruce didn't like what he was hearing. He wasn't cutting Tyler in on the action.

"Naw. That's why I asked for bitcoins. Once he transfers those to my anonymous account, I'll give him the video. That's the part of the swap I have to figure out."

"Go to the bus station and rent a locker," Tyler said. "Put the original video in and mail him the key."

"Yeah, but what if he insists on swapping at the same time?"

"Tell him no way. He gets it after you get the money, or else."

"Maybe. I just have to think about this," Bruce said. "Because one way or another, I'm going to get the money from that bloodsucker."

The microwave *dinged*, and Tyler swung around to grab two plates from the cupboard. "Ya know, three and a half million isn't that much money. You should have asked for a billion."

Tyler slid the steaming burritos out of the microwave and snatched back his burned fingers, shoving them in his mouth. Served the freeloader right.

Bruce took his plate from Tyler and used a fork to peel back the steaming wrapper. "Well, even if he pays, I could still put it on one of those dark web pay-per-views. I mean, how would he ever figure it out if I did?"

"Now you're thinking, dude."

Yeah. No reason not to wring every last dollar he could out of the guy's perversion. Then he'd have enough to do what he always wanted to do: start a video game company. But how to get the money out of Bautista? If he thought long enough, he was sure he'd come up with something that'd work.

Chapter 41
A New World

Town hall—The next day

After braving the freeway for the drive from Los Angeles, Christine Dunne arrived midmorning on Thursday and toured the office Nicholas assigned her. It was a short tour, but a nice office.

On one end, there was a large desk and computer terminal. On the other, a round conference table with four chairs. A door by the table opened into a huge walk-in file room with racks of shelves. At a guess, the file room could hold over a hundred boxes of documents. About thirty boxes already occupied the shelves.

Good.

It told her Marcus and Nicholas had worked with outside counsel before. Coming into a new situation, she never knew what to expect.

A small cupboard just inside the closet door held office supplies. Yellow pads, pens, sticky tabs, binder clips, staplers—just about everything they'd need. She liked their attention to detail.

Nicholas took her to the typical break room down the hall from her office, near the restrooms. A stack of menus from local takeout restaurants were in a file folder that sat near the sink. Sodas and snacks were in the refrigerator and the cupboards.

Uh oh. Takeout food and free snacking were a hazard of the job. They put pounds on faster than she could count if she wasn't careful, especially at her age.

She checked the refrigerator, and they had almond milk. Better than those sweetened artificial creamer cups.

And bingo! An espresso machine. Manual. A bag of espresso beans in the freezer, a grinder on the counter. *Perfect.*

"Help yourself to anything," Nicholas said. "I keep a running shopping list when we start to get low—add whatever you need to the list, and I'll have the delivery service pick it up."

"Anything? No one has private stock in here?"

Nicholas laughed. "It's usually just me and Marcus. Marcus swore off coffee and snacks years ago. So you're sharing with me. The town pays for the supplies. Just be sure to write down what you need before we run out. If you have leftover food from lunch or dinner, put your name on the box."

"Those are easy rules. Thanks, Nicholas."

She'd worked in enough guest offices to get the basics, though every business—or public entity—had different twists on their break room culture. "I'll check into my hotel later tonight. Why don't we get started?"

"Works for me." As they left the kitchen, he paused in front of a mirror by the door and carefully scratched around the bandage on his scalp. "Sorry. I got this from the earthquake. Solon landed on me."

"You named a pet after the ancient Greek lawmaker?"

"No, I had his solid marble bust on a tall chest of drawers near my bed. One of our residents carved the bust and gave it to me. I was sleeping when it toppled."

"And you weren't injured worse?"

"I spent a night in the hospital but got lucky—ah, Cerissa—Dr. Patel—was part of the search-and-rescue team. Anyway, the ER doctor shaved the area to stitch the gash. Now my hair is starting to grow in, and it itches."

Christine had noticed the uneven haircut. "I hope your scalp heals quickly."

"Thanks."

Still, it seemed strange that he wasn't more severely injured—a solid marble bust could have cracked his skull.

Back in the office, Nicholas took her through the boxes delivered by the document storage service yesterday. She slipped on her black-framed reading glasses. A few hours later, they were hip-deep in the third box when a pretty young woman with striking green eyes and long coffee-colored hair tapped at the open door.

"Hi, Nicholas." The woman entered the office, rolling a hand truck with four boxes on it. "Here are the files Uncle Henry wanted brought over."

"Super—thanks, Cerissa." Nicholas unloaded the hand truck against the wall. Then he gave her a hug and turned to Christine. "Dr. Cerissa Patel, I want you to meet Christine Dunne."

"It's nice to meet you," Cerissa said, extending her hand.

"It's a pleasure to meet you too. You must be Enrique's fiancée."

"Yes. Although it still feels strange to be introduced that way."

Christine hadn't yet met Henry's nephew and looked closely at Cerissa. She had to be in her twenties, although that was an estimate—it got harder each year for Christine to judge ages. "Enrique is lucky to have such a pretty fiancée."

Nicholas nudged the young woman affectionately. "Yeah, Enrique has an eye for arm candy."

Cerissa rolled her eyes at Nicholas, then turned to Christine. "Please ignore the 'arm candy' comment. I'm a doctor and research scientist."

"That's fantastic." Women had always been professionals, but when Christine went to college, those doors were just beginning to open wider. It was nice to see accomplished women in the current generation of young people. "Henry sent me an email instructing me that I could talk with you or Enrique about the case without violating privilege. He thought you might be able to help."

"I hope I can. I went through the boxes, and I think I found the document you're interested in."

"That's great." Nicholas clapped his hands together, excited. "Where is it?"

Cerissa took the lid off the top box. "Here."

Christine looked at the agreement, Nicholas hanging over her shoulder. So far, she'd only seen a photocopy—they were still looking for the original that was supposed to be in the town's boxes.

The one Cerissa had found was a carbon copy original—the type made by slipping a purple carbon sheet between pages. The carbon copy was still attached to its traditional blue-backed heavy paper cover and typed on onionskin paper using an old IBM Selectric typewriter. Christine recognized the typeface; she'd started practicing law in the 1980s, when such typewriters were used.

She handled the fragile paper carefully, turning the pages so they remained rounded over the two top staples, and didn't crack, crease, or tear them. Typical of the paper, turning the pages emitted a sharp, crisp, crinkling sound. The texture felt both familiar and strange after years of handling the heavier—and quieter—paper used in computer printers.

When she got to the page that held the dispute resolution clause, outlining where the case would be heard if there was a disagreement between the parties, she stopped. It clearly spelled out that disputes would be heard by the local Mordida courts, instead of an arbitrator. She checked the preceding page and the following page, and the words flowed from one to the other and made sense.

She checked the signature page. All four slots were filled in, signed by the representatives of each water company, and their attorneys.

Could Henry's memory be wrong? Perhaps the document never contained an arbitration clause. She rubbed her chin, uncertainty creeping over her.

Yet he'd seemed so adamant.

Then she noticed it. The watermark on the onionskin paper was upside down on the dispute resolution page.

"Do you see it, Nicholas?" Christine asked.

"Ah—see what? The phrasing flows perfectly from one page to the next."

"It's not the phrasing. Look closely at the paper."

"It's just old-fashioned typing paper."

"But with a watermark. A manufacturer's watermark. It's upside down on this page only," Christine pointed out. "And, if I'm correct, slightly different, too. We'll have to check the watermark's date."

Nicholas leaned in closer. "I don't see a date."

She smiled at him. Youngsters were so cute. Raised in the digital age, they didn't have the background to know about this stuff. "You're familiar with computer metadata, right? The properties an electronic file is given?"

"Yeah."

"Back in the day, the paper manufacturers changed their watermark slightly each year. You could tell by the watermark what year the paper was manufactured in. They did it on purpose, to help lawyers in case the integrity of a document was called into question. We'll have to contact the manufacturer to get their date records."

"You think…"

"Yes, I think someone carefully rewrote this page so it fit and used paper from a different year batch. That would explain the dispute resolution provision." She pointed at the massive paragraph. "It's much too wordy for this kind of provision. They had to make up space the arbitration clause had originally filled. But they weren't as careful as the original typist."

She didn't want to take the document apart yet. She wanted the original staples where they were, so no one could question its integrity. Holding the document awkwardly, she compared the upside-down page to the others—the carbon color looked similar enough to the naked eye. They'd need an expert to compare it.

"Whoever typed this probably wasn't used to typing. They put the paper into the typewriter upside down and didn't think to check the manufacturer's watermark to make sure they were using paper from the same year."

"Then we have a claim of fraud?" Cerissa asked.

"Maybe. We'll hire an expert to make sure."

Nicholas nodded. "Do you want me to find one? The board has pre-approved the litigation expenses."

"Please research those in the area. But I want to make the final decision after I see their qualifications." The person they hired was key to winning, and she'd have to defend their expert status to the court. "Let me see their CV before you retain them."

"Got it."

Cerissa frowned. "What happens if you prove fraud?"

"Fraud would vitiate the contract—nullify it. No meeting of the minds. If we have a statute of limitations problem with the fraud claim, we could even argue there was never contract formation in the first place, because of the lack of mutual agreement. Make a note, Nicholas. We'll need to research the statute of limitations."

Her main concern was that a court could rule that, since the document had been in their hands all these years, they should have discovered the fraud before this.

Nicholas wrote "Fraud SOL" on his yellow pad. If the statute of limitations had run—the time in which they had to file a legal complaint—they'd be out of luck on the fraud claim.

Christine continued to think out loud, and Nicholas took notes. "We'll need to get MWC to submit their copy to the expert for analysis. So we'll have to figure out strategically how to release this information." She lowered her reading glasses and glanced Cerissa's way.

Cerissa nodded. "I'll tell Henry, but no one else."

"Good girl. This has to be kept our secret until we figure out how to handle it. I'm thinking we make a demand for arbitration anyway and let them reject it. That will set up our reason for wanting to see their copy of the agreement."

Nicholas picked up the faked page and, studying it, smiled. "Marcus is going to be very pleased."

"I'd say we earned our fees for the morning." Christine sighed, feeling the fatigue catch up with her. "I could use some lunch."

"Let me get the menus and you can write down what you want," Nicholas said, heading for the door.

"Sure." Christine didn't really care which restaurant they ordered from at the moment, as long as she had food. She was too tired to worry about the calories. There would be time to scope out healthier options later.

He returned quickly, and Christine wrote down her order.

"You want anything, Cerissa?" Nicholas asked. "I'm ordering from the deli."

"The one near the winery?"

"Yup."

"Then I'll take a turkey sandwich and an iced tea, please."

"Done deal," Nicholas said, and went to the front office to call it in.

Christine sat back and tapped the pen on her lips. "I wish Henry were up right now. I'd like to talk to him about this."

Cerissa picked up her phone and checked something. "He'll be awake around five fifteen tonight. I'm sure he'll want to talk with you then. Or you could come by the house at seven."

Christine thought carefully about her next comment. "It must be awkward to live in the same house with Henry."

"Pardon?"

"His skin condition. His inability to go out in the sun. He's a day sleeper because of it—you must have to be very quiet during the day."

"Oh, that." Cerissa shrugged. "I've gotten used to it. Enrique has the same problem. Um, it runs in their family, apparently."

"I see." Henry hadn't named the condition, and Christine had meant to research such skin aliments, but ran out of time. "So the condition isn't contagious?"

The judge would want to be reassured about that.

"No." Cerissa's brow furrowed like the question didn't make sense to her.

"Ah, so it's genetic?"

"Something like that."

"It must have struck you as unusual when you first met him."

"Not really. I'm a doctor, and familiar with his condition. He's adapted quite well under the circumstances."

"Sorry about my questions. His illness has limited how we can approach the case, and I was curious about it. He didn't tell me the name of the condition, so I haven't been able to research it myself."

"It's all right, but you should ask him. Doctor-patient confidentiality, you know." Cerissa scrunched her eyebrows and looked at her watch. "I suspect he'll want to talk with you once he's awake, but he may have winery business to take care of first. In the meantime, we should get back to reading through the rest of the documents. Who knows what else we might find?"

Chapter 42

Sorrow

Robles Road—Later that afternoon

Cerissa lost most of the day working with Christine and Nicholas, letting herself get sucked into the hunt for key documents. When they took a break so Christine could check in at her hotel, Cerissa passed on the offer of dinner and took her leave.

She chuckled to herself as the two lawyers tried to arrive at a consensus regarding cuisine. Because of the garlic, Nicholas had nixed Christine's first choice from a Thai restaurant. They ultimately settled on Mexican food to be delivered later.

After saying goodbye, Cerissa hurried to the town center parking lot. She figured she could get back to the lab and still have an hour to work before Henry woke.

Ever since the quake, she'd found it impossible to say no to anyone who asked for her help, and it left her short on time to complete everything. Maybe she should practice saying no to the next person who asked her for a favor.

She had just turned right onto Robles Road when her phone rang. She tapped the call answer symbol on the steering wheel. "Hello?"

Over the car's speakerphone, she heard, "Hi, it's Shayna."

Yacov's widow. Cerissa had been helping Shayna through the grieving process, but after they went to the circus together, her friend had gone to Beverly Hills to visit family, so Shayna avoided the earthquake.

"Are you back?" Cerissa asked.

"I got in yesterday. It was nice to see my family, but they are all so worried about me, it makes me uncomfortable to be there. I just wanted to come home. Besides, I needed to see if my home was habitable after the earthquake."

"Are you there now?"

"Yes, that's why I called. Our house—I mean, my house—is in good shape, if you want to stop by."

"I just left Marcus's office." She couldn't say no to Shayna. She'd start her new resolution with the next person who asked for something. "I'll be there in five minutes."

Shayna greeted Cerissa at the door. The two women hugged, and Shayna led the way into the living room. She had tea set up for the two of them. As she poured from a china pot decorated with violets, she told Cerissa about her trip to Beverly Hills, and Cerissa filled Shayna in on all that had happened since the earthquake.

Shayna looked well, but Cerissa knew looks could be deceiving. "How are you feeling?"

"Some days are better than others. Yacov's death doesn't always seem real, particularly during the daytime." Shayna sighed and took a sip of her tea. "It's easy to forget that he isn't downstairs asleep. But at night, that's when it really hits me that he's gone."

Cerissa's eyes started to mist. "I'm sorry. I can't imagine…"

"I know. Now don't start crying or I'll be doing it too," Shayna said. "And I called you for a reason. I'm trying to figure out what to do about these." Shayna held up a stack of envelopes.

"What are they?"

"Letters of introduction," Shayna said, handing them to Cerissa.

"Letters of introduction?"

"It's all so old-fashioned. Vampires who want to be introduced to me have asked a respected friend or colleague to write a letter introducing them. All of them offer their condolences, and acknowledge it's too soon, but they want me to keep their 'friend' in mind when I do start entertaining offers. It's just too surreal for words." Shayna fiddled with the hem of her blouse, looking lost. "Yacov hasn't been dead two months. I don't know what to do with the letters."

"Perhaps I could ask Henry," Cerissa said, hopeful he would know the protocol. "But more importantly, what do you want?"

"I don't know." Tears formed in Shayna's eyes, and she used her tea napkin to blot them. "This is my home. I know I'm welcome to stay here a year, but I don't want to leave at the end of that year. Still, that's no reason to meet these gentlemen. I don't want to enter into a relationship just to remain in the community. And I'm not ready for anything. I consider it a good day when I can get through without a major cry."

Cerissa leaned over to hug her. "Oh, Shayna."

"It's okay. I know it's part of the process, but sometimes it's hard to keep going. Anyway, I'm definitely in no shape to deal with these kind gentlemen."

"Do you really have to leave after one year?"

"Winston—the mayor—explained that it's possible to get an extension if I really want to stay, even if I haven't started dating another vampire yet. Yacov was so well respected, I have a feeling they'll bend over backward to make an exception."

"I'm sure they will."

Cerissa set down the letters and nibbled on one of the double-fudge cookies Shayna had freshly baked to go with their tea. If she wasn't careful, she'd power down the whole plate, they were so tasty.

"Look, I've got an idea." Cerissa waved the cookie at the letters. "These gentlemen had someone write for them. Why don't I write a response for you? You know, thanking them for their concern and we'll keep you in mind, but don't call us, we'll call you. That sort of thing."

"Would you? I just can't seem to cope with it right now."

"I'd be glad to." She stifled a sigh, adding the correspondence mentally to her overflowing to-do list. "Are there any that you want me to give special attention to?"

"There was one introducing a rabbi from Kiev. Be very respectful to him."

Cerissa flipped through the letters and found the one Shayna was referring to. She opened it and found a picture enclosed. Not bad looking, although a little nerdish. She skimmed the letter. He had become a rabbi after being turned. Interesting.

"According to his letter," Cerissa said when she finished reading, "he's trained his successor and is interested in immigrating to America. It never occurred to me that there would be organized communities in the former Soviet Union."

"They had a harder time surviving under a totalitarian regime, but they did survive." Shayna took a sip of her tea. "Now that Russia is no longer a superpower, and with corruption so widespread, they are able to buy their privacy—they have a small enclave and are left alone."

Cerissa returned the letter to its envelope. "I'll respond to his first. Anything else?"

"Not to do with the letters. But I have something for Henry. Would you take it home to him? It's Yacov's chess set."

"Shayna, are you sure you want to give it away? You have time to decide."

"I can't hang on to everything. I've been setting things aside for Yacov's close friends. And I know he would want Henry to have the chess set. They were chess partners for over a hundred years. It seemed the right choice."

"I'm sure it will mean a lot to Henry to receive the set."

"Then it's settled. And I have something for you, too." Shayna got up and, walking stiffly, went to a bookshelf. She took down a small brown book. "I know you and Yacov met discussing religion. I think he would like it if you had this."

"It looks like a prayer book," Cerissa said.

"You're right. He had several, but this was his favorite."

"Shayna, you should keep this."

"No, I have my own prayer book, and I have others that he used as well. But this one has both the Hebrew and the English versions of the prayers. You start at the back. It opens the reverse of what you're used to."

"Thank you, Shayna. I will treasure it." Cerissa held the book to her heart as she spoke.

"When you come over for Shabbat, or for any of the holidays, bring it with you. You can read the prayers from it."

"I'd be proud to do so. Thank you." Cerissa stood and hugged her friend. "Is there anything else I can help you with? You know that if you ever want company, or just need to talk, all you have to do is call."

"I'll keep that in mind. Right now, I have a full social calendar. Everyone is determined not to let me be alone if I don't want to be. And the theater group made a point of asking me to be involved in the next production. So I'll have things to keep me busy."

"I'm glad your friends are reaching out to you. But I mean it. If you need anything, just call."

"Thanks, Cerissa. It's good to have friends at a time like this. But I just need to work through the grief my own way. I think the hardest part will be clearing out his room. I've left it just the way it was when he died. I want to give his clothes away to the homeless shelter, but I just haven't gotten up the energy yet."

"When you're ready, I can come over and help."

There she was, volunteering again. But this was important.

"We'll see. Thanks for stopping by on such short notice." Shayna picked up a plastic container and slid the rest of the cookies into it. "Take these, too," she said, and walked Cerissa to the door.

Cerissa carefully placed the letters in her purse, accepted the cookies, and carried the chess set and prayer book to her car as if they were precious relics. And in many ways, they were.

But how would Henry feel? She knew he struggled with his own grief over Yacov's death. And right now, he was burdened by the earthquake damage to the winery and the water issues, too.

But she couldn't hide the chess set from him, either. It wasn't right to hide things to protect the ones we love.

She just hoped it didn't upset him too much.

Chapter 43
Metadata

Rancho Bautista del Murciélago—Early evening the same day

Henry swiped to answer the call, smearing a drop of shaving cream on the screen. He bit back an annoyed growl. His beard was only half off, and he didn't welcome the interruption of his evening routine.

"Henry, it's Tig."

He tried his best to sound pleasant. "Good evening, chief. How may I help you?"

"We have an appointment this evening to use the Mordida crime lab's computer expert. Can you meet us there to open the evidence envelope as we agreed?"

Dios, dame paciencia. He did not want to fib to Cerissa again. It was getting harder to stretch the truth. "Must we?"

"Henry, if you want to catch whoever did this, then yes, we must."

"But we have not heard anything more from the blackmailer. Maybe they have forgotten about it."

"They will not forget." Tig huffed loud enough that he heard it. "They may be waiting for something else to happen, something we don't know about. We need to obtain all the information we can now. Our undercover officer from the San Francisco Police Department will begin interviewing your employees over the weekend. Between what we discover about the flash drive, and the fingerprints, we should be able to identify our target."

"Very well. I will meet you in Mordida. How do I get past the blockade?"

"I'll leave your name with the sergeant on duty. Take Robles Road and you'll be fine going and returning. Tonight is the last night of the curfew."

"Thank you."

After Tig hung up, he wiped the phone clean and returned to shaving. He had planned on spending the early evening going over his personal budget. Now, that would be delayed.

He found Cerissa in her basement lab and gave her a kiss, and she immediately returned her attention to the beaker heating over an open flame.

"What is in there?"

"Ah, my first attempt at a topical solution for sun exposure." She measured out a powder on the scale next to her and dumped it into the mix. "Do you mind if we talk later? I got hooked on helping Christine and Nicholas search for documents they needed for the case. But now I'm behind schedule."

"Of course, *cariña*. But I must go into town. Afterward, I have an appointment with the attorney."

"Then I should tell you what she found. She's a smart lady." Cerissa filled him in on Christine's discovery about the onionskin paper. "And before you leave, I have something for you. A few things, actually." She looked over her shoulder at him. "I have a stimulant I want you to try later to see if it will stop you from falling asleep. You should take it right before sunrise."

She handed him a white pouch with a red cross on it. "Stimulant" was handwritten at the top.

He gave a little bow, taking the pouch from her. "Thank you for this."

"And Shayna wanted me to give you something."

She reached for a box on the shelf. He knew that box. He didn't need her to tell him what it was.

Yacov's chess set.

She held it out, and he just stood there.

For a few moments each night, he'd forget that Yacov had been killed. Then it'd come back to him. His mentor and most trusted friend was gone. His guiding light now snuffed out.

Staring at the chess set, he thought of the hours they'd spent together, playing chess and talking into the early hours of the morning. The hours together he would never have again. The great loss of their camaraderie. The great loss of Yacov.

"I— Are you sure Shayna didn't want to keep it?"

Cerissa continued to hold the chess set out to him. "She phoned and asked me to come over for the sole purpose of giving you this and giving Yacov's prayer book to me. I know it's only been nine weeks, but she's sure."

Henry stared at the black box, the nubby texture catching the light, a leather thong hooked around a brass button that held the box together and was worn from repeated use.

He suddenly wished Yacov was still here to discuss the blackmail situation. A selfish wish—if anything, he should be wishing Yacov was still here for Shayna's sake—but a strong wish nonetheless.

"Please, Henry. Take the chess set. She wanted you to have it."

He curled his fingers around the box and then tucked it under his arm. "Thank you, *cariña*. I will send Shayna a thank-you note."

"I'm sure she'll appreciate that." Cerissa averted her eyes. "If you want to play a game, I'm a decent player. Not great…"

Tears pricked his eyes. Cerissa stepped in close, and he took her into his arms, burying his nose into her hair, pressing his lips to her neck.

"I will see you later when I return," he whispered, his voice rough from unshed tears.

He kissed her goodbye, stopped by a crypt and dropped the pouch filled with stimulant-infused blood on the cot—so he wouldn't forget—and then went to the kitchen to grab a self-heating pouch of dark wine for his dinner, taking it upstairs to his office. He put the chess set away, but before he could leave, an email *dinged*. The engineer's structural report.

Finally.

Yes, Tig was expecting him soon, but this was important too. He opened the PDF and scrolled through it, reaching the executive summary. The extensive damage could be corrected, but the price tag was high, estimated at over five hundred thousand dollars.

He didn't have that kind of cash available right now. Was it worth filing an insurance claim? Maybe they should include loss of use and the destroyed wine. That would surely put them above the high deductible amount.

Besides, first come, first served. If the insurance companies went bankrupt, the first in line were more likely to get paid.

He sent off a quick email to Suri with a copy to Rolf. *File an insurance claim. Report the losses. Details to follow later.*

And if the insurance company didn't pay? What would he do then?

It felt like the bottom had fallen out from under him.

Another email popped in with Rolf's reply. *Let's meet tomorrow night at the winery.*

Henry sent back his acceptance. He feared what Rolf would say—they'd have to come up with the money to pay for the repairs even if the insurance didn't cover the damage. But he had no time now to dwell on it. He was late to meet Tig.

He aged himself, since he would be seeing Christine later, and drank another pouch of blood to fuel the change as he walked downstairs.

Cerissa hadn't left any mail on his desk, so on his way out he checked the mailbox and found a plain letter-sized envelope with no return address. His stomach tightened. Turning the envelope over, he started to slide his finger under the flap, and then thought better of it. He would hold off in case it was from the blackmailer and Tig wanted to see it opened.

When he arrived at the crime lab, Tig and Jayden were waiting for him. They introduced him to Ynez, the crime scene tech.

"I think I received something new from the blackmailer." Henry handed the envelope to Tig. "No return address."

Tig examined it and then handed the envelope to Ynez. "Please open it."

Wearing gloves, the forensic tech used a sharp blade to slice the bottom open, not disturbing the sealed flap. "If they licked the envelope to close it, I might be able to lift DNA."

Ynez then unfolded the contents—a one-page letter—and read it out loud. "'You have three more days to purchase one hundred bitcoins. I will send the account number to your email address on Monday ten minutes before sunrise. Pay within five minutes or the video goes on porn pay-per-view.'"

Counting tonight, that left him with four nights to come up with the ransom. Henry scowled at the letter. He didn't have that amount in liquid assets. No one did typically, but at this point, between the earthquake and the winery, his finances were a dumpster fire. He couldn't put the money together even if he wanted to. What was he going to do if they didn't locate the blackmailer?

Tig *tsked*. "Why is the blackmailer sending the account number by email?"

"Maybe he doesn't have a bitcoin account set up yet," Jayden replied. "If this guy's an amateur, he may not have been tech-savvy enough to already have the number when he sent the letter."

"Possibly." Tig focused on the letter. "That, or he thinks giving Henry only ten minutes to transfer the bitcoins buys him extra security." Then she turned and stared at Henry. "How did the blackmailer know sunrise—"

Henry cleared his throat loudly. "We can discuss that later." His phone chimed, and he checked the alarm. "I don't mean to be cavalier about the situation, but that was the reminder that I have a meeting with the SEWC lawyer in thirty minutes."

"We can dust the letter for prints after you leave," Jayden said. "Examining the flash drive shouldn't take long."

Henry watched as the lab tech broke the seal on the evidence bag. Before she could plug the drive into the USB slot, he stopped her, his hand blocking the port on the laptop. "Do not copy the video."

Tig gripped his arm and pulled him back a step. "Don't worry, Henry, she won't copy it. She is just going to examine the file."

Ynez plugged in the drive and opened the file directory. A moment later, she laughed. "What an idiot."

"Why do you say that?" Tig asked.

"The blackmailer named the flash drive 'Lady Killer.'"

"Rats," Jayden said. "So the perp didn't use their real name."

"Yeah, but he just made your job easier. Give me a few minutes, and I'll explain."

Ynez returned to examining the drive, running various programs. After about fifteen minutes, she summed it up. "I'll give you a printout of the information I've been able to get from the flash drive." She picked up a cable and connected the laptop to a nearby printer. "Most of it is technical. But for your purposes, the useful information is the name and serial number."

"Why is that important?" Tig asked.

"If you find the perp's computer, check the registry. I'll give you a program. You can use it to pull up the list of all flash drives by name and serial number that have been plugged into that computer." The tech collected a page from the printer and pointed at a long-string number. "If what you find matches the serial number here, and the name 'Lady Killer,' then you have confirmation, you found the right computer."

"Thank you," Tig said, "you've been most helpful."

Ynez returned the flash drive to its bag, then resealed and signed the evidence log taped to it. "How bad is it? The video?"

Henry sighed. He so didn't want to discuss it with a stranger. "It is a sexual encounter of the standard nature. The person who made it did so covertly."

"That's a terrible thing to do. Revenge porn is the worst. I hope you catch them."

"Do not worry. We will."

Henry added his signature to the evidence bag and left for his other meeting. Clenching his jaw shut as he strode to the parking lot and feeling the muscle bulge, he fisted his hands. Lady Killer would no longer qualify for that title once Henry got through with him.

At some point he'd decided that justice would be his to mete out. He simply wasn't going to tell Tig about his plan.

CHAPTER 44

FIRST IMPRESSIONS

TOWN HALL—LATER THAT NIGHT

Christine stood when they entered her temporary office. She'd seen them both during the videoconference, but now in person, she sized them up quickly.

Henry was taller than Rolf, with more gray in his black hair than Rolf had in his blonde, but then, blondes tended to hide gray better. At fifty-five, Henry looked very good. In comparison, she guessed Rolf was in his late forties. But looks could be deceiving.

"Good evening, Christine," Henry said with an accent.

Between his accent and his facial features, she guessed he was originally from Mexico or Central America. She took his hand when he offered it. A bit cool. Perhaps he had the air conditioning in his car turned up high. After all, it was a warm evening.

"It is nice to meet you in person, Henry," she replied.

"Indeed, it is much preferred to a screen." He gave a smile and a formal nod. Almost a bow.

Cerissa hadn't mentioned whether Henry was married. A good-looking man, but a bit young for her. Still, she liked the way he carried himself with a sense of confidence, and his smile spoke of an old-world charm.

He'd do great on the witness stand.

After shaking her hand, Rolf was curt and down to business. "Shall we?" he asked, checking his watch and then motioning toward the conference table.

Clearly, Henry was the face man of the two.

Marcus—who was younger than the two board members—was already at the table with Nicholas, who seemed a shade younger than Marcus, mainly from his demeanor and occasional use of twenty-something slang.

She grabbed her desk chair, rolling it to the table so there would be enough seats. "We were discussing the estoppel argument just before you arrived," she said as she sat down.

Marcus had been involved in another matter all day, so she had taken him on a deep dive of what she'd learned, lawyer to lawyer, as soon as he arrived at her office.

For the board members, she gave a brief update on the carbon copy contract and what she'd discovered, covering the same material at less depth.

"After Cerissa left, we found a photocopy with only SEWC signatures. It was attached to the file copy of the transmittal letter. It had what Marcus believes to be the original version." She handed copies to Henry and Rolf. "Can you confirm, Henry?"

They took five minutes to review it in silence.

Henry finished first. "Yes, this looks like the original language we used back then."

Rolf grunted. "This is what I was shown when I was appointed to the board."

"With any luck, we should prevail on the fraud claim," she said. "But we have to be ready in case we don't. For that reason, we have to be prepared to defend against MWC's claim that you waived the right to stop their take of the water."

"But it is clearly fraudulent what they did." Henry flapped the photocopy and tossed it disdainfully onto the table.

Marcus laid a hand on Henry's sleeve. "Of course it is. And we're working on finding an expert to testify to the fraud. But we must be prepared on each issue if this goes to trial."

Rolf crossed his arms and leaned back. "That makes sense. But how can they interfere with our right to control the water? We own the water in the aquifer beneath our land."

"Under the English common law rule, you'd be right," Christine said. "The owner of property had absolute control over their groundwater. But not in California."

Henry nodded. "We don't follow English common law because we were once a part of Mexico."

"Close, but not quite." Christine thought for a moment. How to explain this to her clients without sounding condescending? "You have rights in the water, but you don't own it."

Rolf's brow furrowed. "If we don't own it, how could we have sold it to Mordida?"

"You didn't sell the water—you sold the right to use it. Water law in California grew out of the gold rush days, in response to miners' claims on water near their mines. So the owner of property has certain rights in the water that lies underneath their property, assuming they haven't relinquished them by deed."

She collected the two copies of the contract from where Henry and Rolf dropped them on the table. She didn't want them leaked to MWC prematurely.

"In your case," she continued, "a trust owns all the land, and gave its rights to the Sierra Escondida Water Company, but that doesn't change things for the purpose of my explanation."

She slowly turned as she spoke, making eye contact with each person at the table to make sure no one had glazed over. This stuff could make the best lawyer fall asleep.

"So, you have the right to take the water out of the ground and use it, provided you put it to a reasonable and beneficial use. But you don't own the water itself. Instead, you have a property right to *use* the water that is part of the rights you purchased when you bought your land."

She picked up a container of bottled water that she'd been drinking from. "When you package water, separate it from the land and put it in a container like this, then it becomes personal property and can be owned. But not while it's still underground."

Henry scowled. Was she losing him? He seemed bright enough, but it was a lot to take in. Or perhaps he was unhappy about the reality of the law.

She waited a moment, but no one spoke, so she continued. "Now, the water that you don't reasonably need for a beneficial use, well, that water is called surplus water."

"*Ja, ja.* But we will no longer have surplus," Rolf said.

Was his accent German or Eastern European? She had a friend from Germany whose accent sounded harsher—more of a percussive "ch" sound than Rolf spoke with—but that could be attributed to regional differences.

"Correct, there isn't enough water to go around. Even with a contract provision like you have—one that would allow you to stop their take of water—a court could conclude that they are still entitled to a proportionate share based on their current reasonable and beneficial need for the water."

"Even with the contract provision?" Henry asked, his voice rising in disbelief.

"Yes, and here's the problem that you face then: courts view domestic use as having priority over agricultural use. Mordida is using the water for domestic use. You want to use it for agricultural. In a battle between the two, they will win by priority."

"But that's not fair." Rolf pounded his fist on the table. "We own the water."

Boy, he's excitable. She'd have to watch out for that when he took the stand.

For now, she'd see if he responded to reason. "I understand why you feel that way, but you don't own the water. You own the right to use the water. And you also gave Mordida a right to use the water by contract."

"But we were here first," Henry said.

"Precisely. You established your use of the water for agriculture first. You have the right to that continued use. But you sold a part of your right to *use* the water on an annual basis. That is what we are trying to terminate. The good news is that they can't claim a right to the water that's separate from the contract because you've always granted them the right to use the water."

Marcus nodded. Of course he would understand immediately what she was alluding to. "You mean," Marcus said, "because of our contract, they can't claim a prescriptive right."

"Correct. If we prove the contract is void because of their fraud, they could then try to claim they acquired an adverse right to the water over time, what's called a prescriptive right. I don't think they'd get very far with that, because of their own fraud. It's as if they are saying to the judge,

'Yes, we cheated, and we should be able to benefit from cheating the Hill.'"

"That is right, they cheated," Rolf said with a scoff.

"And no judge in equity is going to reward them for defrauding you. Besides, they used the water under the pretense that you had granted them a contractual right to do so, they weren't claiming they had an independent right to it, so that's another reason their prescriptive claim would fail. But we're in a better position if we get the contract voided completely and terminate any contractual claim they have for the water."

Henry nodded. "If we do not, though, what of their argument that we waived our termination clause? That is what started this mess, is it not?"

Good. He'd been following her clearly.

"The waiver issue," she continued, "is a highly technical argument, and I won't bore you with it. Suffice it to say that they'll be able to withstand summary judgment—that means we'll have to hold a trial and prove that you haven't waived the termination clause. But again, if we prove fraud, we never get to the waiver argument."

"I see," Henry said. "Why did you want to speak with us tonight?"

"We should put together a settlement offer. I know you aren't happy with MWC right now, but we should be prepared to put the best offer we can on the table to keep us out of court."

CHRISTINE'S TEMPORARY OFFICE—MOMENTS LATER

Henry understood most of what Christine had said—he'd been involved on SEWC's board for over a hundred years and discussed such matters enough times with Marcus. And he himself had lived through the water wars. At a real-world level, he knew this battle better than the lawyers, even if he didn't always use the same terms they did to describe it.

He even understood why Christine was suggesting a settlement proposal.

It was partly his fault. His insistence that they stay out of court had made an impression on her.

"Christine, do you think you can convince the court to hold its hearings at night? Marcus tells me that courts will accommodate a disability."

"I think we have a good shot at it, at least when you need to testify. The rest of the hearings would probably be during the day."

Henry leaned back in his chair and considered the matter. Although he'd prefer to be present for the entire trial, he could live with that resolution.

"In that case, I do not see any reason to make a settlement offer. MWC is not entitled to the water. I will not give in to blackmailers."

He felt rather strongly about that—especially after what he was going through with that scurrilous video.

"Blackmailers? That's an interesting way to put it." Christine crossed her arms. "Are you sure you don't want me to draft a settlement proposal, just in case?"

"I am certain." Henry gave a polite nod. "Wait for them to come to you. They should be the first to blink."

Rolf tapped a finger on the table. "Henry's right. We have the better poker hand. We just need to show them how bad their hand is, and they'll be more reasonable."

"You're the client." Christine shrugged. "I just wanted to make sure we explored the option."

"Thank you." Henry stood. "We appreciate your thoroughness. But the one thing Rolf and I know well is how to negotiate, and in this case, we will let them crawl to us."

CHAPTER 45

THE PERFECTIONIST

HILL CHAPEL—LATER THAT NIGHT

Marcus strolled along the pathway, briefly admiring the river-stone chapel as he did so. It was a miracle that the old mortar and stone building had survived the earthquake with minimal damage.

As he headed to the more modern buildings located behind the Hill

Chapel, which included Father Matt's office, Marcus squeezed Nicholas's hand affectionately.

I'm so fortunate he's all right.

Marcus no longer cared what Cerissa was. Her quick thinking had saved Nicholas, and for that, he'd be eternally thankful.

Gratitude. Before the quake, the word had never been meaningful to him. Now, his gratitude that Nicholas had survived filled him with happiness. As they reached Father Matt's door, the pleasant warmth in Marcus's chest increased.

It hadn't always been like that. His initial reaction to the counseling sessions with Nicholas had been a cross between trepidation and shame—like he was a child being taken to the headmaster for a whipping.

That was no longer the case. The office didn't feel like a place of punishment anymore. It was a greenhouse where the emotions he'd long buried could flower.

Once they were inside and seated comfortably, Father Matt asked, "How are you feeling, Nicholas? I heard you spent a night in the hospital."

"One hundred percent better."

"Good to hear. Then let us begin with the same question I've asked at the start of each session: what is your goal today? Do you want to work toward rebuilding your relationship, or do you want to work toward saying goodbye?"

They were no longer taking opposite ends of the couch—Nicholas sat close to Marcus, their hips touching, their hands resting on each other's thighs. Looking at his partner with all the love he felt, Marcus waited for Nicholas to go first, watching the chiseled cheekbones and sensuous lips of his mate as he spoke.

"I want to rebuild."

"And you, Marcus?"

"I want to rebuild."

"Very good." The gentle smile on Matt's face reassured Marcus. They were going in the right direction. "Before we get to your trust journals, is there anything you want to talk about?"

"Ah," Nicholas began, with a glance at Marcus, "Ari is sleeping with Gaea."

Marcus held his tongue. Matt already knew about Gaea and Ari. The council notified him when Gaea took over the loyalty bite. But Marcus stayed silent. He'd learned to let Nicholas finish what he had to say before jumping into the conversation.

Matt adjusted his wireframe glasses. "How does that make you feel, knowing Ari is with Gaea now?"

Nicholas's eyes brightened. "It makes me feel great."

"Why do you think that is?"

"If he's with Gaea, he'll quit sniffing around Marcus."

"So it makes you feel more certain in your relationship with Marcus?"

"Yeah." Nicholas squeezed Marcus's hand. "It feels more final. That he won't be back."

"It sounds as if you still don't trust Marcus."

"I'm beginning to. I just—I just feel better knowing the temptation is gone."

"That's entirely understandable, but it also means we have more work to do on rebuilding the trust between you. Does that make sense to you?"

"Yeah, I guess."

"Marcus, hearing Nicholas's reaction, how do you feel?"

"I hope to earn his full trust. I wish I had it now, but I understand."

"Is there anything you want to tell Nicholas?"

Marcus turned to face his partner. "Ari is no threat to you. No one is. I love you, and I'll do whatever I have to do to rebuild your trust in me."

"Nicholas?" Matt prompted.

"We're not there yet, but I hope we get there too."

"All right. Now, Marcus, is there anything you want to raise before we start discussing your trust journals?"

"We've had to cancel a few sessions—"

"Understandable. The aftermath of the quake has kept everyone busy."

"I'm feeling sucked back into the stress of the job—being the person everyone relies upon to fix their problems."

When Marcus paused, Father Matt nodded. "Go on."

"I'm afraid. Afraid I'll lose control over the council and something bad will happen. Afraid that I'll do something stupid in the name of saving the Hill."

"Okay, we've touched a bit on this already. It sounds as if you're codependent with your job."

"I beg your pardon?"

"You see your well-being as intricately tied with the Hill. Have you ever considered your boundaries?"

Marcus scrubbed a hand over his face. Sometimes Matt's jargon was a bit too much to take in. "I'm still not tracking…"

"Where you stop, and the town begins."

"I— No."

"Marcus, when was the last time you took a break from being town attorney?"

"After the war treaty was signed in the early seventies, I took six months to get my personal business in order and make arrangements for my next identity to pass the bar. By the time I returned, the newly elected council had started adopting all sorts of ridiculous laws."

Matt nodded. "I arrived in the community a few years after that. If I recall, you were able to undo those laws when you returned."

"Yes, but the stress, the fear I couldn't—it ate at me."

"Hmm, it sounds like you could use a second resident lawyer to trade off with—to give you a break."

That was the same thing Nicholas said last week before the earthquake. But it was a pipe dream. The Hill's survival relied on a careful balance between the interests of the vintners and the interests of the residents in other occupations. How could he ever find someone he could trust enough to hand over the reins to?

An image of Christine suddenly popped into his mind. She had the legal background, certainly, along with a track record of competency and litigation wins. But it was too soon—much too soon to consider her. He barely knew her. And yet…that didn't mean he couldn't observe and evaluate her with the possibility in mind.

He pushed the idea away for the moment and came back to the heart of the issue. "No one will do as good a job as I do." Especially not a mortal who didn't yet know about vampires. "I don't see a way around it."

"I think his trust issues are getting in the way," Nicholas said.

Marcus remained silent, unable to confidently argue against the point.

"Could it also be an issue of perfection versus what's good enough?" Matt asked.

"He's definitely a perfectionist." Nicholas chuckled. "It's why we all call him the legal wizard."

Marcus couldn't deny the truth. "I am a perfectionist, but I think the perfectionism isn't the problem—it serves me too well. It makes sure nothing destroys my way of life here."

"Perfectionism is a heavy burden to carry."

"Perhaps, but without me and my perfectionism, I don't know if this community would have survived this long."

Matt nodded. "That's a lot to unpack. You've made a good start bringing it up. I'm happy to meet with you individually if you want to work on this issue more intensely. Now, we have about twenty minutes left to your joint session. Is this a good place to pause Marcus's issue and move on to your trust-building work?"

Marcus nodded. The way Nicholas looked over to him, to get his response first, was so endearing. That in itself showed him how much work they'd accomplished on trust.

As to his more personal issues over being town attorney, and his desperate need for a break, well, he may take Matt up on the offer to talk more about it—later. Right now, adding anything more to his calendar was impossible. Not with the water issue breathing down his neck.

Maybe when that was resolved, he'd be able to take a vacation and figure it out.

Chapter 46

Tricking the Sun

Rancho Bautista del Murciélago—Shortly before dawn on Friday

At six fifty in the morning, Henry let Cerissa walk him to his crypt. It felt odd, given that normally he refused to let her be present when he fell asleep. But she wanted to be there when he tried the stimulant, and so after he returned home from the winery, he woke her, per her request.

"Oh, I meant to tell you." She rubbed the sleep from her eyes and yawned. "I used the credit card you gave me."

"That is good, *cariña*," he replied, even as he clamped down on the crystal's connection to hide the anxiety blooming in his chest.

He didn't want Cerissa to pick up on his reaction. After all, he had told her to use the card. He couldn't begrudge that she did so, no matter how tight his finances were.

Besides, he'd seen her personal credit card statements. She hardly spent anything.

She followed him down the stairs to the basement. "I needed more equipment for the basement lab, and between helping the circus performers, and then Nicholas, my supplies were starting to run low. And I bought a machine that will encapsulate vampire blood faster."

"I see. How much did you spend?"

"Well, the compounds I use to make the encapsulations aren't exactly cheap. I would have used my credit card, except the machine's cost exceeded my current credit limit, and I had to charge it, so I used the card you gave me. But if it's too much, I can pay you back."

"How much, *cariña*?"

"I don't remember the exact amount."

"*Cariña.*"

They were passing her lab door. "Let me get the invoice."

She jetted into her lab and returned, handing it to him. He glanced at the bottom of the page.

"Twenty-five thousand dollars!" he said, his voice rising.

"Yes. I also needed chemicals and equipment I didn't have before that might help with the sunlight problem. All of it costs money. And I can take only so much from the Enclave without the Protectors noticing."

"I understand. I just didn't think—"

"If it's too much, I can get an advance from Leopold. The business will ultimately benefit from the work I'm doing. There's no need for you to finance these expenses..."

Henry's mind was spinning. How would he pay a bill this size with his finances in disarray? Credit card interest rates were astronomical. He'd always paid off his cards at the end of the month. Until now.

Cerissa was still speaking. "...really. I shouldn't have charged it on your card. I'll talk to Leopold."

"No." The idea of letting her pay, after he'd given her the cards and insisted she use them, shot feelings of inadequacy through him. "I told you to charge your expenses to the credit card, and you did. I won't go back on my word."

"But Henry, you're upset. I can tell. It's too much money. I'll pay the credit card bill."

"No, you will not." He unlocked the crypt door and opened it so she could enter first. "You are doing this research for me. I will pay for your supplies."

"But Henry—"

"No. I told you I would pay, and I will. I do not go back on my word."

"Something's wrong. Something more than the water. What is it?"

"It is none of your business."

"Henry!"

"I'm sorry." He scrubbed a hand across his face. "Of course it's your business. But now is not the time to discuss it. I'm about to go to sleep for the day—"

"Not if this works," she said, picking up the white pouch with a red cross from where he'd left it on his cot.

He slumped onto the cot, his shoulders drooping. The one thing he could always count on was a restful sleep. And now, he'd be up all day, trapped in the house with the blinds shut.

Cerissa could read the anxiety in his posture. And his harsh response—he'd never spoken to her that way before. What was going on? Was it simply all the stress they were under?

She produced the coffee mug she'd carried with her, opened the pouch, and poured in the medicated blood. "Even if this works, we can't do it too often. It's the strongest stimulant I can give a human, and it killed the clone."

"I am sorry to hear that."

"I have another batch of clones incubating, so I'll be able to replace it in a few months. But they use a lot of resources to grow to the point they are useful, so I hate losing even one." She handed him the mug. "If this works, it will be worth it. Bottoms up."

He gave her side-eye and pointed at the doorway. "You should go stand over there. We don't know how this will affect me."

It was so cute how he felt like he had to protect her. Even though it wasn't necessary, she complied with his request and stopped in the doorway to lean against the frame and yawn again. The Lux may need less sleep, but even for her, dawn was too early to be up.

Henry took a deep drink from the mug and shivered. "Yes, I can feel it."

He squeezed his eyelids shut, only to open them very wide and look her way. His pupils were blown out.

Good. That was the reaction she was hoping for.

"I do not like this feeling." His grip on the mug had turned his knuckles white. "It feels like ants under my skin."

"Go on, finish it. I want to make sure we give this all the chance we can to succeed."

He leaned against the wall behind him, and then sat erect, vacillating like he couldn't get comfortable. His knee bounced a mile a minute, and he gulped the rest of the mug. Then he looked up at her. "If this doesn't work, you'll leave immediately, as agreed?"

"Yes, Quique." She held out her phone so she could split her vision between watching him keep his eyes open and watching her phone, which was counting down the seconds to sunrise.

Five, four, three...

"This is not very pleasant." Still holding the mug, he ran his free hand over one arm as if trying to warm himself. "I really do not like—"

Her phone announced sunrise, and he flopped back, banging his head against the wall.

She raced to his side and shook his arm. "Henry, stay awake!"

His eyelids opened once, then fell shut again.

She tried for another minute or so but couldn't rouse him.

She sighed in disappointment.

Well, that was a failure.

Nothing left to do but put him to bed.

His fingers still gripped the mug. With a little effort, she unwound them, and then gently guided his head back to the pillow and lifted his legs until he was stretched out on his back.

She placed his hands flat on his stomach, the way he normally slept. Why he always lay that way slightly bothered her—he looked like a posed corpse.

Shrugging to herself, she took the mug and locked the crypt door before climbing the stairs to the kitchen.

Back to the drawing board.

Hmm. Maybe she was trying too hard. Tomorrow night, they would try the adrenaline-enhanced blood that Rolf drank. Maybe a more organic solution would work to keep Henry awake. The clones' own bodies produced the stimulant in response to stress—maybe drinking a sufficient quantity would do the trick.

She hoped so. Because she was running out of ideas.

Still, she had two problems to solve if Henry was going to testify during the day, and for the second one, she had a different guinea pig in mind.

Chapter 47
A Bit of Help

MIAMI BEACH, FLORIDA—TEN MINUTES LATER

A quick exchange of texts confirmed Ari had flashed back to his Florida home for the day. As soon as Cerissa transported to the backyard dock of his sprawling one-story house, it was as if she was walking through water. The air felt heavier in South Beach than in Sierra Escondida, thanks to the high humidity.

"Ciss!" Ari called out, jumping up on the dock from the boat he had tethered there. He grabbed her in a bear hug, twirling her off her feet. "This is a welcome surprise."

"I need to talk."

"Of course you do. I was just heading out for breakfast. Let's go." He led her away from the dock and through the patio, opening the sliding glass door, past the living room and the entryway, and out on to the street. At close to ten in the morning local time, it wasn't too hot yet, and they walked the three blocks to a restaurant that guaranteed genuine Southern cooking—at least, according to the sign out front.

Delicious smells of sugary baked goods and fried bacon infused the air the minute she walked in. A friendly waitress greeted Ari by name and got them seated quickly.

"So, what are you hungry for?" he asked, not bothering to open the menu.

"I don't know. Why don't you order and surprise me?"

"Don't tell me you let Henry pick what you eat? That's so old school."

"No, he doesn't select my food for me. Well, not really," she said, lowering her voice. "Not unless he wants my blood seasoned a certain way."

"Do tell. So what you eat matters?"

"Yes. Anyway, I just thought you might order for me because I don't know Southern cuisine that well. I wouldn't know what to try. But if you're going to be a shit about it..." She opened the menu, propping it between them.

"Touchy, touchy," he said. "I'll be happy to order for you. Hey, Benita." He stopped the waitress as she tried to breeze by. "How about taking our order before we starve to death?"

Benita took out her pad and pen. "The way you eat, honey chile, that will never happen."

"It's all your fault. I eat so much just to have an excuse to see the most beautiful waitress in this city."

She tapped her pen against the pad. "Sugar, they sell that by the pound where I come from."

"Well, in that case, can we talk about food? My cousin here will have the eggs and chicken-fried steak, with grits. I'll have the Cajun omelet, and we'll both have a basket of corn fritters—and throw in some calas, too. Plenty of honey butter to go with that."

"How does your *cousin* want her eggs?" Benita asked.

"Ciss?"

"Scrambled, please."

"Coffee?"

"I'll have iced tea."

"Coffee for me," Ari said. "So, when do you get off work?"

"Keep that up and you'll be in a mess of trouble with my boyfriend."

"Now you've gone and broken my heart, Benita."

Tilting her head in Cerissa's direction, Benita asked, "How do you put up with him?"

Cerissa smiled. "He's family. You know how that is."

"I surely do." Benita stuck the pen behind her ear and walked off toward the kitchen.

"You're an incurable flirt, Ari."

"Yes, but it keeps me occupied on this little backwater planet." He leaned against the booth's cushion and stretched. "You know, there's a story they tell about a guy who would walk down the beach and ask each woman he met if she wanted to go to bed with him. Nine times out of ten, they'd say no. But all he needed was for the tenth one to say yes. It's a matter of playing the odds, Ciss."

She rolled her eyes. Gaea better not catch wind of his shenanigans. "I wish you well with your adventures."

"And how goes it with your little experiment? Still happy with Henry?"

"Yes, although a lot has happened lately." She filled him in on the dispute over water rights. "Change of topic. I know you're more into computers than biological sciences, but you have some science background. I'm trying to figure how to approach a research project."

"Okay, what do you have in mind?" he asked, as Benita arrived with their order.

Cerissa held her response until the dishes were on the table and Benita was out of earshot again. "One of the problems Henry faces with the lawsuit is the courtroom. He and Rolf may have to testify. If court is held during the day, he can't do that. If I could come up with something—either a topical or oral medication—that protects him from the sun, it'd help."

She paused to take a bite of the chicken-fried steak. "Umm, this is good."

"Try some pepper sauce on your eggs." He handed her the bottle.

She sprinkled some on. "Anyway, I've gotten access to the few research reports there are on vampires. Commercial sunscreens don't work."

"Research reports written by vamps? You go, girl. How'd you get that?"

"I'm working on a problem for a client of Father Matt's, and he got me access to their secret online magazine called *Living from Dusk to Dawn*."

"What does Henry think of your goal?"

"He encouraged me to do the research." She took a bite of the eggs with hot sauce then quickly reached for her iced tea and drank it down. The label should have rated the sauce a ten-alarm fire.

Ari grabbed a corn fritter and then held out the basket to her. "One of these will help with the flames."

"Thanks," she said, spreading honey butter on it and then taking a bite. He was right. The fritter counteracted the pepper sauce, too.

"Back to your other problem." Ari scrunched his lips together, looking puzzled. "I'm surprised Henry wasn't concerned about the greater ramifications."

"Like what?"

"Like, how it might reveal what you are, that you're—"

He stopped abruptly when Benita came by to refill Cerissa's iced tea.

She took advantage of the break to think through Ari's concerns. She couldn't see how her research might reveal her Lux origins. Sure, if the fix required gene surgery, she could see how revealing that *technology* would put them at risk of being found out—the Lux were years ahead of humans. While humans had the ability to take a bacteria, edit the genetic structure to supercharge it, and release it on the populace, the Lux were much more proficient and subtle with gene surgery.

But even if the fix required her to make a change at the genetic level, there was no reason to believe she'd be found out. No one else in the vampire communities was doing the kind of research she was. They wouldn't examine her work to deconstruct it.

Once Benita finished refilling their drinks, Ari devoured a corn fritter and reached for a cala. The rice fritter was dusted with powdered sugar. As he ate it, he licked the sugar off his fingers. "You know, if you keep fixing every problem, they might start suspecting you. Marcus did."

"He doesn't anymore. Henry took care of that problem."

"Whatever you say—"

"Let's get back to how you would approach the problem."

"Have you tried different light spectrum filters? Perhaps a certain wavelength causes the reaction?"

"It doesn't matter, as long as the skin is exposed to real sunlight. Father Matt told me sunlamps produce no reaction—he even recommends daylight spectrum lights for his clients with depression. It must be something unique about the sun itself, but that makes no scientific sense."

"There could be another explanation." Ari took another big, sloppy bite of his omelet. Lowering his voice, he added, "Vampires may be outside the laws of physical nature."

"If you're suggesting once again that they're 'supernatural,' you know better. Vampires are a Lux genetic experiment gone wrong."

"That's my point. Who knows? If we're supernatural, and vamps are made from our genetic material, then, *ipso facto*, they are supernatural."

"Oh, Ari." She felt a headache coming on. Talking to him frequently did that to her.

"Hey, if I'm right, they aren't truly alive. The soul of the real Henry Bautista may not inhabit that body. It may have fled when the body died. The entity you call 'Henry' may just be a dead body reanimated by a demon, kept alive by human blood. Mortal mythology says demons are afraid of the light, you know."

"That's a terrible thing to suggest. You've spent way too much time in the era when humans believed in all that superstitious junk. Besides, Henry makes very moral choices about how he lives his life."

"Even in theological terms, demons have free will. Nothing stops a demon from cutting ties with evil and living a moral life."

"Ari, that's just ridiculous. Henry has memories of being human. Look at Marcus—he was a lawyer and retained that knowledge after being turned."

"So?"

"He's a lawyer, not a demon."

"There's a difference?"

"Very funny. I'll tell him you said that next time I see him."

"He likes lawyer jokes—so be my guest."

"Can we get back to my original question?"

He took another big bite of his omelet and shoved it down with another corn fritter, but had the decency to swallow before he continued. "Okay, kiddo, here's my point: there may be no 'laws of nature' that apply to guide you in constructing a theory for protecting him from daylight. It may just be magic."

"'Magic' is the word humans use when they haven't figured out the real explanation yet." She finished off the last of her eggs and chicken-fried steak. "Besides, there are certain 'laws of nature' that apply universally to all vampires. In addition to sunlight, they all react badly to garlic and silver."

"True. But there might not be a scientifically verifiable explanation for those patterns."

"Well, if there isn't, then there's no harm in my trying. But I'm absolutely frustrated. If I only had the prototype's genome, then I could run comparisons to Henry's DNA—"

"When you turn in your next report to the Protectors, include what you're working on and indicate that it would help if you had the original genome."

"Yeah, sure. I might as well walk up to Agathe and confess that I broke into the library and read the original Ninevah journal."

He reached across the table and rapped his knuckles on her head.

"Hey!" She sat back and rubbed her forehead. "Why'd you do that?"

"Sometimes I wonder about you. Be subtle. Get the point across that you wish you had the original vampire to test, not that you suspect the Lux might actually have a sample."

"Fine. But I have to do something to help Henry—not being able to go out in the daylight really puts him at a disadvantage in the lawsuit."

"Cerissa, don't take this the wrong way, but that's Henry's problem, not yours."

"As you pointed out, he's my fiancé. Of course it's my problem."

"Nuh uh. I see you have yet to learn an important relationship lesson. Being a couple doesn't mean you should solve his problems, and it doesn't mean he should solve yours. Sure, you share your problems with each other, but at a certain point, you have to let go."

"I still don't get where you come off giving relationship advice, considering your lifestyle."

"I know things." He waggled his fingers at her. "And there's a fine line between caring and thinking that you have to take care of all of Henry's problems. It's not healthy."

"And what do you know about healthy relationships?"

He laughed and flagged down Benita to pay the check. "I wondered when you were going to ask."

"Ask what?"

"Come on, you have to be dying to know. Go on."

Busted. Yes, she did want to ask about Gaea. She raised her iced tea glass to cover her blush and took a long, cooling drink.

"All right." She set the glass on the table. "What is it with you and Gaea?"

"Ah ha! I knew you had another reason for coming here today."

"Ari—"

"Gaea's filed with the council for permission to continue seeing me casually, and to take over the bite bond from Father Matt, without becoming mates. She's just not ready for that—but some consolation sex is definitely on the table."

Cerissa's protective feelings over Gaea warred with her recognition that the six-hundred-year-old vampire could take care of herself—even against Ari's whimsies. "You better be right. If you hurt Gaea, I swear—"

"Don't worry about that. She won't let me hurt her. On the other hand, the lady swings a mean hairbrush."

Cerissa did not want to hear any more about him and Gaea's hairbrush. Last thing she needed was another giggle fit.

"That's it." She pushed to her feet. "I'm going home."

"No, you aren't."

Crap, he was right. She still needed his help to test her latest batch of vampire sun protection. She dropped back onto the booth's bench.

"But speaking of home"—he paused to polish off his coffee—"I've rented an apartment in Mordida. Easier to convince Gaea to let me go home to sleep but be around when I want to."

She couldn't believe it. "Of all the… Ari, the council watched me like a hawk, and they refused to let me take an apartment in Mordida. What makes you think they're going to let you?"

"Hey, second children aren't watched as closely. You broke the ground, and I get to capitalize on it."

"Quit gloating."

He slid out of the booth, still smirking. "Let's get out of here. I want to go for a swim—in the Everglades." He grabbed her hand and led her out of the restaurant.

She tried to keep up with the fast pace he set. "The Everglades? How do you swim in a swamp?"

"Easy, if you're an alligator."

Oh, this again.

Staying here for the day would eat up a chunk of time she could have spent researching Henry's problem. On the other hand, staying here would take her away from any aftershocks for most of the day. And she did have that test she wanted to run on Ari…

They arrived back at his house, where his Pontiac Firebird beater was parked at the curb—the car was over twenty years old—and he opened the door for her. "Ever morph into a gator?"

"Can't say that I have." She brushed the sand out of the front seat and got in.

"Then you are in for a treat. Scaring the tourists is *fun*. And it will be just the thing to get you out of that overactive brain of yours. Gators don't think that much. Their brains are about the size of a walnut. The deepest thought you'll have as a gator is wondering if something's edible."

"Why am I not surprised that's the reason you like becoming one?"

"Just try not to eat any dogs or cats. Humans get really upset if you chow down on their pets. 'Gator's got my dog' is usually followed by the blast of a shotgun. So be careful."

"Ari, you're really terrible sometimes."

"True, but I do have fun."

Chapter 48

Walnut Brain

SOUTH BEACH, FLORIDA—LATER THAT AFTERNOON

Cerissa used the shower at Ari's house to clean up, then hurried to get dressed. Time meant nothing to an alligator, and the day had escaped her.

Ari wasn't lying when he said alligators weren't deep thinkers. Except for the driving need to eat, very little had flowed through her mind. And since she started the day with about a thousand more calories than she needed, thanks to the breakfast Ari ordered, she wasn't inclined to accept the raw chicken handouts from the tour guides, which had the fishy smell of meat months past its expiration date.

All in all, she had given her brain a nice rest for the day—something she'd needed. She hadn't realized how much anxiety she'd been holding in her body until she'd morphed back to human. It almost felt like everything reset. Almost.

Then the worries started pressing down on her again.

"Hey," she said, emerging from the hallway into Ari's computer workroom, which would be a family room in any normal household. He sat at his desk, which looked like a NASA command station, with multiple monitors and two keyboards. And, of course, the kitchen refrigerator was only ten steps beyond his chair.

Typical Ari.

"Before I leave, can you help me with something?"

"What's that, sweet cheeks?"

"Well, I've created a super sunblock mixture. I wanted to test it on you."

"You want me to morph into a vampire and go out in the sun. Are you crazy?"

If anyone in their family was crazy, it was Ari. "Not all of you"—she waved at him dismissively—"just part of your arm. We slather on my formula, stick your hand outside, and see what happens."

"And why aren't you doing this with Henry?"

"I don't know what might happen if it doesn't work. He could die. I'm not taking that risk."

Ari got bug-eyed. "But I'm disposable?"

"No. You'll be able to morph before anything really bad happens."

"Why don't you test it on yourself? You can morph too."

"I need to be able to observe the effect." She smirked at him. "Can't do that if I'm the test subject."

"You're putting a lot of faith in my morphing abilities."

"Come on, Ari. You know it can't permanently injure you."

"If I do this, you owe me big time."

"Sure, whatever. Like I haven't already done you enough favors to last a lifetime. I mean, have I yet to tease you about Gaea—"

"Damn, girl. I wondered when you'd get back to that."

"Well, I don't have to go there if you'll just morph."

Ari took a deep inhale and huffed it out. He led the way to the living room and closed all the blinds. Moments later, he was vampire.

He yawned and plopped down on the couch. "All I want to do is fall asleep."

She pulled him to his feet. "No falling asleep. Keep those eyes open."

"Yeah, yeah, nag, nag. What is it you want me to put on?"

Cerissa took a jar out of her purse and unscrewed the lid. Dipping her fingers into the mixture, she spread it on Ari's hand. The thick white layer, with a base of zinc oxide and a mixture of UV-blocking chemicals, filled every pore. She stepped back. "Let's try that."

"This isn't practical, even if it works." He flexed his hand. "It's like being covered in greasy goo. If I touch anything, it'll rub off."

"I want to start with the thickest application and work backward from there until we find the bare minimum that works."

"Okay, I get it. So how do we do this?"

"If you'll stand against the wall and slip your hand between the blinds and the window, it should limit the exposure."

He leaned back, closing his eyes and yawning again.

Cerissa lifted the blinds to make space. "Now. Stick your hand out."

Ari did. A split second later, he yowled. "What the everlovin' fu—"

"Let me see."

Ari yanked his hand back from the window. His skin was covered in big red blisters pushing through the white film. "That hurt like a son-of-a-bitch."

She took a quick photo of his skin for her records, then lifted his arm to examine it more closely.

"Ow." He jerked his hand out of hers and morphed.

"See, you're fine."

"Except for the memory of being fried. I'll be forever emotionally scarred."

"When you get done feeling sorry for yourself, think about someone else for a moment. The mix didn't work. That means I don't have a solution for Henry's problem."

"Oh. Sorry, kid. I know it was important to you. I'm happy to suffer a little pain for the cause."

"Good. Because if I come up with any new ideas, I'm heading back here to try them on you." She tapped her watch to flash home before Ari could refuse. When it came right down to it, no matter how much he complained, her cousin always had her back.

Chapter 49

Suspicion

Marcus and Nicholas's temporary home—Early evening

Marcus rose at five forty-five due to the early moonrise. The temporary home they'd moved into was well-appointed with blackout curtains. Even though the sun still shone outside, he could move about without fear of being burned.

Nicholas was nowhere to be found. Probably still at town hall working with Christine. Marcus dressed and was heating dark wine when he heard the front door close.

"I'm in the kitchen," he called out.

Nicholas strode in and tossed his briefcase on the kitchen table, then swept into Marcus's arms for a kiss. When they broke, he said, "We have to talk."

"About the water case?"

"About Christine." Nicholas opened the refrigerator, took out leftovers, and began heating them. "She is asking questions."

"What kind of questions?"

"It really started last night. When we ordered dinner, she wanted a heavily garlicked Thai dish. I told her I was allergic to garlic. She seemed to accept it. Then, on her way back to her hotel, after we wrapped for the night, she stopped by the chapel. Matt found her reading the bulletin board. She asked him why so many services were scheduled in the evening and made a comment about the gold cross he wore. He texted me after she left."

Marcus frowned. It felt like she was poking at the outer limits, looking for an answer to explain why they were unavailable during the day. "And you didn't think to tell me last night?"

"You have so much on your mind right now, I didn't want to bother you with it."

That's what he got for complaining about his workload during their therapy session. If only he hadn't. "So what happened?"

"She ran a background search on Henry for the express purpose of making sure he didn't have any skeletons in his closet before he testified."

Marcus *tsked*. Understandable; it wasn't that far from the usual practice—no lawyer liked to be surprised at trial—but in this case, it was bad news. "I take it she found something?"

"It's what she didn't find. Records of Henry's prior identity—the one he allegedly inherited from—threw up some red flags."

"Damn it. What kind?"

"Holes in his background, including a missing death certificate. Newspaper photos associated with the winery in 1986 showing a gray-haired man who looks exactly like our Henry."

Marcus didn't like any of that. A smart woman like Christine would soon put it all together. Not to mention this rushed his hand—she might have made a good candidate for one of the spots being held open for essential skill sets, given her credentials and areas of expertise. He wanted more time to get to know her before revealing what the Hill hid or asking if she had any interest in becoming one of them.

Marcus huffed his frustration. "You can't blame Henry for the holes in his background. Before the internet, some aspects of identity swaps could be handled less carefully."

"I understand. But now, with everything on the web—"

"We must be more precise. Indeed."

Nicholas scrubbed a hand through his hair, the fine jaw-length strands falling back into place, momentarily covering the shaved gap. "And as much as I hate the idea, I think you're going to have to bite her."

Marcus took out his phone. "I'll need to talk with the mayor first."

He took a moment to text Winston to meet him at town hall.

"When your meeting is over, call me," Nicholas said. "You may have to bite her, but I plan on being there when you do."

"Now, Nicholas—"

"No. No ifs, ands, or buts about it—I will witness any biting of someone else. That's a hard line. Don't even think of arguing it."

Marcus sighed. "All right. I understand. I'll call you when I finish with the mayor."

Chapter 50
Testing a Theory

The Lux Enclave—Around the Same Time

After leaving Ari's place, Cerissa worked nonstop in the Enclave's lab, once again avoiding an aftershock. She'd programmed her phone to notify her when a significant one occurred.

At sunset, she returned home and rushed to get ready for an appointment at the Hill Chapel.

She kissed Henry goodbye, took her prepacked medical bag, and drove to Father Matt's office. Dr. Clarke had taken x-rays last night. Seaton's fangs were solid, no canal for fang serum. When his x-rays were compared to a set of films for a vampire who produced fang serum, even a layperson would see a clear difference.

Seaton was waiting for her when she arrived, and Matt had an empty glass ready.

She picked up a silvery red blood pouch, smaller than the ones she usually used, tore off the corner, and poured. Using apheresis, she had collected twice the number of red blood cells than normal from a clone and packaged the results in a shiny red pouch. The concentrated blood filled the bottom third of the glass, and looked darker, more scarlet than regular blood. "I want you to try this and tell me what you feel."

Seaton took the glass from her and eyeballed the contents. "Not much there."

"I know. Just try it."

She had yet to determine which triggered sexual desire in vampires: drinking blood, or the exposure to fang serum when they bit. This was an experiment to determine if concentrated blood alone could provoke a sexual response. In theory, if they could revive his flagging libido, he might see mortals as something other than food alone, which, in turn, might lead him to bond with them.

Seaton took a sip. He frowned, as if he was trying to figure something out. He took another sip. "What is this?"

"It's blood. Just more concentrated. A much higher number of red blood cells and less plasma. Go ahead and finish it."

Seaton drank the rest of it down. He placed the glass back on the coffee table.

"Tasty. Very tasty. Filling."

"Nothing else?" Cerissa asked. Henry had reacted strongly, and blamed his reaction on the concentrated blood, so she'd nicknamed it "Viagra for Vampires."

Seaton shrugged. "Other than satisfying? No."

"I see," she said, disappointed her experiment had failed. The solution would not be as easy as concentrated blood alone.

"What were you hoping it would do?" Matt asked, running his fingers over his closely trimmed beard.

"Those who've tried it say concentrated blood increases the libido. I was hoping it alone would elicit a sexual response."

Matt nodded. "So that Seaton might see mortals as something other than a food source."

"Correct."

Matt adjusted his eyeglasses by lifting and reseating the gold metal frames, looking thoughtful. "How can blood alone do that?"

"I don't know why concentrated blood works that way, just that it does."

"Do you have another sample? I'd like to see for myself what you're talking about."

"I'm not sure that's a good idea."

"Why not?"

"It can have a very strong effect."

"But you gave it to Seaton."

"I felt comfortable doing so because you are here."

Matt raised his brows above his eyeglass frames, and she considered the idea for a moment. She trusted Matt. If anyone could restrain himself, he could.

She reached into her bag and brought out another pouch. Matt produced another glass from a cabinet behind his desk, and she poured the blood in.

He sniffed it. His fangs instantly became visible, and he gulped down the thick liquid, then dropped the glass on the coffee table, his hand shaking. He gripped the armrests of his chair, and his white knuckles looked even whiter as he squeezed.

Uneasiness invaded her stomach.

Oh, this is not good.

She worked up the courage to ask, "Matt, what's wrong?"

He opened his eyes and looked at her. His pupils were blown out, his breathing labored, and he looked at her with, well, lust.

"Leave," he replied, panting. "Quickly."

She instinctively morphed her blood to take on a garlicky smell, and moved toward the door, stopping short of it, too concerned to abandon him. "Will you be all right?"

He jumped to his feet and took two steps in her direction before stopping and clenching his hands, obviously struggling for control. He started to lurch toward her again but veered at the last moment toward the door. He pulled it open, slamming it against the bookshelves, and fled the office.

A much stronger reaction than Henry had.

She looked over at Seaton, who was still seated on the couch, watching it all.

"That's what you wanted to happen to me?" he asked, disgusted.

"Well, no—"

"Go away, doctor. I don't want your help. I'm done cooperating with this nonsense. Sex has nothing to do with being a vampire. It's all about the blood. The blood and only the blood. The council thinks I'm crazy, but I'm the sane one. I don't fuck my food, and I don't fall in love with it either. You'll never be anything more than a meal to me. That's the way I like it, and that's the way it's going to stay."

He got up and started to walk out. Then he stopped. "I take that back. *You* will never be a meal to me. You don't smell right. I don't know how you do it, how you change your blood at will, and I don't care. Just leave me alone."

He stomped out the door, leaving Cerissa worried. Her defense reflex had given her away again. But how did Seaton sense it when Matt didn't? Did the ability to generate fang serum somehow blind normal vampires?

Then a different idea hit her. The morphing compound in fang serum may have been in the original protype, but was the sexual stimulant also present from the start, or a later mutation? If so, was Seaton a throwback, a glimpse into what vampires were like thousands of years ago? Sexual bonding between vampires and mortals may have been a mutation, one that prompted a vampire to mate, and then turn their mate, so the trait was reproduced over time.

Hmm. What was it like for the first vampire who produced the sexual stimulant in their fang serum? Was there a population explosion after that? Or a decline in population, as vampires slowed their reproduction to stay with their mate? Perhaps she could trace it by finding out when vampire myths became popular.

She needed to write this down, map it out like a logic tree, and figure out the different possibilities. If only she had the first genome, then she might know for sure.

She glanced at the door. Matt hadn't returned yet. Would he be all right after a few minutes? Henry had been. The last thing she wanted to do was embarrass Matt. She finished cleaning up, stuffed the empty pouches into her medical bag, and waited outside his office door.

When he didn't come back, she retrieved her phone from her purse. Should she call someone to check on him? Before she could, he appeared in the hallway, looking a little embarrassed.

"Seaton left," she told him.

"Thank you. And, ah, please don't mention my reaction to anyone?"

"Don't worry, I won't. Goodnight." She began to walk away, but then stopped and turned. "Matt, before I leave, can you tell me what happened? I'm trying to figure out why it has that effect."

He looked sheepish. "I've never had it happen before."

"And 'it' being?" She gestured for him to continue.

"I think the blood triggered a release of fang serum." He paused and looked like he was pressing his tongue to the roof of his mouth. "The gland is completely empty."

"And you swallowed all that serum with the blood?"

"I think so. Very overwhelming."

"Thank you for telling me. If you think of anything else to report about the experience, please call me."

He looked away. "I'd just as soon forget."

She waved goodbye and hid her smirk until he disappeared into his office.

Now to head home. She hadn't spoken with Henry about how testy he'd been this morning. Since he'd passed out at dawn, their discussion was cut short. She couldn't help wondering what he was hiding.

Maybe when she got home, she'd ask him. If she got up the nerve...

Chapter 51

No Fear

Town Hall Offices—Around the Same Time

Marcus stormed out of the mayor's office. He'd spent a contentious hour arguing with Winston. Although he would brief Henry and Rolf later about the situation, averting a threat of exposure fell under the mayor's jurisdiction. Based on Christine's questions, something had to be done about her, and it had to be done now. When he got back to Christine's office, it was almost eight in the evening.

"I sent the demand for arbitration today," Christine said as Marcus strode in.

He grabbed the chair opposite her at the conference table. "Good. We should hear something in the next day or two."

"That's my thought."

She picked up a stack of files, and his gaze followed as she stuffed them into her leather briefcase, the kind with a flat bottom and a wide hinged entry at the top, and she left it open.

"Glad we're on the same page," Marcus said, making sure to adopt a friendly tone. "Have you seen Nicholas around?"

"I haven't seen him for a couple of hours—not since he left to grab dinner."

"Oh." Marcus tugged at his mustache. He'd phoned Nicholas after leaving the mayor's office, but his mate hadn't answered. Should he call again? "Give me a moment."

He decided a text would be faster. It took no time for his thumbs to type out, *Bite imminent. Where are you?*

Nicholas's response was immediate. *On way.*

Something must have happened to delay him.

Marcus looked up at Christine. "Ah, he'll be here shortly."

"Oh, that's not necessary. There isn't anything else for us to do tonight. I just wanted to touch base with you in person before I went back to the hotel."

Dammit. He wanted his mate to be present for the bite. How to stall her?

"That was kind of you to wait. Are you certain there's nothing we can get ahead on now?"

"Not that I can see."

Marcus bit back a sigh. He didn't have a choice. He couldn't let her leave without initiating the loyalty bond. If she figured it all out, she might say something to a colleague about them, or decide not to return.

Later, they'd schedule the booster bite with Nicholas present.

He made eye contact with Christine, the first step to mesmerize his prey into passivity, and edged around the table, using his splayed hand for support as he leaned toward her.

But she didn't sit frozen. She reached into her open briefcase and pulled out a spray bottle. "I wouldn't come any closer if I were you."

He furrowed his brow, restraining a laugh. Why would he be afraid of a spray bottle? He moved closer.

She sprayed the table next to his hand.

Marcus recoiled. The drops burned like acid, raising blisters on his hands where the liquid splashed onto him. He hissed at the sting.

A pungent odor fouled the air—garlic.

He stared at the drops on the table. "Wipe that up."

"Go back to your seat and I will," Christine replied.

He backed up and considered his options. He could try to take the bottle from her, but if she hit his eyes with the spray, he'd be in deep trouble. Even at supernatural speed, he risked being blinded.

"Well, well." She ran her fingers through the splatter on the table and anointed her neck with it. "Whatever are we going to do about this turn of events?"

Marcus glanced at the briefcase he'd carried into the room and reached for the latch. If they were going to talk, he needed to stop the burning pain radiating up his arm.

Christine raised the bottle. "Freeze."

"I just want to get—"

"A weapon? I don't think so."

"No. I have a medication that will stop the blistering." The blisters had continued to appear, crawling up his arms despite the long-sleeve shirt he wore. The fabric must have absorbed the noxious liquid and plastered it against his skin.

"Slide the briefcase over to me and I will get your medication for you."

Marcus did. "It's a round jar."

With one hand, she snapped open the case and found the jar. She unscrewed the lid. "What is it?"

"Vampire blood in a preservative suspension. Vampire blood has healing properties. You've met our resident research scientist, Dr. Patel—Cerissa. She came up with the idea of using a microencapsulation process to create a healing ointment for us. Normal medications don't work."

"Well, it's nice to hear the truth." She slid the jar across the table to him.

He unbuttoned his cuffs, rolling up the sleeves to expose the burn, and applied the salve to the red welts, giving a sigh of relief as they faded. "I can tell you the truth now, because you will either submit to me tonight or you won't leave the Hill alive."

"Counselor, there may be another option. Never underestimate the creative solutions that two bright minds might conjure."

Creative? He was as creative as the next lawyer, but there was no other option. For her own sake, he had to convince her that her only choice was to submit to his bite.

"You don't seem to understand the situation you're in," he said. "If you leave here without my permission, you won't be allowed past the gates. The guards are mortal and loyal to us. If I don't call down to the gate, clearing you to leave, they will detain you and take you to our chief of police. She is not known for being gentle with mortals who are a threat to our survival."

"And just how am I a threat to your survival, Marcus? Do I look like I want to be considered a total Froot Loop at this stage of my career? I can just hear my colleagues: 'Christine thinks she's seen vampires.' Yes, that's a real career booster."

Marcus shook his head. He could hear Winston's response in his mind, and it wasn't good. "The mayor would never buy it. Your fear of being thought a fool isn't a sufficient deterrent. It does not guarantee your silence the way my bite would."

"Your bite?" She raised an eyebrow. "I don't think so."

"Look, Christine—"

"Marcus, I learned you are a vampire through the attorney-client relationship. I couldn't legally tell a soul if I wanted to. Attorney-client privilege protects you. I have no desire or reason for breaking the law or my word."

"I'm sorry," he said, returning the lid to the jar he held. He had to persuade her, for her own sake. "We can't take the chance."

"Because you live here on the Hill and can't easily relocate."

"Precisely."

"I understand, I really do. You're hiding in the open. It's marvelous, really. Once I figured it out, I had to admire you. Creating your own incorporated town. Making the community a private association with privately owned roads and using guarded gates to keep intruders out. I'm quite impressed. Are you the architect behind it?"

She was as bright as he gave her credit for, even more so. "There were five of us, but I came up with the town structure and other ways to use the law to achieve our purposes."

"Well done."

Marcus leaned back in his chair. "Why aren't you afraid of me?"

"The garlic will keep you at bay for the moment."

He *harrumphed*. It wouldn't keep him away forever. "You know, most mortals make the mistake of using a religious icon."

She smiled ruefully. "I believe in researching the territory thoroughly. I visited Father Matt last night, and noticed he had the same characteristics as others of your kind: the sallow pallor, the slightly flat affect. But he was wearing a cross. We chatted for a few minutes, and it became obvious he was a religious man. I concluded that religious icons would not repel a vampire."

But she hadn't noticed the chapel crosses were made of gold, not silver. So, she caught certain things but not others.

"When it came to the vampire myth, I reached the opposite conclusion regarding garlic," she continued. "Nicholas was a little too adamant about his severe garlic allergy story when I wanted to order the Thai garlic chicken."

"If you figured out what we are, why take the risk of coming back here?"

"I was too intrigued by the possibilities."

"But weren't you afraid? Usually fear overcomes curiosity."

"Of course I was afraid. But I'm used to overcoming my fears. I've never let them stop me before."

Marcus tapped his fingers on the table. He could see that to be true. He also knew she was too smart not to have a plan in effect if he didn't let her leave.

"How long have you suspected?"

"I first knew something was off because of the way Henry reacted in our initial video call. He probably would have been subtler, but it was clear the missing arbitration clause put him off his game."

"Yes, he knew he'd blown it at that point."

"It was enough to make me hyperalert to oddities. When no one would tell me the name of the illness he had—everyone dodged it, including Dr. Patel—I grew suspicious. Add to it the other curious details, and though I still wasn't absolutely sure, it was better to be safe than sorry. So I put together the spray bottle when we took a break this afternoon."

Marcus frowned. "Henry almost fired you that first night. I convinced him I could control you."

"So you decided you'd hypnotize me and make me one of your human slaves?"

"They aren't slaves," Marcus said. The idea was abhorrent. "The taking of blood instills a loyalty bond. A mortal who has been bitten can't reveal our existence; they can't reveal our world to uninitiated mortals. But they are always free to leave. We keep no captives here."

"Taking of blood?" she repeated. "So that was what you were trying to do? Bite me and drink my blood?"

"I was trying to mesmerize you in preparation, to make you passive so I could feed on you and initiate the loyalty bond. But you weren't mesmerized."

"A disciplined mind can't be mesmerized."

Yes, some mortals were resistant, and others could be trained to resist. He hadn't guessed she'd be immune to his mesmerizing powers. "Here are your choices as I see them. Option one, you can let me take your blood and bind you to me. I won't harm you. You're too valuable to us, and I don't harm those who cooperate. Then, when we are done with the lawsuit, I will wipe your memory of vampires and release you."

Her eyebrows quirked up. "And I'm supposed to take it on faith that you won't harm me and that you'll release me? After I caught you trying to do something against my will?"

"Option two," he continued. "I go to the town council and get their permission to kill you." That was the mayor's preferred route, as he wanted to blame the entire mess on Henry. Marcus managed to talk Winston off the ledge, but death was still on the table. "Your knowledge of us and my inability to mesmerize you makes you a threat to us. We must neutralize that threat in some manner."

"There is another alternative."

"And what is that?"

"You trust me and my commitment to the attorney-client relationship."

"*Trust you?*" Marcus asked. Pure poppycock. Her suggestion was not going to fly with either the mayor or the town council.

She shrugged. "You want me to trust you."

Just then, the door banged open, and Nicholas rushed into the room. "Marcus?"

He read the question in Nicholas's eyes. "Not yet. She has garlic spray."

Nicholas looked relieved, angered, and concerned all at once. "Did she hurt you?"

"I am fine, but it appears we are at a stalemate." Marcus eyed Christine for a moment. "I know what the town council will say, so, Nicholas, if you could remove that bottle from Christine's hand—"

"Wait, I don't want to use this on Nicholas, but I will," Christine said, holding up her other hand to show them a canister of pepper spray.

Marcus wouldn't let Christine use the caustic aerosol on Nicholas. If he had to, he'd brave the garlic himself.

"Don't even think of it," she said, and leaned back, looking like she was considering something. "What would you say to using a mediator to resolve this?"

"Mediation?" He tugged at his mustache and looked up at Nicholas, who gave a slight nod.

"Yes, Marcus," Christine said. "Let's give mediation a shot."

"And just who would you suggest we use as a mediator?" It's not like they could call the Mordida Mediation Association and hire one through them.

"Well, Cerissa struck me as someone who was fully awake and aware."

Cerissa? Really, what good could it possibly do to bring her into the mix? But then the whisper of an idea about Christine's qualifications came back to him, about sharing his responsibilities with her if she became one of them.

If Christine wanted a mediator, why not? He was willing to indulge her up to a point. After all, it might convince her to submit to the bite.

Before he could answer, she said, "Why don't you invite Cerissa and Henry over? After all, Henry is the official representative of SEWC—that makes him the client." Christine glanced up at Nicholas, and then smiled at Marcus. "Henry should have a say as to whether we terminate the attorney-client relationship, don't you think?"

Chapter 52

Another Threat

Outside Christine's temporary office—an hour later

Henry strode through town hall, Cerissa trying to keep up with him. When he found Marcus and Nicholas outside Christine's door, he tried to keep the panic from his voice. "What do you mean, she knows what we are?"

"Precisely that," Marcus replied. "And she won't let me take her blood."

"It is not up to her. Go in there and force the matter."

"Henry!" Cerissa said, crossing her arms.

Marcus patted the air. "Calm down, everyone. She wants to speak with Cerissa first, have her mediate. If Cerissa can convince her to do the loyalty bite, I think—"

Henry waved his hand in the direction of the office. "Do not waste time with that. You have to mesmerize her, make her forget, and hire a new attorney."

"Won't work. I can't get a foothold in her mind without taking her blood first. She's a very strong-willed person."

Anger flooded through Henry, and his eyes stung as his pupils enlarged. Between the blackmailer and money pressures, his pretense of being civilized was over. He reached for the doorknob. "Then I will take care of it."

Marcus stopped him with a squeeze on his arm. "I would prefer that we try another way first. She is locked in there and not going anywhere."

"Marcus, you cannot—"

"She has a spray bottle of garlic. I don't know if she has figured out that silver kills us. She could be armed. I wouldn't put it past her."

Cerissa stepped between them. "Let me talk with her."

Henry growled. "Cerissa—"

"Your concern is whether you can trust her, right? And she said she won't say anything about us because of the attorney-client privilege and because she'd sound crazy. Let me question her about the first point."

Henry pinched the bridge of his nose, trying to focus on the meaning behind her words. "What good will that do?"

"You know my methods. It might give us some reliable information—so you can decide whether to trust her."

Marcus motioned to get his attention. "Before you agree, Henry, you should know that Christine also has pepper spray. She threatened to use it on Nicholas if we tried to disarm her."

"Christine won't hurt me." Cerissa took Henry's left hand and pressed her lips to his wrist where the crystal was embedded. "Please, Henry?"

The warmth of her love followed the press of her lips, her aura calming him. *¡Ave María Purísima!* She had learned a new trick with the crystal.

"Very well, I'll allow it," Henry said, still feeling a little dazed by the effect. "But if it does not work, we will solve this using less civilized means."

Marcus nodded. "You aren't alone. The mayor wants to kill her if we can't make this work."

⁂

Cerissa rounded on Marcus. "He what?" she demanded.

What an idiot! Her opinion of the mayor couldn't get any lower.

Marcus patted the air. "I talked him out of it for the time being. But if we can't control Christine—"

"I'll fix this. Wait here; don't do anything. I have to get something first." She ran out to the car and returned with her medical bag in hand, then tried Christine's office doorknob, which wouldn't turn. "Do you want to unlock the door, Marcus?"

He produced the key and opened it.

She caught Henry's gaze and gestured at Marcus. "Don't listen. I'll explain afterward."

Marcus sputtered unintelligibly for a moment. "You're not closing that door. It's not safe."

She ignored him and pushed the door shut in his face, then walked toward the conference table, carefully watching Christine. The attorney didn't move. In fact, she looked relaxed and faintly amused.

Cerissa took the chair opposite Christine's. "We have an interesting situation on our hands."

"I'm surprised they sent you in alone."

Cerissa smiled at that. "I didn't give them much choice." She set the medical bag on the table but didn't open it. "You suggested to Marcus that we trust you, but we don't know anything about you. We have no way of knowing whether you're trustworthy."

"Henry and Marcus trusted me enough to hire me to represent them against MWC." Christine eyed the bag but didn't comment on it.

"True, but that was a small trust in comparison to what you're suggesting now."

Christine pressed her lips together, then said, "You don't seem to be under their influence. At least, I get the sense that you aren't being controlled by Henry."

"You are correct. I can't be mesmerized. I'm an envoy."

"And that is?"

"I've been trained in the ways of vampires and have developed a tolerance to their mesmerizing practices. They know me to be loyal, and I was vouched for by a very respected vampire before I was ever allowed past the gates."

She felt strange every time she told her cover story. In reality, she couldn't be mesmerized because she was Lux.

Christine set the garlic sprayer on the table and laid the pepper spray cylinder next to it. "Perhaps envoy status is the solution to our dilemma."

"If we weren't in the middle of litigation, I might agree," Cerissa said, shaking her head. "But we can't take time away from the lawsuit to allow you to be properly vetted and trained. It takes years."

"Any other ideas?"

Cerissa raised an eyebrow. Why was Christine so cool in the face of danger? It seemed real and not a façade. "You're awfully calm for someone in your situation."

"I have a backup plan. I've never violated a client confidence. But if I'm dead, all bets are off. I've left a very detailed letter that my partners will find if I'm killed. And one of them is as strong-willed as I am. He may not be able to completely expose all of you, but I'd bet that he makes your lives very difficult."

Cerissa pursed her lips. It left her with no choice but to use the method she'd hinted at to Henry.

"I do have another approach we could try. One of my research projects is memory reading—the linking of computer technology to the human mind. With the device I've developed, I can link to your memories. With your permission, I'd ask you questions and read the results. It will help everyone determine your trustworthiness."

"Why do you need my permission?"

"It doesn't work with someone who isn't willing. They can resist it. It can only be done with consent."

"And I don't give it. You would be able to see other client confidences." Christine shook her head. "No, I won't permit it."

"I will ask three very limited questions." Cerissa took the legal pad that was lying on the table and wrote out the questions. She flipped the pad around so Christine could see it.

The attorney's eyebrows shot up in response. "Those are three very good questions."

Cerissa waited, letting Christine consider her proposal.

"How does the memory link work?" Christine asked.

Cerissa unlatched and reached into her medical bag. This was a big gamble. Only Henry had ever seen her use the Lux touchstone. But showing how it worked to someone who wasn't loyal to the Lux? Her throat tightened at the risk she was taking.

Ari is right. If I keep jumping in to fix things, people are going to guess what I am.

Still, a life was at stake. She couldn't sit on the sidelines while the town council ordered Christine killed. Not if she could do something, even if it made others suspicious.

Cerissa took the device from her medical bag and showed it to the attorney, setting it on the table in front of her.

Christine eyed the touchstone. "It looks like a solid granite ball."

"Do you understand how a computer works?"

"I know the basics."

"Okay. That ball contains a very advanced...integrated circuit chip." Cerissa picked it up. "You hold it in your hand."

"I see. And with this, you can read memories?"

"Yes. The technology is somewhat primitive, so it isn't perfect."

Cerissa returned the ball to the table, and it rolled toward Christine, who stopped it with one fingernail and quickly pulled away, like she was avoiding a red-hot stove.

"But I will be able to tell how closely you've guarded secrets in the past," Cerissa added.

Christine studied the ball, hovering her hand over it without touching the stone surface again. "How do I know this isn't going to harm me? As soon as I pick it up, it knocks me unconscious."

"You saw me hold it, and you already touched the ball. Nothing happened. At some point, you'll have to trust me. But before we start, I have to make a call." Cerissa retrieved her phone from her purse. "Ari? I need the app that you used to read the Cutter's memories."

"Not if you're about to do something stupid," Ari replied.

"Ari..." she said with a growl. "I have my reasons."

"Bending the rules again, are we? Does Henry like it when you're a naughty girl?"

"Ari, either help me or don't. But don't waste my time."

She heard a big, put-upon sigh over the line. "Don't worry, Ciss—I'll take care of it."

"Thanks. I knew I could count on you."

"Of course. You can fill me in later. Bye."

"Who was that?" Christine asked.

"Another scientist. I didn't have the phone app, and I didn't want to take you to my lab in Henry's basement." Cerissa tapped the link Ari sent and loaded the app to her phone. "There." She laid the phone on the table so Christine could see, then wrapped her hand around the touchstone. "Okay, ask me a limited question."

Christine picked up the phone, tilting it toward her. "What's your first memory of seeing Henry?"

Cerissa smiled, the memory filling her chest with warmth. The phone replayed in low resolution the first time she saw Henry and Rolf talking to each other, both dressed in tuxedos. It was the spring dance, over six months ago.

"Do you want another question? Keep in mind it must be a memory."

"A childhood memory—your father or mother."

Cerissa's smile turned wistful. Her father was very special to her. The memory played of him teaching her about the Hindu gods and goddesses.

"How is it I understand what he's saying?" Christine asked. "I don't speak…"

"Hindi. I was born in India." Not that it resembled the language spoken in Surat today. "I set the default to English. The touchstone translates the memory so your mind can comprehend it."

Christine sat there for a moment, staring at the ball.

"Convinced?" Cerissa asked.

Christine met her gaze, a sparkle in her eyes. "Quite convinced."

Something in her tone alarmed Cerissa.

Whatever possessed me to take this risk? Henry could have handled it once he calmed down. I know he would have. Even Marcus might have swayed her eventually.

What am I doing? I didn't have to rush to the rescue—

But it was too late to do anything about it now. Well, she could try to mitigate the exposure, at least. "There is something else. I need your assurance that you won't mention this technology to anyone. Right now, I'm not supposed to use it on subjects who haven't signed a waiver. It's safe enough, it's just not been cleared for general use, so you would put me in a bad spot if you revealed it."

"If I was your attorney, it would be covered by attorney-client privilege."

That worked for her—if she was right, they'd all be relying on Christine's honor anyway. Cerissa reached into her purse to retrieve her wallet. "What's your hourly rate?"

"Five hundred dollars."

Cerissa counted out six twenties and a five. "Here's one-hundred and twenty-five dollars for a quarter hour. Does that work for you?"

"It isn't necessary." Christine started to push the money back across the table. Then she paused. Taking the five-dollar bill, she left the rest. "A new client discount for the first consultation. If you need any further advice, it's my standard rate."

"Thank you." Cerissa scooped up the remaining money and slid it into her purse. "Let me get Henry. He'll want to see your memories too."

"Just three questions, correct?"

"Yes. If I feel I need to ask any other questions, you'll set down the device, and I'll tell you what the questions are so you can freely consent."

"I guess one of us has to trust the other first."

"Yes."

"And you want me to go first."

"I don't see another way. Vampires are a paranoid lot. They've had to be to survive."

"Just remember. If something happens to me, my partners will know all about this place," Christine said.

"You won't be harmed by what I do."

Christine looked off to the side, as if contemplating something. "The other mortals on the Hill. How did they come to be here?"

"Voluntarily. We are all free to leave when we want to."

"Um, why, I mean, what is the motivation for having a relationship with a vampire?"

"Like any other relationship—love, companionship, and sex." Cerissa's lip twitched into a smirk. "For some, it's more one than the other. In addition to being paranoid, vampires are a horny bunch. And they are extremely good in bed. They've had hundreds of years to learn. There is also something more alive about the undead. They are very charming and intense people. Life here is never dull."

Christine locked eyes with Cerissa. "I've asked you to trust me, so I guess I'll have to trust you."

"Yes, thank you," Cerissa said with a nod. That was the only way they'd get through this. "Let me get Henry."

"Wait." Christine needed a bit more evidence before agreeing to submit to Cerissa's device. "Before you bring them in, ask me a question. I want to see what they'll see."

"All right. I'll use the first question I listed. Pick up the touchstone. I want you to relax and let your mind go where it wants."

"Let me see the phone's screen."

Cerissa propped it up against a coffee mug on the table.

Christine stared at the blank screen. "Now what?"

"Wrap your fingers around the touchstone, so they all make contact."

She squeezed the…touchstone. That was what Cerissa called it. What would it feel like once the process started? Christine didn't feel any different so far.

"What is the biggest risk you've taken to avoid revealing a client confidence?" Cerissa asked.

Christine considered the question. She saw her memories on the phone's small screen like they were pictures hanging on a wall. Then one flew open in response to the question. She watched as the movie played out.

In that moment, she realized that Cerissa was lying. The touchstone was beyond any possible technology being developed. Christine was an avid follower of science bloggers who wrote about leading-edge scientific breakthroughs. Nothing like the touchstone was even hinted at. No one could read memories like this.

She made the quick leap. If vampires existed, then it was possible Cerissa's touchstone wasn't technology. Could it be *magic*? Was Cerissa a witch?

Christine shut her eyes, storing the thought away to consider later. Contemplating any other impossible things right now would make her mind explode.

CHAPTER 53
TOUCHSTONE

CHRISTINE'S TEMPORARY OFFICE—MOMENTS LATER

Cerissa took the phone back. "Henry knows about this device, but Marcus and Nicholas don't. I'm going to tell the lawyers it's a lie detector, which is true in a sense. You'll describe the memory that answers my question. I'm going to watch on the phone, so I will know if you're lying."

"I see."

"As I mentioned, it hasn't been cleared for general use. You can't tell them it's true nature. Attorney-client privilege."

"Got it."

"Okay." Cerissa scooted her chair away from the table. "I'll be right back."

She returned to where the three men stood in the hallway, shutting the door behind her. "I think Christine can be trusted. She spent six weeks in jail rather than give up a client confidence. She has an extremely strong sense of pride."

"Is that what she told you? That she went to jail? How do you know she isn't lying about that?" Marcus asked.

"Because I've developed an advanced lie detector. It's in the process of being patented, so you can't tell anyone about it. Understand?"

Marcus squinted at her. "How do we know it works? Have you tested it widely?"

Why couldn't a vampire simply take a mortal's word? "It works. It's been through a Phase III clinical trial." Or at least, the Lux equivalent. "It's 99.8 percent accurate."

"Are you cer—"

"Marcus, I'd trust my technology before I'd trust your loyalty bond, particularly after what we saw happen with Dylan."

Just saying the name of the mortal who killed Yacov brought angry tears to her eyes.

Marcus dropped his gaze. "Ah—right."

"*Cariña.*" Henry stroked her arm. "We believe you. Lead the way."

Cerissa knocked to let Christine know they were coming in, and then opened the door.

"Wait." Christine gestured for them to stop. "You only said Henry, Cerissa."

"Ah, yes, but—"

"Marcus and Nicholas can come in, but they have to move slowly and sit down in those chairs"—the chairs had been repositioned away from the table—"and not move."

"What—" Marcus began.

"You asked me to trust you, and it's a work in progress."

"Very well," Marcus said.

Henry sat down next to Cerissa. "We will not harm you."

After Marcus and Nicholas were seated where Christine had pointed, Cerissa said, "All right. Pick up the ball so we can return to the first question."

Christine clutched the touchstone, and Cerissa looked at the phone's screen, tipping it in Henry's direction so Marcus wouldn't see. She put one earbud in her ear and slipped Henry the other one when the guys weren't looking.

Turning to Christine, Cerissa asked, "What is the biggest risk you've taken to avoid revealing a client confidence?"

Cerissa watched and listened via the phone as Christine described the situation, how she went to jail rather than reveal a client confidence.

When that memory finished, Cerissa looked over at Marcus. "She told the truth. Now, the second question." Cerissa focused on Christine again. "Have you ever lied to a client?"

"Never."

Cerissa watched. Nothing appeared on the screen. "You've never lied to a client?"

"Correct. I've never lied to a client."

"Have you ever broken a promise to a client?"

Christine laughed. "Umm, I've a tendency to be late. You must understand yourself, Marcus. Clients compete for your time, and sometimes, no matter what you promise or how hard you try to fulfill that promise, being on time can sometimes be challenging."

As Christine spoke, Cerissa watched memory after memory surface, each of them revealing how Christine had a tendency to be late to client meetings. Even when she'd promised to be on time.

Cerissa tapped the screen to stop the memories. "Christine, I'm going to reframe the question. All right?"

"Go ahead," Christine said, with a light laugh.

"Excluding tardiness, have you ever broken a promise to a client?"

"Never."

With that answer, no memories surfaced. Aside from being late, apparently Christine didn't break her promises. "She's telling the truth."

Marcus jumped in. "Ask her what she wants most out of life."

How would that question help them determine if Christine was trustworthy? Cerissa turned the phone over and gestured for Christine to wait. "I promised her that we would tell her the question before asking it, so we don't ask something that would reveal a client confidence."

Christine smiled in Cerissa's direction. "I'm okay with the question."

"But I'm not," Cerissa replied. "Marcus, your question requires a prospective answer—you're not asking her about something that happened in the past. My lie detector isn't designed to respond to questions like that."

"For what it's worth," Christine said, "I think there is an answer to Marcus's question. It's already happened."

Cerissa turned the phone over so she and Henry could see the screen and asked, "All right, then. Christine, what do you want most out of life?"

They watched as the memory formed itself. Christine was arguing in front of the United States Supreme Court.

And she was very good at it.

When the memory faded, Christine said, "I've always wanted to be the best lawyer I could be. When I was admitted to the bar of the Supreme Court, I knew I had arrived."

Henry nodded at Marcus, and the three men stood and walked out of the conference room.

"Please wait here," Cerissa said to Christine.

Christine chuckled. "I have no place else to go."

Once the door was closed, Cerissa said, "I think she'll keep your secrets."

"Even without the loyalty bond?" Marcus asked.

Henry nodded. "I am inclined to trust Cerissa's evaluation of the situation."

"Well, you're the client," Marcus said, still looking uncertain. "But it's all of our necks on the line."

Henry gave his friend a stern look. "I made this community what it is, and if I want to take this risk, I will."

"Wait a minute, Henry." Marcus pointed a finger at him. "All of us are invested in this community. It's not just your baby. Perhaps we should take this to the whole council and let them decide whether to trust her."

Adrenaline coursed through Cerissa, sending her heart into a tizzy. The last thing she wanted was to explain to the council what she did with the touchstone. "No, we can't—"

"They will dither it to death," Henry spat, beating her to it. "Sometimes, Marcus, you have to make an executive decision. Take the risk and the responsibility."

"But it's not your decision to make alone."

"As chairman of the water board, it is, and I'm choosing this method. We will trust Christine."

"But the mayor—"

"I'd like to see Winston tell me I cannot make the decision. And you know as well as I do, he'd relish having me take the risk, so he can blame me if it fails."

Cerissa breathed out a silent sigh of relief. Henry had come to her rescue.

Marcus tugged at his mustache. "Christine is your attorney, I suppose. But I think it's a mistake not to sway her to accept the bite. If trusting her backfires, it's on your head, not mine."

"I can accept that." Henry turned to Cerissa. "Please wait out here. I want to talk with Christine alone for a moment."

A cold sensation swept through Cerissa when the crystal transmitted Henry's emotions. "Wait. Promise me you won't bite her against her will."

"I cannot make you that promise. I plan on talking with her further, and if I don't like the answers I hear, I may have to take her blood in order to force the bond or to mesmerize her to forget."

Marcus made a sound of approval, and Cerissa narrowed her eyes at him.

"But as I said," Henry continued, "I am inclined to trust your evaluation."

"Fine. Just promise me you won't do anything too foolhardy."

He chuckled grimly. "*That* I can promise."

Chapter 54

Truth or Bluff

CHRISTINE'S TEMPORARY OFFICE—MOMENTS LATER

Henry crossed the room to the conference table, moving a chair so it sat directly across from Christine. The spray bottle of garlic was next to her, along with the pepper spray. He took a deep inhale. No smell of gun oil—so she probably didn't carry a firearm—and no smell of silver, but that wasn't definitive. Liquid or molten silver, including a recently fired silver bullet, would give off a telltale scent. But solid silver couldn't be detected by smell.

Also missing from the room was the tart smell of adrenaline, an intoxicating scent like limoncello. Why wasn't she afraid?

She should be.

With everything going on, he was wound up tight enough to kill. If he had to, he could lunge across the table and have her by the throat before she could pick up her weapon. She clearly knew nothing about supernatural speed.

And the garlic would not deter him as it had Marcus. After all, it would not kill him. It'd simply hurt like hell. And Marcus had been caught by surprise. If Henry had to attack, Christine would never see it coming.

But killing her wasn't on the agenda.

Christine eyed him as he sat down. She didn't say anything. Was she waiting for him to make the first move? She may be a good lawyer, but he was an expert negotiator. He'd wait for her to show her hand first.

When he remained silent, she said, "Mr. Bautista, you look like you've made up your mind."

"Not entirely. And why the sudden formality? As I told you before, you may call me Henry."

"I'm usually not on a first-name basis with people who plan on killing me."

"Then you are fortunate that is not my *plan*, Christine. My mistake has put you in this uncomfortable position, and for that, I offer my apologies."

She appeared surprised by his admission. "Thank you. Once we have resolved this, I look forward to working on your case and winning it for you."

Did she? They would see. He sat back, studying the attorney's reaction as he spoke. "I have considered your request. Past behavior is not always a predictor of future behavior when it comes to mortals. But sometimes it is the only indicator we have."

"So you are convinced by what you've heard?" she asked, sounding hopeful.

"For the most part." Henry fell silent for a moment. "You want us to trust you. Fine. I agree. You will continue to work as SEWC's attorney, and you are free to come and go on the Hill as you please. You will not be our prisoner."

"So you'd considered that option?"

"Yes, all options were discussed. I could have had one of our mortal police officers wearing a face shield come in to disarm you of both substances. I didn't. I also concluded you would not work effectively on my behalf as my prisoner. And I did not like the idea of bonding you to Marcus, either, because—"

"Because you'd prefer to be the one to *bond* me? Though you can't because of Cerissa."

"Did she tell you that?" he asked, his face clouding over. He did not believe Cerissa would have been so inept.

"No, she didn't. But the way she loves you, I suspect it might bother her if you did."

"You've figured it out, then."

Not that he'd made it hard for her to guess. He hadn't bothered aging himself for this meeting.

"There is no Enrique," she said, holding his gaze. "Or should I say, you are both Henry and Enrique. How old are you, really?"

"Over two hundred years."

"And Marcus and Rolf?"

"They are younger. Marcus is a shade over a hundred and fifty, and Rolf is approaching his first century."

She looked unruffled by this information. Clearly, she had an excellent mind, one accustomed to reasoning out the facts to arrive at the truth, no matter how improbable. He relaxed for the first time since learning Christine had figured out what the Hill hid.

"It is not a good idea for you and I to share the loyalty bond," he continued, "because you have to be impartial, objective, in your work for me. The loyalty bond would interfere with that. It is the same reason Marcus was less than ideal—it might distract you from your working relationship, make you less independent and too focused on pleasing him. I did consider another alternative."

"And that was?"

"Father Matt. I understand you met him and found him to be a religious man. If he formed the bond with you, I know he wouldn't interfere with your work. And you might find it easier to believe that he would not harm you."

"If I were a religious woman, perhaps. But I'm a bit too jaded—priests are human, as we all know."

Yes, he'd read about the sex scandals in the church. The whole mess had left him angry with his church. Parents had entrusted their children into the church's care, and the church had failed them.

"Father Matt is not like that—he would not take advantage of you," Henry said. "But I understand how you feel. It was an option worth exploring."

"Which leads us to your decision."

"I have decided to trust you without the loyalty bond. But know this: if you betray us, we will not waste our time reporting it to the attorney ethics bar. We will hunt you down and kill you. After getting the town council's approval, of course."

"Of course," she replied.

He didn't miss the sarcasm in her tone.

"Now," he said, folding his fingers together and considering his next words carefully. "We are willing to trust you. But in return, I want you to do something that shows your trust in us. I want you to allow Cerissa to draw a sample of your blood."

"And just why would I allow that?"

"Do not worry—it cannot be used to form the loyalty bond. That requires *direct* contact."

"Direct contact?"

"I—one of us—would have to bite you."

"I see. Then why do you want my blood?"

"Because with it, I can track you down anywhere you go on this planet. If you betray us, there will be no place to hide."

"And since I have no intent of betraying you, you think this is a reasonable request."

"Precisely." He gave a confident grin, one that said he was being perfectly reasonable. Now it was her turn to trust him.

"Who would have possession of the blood sample?" she asked.

"Cerissa has a lab in my house. I imagine it could be stored there."

"I will permit the blood draw if Cerissa agrees to keep the sample under lock and key until the town council issues an order to release it."

"Done. I will send her in here, and you can then return to your hotel tonight." Henry stood to leave.

"Before you go, Henry, would you indulge my curiosity with one request?"

"And that would be?"

"I hope in your society this isn't a rude question. And if it is, I apologize in advance for my ignorance. But I would like to see your fangs. Can you show them to me? Assuming vampires have them."

"Give me your hand," Henry instructed her.

She clutched her right hand with her left and looked at him skeptically. "I will not bite you; you have my word. But I will need your hand."

It took another moment for her to make up her mind. Holding the garlic spray bottle in the other hand, she extended her arm. He turned it over and took a deep inhale of her wrist. Human blood. Not as sweet as Cerissa's, but still, enticing.

He looked up at her and smiled. "It is a reflexive response to the scent of blood."

Unable to resist the whim, he lowered his mouth to her hand and allowed his fangs to gently touch her. As a child, he'd teased his sisters with stink bugs and lizards. He never outgrew the impulse to tease.

She jerked back, withdrawing her hand from his. "Thank you, Henry. Most instructive. Now, if you'll send in Cerissa, I'd like to leave soon."

He bowed to her and left the room, closing the door. Marcus, Nicholas, and Cerissa were still in the hallway. "I believe we have arrived at a solution," he lisped.

Cerissa stared at his mouth. "Why are your fangs out? Did you attack her?"

"No, I did not. She wanted to see them." He shrugged. He did not always understand the ways of mortals. "We have reached an understanding. We will trust her. If she betrays that trust, her life is forfeit." He closed his mouth, willing his fangs to retract. He hated the slight lisp created when he spoke with them extended. "And Cerissa will draw a sample of her blood tonight."

Cerissa furrowed her brow at him.

"Please."

Once the door closed behind Cerissa, Marcus asked, "What's the blood sample for?"

"I told Christine we could use the blood to track her down, that with it, she could not hide from us."

Nicholas snickered, and Marcus looked faintly disgusted. "That's a bunch of poppycock, Henry, and you know it."

Henry smirked. "You know that, and I know that, but she does not know that."

Chapter 55

The Bottom Line

Outside Christine's temporary office—Moments later

Henry checked his watch. He had fifteen minutes to make it to his meeting with Rolf.

Once Cerissa finished collecting Christine's blood sample, she kissed him and left for home in her own car. Christine then scooted out of the office right behind Cerissa—giving Marcus and him a wide berth when she walked by.

Henry wasn't offended by her maneuvers. She'd relax around them over time.

With a goodbye to Marcus and Nicholas, Henry left and drove his Viper to the winery. One of the winery's party rooms doubled as a conference suite, and Rolf had agreed to hold their discussion there. In the past they would have met in the owner's tasting room. Henry couldn't stand the idea. That room felt soiled to him now.

Rolf stormed in and stopped on the other side of the table, leaning on his fists and screwing up his face into an angry scowl. "Marcus just phoned me. What the *Hölle* were you thinking?"

Henry leaned back in his chair and crossed his arms. Staying calm in the face of Rolf's anger was the best way to deal with him. "I believe Christine is trustworthy."

"How can you possibly know that? We've only just started working with her. If she spills the truth about the Hill, the council will have you at the whipping post, at a minimum."

Henry was getting fed up with that threat. Another seven months to go on his suspended sentence before he was free of it. "Cerissa confirmed Christine's trustworthiness with Lux technology."

"*Scheiße*, how can she do that?"

"She has a device that can read memories."

"Seriously?"

"Yes, seriously. Now, may we focus on what we came here to discuss?"

"*Ja, ja.*" Rolf took his seat, set his tablet on the table, and swiped at the screen. "I've looked over the budget. As a starting point, we should delay buying the automatic bottling system."

Now that Henry had seen the damage wrought by the old-fashioned method—and losing almost half the vintage they were about to bottle because of it—he hated the idea of delaying the update for another year. They wouldn't be in this situation now if they'd completed the upgrade already.

"Are you sure?" Henry asked. "You were right last year, that we should have made the capital improvement then."

A flash of pride swept across Rolf's face, before he returned to scowling. "That was then, this is now."

As much as Henry hated admitting it, Rolf was correct. The earthquake had shaken their business plan to its core. Changes had to be made based upon today's situation.

"Are you suggesting we move the entire fund from capital improvements to operating expenses?"

"Half of it. If we recover, then in a few years we'll have the money saved again and can make the improvement."

Henry sighed and looked at his notepad tallying the losses. "That means we must make additional cuts. Between the structural repairs, and the destruction of almost half our Cabernet inventory, we're over a million dollars in losses—that is, if the insurance company doesn't cover it."

Rolf tossed the policy across the table to Henry. "I looked it up. We have a three-million-dollar coverage limit, and our deductible is twenty percent of that. Six hundred thousand out of our pockets before insurance pays a dime."

Henry skimmed through the document. Rolf was right. And they'd need to get an expert to do an estimate of their lost profit. Another expense. His head swam, trying to keep track of the figures. All this on top of the money the blackmailer was demanding.

If Tig's plan didn't work, what would he do?

"Henry." Rolf rapped his knuckles on the table. "Have you looked at the Excel spreadsheet Suri sent?"

At Henry's request, their manager had created a chart showing the average high and low times for the wine bar. If they closed Tuesday through Thursday—both the wine bar and the gift shop—they could lay off three or four workers.

The recommendation was not surprising. He'd been in business long enough that he'd gotten accustomed to the rhythms of tourists. Mondays and Fridays were popular with the Los Angeles and San Francisco crowd who drove through the San Joaquin Valley on their way to and from a long weekend.

"If we do that, will we have enough people on the payroll for weekend events?" He had every reason to be concerned. Weddings and parties were a significant source of income.

Rolf slid a printed email across the table. "I asked her. She's suggesting we use our regulars for weekend events—to keep those customers happy—and hire part-time college students to staff the wine bar on the weekends."

"So, our regulars would be on a ten-hour workday, four days each week?"

"That's her recommendation."

"But only for the winter—"

"Henry, we'll have to wait and see. It's for the foreseeable future."

Henry hated the idea of putting anyone out of work. "Who do we lay off?"

"Let's leave the decision to Suri. She knows who is good and who is"—Rolf wobbled his hand back and forth—"marginal."

Henry nodded. "I think we should also raise our rental rates by ten percent for our next high season."

"Fifteen percent across the board would be better."

"We do not want to price ourselves out of the market." Henry frowned as he considered the variables involved. "We are headed into the winter months. Let's do ten percent for now, and beginning the first of January, raise them by another five percent and see how we're doing. We usually are booked six months to a year in advance for our high season."

"All right. What about the harvest?"

"I've looked into our options, and we could do the picking ourselves."

"*Nein*," Rolf said with a flip of his hand. "With everything going on with SEWC, you and I won't have time."

Moving at supernatural speed, they were faster than mortal pickers, but it meant taking time from their other duties. Henry made a note on his yellow pad. "I've checked with the company we usually use to hire temporary workers, and they are having a problem getting enough people for harvest season. Americans don't want to do the work, and the government has been targeting the immigrants who are willing to."

Rolf scoffed. "Tell me something I don't already know."

"I've looked into another option. Mechanical harvesting. The price per acre is much less, and as much as I dislike them, the machines have improved."

"That should work." Rolf swept his bangs back. "Now, the capital infusion—do you have the money?"

"I am tight right now."

"That's not my fault. Sell something."

"I've spoken to both my accountant and my financial adviser. Both advise against selling anything to save the winery."

Rolf drummed his fingers on the table. "Do you intend to break up our partnership?"

"I did not say that. I told you what advice I received. I'm still considering it."

"Well, don't think too long. If you're going to bail on me, I need to find someone to buy you out."

Henry hated that idea. He loved being a vintner. "Rolf, this is my winery. Do not make demands."

"This is *our* winery. But only as long as each of us pull our own weight."

Henry clamped his jaw shut on the angry words he wanted to say. They'd been partners for seventy years, and equal contribution was the foundation of their partnership. "We don't have to make a decision today. We need to hear back from the insurance company first."

"Damn it, Henry. We have to cover the deductible at least, and you need to make a decision, and soon. If you don't, I'm going to start putting out feelers for investors to buy out your shares."

"And what will you do for a winemaker? William is good, but we both know it is my superior senses and expertise that produces our fine wines."

Rolf scoffed and shot out of his chair. "We can always *hire* you as an employee," Rolf said, and stormed out.

Henry sat there, staring at the door Rolf had slammed shut. As distasteful as Rolf's outburst was, his anger wasn't surprising—pretty typical for how Rolf responded to fear.

And they were both afraid the earthquake had ended their partnership.

Henry pounded his fist on the table. This was his winery, damn it. He'd run the business himself before bringing Rolf on as a partner. There had to be a way to save the partnership, to remain an owner in it.

There just had to be.

Chapter 56
Eyes Wide Open

Rancho Bautista del Murciélago—Four in the Morning

Henry returned home. His argument with Rolf had left him raw, but he had to keep working. Cerissa was already asleep—she planned on waking before sunrise to try another theory for keeping him awake—so he went to his home office to place the call without disturbing her.

"Good morning, Ari," Henry said into the phone.

"This is a bit of a surprise, cousin." Ari had already started referring to Henry that way, even though the official marriage was a year away. "Is Cerissa all right?"

"She is fine. But I have a bit of a problem." Henry rubbed his eyes. He'd given the matter a lot of thought in the hours since his discussion with Christine. "Would it be possible for you to monitor Christine Dunne's communications? Telephone and email? She is our outside attorney, and she's figured out what we are."

"Whoa. That's bad news. But it explains why Cerissa used the touchstone."

"Indeed. Anyway, Christine has promised to keep our secret—still, we want to make sure she does not reveal our nature to any other outsiders."

"Hmm," Ari said. "You sure your last name isn't Kissinger?"

"Beg pardon?" Henry replied, puzzled.

"'Trust but verify.'"

"Aah, yes, I understand now. That is precisely it. We want to verify she is not telling others about us."

Ari paused. "What the hell, consider it done. I can set it up on a limited basis, so we don't intrude on privileged conversations."

Henry felt a weight ease off his shoulders. After meeting with Rolf, uncertainty had been riding him. The lie he'd told about tracking Christine by blood might not be enough to protect their secret.

"Are you sure such a limited monitoring will work?"

"It's not foolproof, but I can do something like the NSA does. Monitor for specific key words. *Vampire, undead, Dracula*—you get the idea. I have to look for unique words that would not come up in a normal conversation. Fortunately for you, I've written a program that would make the NSA green with envy. It can separate context-specific uses. Take the word *stake*—an attorney may use it, as in *stakeholder*, to indicate someone who has an interest in a transaction. My program will ignore that context and look for stake as a weapon. You get the idea."

Henry did indeed understand, although the particular example Ari chose made him a bit uncomfortable. "That sounds like it would work."

"Email me all the contact information you have on her, and I'll do some additional research to see if she has any other email identities."

"Thank you." They ended the call.

There was nothing more Henry could do. No matter how hard he tried, he could never make the Hill a completely safe place to live.

Because this side of the grave, absolute safety was impossible.

HENRY'S BASEMENT—MINUTES BEFORE DAWN ON SATURDAY

Cerissa yawned. Something about waking before sunrise challenged her ability to keep her own eyes open and her mind on task. Was this what Henry felt like when the sun began to rise?

She normally needed about six hours of sleep each day but could get by on four if she had to. So it wasn't the amount of sleep that made her feel like crawling back into bed—she'd gone to bed early enough and slept for six hours.

As Henry requested, she stood near the door to his crypt, while he sat on his cot, his back to the block wall. He poured the first of three bags of adrenaline-enhanced blood into his mug. "If I make any move toward you, you will slam the door shut and lock it, understood?"

"Yes, Henry."

He'd only repeated that for the umpteenth time. The last time he'd tried full-strength adrenaline-enhanced blood, he had a hard time restraining himself from attacking her. And she expected him to drink three bags this morning. So his fear made sense, but time was the real enemy now.

She glanced at her phone. "Drink up. Sunrise is imminent."

He chugged down the first mug, gripping the edge of the cot with one hand as his knuckles turned white.

"Open your eyes, Henry. Try to keep them open." She mentally started counting the seconds. "Quick, drink the next one."

He did, and when finished, he placed the mug on the floor and gripped the cot with both hands, like he was trying to keep himself from leaping to his feet.

"Now, the third."

"I don't think I safely can."

"We need to see if it will keep you awake."

"Cerissa—"

"Drink it. Now."

He ripped off the corner of the pouch and, instead of pouring it in the mug, brought it to his lips and drank. A small amount spilled down the corner of his lips, and he wiped it away with the back of his hand.

"More." She could tell he hadn't finished the pouch.

He raised it to his lips again and drank, then crushed the pouch, dropping it into the wastebasket she'd left by the side of the cot.

Once again, he squeezed his eyes shut.

"Open them, Henry."

He shook his head. "I can hear the sound of water running past my ears."

He was hearing his own blood as his pulse rate increased. The pulse oximeter she had clipped to his index finger was sending its reading to her phone. She kept her vision split between the readings and him. It was past sunrise, and he still seemed conscious.

"Henry, look at me."

His eyelids fluttered open, and his head turned, his pupils blown out.

"How do you feel?" she asked.

"Terrible. The sun. Is. Pulling. Me. Down."

"Fight it."

"I. Am." He gritted his teeth, his jaw bulging. Then his eyelids slowly drooped, and his chin dropped forward.

"No, don't close your eyes!"

Henry thumped back against the block wall. He'd made it for thirty seconds after sunrise.

"Henry, listen to my voice. You can do this. Open your eyes."

He did. He reached in her direction, his fingers slowly straightening—

Then he toppled over onto his side, his head landing on the pillow, his eyes shut, his body in the stiff posture of the dead.

Failure, again.

She tiptoed to his side and lifted his legs, turning him onto his back. After picking up the mug and removing the pulse oximeter from his finger, she backed away, shut the door, and locked it.

Now what?

She was out of ideas. Thirty seconds after sunrise wasn't enough to make it to court. Christine had better convince the judge to accommodate them, because so far, nothing was going to keep Henry awake long enough to testify.

Chapter 57
Insider Information

MORDIDA WATER COMPANY—FOUR HOURS LATER

Jackson Aldridge sat at his desk at MWC's headquarters, fuming. He'd come in on a Saturday morning to get caught up on some paperwork and couldn't believe what his attorney had just told him.

"What do you mean, they're suing us? We should be suing them. If those rich bastards on the Hill think they can take our water whenever they want to, well, they have another thing coming to them."

Dick Peters sat in the guest chair on the other side of the desk. "Look, Jackson, we'll do everything we can to stop them."

"You're MWC's attorney. You're paid to say that."

"You worry too much." Dick raised his hand, gesturing for calm. "I have this."

Yeah, right.

That condescending twit could just put his hands right back in his lap. Jackson hadn't stayed at the top of the organization by being calm or relying on others. He'd stayed there by being the bastard everyone was afraid of.

"Their arbitration demand arrived this morning," Dick continued, "and I've already told their new attorney to pound sand. It was the strangest thing. She thought they not only had a right to arbitration under the contract, but a right to hold the arbitration at night. Something about Bautista having a skin disorder. He can't go out in the daylight."

"Yeah, I've heard that before." Jackson gnawed on a lollipop—the hard candy was the only thing keeping him from going outside for a smoke. "Any time we have to meet with them, it has to be at night."

"Well, I've looked through the agreement, and nothing in it requires us to arbitrate. So they filed for a preliminary injunction—"

Jackson bit down hard on the sucker, making a crunching noise. "They what? How'd they get it written this quick?"

"My guess—Dunne had it drafted and ready to go." Dick passed the document over to Jackson. "The filing asks the court to order MWC to stop drawing any more water from their aquifer. It also asks the court to enforce the so-called arbitration clause. We'll probably litigate that first." Dick paused, like he was pondering something. "If Bautista can't go out during the daytime, do you think they'll cave?"

"I don't care what kind of skin disease he has. He'll show up. He has to, or he loses, right?" Jackson asked.

"True. He signed the agreement. His attorney is going to have to put him on the stand to testify about it."

"Then he'll be there. I just—" Jackson was interrupted by the sound of his cell phone. "Damn thing."

He chomped down on the white stick his sucker had been attached to, keeping the stick in place. It took two hands to hold the phone and swipe the accept button. He brought the infernal device up to his ear and removed the mangled sucker stick from his mouth.

"Hang on, Tyler. I'm meeting with my attorney right now." Jackson hit the mute button and looked at Dick. "It's my sister's kid. Not too bright, but means well. I'll get rid of him quickly."

Dick nodded, and Jackson unmuted the call. "Okay, Tyler, what is it?"

"Sorry to bother you, Uncle Jackson, but you know that guy you were swearing about when you came by on Tuesday? Henry something?"

"Yeah, Henry Bautista."

"Well, my friend, Bruce, he took some video of the guy. I don't know if you can use this, but he's a pervert."

"He's a child molester?" Jackson asked, his hopes rising. Something like that could be used to get Bautista to drop the lawsuit.

"No, she looked like she was old enough. But get this—he likes to suck women's blood when he has sex with them."

"No shit." Jackson thought he'd heard of everything—but a blood fetish?

"What is it?" Dick mouthed.

"You're not going to believe this," Jackson whispered back. To his nephew, he asked, "How do you know it's true?"

"Like I said, Bruce has the whole thing on video. I've seen it. Real gross."

"How did your friend get this video?"

"He put a camera in this room at the winery, and Bautista did the girl right there, and he bit her neck. His mouth was, like, full of blood. You could see it drip on the video."

"Can you send me a copy of the recording?"

"I don't know. Bruce doesn't want anyone to know he has it. He's trying to get money out of the guy. You know, Bautista ponies up millions of dollars, and Bruce gives him the only copy of the video. But I remembered you were really pissed at the guy, and I thought if I could help...."

"How much money do you need, Tyler?" Jackson asked. He knew that was the bottom line with his nephew.

"I could really use five hundred dollars to make my car payment. I'm kinda two months overdue."

"I'll mail you a check," Jackson said. "You've done good, boy."

"Thanks, Uncle Jackson."

Jackson ended the call and whistled in disbelief. "You are not going to believe this. I'm not even sure I do. My nephew swears he's seen it on video. Henry Bautista has a blood fetish."

"A what?" Dick asked.

"Tyler's friend put a hidden camera in a room at Bautista's winery and got our boy on video screwing this girl and biting her neck. I've heard about it on television—there are people who think they are vampires and suck each other's blood. Really sick stuff."

"Quit pulling my leg. This is one of your practical jokes, right? You put your nephew up to calling."

"No, no joke."

"You're trying to tell me that Henry Bautista—the Henry Bautista who refuses to go out in the daylight—also sucks blood?"

The statement sank in. "I'll be damned."

"I'm done here. You're not going to make me the butt of your joke." Dick threw the papers back into his briefcase and slammed it shut. He stood. "When you want to have a serious conversation, Jackson, I'll be back."

"Sit down."

"I will when you stop talking nonsense."

"I'm not talking nonsense. Sit down. I've got an idea." He stuck the stick back in his mouth, working it with his molars, biting the last of the candy residue off it, the germ of an idea growing.

Knowledge was power. And Jackson liked power.

"I'm not saying Henry is a vampire"—he tossed the stick in the trash and picked up a new sucker—"but he may think of himself as one. We can use this information to our advantage."

"Okay." Dick sat back down. "What did you have in mind?"

Jackson waved the new sucker in the air. "They've been asking for a nighttime meeting to discuss the situation. Let's give them what they wanted."

"I don't know. It sets a bad precedent."

"No, it'll catch them off guard. I have an idea, and you're going to go along with it, because if I'm right, the information my nephew provided gives us the upper hand. So, let's use it."

Chapter 58

Trick or Treat

Town hall—Shortly after sunset

Christine still couldn't believe what her clients had confirmed last night. Civilized vampires existed, living in a town of their own making. And Henry's fangs—she hadn't hallucinated them. The sharp prick when they touched her palm had been all too real.

But Marcus surprised the crap out of her when he phoned before the sun set. Now that she was in on the Hill's secret, he appeared relaxed enough as he explained how a late moonset or early moonrise affected their day sleep. And today there was an early moonrise. With everyone awake, she sent an email inviting them to join a videoconference.

"MWC wants a meeting with us," Christine said, as soon as Henry and Rolf logged on. SEWC didn't have much time to decide. She had to push her clients in the right direction. "Dick Peters said they're willing to meet tonight."

Rolf frowned at the camera. "On a Saturday night?"

"I guess everyone is working the weekend thanks to the earthquake," she replied.

Marcus rolled his lips together, looking thoughtful. "Did he say what MWC wanted to talk about?"

"No, and something about it didn't feel right to me. They've been refusing any meetings, and insisting that if we have a meeting, it has to be a daytime meeting. But now they suddenly give in. Something is up." She took a sip of her coffee. After going to the hotel last night, she'd stayed awake most of the night thinking about vampires. She needed the caffeine to keep going. "But I can't come up with a good reason to say no."

Henry folded his hands on the desk in front of him. "Perhaps they are ready to negotiate in good faith."

He really was an optimist. She shook her head. "I doubt it."

"What is the worst thing that can happen?" Rolf asked. "We show up, we talk, they talk, we don't reach agreement. At most, we've wasted a few hours of our lives."

Despite the red flags, Rolf had a point. "If you're both in agreement, I'll confirm."

Henry nodded. "Do it."

She picked up her phone and sent the text message to MWC's attorney. "Done. We'll listen to what they have to say, take a break, and discuss it. Don't make any commitments. We're too close to our hearing date. Injunctions are fast-tracked. This may be our only opportunity to settle this short of litigation, but we can't seem eager."

"You do not need to lecture Rolf or me on how to negotiate. We were negotiating business deals before your grandmother was born." Henry glanced down and pursed his lips. "Or at least, I was."

RANCHO BAUTISTA DEL MURCIÉLAGO—SEVEN AT NIGHT

MWC's reply insisted the meeting take place at their headquarters. Henry aged himself to resume the role of the man who'd signed the water agreement in 1987. Now that Christine knew what he was, he hadn't bothered to waste the blood to transform himself into older Henry before logging on to the videoconference. But MWC needed to see his older self at the meeting.

Though he'd slept peacefully and drunk his usual amount of dark wine when he woke, he still felt, well, hungover. The sheer amount of the adrenaline-enhanced blood he'd consumed before going to sleep made him feel antsy, and his ears still buzzed from the stimulant.

At the agreed-upon time, he met Rolf, Christine, and Marcus at town hall, and they piled into Rolf's white Escalade for the drive to MWC's three-story office building. He'd been there before, so there was no difficulty finding the sandstone-colored edifice next to the large water purification plant. Neither showed any signs of damage from the earthquake.

The MWC's board had appointed two of its members to serve as a negotiating committee. When Henry's team entered the conference room, board members Roger Chimera and Jane Neumann were already seated on one side of the long table next to MWC's general manager Jackson Aldridge and attorney Dick Peters. Jackson invited the Sierra Escondida representatives to sit on the other side.

It was then that Henry noticed the large mirror. The decoration had been added to the room since the last time they were there and was positioned directly behind where Henry and Rolf would sit. Henry paused to check his reflection; his hair was fine. He wasn't afraid of mirrors, thanks to his sprayed-on tan.

He leaned over and whispered to Rolf, "Why did they install a mirror for our meeting?"

Rolf whispered back, smiling, "You're getting paranoid."

Henry plastered on a placid smile in response, even as he assessed the possibilities.

Of course, it could mean nothing, as Rolf suggested. Perhaps whatever had hung there before had fallen off in the earthquake.

On the other hand, maybe they'd positioned the mirror to see the notes and strategy papers of the SEWC team. Henry would have to check the angle later, to see what could be seen in the reflection from Jackson's perspective. Henry wouldn't put it past the *gilipollas* to try such a trick.

"Well, ladies and gentlemen," Christine said. "It's your dime. You called the meeting. Tell us what you want to talk about."

Jackson spoke up first. "We've read your pleadings. You think there's been some kind of forgery. I personally signed the agreement, and I knew the old water company attorney, and he wouldn't have done something like that. We think you might have meant to send a contract with a nighttime arbitration clause, and then screwed up, and sent the wrong one."

Marcus visibly bristled. Christine jumped in before Marcus did. "I've been through the files. Our expert examined the originals today. It's clear there was a forgery."

Jackson took out a small pocketknife and began cleaning his fingernails. Henry frowned at the rude gesture, but then, what could he expect from someone like this *pendejo*?

"The way we see it," Jackson said, running the knife under his thumbnail, "your boys don't want to testify during the daytime. We think the judge is going to insist that the trial be held during the day. So we're willing to listen to whatever offer you want to make. After all, you're the ones with the most to lose."

"I don't believe so, Mr. Aldridge," Christine said. "If we prevail on the forgery issue, the contract is nullified. It's MWC that will lose."

"Then your boys will have to testify. Are they prepared to do that during the day?" Jackson looked up, his eyes on Christine, but he continued to clean his fingernails.

Henry pursed his lips in disgust, not believing the lack of respect.

Suddenly, the knife slipped, slicing the ball of Jackson's finger. Blood welled up in the wound, and Jackson squeezed his finger, which made it bleed more.

Henry froze. Time slowed. Hunger growled through his veins. The scent and sight captivated him. He stared at the bright red liquid and willed himself to look away. It was harder than it should have been.

¡Hijo de puta! *I should have drunk a third pouch of blood before this meeting.*

Christine cleared her throat. "Mr. Aldridge, you've cut yourself. We'll take a recess while you attend to that." She stood up. "Henry," she said, touching his shoulder, "let's go outside." She cleared her throat. "Marcus, Rolf—come with us."

Henry was on his feet and moving before he realized what he was doing. He was furious—furious with himself for his reaction and furious at Jackson for setting him up. As soon as they were outside, he turned to Christine. "They know. The mirror, the blood. They *know*."

"What was that all about?" Rolf asked as he caught up with Christine and Henry.

"That, Rolf, was a trap, and I walked right into it."

"Now, Henry," Marcus said, gripping his shoulder, "you're overreacting."

Henry clenched and unclenched his fists. "I am not overreacting. He knows what we are. We have no choice. His memory of us must be wiped."

"You may be right," Rolf whispered. "But not without the council's approval."

Marcus furrowed his brow. "You're sure he knows?"

Henry couldn't believe Marcus was being so dense. "Yes, he knows. They hung the mirror to see our reaction. And where the mirror did not work, the blood did."

"Then we need to tell the council," Marcus said.

"Those weaklings. They will never agree to it," Henry shot back. "We will lose our water."

Christine *tsked*. "No, you are not going to lose the Hill's water."

"They lie and they cheat," Henry said with a growl. "What can you do?"

Christine looked at them firmly. "Take a breath, everyone. We're going to go back in there. We still have a shot at winning."

"What good will it do to return?"

"If we don't go back in, it will confirm what they suspect. If we leave now, you might as well say, 'Christine, we're folding the tent and giving up.'"

"I will not give in to those people." Henry clenched his jaw. "Ever."

"Then calm down." Christine frowned. "I think Henry's right—it was a trap. For some reason, they suspect you are what you are. But it doesn't matter. We've told the judge that we need a night hearing. You have signed affidavits from Dr. Clarke about your inability to go out in daylight. The Americans with Disabilities Act provides all the justification we need. The judge will see it our way and hold court at night when you two have to testify. So we aren't out of the ballgame yet. Let's go back in there, heads held high, and act like nothing happened. Do you think you guys can pull that off?"

Rolf thumped Henry on the back. "*Ja*. We can do this. If we don't, we look weak."

Between all the disasters that kept piling on him—the earthquake, the blackmailer, the expenses, the loss of water, and now this, the possible exposure of Hill vampires to their adversaries—Henry felt like a dry twig ready to snap.

"Yes, we can put on the performance you seek," he replied with a growl. "But when this is over, Jackson is mine. I claim him. He drew blood to entice me. He will pay the price for that."

"Henry, we'll deal with Jackson when the time comes," Marcus said. "For now, we need to get back in there and act like nothing happened."

"Wait a moment." Christine held up her hand. "Henry, you wear a crucifix under your shirt?"

Henry scowled. "How do you know that?"

"Cerissa mentioned it. I think she was trying to misdirect me when I started asking questions. Before we go back in, I want you to move the crucifix to the outside of your shirt, so they can see it."

"You think it might help confuse them?" Marcus asked.

"Yes. Between the mirror and the crucifix, they might talk themselves out of believing you are vampires."

Henry reached inside his shirt and pulled it out, where it hung awkwardly. "It will look strange over my tie."

"Now isn't the time to be fashion-conscious," she scolded him.

"Give it to me." Rolf held out his hand. "I'll wear it. I knew there was a reason I didn't want to wear a tie to this meeting, aside from my total disdain for MWC." He took the gold icon from Henry and fastened the chain around his neck. "There. How does it look?"

"Like blasphemy on the neck of a nonbeliever," Henry replied.

Rolf rolled his eyes. "Now is not the time for a religious debate, Henry."

"It isn't straight." Marcus reached for it and centered the symbol, so it was visible above the open V of Rolf's camp shirt. "There. They can't miss it."

Henry nodded his approval.

Christine swept her hand toward the conference room. "Then let's go back in and convince them that they are dealing with normal human beings, shall we, gentlemen?"

MWC HEADQUARTERS—SAME TIME

"Did you see the look on Henry's face?" Jackson asked his attorney.

Dick had accompanied him to the kitchen to get a bandage for his finger from the first-aid kit in the cabinet above the coffee maker.

"I wouldn't have believed it if I hadn't seen it for myself. He was hypnotized by the sight of your blood. It was like he was watching a stripper—there was desire in his eyes."

"All three men seemed to react to it," Jackson replied. "Dunne didn't—so she doesn't have the same *problem* the other three do."

Dick shook his head. "I don't know. Henry definitely reacted. I'm not sure about Marcus and Rolf. They may have just been startled to see you cut yourself. But Henry, something about him looked hungry."

"Hard as it is to believe, my nephew was right." Who would have thought Jackson's idiot nephew would come up with the answer to their problem? "Henry Bautista has a blood fetish—he thinks he's a vampire."

"You don't believe—"

"Nah. No such thing exists. And besides, he couldn't be a real one," Jackson said with a laugh. It had been his idea to hang the mirror to see Henry's reaction. "After all—he has a reflection."

Dick took off his glasses and rubbed his eyes, before returning them to rest on the Roman bump in his nose. "This has got to be the strangest case I've ever worked on."

Jackson smirked at him. "And it's only going to get stranger."

Chapter 59

Aftermath

Robles Road—Thirty minutes later

Henry was furious as they drove back to the Hill. The negotiations with MWC had been a sham. Nothing further was accomplished when they returned to the table after the break. It had all been a ruse to trap him into revealing his true nature.

Sitting next to him in the SUV's back seat, Christine was the first to break the uncomfortable silence. "This wasn't fatal to our case. Jackson can suspect whatever he wants about you. It doesn't change the strength of our claim."

"You do not know what it's like," Henry said. "We have carefully guarded what we are, so that we may live in peace here. If an idiot like that thinks we are vampires, he may dig deeper."

In the rearview mirror, Henry caught Rolf giving him side-eye from the driver's seat, but Henry refused to tell Christine or Marcus about the blackmailer's video. He was too embarrassed that his error in judgment had been recorded.

But what had clued Jackson to try the knife cut? Could he be in league with the blackmailer?

Rolf *harrumphed*. "Don't worry. We'll take care of it. This won't threaten the community."

"I am not as certain of that as you are, Rolf."

What if they couldn't contain it? Three people in a short period of time had figured out their secret—Christine, Jackson, and the blackmailer. What if it expanded exponentially from there? In a month, they'd have conspiracy theorists driving by the Hill's gates, trying to catch a glimpse of the vampires. Groupies would be next. Then a journalist would write some curiosity piece, and another would dig deeper and write a proper exposé.

After that, all hell would break loose as government agencies like the FBI figured out the truth. And if that happened, would they lose the Hill?

Rolf caught his eye again in the rearview mirror. "Look, I'll drop you off at your house first. Spend the evening with Cerissa. Chill out."

No, Henry needed time to calm down before seeing his mate. "Please drop me off at the driveway. I will walk from there."

Rolf stopped the SUV where directed, unlatched the crucifix, and held it out. "Here, don't forget this."

Henry let the necklace drop into his palm. "Thank you."

Walking up the curving driveway to his home, he ran his thumb over the hard body on the instrument of torture, trying to find peace again. Life came with all kinds of tribulations. At least his weren't as terrible as what some went through.

Christine watched the despondent vampire walk up the curving driveway to his home. "Is he always so intense?"

Marcus sighed. "He's been under a lot of strain lately. The community was attacked by a former protégé of mine not long ago. One of our close friends was killed before Oscar was caught. And then came the earthquake and the threat to his livelihood by the water shortage. I'd say he's wound about as tight as I've ever seen him."

Yeah, wound up tight was one way to put it. Christine phrased her next comment carefully. She didn't want to piss them off. "I wasn't sure if it was the circumstances or inherent to being a vampire."

Rolf put the SUV in drive and headed back to town hall. "We do tend to be more intense after the change than we were as mortals. And paranoia is not uncommon, especially since we have been hunted and killed by mortals as long as we've been in existence."

"Just because you're paranoid, doesn't mean they aren't out to get you," Christine said, not believing she'd let the hackneyed quote roll off her tongue.

"Exactly." Marcus tugged at his mustache. "But it's a good existence. We will never grow old and die. We will live a long time, assuming we don't meet up with a vampire slayer or an unfortunate accident."

It almost sounded like Marcus was trying to sell her on the idea.

"Although I knew this one Vietnamese vampire who was killed when he fell into a pit filled with punji sticks during the war," Marcus continued. "One went through his heart. It wasn't pretty."

Christine cringed. Maybe Marcus wasn't trying to sell her on it after all. "That sounds like a terrible way to die."

"Especially to one who expects to live a very long life. Such a waste."

Henry had already told her their approximate ages. "How long is long?"

Marcus and Rolf exchanged looks, and then Marcus said, "It depends."

She laughed. Leave it to a lawyer not to give a straight answer. "How old are the oldest vampires?"

Marcus looked over the seat. "We suspect there are some who exceed two thousand years old, but they are elusive."

"You mentioned accidents and slayers. What are the other limiting factors, then?"

"Some vampires, as they grow older, can slip into a form of dementia—you'll hear them called revenants. When they do, the communities have no choice but to put them down before they go on a killing rampage."

It was good to know the communities policed their own. She wasn't sure whether she should ask any more questions, but her curiosity was getting the better of her. At fifty-nine, the ache in her knees, the tendency to fatigue easier, the downswing in her own libido, in addition to the hot flashes, reminded her that the last third of her life had begun—if she was lucky enough to live into her eighties. Not everyone was.

Did she want more years? Quality years, where she wasn't in arthritic pain and her mobility wasn't limited? Where she didn't live in fear of developing cancer or having a stroke?

There was so much she still wanted to do. So many things she'd sacrificed by having a demanding career. What would it be like to relax more? She could read, garden, socialize. Maybe create something. She had considered writing fiction while in her twenties. Or maybe go to college at night and study something just for the pleasure of learning?

The idea of becoming one of them was worth exploring.

"What else is different about being a vampire?" she asked.

"The craving for blood, and complete lack of interest in food."

Christine studied Marcus as he spoke nonchalantly, still not believing how much he'd let down his barriers.

"Sexual interest is heightened," he continued, "and sex is better, hard as that might be to believe. At first, adjusting to being awake only at night was difficult for me. With our sleep controlled by both the sun and the moon, we may sleep only four hours some days, up to twelve hours on others. But we make up for it with the added years, so I have no complaints."

"Do you sleep in a coffin?" she asked. Drinking blood and sleeping in a coffin both sounded awful to her.

Rolf laughed, glancing at Marcus. "That one never dies, *ja*?"

Marcus smirked and then looked back at Christine. "No, that's just part of the myth. We need a completely dark place—if any daylight hits our skin, we suffer from burns. Most of us just use a single-wide bed or a cot in a windowless room. Nothing fancy. All very civilized."

That was a relief to hear. "How does someone become a vampire?"

"The mechanics are simple enough."

"And they are?"

He smirked at her. "Now, Christine, we have to have some secrets."

Well, maybe he wasn't quite as open as she thought. "Can you turn whoever you want to?"

"No," Rolf scoffed, and Christine waited for Marcus's fuller reply—she was sure he'd have one.

Marcus quirked his mustache and shot Rolf a look. "The politics are a little complicated. In Sierra Escondida, the town council votes on it, and the board of directors for the homeowners' association must approve as well. No one can be turned here, and stay resident on the Hill, without the approval of both entities. Otherwise, we'd have a population explosion that we couldn't accommodate with the limited supply of expired mortal blood we harvest from hospitals and blood banks. Also, a vampire under two hundred years old is not allowed to have children."

"Have children?" she asked.

"Our phrase for it. They aren't allowed to make a vampire. When a vampire under two hundred years turns a mortal, the results can be very bad. Not always, but the children of younger vampires are often emotionally unstable."

Christine smiled. "If only mortals had to get certified as capable parents first, there would be fewer children with emotional problems."

"Indeed," Marcus said, laughing. "And right now, there is a moratorium on expanding our numbers, although we are permitted to replace those who die. Currently, we have fourteen openings."

Fourteen? Were they slow to fill their ranks, or had some tragedy befallen the community? Marcus had mentioned one death, caused by a vampire named Oscar. Had there been others?

Still, with fourteen openings, the possibilities were interesting. Christine mulled them over as they finished the drive to Marcus's office.

RANCHO BAUTISTA DEL MURCIÉLAGO—SAME TIME

The walk had been good for him. Henry arrived back at his front door a little less angry and a little less panicked.

But not by much.

He opened the door and went in. Cerissa did not come to greet him as she normally did.

He went downstairs to the lab and knocked on the door. "Cerissa?" he said, announcing his presence.

"You're back?" she asked over her shoulder. "I've been so busy I lost track of the time. How did it go with MWC?" She turned back to her lab bench and continued to mix chemicals together.

"It did not go well. They did not negotiate in good faith." He didn't want to trouble her with more of his problems, especially when this new one might be linked to the blackmailer, so he didn't provide the awkward details. "We will have to go to court."

"I'm sorry to hear that. I was hoping this would be the break you needed."

"It was not. If you'll excuse me, I need time alone."

"Are you going for a motorcycle ride?"

Not a bad idea. He kissed her cheek—both of her hands were occupied with the chemicals she was mixing—and then went outside.

Moments like these, he wished they still hunted, or at least were allowed to live-feed on strangers near their community. Although dark wine from Cerissa's clones was far superior to banked blood, nothing beat an occasional live feed when stressed—and while the thought of sharing *his* blood with someone else felt like he would be cheating on Cerissa, feeding on a stranger didn't.

Yes, he recognized the double standard. But he had to feed to survive. And giving anyone else the privilege of tasting his blood violated what he and Cerissa had together—with two exceptions: the first was, he'd allow it to save a friend in an emergency, and the second was his maker, who insisted on the right to take his blood under vampire law.

He sighed to himself, stripped off his tie and suit coat, left them in the garage, and loosened the top button of his white dress shirt. Sliding his leg over the leather seat, he started the bike.

No matter what he'd said to Tig, when they caught the blackmailer, he'd satisfy both needs at once. Whoever said revenge is best served cold was wrong. Revenge served hot from the vein was much more satisfying.

Chapter 60

Conning the Con

Vasquez Müller Winery—The next day

Bruce entered the wine lab wearing his white shirt, black tie, and matching pants—the uniform of the wine pourers. He still didn't understand why he was there, why they'd called him in on his day off to work.

It couldn't be about the whispers of layoffs. Why call him in on Sunday and pay overtime for that? They could have waited until Monday and fired him then.

And it couldn't be about the video, either, because he wouldn't be in the wine lab—he'd be in Suri's office being yelled at and getting his walking papers.

"Please have a seat," the preppy-looking man said.

The guy wore a striped shirt with a button-down collar, perfectly ironed. Geez, what a dweeb.

A small table stood in the middle of the room, with fancy wineglasses on each side of a plate setup. Bruce took the empty chair the dweeb offered.

"I'm Devin Carlson," the guy across from him said. "I'm a marketing research specialist. The owners have hired my company to advise them on some changes they've been considering. You're one of the servers, right?"

"Yeah, isn't the outfit a dead giveaway?" Bruce said, making the joke because he was uncomfortable. He hadn't gone to college, and from the lingo used, it was clear this guy had.

But even so, he felt himself relax. At least they weren't here to fire him. He hadn't really believed they'd call him in for that, but until he got his bitcoins, he feared something would go wrong.

"Your name is Bruce Howell, right?"

"Yeah, that's me. Why?"

"Don't worry, I don't bite," Devin said.

Bruce laughed uncomfortably. Why would the guy say that, exactly? Or were they onto him after all?

"I'm going to ask you a few questions, and then you can get back to work. How does that sound?"

"Okay."

"You work at the wine-tasting bar, right?"

"Yeah. And I double as a server for the jazz concerts and other special events."

"Like the private engagement party last weekend?" Devin asked.

"Yeah, I worked that event."

"What do you think of the special events? Do you think the guests who attend feel they are getting their money's worth?"

"Sure. I heard only good things about the food we served. Although the dessert wasn't popular. We might want to rethink that next year."

"I'll make a note of it." Devin typed on his tablet. "Anything else that the guests commented on?"

"They liked the wines, but I guess they wouldn't book here if they didn't. And the band. We might want to consider putting pitchers of water on the table once the dancing starts. We had a hard time keeping up with all the requests for refills on water. People get thirsty, and they don't want just wine."

"Another good point," Devin said. "How late did you work the event?"

"I started around five, and I don't think I left until after two in the morning. We had a lot of cleanup to do."

"And the guests, did they stay until the event was over, or did they start leaving sooner?"

"Most of the tables near my station were full right up to the end."

"Good. That means people were enjoying themselves."

Bruce nodded. "Sure."

"One of the things we've considered is switching to a new type of wineglass." Devin motioned to the two wineglasses in front of Bruce. "I want you to pick up one with your left hand, and the other with your right. Get an idea of the way they feel in your hand."

Bruce picked them up by the stems.

"Set them back down—now, pick them up again, but by the bowls, like this." Devin demonstrated on the one in front of him, sliding the stem between his fingers and wrapping his fingers around the bowl. "That's it— now compare how they feel, the weight, the roundness. Which do you like best? The one in your right or left hand?"

"Ah, the one in my left feels fragile. As a waiter, I'd be afraid of breaking it too easily. The one in my right has more substance to it. I bet it goes through the dishwasher just fine."

"Good observations." Devin made another note. "Go ahead and set those down, and then pick up the two plates in front of you. Which do you think would be better for serving appetizers on? The owners are considering expanding the food service at the wine-tasting bar, to encourage people to hang out, eat, and buy wine by the glass."

Bruce picked up the plates. "I like the more modern-looking one. I think people my age will like it better."

"Thank you, Bruce. Go ahead and set those down. That's all the questions I have. Is there anything else you'd like to add? Are you happy working here?"

"Sure. It's a job. In this economy, I'm glad to have it."

"That's good. If you think of anything else, here is a preaddressed envelope. Just put your ideas on paper and mail it to me. I'll go through them and collate the responses for Henry and Rolf."

Bruce took the envelope. This had been the strangest experience he'd ever been through. He couldn't put his finger on it, but it just didn't seem like a marketing interview.

Jayden watched from William's office. The assistant winemaker was busy in the cask room and had offered them the use of his office to hold the recording equipment for the remote camera. William thought they were a marketing crew, recording bits for a potential ad campaign.

As soon as Bruce left, Jayden stepped into the wine lab—a large room with a long white counter holding lab-like equipment to test wine. In the middle of the room was the table Devin sat at, with his back to the camera, so they recorded each person as they collected fingerprints.

Devin filled out the labels for the plates and glassware. Jayden then dusted the glasses with carbon powder and, using fingerprint-lift tape, carefully removed the fingerprints and labeled them. He did the same for the plates.

"Looks like you got a good set," Jayden said. So far, his idea was working. "Probably all ten fingers. What did you think of Bruce?"

"Guy seemed nervous when he first walked in, but then he settled down after he heard the pitch."

Jayden bagged the glasses and plates and took the fingerprint results to William's office. He'd scan them and start comparing the prints while Devin worked with the next interviewee.

Devin took clean glasses from the two crates sitting on the floor near the table. He wiped them down so they were really clean and treated them with a spray that made fingerprints adhere to the surface without feeling sticky. He did the same thing with two new sample plates.

Jayden pulled the door shut to the office just as the next victim, er, interviewee, arrived. He slapped Bruce's fingerprints onto the scanner. They should have the results, positive or negative, in no time.

Chapter 61

The Eyes Tell All

Vasquez Müller Winery—That night

Tig waited with Jayden in the parking lot of the winery. It was after nine. Rolf's SUV was parked nearby, but there was no sign of him. Henry was late as well. Where were they?

The sound of a motorcycle engine grew closer. The bike turned into the driveway and stopped by the police van.

When Henry dismounted and removed his helmet, she said, "We now have a name, thanks to Jayden's plan. The fingerprints on the back of the bookshelf match those of Bruce Howell."

Henry's eyes went wide with disbelief. "One of our employees?"

"Yes." Rolf strode from the direction of the winery buildings to where the three were standing. "He works in the wine-tasting room normally. He's one of our servers. And yes, he was working your engagement party."

"Even more damning," Tig said, "he volunteered to clean the room on Sunday, giving him the opportunity to retrieve the camera."

Rolf nodded. "He had no other reason to volunteer. Suri told me the servers don't think of themselves as janitors, so they never offer to clean the tasting room."

"Do we have an address?" Henry asked.

"I got it from Suri earlier today," Jayden said.

Rolf held up a file labeled with Bruce's name. "And I have his personnel file."

"But no one is going off half-cocked." Last thing Tig needed was for Henry and Rolf to take things into their own hands. "Jayden convinced a judge to sign the warrant. We're going to search Bruce's place and find the original recording."

Jayden showed Henry the warrant. "And even if he's hidden the disc in a safe deposit box, all we need is his computer to make sure we have the right person. If we find Lady Killer and the flash drive serial number in its registry, then we have confirmation."

"You have everything you need." Henry paused to type on his phone, and then used the phone to gesture toward the police van. "Shall we leave for Bruce's?"

Tig frowned. Henry's gray hair and light wrinkles suddenly made sense. His older self had appeared in the video. He intended to confront the perp. But how could she tell a founder he wasn't welcome along?

"Henry, it may be better if we keep our party small. Rolf is a reserve police officer, but you're not officially one."

Henry looked up from his phone, and his lips twisted into a sardonic smile. "Did you forget you deputized me when we were hunting Oscar?"

Crap. How had she forgotten that tidbit? Henry had twisted her arm before he went to San Diego with Cerissa.

"Even if you are on the reserve force, you're the victim here, and the victim is never part of the team when serving a search warrant."

"The only victim here will be Bruce Howell when the Mordida police find his cold, dead body."

Rolf gripped Henry's shoulder. "It will cause too many questions to be asked. He's our employee. And we don't know who he's shown the recording to. We can't do anything to lend credence to the video. It could have repercussions."

"We are wasting time." Henry brushed off Rolf's hand, *whooshed* over to his motorcycle, slapped his phone into a mount on the handlebars, and sped off.

Damn, damn, damn. Tig knew immediately what had happened, though the others seemed confused.

"He's gone after the perp," she yelled while racing to the police van. "Come on—go, go, go."

Henry had probably memorized the address when Jayden showed him the warrant. Tig waited the seconds it took for the other two passenger doors to close behind Jayden and Rolf, and she shoved the van into gear. "We have to get there before Henry does something stupid."

They shot out of the parking lot, siren wailing. Fortunately, she'd already mapped out a shortcut.

CITY OF MORDIDA—MOMENTS LATER

The motorcycle gave Henry an immediate advantage. Leaning forward, he hugged the bike and gained speed by swerving in and out of traffic to beat the rest of them to the destination.

While Tig argued with him, he'd mapped the address on his phone.

When he arrived, he parked the bike at the curb and dropped the helmet into the storage compartment. He didn't want it obscuring his face; he wanted to see Bruce's reaction when he recognized Henry at his door.

Looking at the apartment building, he took a moment to study the two-story four-plex. Based on the numbering, Bruce lived in the upper-right apartment.

Henry *whooshed* up the stairs, covered the peephole with his finger, and knocked. Behind him at street level, the rumble of the police van marked its arrival.

Someone shuffled to the door. A pause, while the occupant realized he couldn't see who was outside.

Open now. Before Tig reaches me.

"Tyler, quit fucking around," Bruce said as he started to crack the door. Then he froze.

"Good evening, Bruce." Henry glared at his blackmailer. "Surprised to see me?"

The terror on Bruce's face said it all. The blackmailer tried to push the door shut, but Henry rammed the door open with his shoulder, rushing in. He clutched Bruce by the throat and pinned him up against the wall.

This *cabrón* had tainted a precious memory, violated the most intimate of moments, risked their very safety with the threat of disclosure. Henry wanted to bring him *pain*.

Bruce had stopped fighting by the time Tig stormed inside. "Henry, release him. Now. You're a founder. You know better." She huffed. "What would Cerissa say?"

A sharp pang of guilt cut through his chest at Tig's last words, and he opened his hand.

Bruce slunk to the floor.

Henry looked at the mortal male, wanting both to rip the throat out of the *pendejo*, and to stop himself from doing the unthinkable.

Madre de Dios, *what is happening to me?*

Chapter 62

Deep Trouble

Mordida Tropical Apartments—Moments later

Bruce coughed and coughed, rubbing his throat and trying to figure out how to get out of this shit without being killed. He should never have messed with a vampire. He should have put the video on pay-per-view and collected the cash as it came in.

He wasn't on the floor for long. The Black woman in a navy pantsuit grabbed him by the arm and stood him up. "I'm Police Chief Tig Anderson. We have a warrant to search your place." She motioned toward the Black guy wearing a police uniform. "Captain Johnson, show him."

The captain held up the paper. "We can search your entire apartment, but what we really want to see is your computer. Where is it?"

Bruce rubbed his throat. He looked at the search warrant. It looked official. Still, he wasn't sure he should cooperate. "I don't have to tell you."

"That's true," the chief said, "but if we have to tear this place apart, we will. You may want to save yourself the hassle and tell us where it is."

The police chief had already moved to the other side of the kitchen's breakfast counter. She started opening drawers and dumped the silverware on the floor.

"Hey, lady, that's not necessary."

"Are you going to tell me where to look, then?"

The two other guys—his bosses—had gone into his bedroom. Bautista called out, "It is in here."

The police chief strode over, grabbed Bruce by the arm, wrenching it behind him, and shoved him ahead of her into the bedroom.

"Hey, don't break my arm, okay?"

She forced Bruce to sit down on the chair in front of the laptop and said, "Log in and give me access."

Bruce rubbed his shoulder. "I don't have to."

"This search warrant says you do. That, or we take it with us to the lab and we break the code there. It may be, oh, *months* before you see it again, though."

Months? Bruce broke out in a cold sweat. He couldn't afford to buy a new laptop. What would he do for fun if they took it?

He punched in a password, his fingers trembling. As soon as the screen cleared, the woman grabbed him by the collar, dumped him on the bed, and gestured to the chair. "It's all yours, Jayden."

Bruce scrubbed his hand over his neck where it still hurt.

The captain sat down and stuck a flash drive in. Moments later, a program opened, showing a grid with words and numbers. Right there on the screen was what Bruce had named the flash drive: Lady Killer.

Shit. What the fuck am I going to do now?

His boss, Rolf Müller, turned to stare at him. "He's the one."

"I already knew that," Bautista said. "It was written on his face when he opened the door."

Yeah, even if Bruce didn't work for the winery, he would have recognized Henry Bautista from the video—right down to the gray hair.

Müller pointed over to the laptop. "But now we have proof."

Fuck, fuck, fuck. He was going to be in a world of hurt. The two cops were friends of the bloodsucker.

Müller stalked over to Bruce and grabbed him by the shirt, pulling him off the bed and slamming him against the wall.

"Ow." Now his head and neck both hurt. "I think you broke my skull."

"It's not the only thing that's going to be broken by the time we're done with you," Bautista snarled.

"Keep the noise down," the chief warned him, "or the neighbors will call the Mordida police. It's better if we don't have to deal with them."

Müller stood inches from Bruce's face. "Do you have any idea what you've put my friend through? Do you understand how much pain you've caused him? Well, if you don't know now, by the time I'm through with you, you'll understand pain."

Bruce's gut growled, threatening to let a load loose in his pants. "What do you want? The video camera? It's over there in the drawer. Take it. Just don't hurt me."

Bautista opened the drawer. He picked up Bruce's tighty whities and tossed them aside. Then his boss held up the camcorder. "Is this it?"

"Yeah."

Bautista pressed play, and the video came on, cued up to the bite. Seeming to be satisfied, he popped the small rectangular drive out of the player and strode back, waving the drive in Bruce's face. "Who have you shown this to?"

"No one," Bruce lied.

"You have shown it to someone." Bautista held the drive inches from Bruce's eyes. "Someone who is connected to the Mordida Water Company."

"Oh shit." Bruce's terror rose another degree, and he squeezed as hard as he could to keep his asshole shut. "That fucker Tyler told his uncle. I told him not to. And now it's Tyler's fault I'm not going to get my money."

"You were never going to get any money," Bautista said, punching him in the stomach.

"Oof—" Bruce doubled over, the muscles in his stomach spasming, the impact ratcheting through him, and he fell to the ground, the air knocked out of his lungs, tears flooding his eyes.

The police chief immediately pulled Bautista back. "Founder."

"Yes." He held up his hands in surrender. "I know."

"Why do you care if this Tyler saw the video or told anyone about it?" the chief asked.

Bruce managed to catch his breath and stared at Bautista through his teary eyes. "She doesn't know you bite people, does she?"

Müller closed the distance, kicked Bruce in the ribs, and *smiled*.

Sharp pain radiated through Bruce's chest, his breath coming in shallow, burning pants. The damn bastard had broken his ribs.

The police chief turned and looked at Müller disapprovingly.

"What? I didn't kick him that hard."

"We do not beat up suspects to stop them from talking, Rolf."

"*Ja, ja.* My bad."

"And we will discuss later what you didn't tell me about the video."

Müller shot Bautista a look. "Sure. But I think there is more Bruce wants to tell us. Right, Bruce?"

Tears leaked from Bruce's eyes as he tried to catch his breath. "I'll tell you anything you want to know."

Müller leaned over and looked at him. "Was anyone else at the winery involved?"

"No, I did it myself."

The police chief brushed Müller aside, grabbed Bruce, and lifted him until his feet dangled in the air. "You wouldn't lie to us, would you?"

"No-o-o," he stammered. "It was just me. I wanted the money all to myself."

"Somehow, I can believe that," Müller said. "So why did you show the video to Tyler?"

"It was an awesome video. The chick in it was hot. I had to show someone."

Chapter 63

Just Deserts

MORDIDA TROPICAL APARTMENTS—MOMENTS LATER

Henry lunged at Bruce, fury sizzling through his veins. This *pendejo* had seen Cerissa naked, violated her with his eyes, lusted after her in his mind.

For that, he should die.

But before he could reach the blackmailer, Rolf blocked him. Face to face, he squared off against his partner.

"Like I said, you'll have your chance," Rolf said. "Let's find out what we can first."

Henry narrowed his eyes. Feeding off Bruce wouldn't be enough to satisfy him now. But Rolf's second point was worth listening to. "Very well. Ask your questions. But he will keep a respectful tongue in his mouth when he answers, or I will rip it out."

"Did you hear that, Bruce?" Tig said. "No more comments about the woman in the video. I'm not sure I can protect you if you don't cooperate. Do you understand?"

Bruce, who was still suspended in the air at the end of Tig's arm, nodded.

"Good. Now, you showed the video to Tyler?"

"Yes."

"Did you show it to anyone else?"

"No, no one."

"Did you tell anyone else?"

"No, do you think I'm crazy? I was blackmailing my boss. I didn't want anyone spilling the beans about it."

"That is probably the only wise thing you did in all this," Henry said, clenching his fists.

Tig shot him a glare and then turned back to Bruce. "And your friend Tyler—he told someone else?"

"He probably told his uncle."

Henry had a sinking feeling that he already knew who the uncle was, but he had to ask. "Who is Tyler's uncle?"

"Jackson Aldridge."

The MWC's executive director. Henry turned his glare on Rolf. "That *gilipollas* knows about the video." Then he swung around to face Bruce again. "And you showed it to him?"

"No, I didn't. Only Tyler saw it. Tyler must have told him what he saw. But his uncle didn't see the video. I swear."

"Henry, the damage is done." Rolf gripped his shoulder. "It doesn't matter if Aldridge saw it or not."

"We will decide later what to do about Aldridge." Henry shook off Rolf's hand, still locking eyes with Bruce. "Where does your friend Tyler live?"

"Ah, you're not going to hurt him, are you?"

"You are in no position to ask questions," Tig said, raising him higher off the ground, holding him by his shirt. "What is his last name and where does he live?"

"His last name is H-Harris," he stammered. "His address is on my phone."

Jayden reached around Tig to lift the phone from Bruce's back pocket. He swiped the screen. "It's locked. Give me your finger."

Bruce didn't.

"Give it to him," Tig snarled, "or I'll break each one looking for the right one."

Bruce stuck out his index finger, and Jayden applied it to the screen.

The phone unlocked. He swiped through screens and punched a button. "Got it."

Henry let out a relieved breath. At least they could wipe Tyler's memory.

"It was wise of you not to lie about that, Bruce." Tig stared into his eyes. "Now, you have one more crucial question to answer. Are there any other copies of the video?"

"No, I swear, I didn't make any others except the one on the laptop I used to make the flash drive. I didn't think you people would find me, so I didn't make another."

Jayden turned off the laptop and grabbed the power cord. "We'll have to take it to make sure the copy's wiped."

"Please, man, don't take my computer."

Tig gave him a shake. "You are in no position to make requests. If you're lucky, we might return it to you—*after* we make sure the video is deleted."

Henry scowled. Return the computer? Tig was being much too nice. After he was finished with Bruce, the *cabrón* would be unable to use a computer—ever.

Tig gestured to the group. "Anyone have any more questions?"

"No, I think you've covered it all," Rolf replied.

"Henry?"

"No questions." Henry stepped closer to the miscreant, rage filling him. "Perhaps we will not kill him. Shall we blind him instead? He has looked on my fiancée with lust. He should not look on any other woman like that again."

"Nice touch, Henry," Rolf said, admiration in his voice. "But I think it makes things too messy. Aldridge knows about the video. If Bruce is blinded, he might suspect you're behind it."

"I would happily take that risk."

"I know you would, but *we* can't. And as you know, Henry, this is not just about you and your fiancée." Rolf gripped Henry's shoulder again. "It's about the community."

Henry growled and shrugged off Rolf's hand. "Then what do you suggest?"

"What the plan has been all along. Strip his memory of it and have a free feed. But that's all." Rolf crossed his arms. "You can't kill him."

Yes, I could. Henry sighed. *Yet I won't. Cerissa wouldn't like it.*

But what he would do was make the *pendejo* suffer.

"Very well." Henry gave a slight bow. "Tig, if you will release him."

Tig lowered the quivering Bruce. Henry took another step forward.

"What are you going to do-o-o?"

"You know precisely what I am going to do. You saw it on the video. I am going to bite your neck and take your blood."

If there was any satisfaction in this, it was watching Bruce cower.

"You fucking freak," he cried.

"That is where you are wrong." Henry gripped Bruce's arms, holding the quivering mortal in place and, with an angry quirk of his lips, displayed his fangs. "You are too stupid to know a real vampire when you see one."

He plunged his fangs into Bruce's neck. As he drank his fill, he exerted his influence. Bruce would wake with no memory of the event, and no memory of the events of the past few weeks. The video would be forgotten completely.

"Okay, Henry." Rolf tapped him on the shoulder. "That's enough."

Henry was ready to break Rolf's fingers if he didn't quit touching him. Bruce deserved pain for what he did to Cerissa. Objectifying her, making that video, sharing it with his friend—the miscreant would be punished for it all.

Chapter 64

Not Enough

Mordida Tropical Apartments—Moments Later

Tig couldn't let Henry do any permanent damage. She grabbed Henry's shoulder and pulled on him—he wouldn't budge. Rolf caught her eye. She realized what he was going to do and readied herself to back his play.

She slipped the special handcuffs out of her pocket. Made from silver but lined with leather, they would restrain without burning the flesh. Since she wore gloves, she could handle the cuffs easily.

On Rolf's nod, Tig moved. One handcuff went around Henry's wrist nearest her. Rolf grabbed Henry's other arm, twisting it back. At the same time, he grabbed Henry's ponytail and pulled on it as hard as he could.

Henry released his victim, gasping, his mouth ruby red, blood dripping from his fangs. Henry turned toward Rolf, trying to lunge at him. But Tig was faster. She slapped the other cuff on his left wrist as Rolf brought the arm back toward her.

Although handcuffed, Henry attempted to ram Rolf with his head.

"Nice try, *toro*," Rolf said as he stepped aside.

Henry lost his balance, fell onto the bed, and, rolling over, tried to get up. Rolf kicked his feet out from under him.

Tig pointed a finger at Henry. "Stay there."

He snarled at her but stayed put.

With Henry under control, Tig looked closely at Bruce, who lay crumpled on the floor, his eyes open but unseeing. Bruce had the vacant gaze of one who'd been thoroughly mesmerized. He still had a strong pulse, and she suspected he would have no trouble recovering from the blood loss.

"Help Henry up," she said to Rolf, "and we'll leave. Jayden, bring the laptop, please. Henry, you still have the disc?"

"Yes, the one that was in the camera is in my pocket," Henry replied, licking the blood from his lips.

Once Rolf had him standing, Tig took Henry's arm. "You're with me."

Rolf turned back to where Bruce lay on the floor, removed an envelope from his jacket, and dropped it in the perp's lap.

"What's that?" Jayden asked.

"His pink slip. He's fired from the winery. And if my plans work out, he won't have a chance in hell of finding a job in Mordida. He'll go broke and have to leave the area. That will be the best for everyone."

Rolf then stabbed the ball of his thumb with a fang and smeared his blood over the bite. By the time Bruce woke, Henry's bite would be healed.

Tig took one last look at the blackmailer and dragged Henry by the arm, leaving the dazed and confused Bruce sitting on the floor of his bedroom.

Mordida Tropical Apartments—Moments later

As much as he wanted to fight her, Henry let Tig lead him out of the apartment.

"Jayden, you'll ride Henry's bike back to the Hill," Tig said.

"That is not necessary." Henry abruptly stopped walking. "I can drive it myself."

"No offense, Founder, but I don't trust you right now." She motioned toward Bruce's apartment. "You may decide to go back and finish the job."

Henry sighed. He wouldn't have trusted himself either. He still wanted to rip out Bruce's tongue for what he'd said about Cerissa and make him watch as Henry sucked the blood from it. "You are correct, of course. I will ride in the van. The motorcycle key is in my front left pocket."

Tig and Rolf exchanged glances.

"If you unlock the handcuffs," Henry continued, "I'll get them for you. I don't think Cerissa would be happy to have either of you reach into my pocket right now."

The involuntary sexual reaction that came with feeding was starting to wane—still, he wanted neither of them in his pants.

Tig bit her lips together and shook her head. The look in her eyes said she was trying to keep from laughing. "All right. Turn around."

After she removed the cuffs, Henry tossed Jayden the key and then rubbed his wrists. He had a minor burn where the leather had been peeled back from the silver during the scuffle, but it would heal quickly. Despite his unhappiness over leaving Bruce alive, warmth flowed through him from the feed, and he felt calmer because of it.

Tig still watched him warily. "Henry, there's no point to avenging something he no longer remembers."

Henry nodded by way of reply. He knew she was right. Nothing more could be done to Bruce. Without his memory of the recording, any further punishment would be meaningless.

"What do you plan on doing with Tyler Harris?" Henry asked as he climbed into the police van's back seat and pulled the door shut.

Tig got in the driver's seat and Rolf took shotgun, then she put the van into gear and pulled away from the curb. "About all we can do is wipe his memory."

"Who will take care of that?" Henry wanted to make sure it was done properly.

"Either Tig or I will." When Tig cleared her throat, Rolf added, "Probably Tig."

"Very good. And Jackson Aldridge?"

Rolf turned to look over the seat at Henry. "Jackson didn't see the video. But he may have told others—at least, that lawyer who works for him seemed to be in on it. So mesmerizing him doesn't buy us anything. I figure we write it off as a loss—he suspects something, but without the video, and without the eyewitnesses who've seen the video, he has no power over us. He can't prove anything."

"I am not so sure. But we can discuss this later." The van had pulled up at the winery. "You can release me now. I will not go back after Bruce."

"Founder," Tig said respectfully, "keep in mind that if you do, you'll jeopardize your standing in the community. The council will have to be made aware of it."

Henry gave a slight bow from the back seat. "I understand you have a job to do."

Tig's duties included keeping the Hill safe from meddlesome mortals, but also ensuring the vampires who resided there abided by the Covenant.

"Henry will do the right thing." Rolf stepped out of the van and opened the back door to let him out. "He always does."

After the events of the past few nights, Henry was less sure of that than Rolf was.

When Jayden got there with Henry's bike, he took the helmet off. "That's a sweet ride. Maybe we should get one like it for the department."

Tig clicked her tongue. "We will see."

Henry donned the helmet and took his leave to ride back to the Hill. If he wasn't experiencing money difficulties, he would have gifted a motorcycle to Jayden for his help.

Tig followed in the police van. He suspected she wanted to make sure he didn't double back. Henry went straight home. Besides, if he wanted to kill Bruce, he could do it some other time, when no one was watching.

Except he wouldn't. In truth, he was too honorable to return and kill the blackmailer.

He stopped in the driveway by the fountain and texted Cerissa, saying he'd been delayed. Knowing the way he was feeling, he couldn't face her. Not with his face flushed from feeding and his anger so close to the surface, making his thoughts tumultuous. He would never forgive himself if he took his wrath out on her.

He started the bike again and headed to the dirt road that ran between his place and Rolf's. It led to the mountain behind his vineyard. If he needed to, he could park at the end of the road and scale the rocky hillside until he exhausted himself. It was better than starting a fight with his beloved.

The road was hard-pack dirt and bare rock, rutted by last year's heavy rains. He took the rolling hills a little too quickly, and almost lost control of the rear tire when he jumped the bike and landed with a thud.

He straightened out and gunned it again, almost reaching the turnaround when his phone rang. He hadn't put in his earbud, so he backed off the throttle, giving a little rear brake so as not to spin out, slowed to a stop, and took the phone off his belt.

"Henry?" Marcus said.

"What do you need? I'm not in a great mood."

"Oh. Then maybe I should hold off telling you."

No, that wouldn't work. Now he was concerned—had something gone wrong with the case? "Go ahead. I'll listen."

"Christine approached me tonight. She wants to join us."

"Do you really need someone else to work with Nicholas? I didn't realize we had enough day work for two assistant town attorneys."

"No, you misunderstand. She wants to be turned vampire."

Henry swallowed his shock. "I do not see how she could have made that decision so quickly."

"Simple. She's a smart woman who knows what she wants. And if I'm to take the long vacation I so richly deserve, I need her."

Henry's heart sped up. "No. I won't support it. Not if it means you'll leave the community."

Marcus chuckled. "I'm glad to hear you still need me."

"How could you doubt it?"

"Look, Henry, no one said anything about leaving the community. But I do deserve a vacation now and again. And so does Nicholas."

Marcus was right. The town did need someone as backup. "I will consider it. But only if you agree not to leave."

"Of course, Henry, of course. I'm not going anywhere, except perhaps a coastal cruise to Alaska."

Chapter 65

Imposter

Rancho Bautista del Murciélago—The Next Night

After a full day's sleep, Henry woke on Monday evening, feeling better about the way they'd resolved the blackmail scheme. It hadn't been perfect, but it would have to do.

Now he felt up to tackling the water issue.

An hour later at his house, Rolf, Karen, and Cerissa joined him in the dining room to discuss their options.

Even though he continued to block the crystal from conveying his emotions, Cerissa's profound sadness leaked through. "Henry, I'm sorry, but my research on how to overcome the sun's effect has hit a dead end. I'll keep trying, but I need more time, and we don't have it."

He squeezed her hand. "I know you tried. For that, I am grateful."

"Specifics, please." Rolf scowled at them. "You asked us here to discuss options. What has she tried?"

"Cerissa has been working on a sunscreen, for lack of a better word, that would allow us to go out in the sun. She used Ari as a test subject, and it didn't work." Given the risk of spontaneous combustion, Henry hadn't volunteered to try it himself. "And she also has been trying to find a stimulant to counteract the effect of sunrise."

"But again, nothing works," she said.

His phone rang. The caller ID indicated it was Christine. He put her on speaker.

"Good evening, Christine. I have Rolf, Karen, and Cerissa here with me, and you're on speaker."

"Good. That will save me a phone call." She paused, and the sound of paper being shuffled became audible over the line. "We heard back from the court. The judge denied our motion for a preliminary injunction. She wants testimony to decide the matter of the fake contract. We're going to trial in two days."

Not good. The moon would rise after sunset for the next week, so he wouldn't wake before dusk. And since Christine had pushed for the earliest dates available, asking the judge to delay another two weeks to when the next early moonrise occurred would likely result in them going to the bottom of the docket, meaning a delay of many months rather than two weeks.

Besides, even if an early moonrise woke him, he still couldn't go out in the daylight.

"Has the judge ruled on the motion to hold the hearings at night when Rolf and I testify?"

"No, not yet. She won't do that until trial is underway."

Henry caught Rolf's eye, who nodded at him to respond. "We must go through with the trial, then. You will win the motion. I will testify after sunset, and Jackson Aldridge will lose."

"I sincerely hope you're right, Henry."

"Oh, I am right. One way or another, Christine, we will prevail."

Henry said goodbye and hung up, scrubbing a hand over his face before looking at everyone. "We will still need options if she doesn't win the motion."

Rolf crossed his arms. "If Cerissa can't come up with a solution, then we'll use actors. We'll fly to Prague and feed the actors answers from there. What's hard to understand about that?"

Sunset in Prague would correspond well enough with the start of morning court hours in California. Henry had researched the matter when Rolf first raised the suggestion a few nights ago. In theory, they would be awake from the time court began until a few hours after it closed. But they could never train actors that quickly to replace them. Impossible.

"I told you already, I don't like your idea." Henry scowled at Rolf, and it wasn't just because the timing made the task insurmountable. "We're trying to prove MWC fraudulently replaced a page in the contract we signed. If we get caught putting on actors, our case will be over. For good."

"How could they detect an actor?" Karen furrowed her brow. "You and Rolf aren't well-known in Mordida. Would they really be able to tell the difference?"

Henry couldn't understand why they kept pressing this idea. "Even if we found two actors who looked like us, there are any number of ways MWC's lawyer could trip up an actor. And have you forgotten already? Both Aldridge and his lawyer saw us on Saturday. They would spot an imposter."

Rolf gave a dismissive snort.

"And even assuming Rolf and I fly to Prague and used some sort of communication device so that we could listen and feed answers to the witness, if the communications failed, they'd be left helpless. Not to mention we'd forever be at risk for blackmail."

And he'd had enough of that lately to last a lifetime.

"Bah, blackmail," Rolf scoffed. "We compel the actors to forget us. Risk eliminated."

Henry shook his head. "We can't do that. What if we need them to testify again? No, if we compel anyone, it should be Aldridge."

"Henry, we already discussed this—" Rolf began.

"Not exactly. I'm suggesting we scare him with what we are, bite him so he can't reveal the truth to others, and then tell him to relinquish the water claim or we'll kill him."

"Now that's not a bad idea," Rolf said with a curt nod.

"Henry, no!" Cerissa exclaimed, coming out of her seat.

"We won't follow through with the threat."

Cerissa crossed her arms. "That doesn't make it any better, and you know it."

He lowered his eyes. He knew how Cerissa felt about such things. Even if he—and every other vampire—had thought this way in the past, she'd shown him why it wasn't right.

Consent was important to her. While she had accepted that vampires sometimes blurred the lines to protect the community, using those powers to force someone to give the vampires a business or legal advantage didn't sit well with her. And, because of her, he did know better, even if it was counter to every instinct screaming at him.

"I've got an idea." Karen twirled a lock of her shoulder-length auburn hair. "What if someone could *be* a perfect physical match?"

"No." Cerissa gestured for Karen to stop. "I can see where you're going, Karen, and the answer is no."

"But it would work."

"What are you two talking about?" Rolf asked.

"I think," Henry replied, speaking slowly and deliberately, the seed Karen planted blooming in his mind, "she is suggesting that Cerissa morph into a replica of me."

Cerissa cringed. The very thought of mimicking Henry made her squirm. The Lux just did not morph to mimic loved ones. And certainly not someone they were *intimate* with.

No.

This was worse than morphing into a vampire.

"And you wonder why I call her *that thing*." Rolf scowled. "But I get the impression she doesn't like the idea."

For once, Rolf was right. She didn't like the idea. At all.

"Although I don't see why not," Rolf continued. "It could be the solution to our problem."

Henry tapped his fingers on the table, looking pensive.

She had no idea how he felt—he was still blocking the crystal. She frowned at the realization.

"But Cerissa," Karen said, sending a perplexed look her way, "you morphed to look like me. Why not Henry?"

"Um, well, we are both women, and…"

It was to protect you from the man who tortured you.

"Is it a gender thing?"

Before she could reply, Rolf jumped in. "So you *can* change yourself to look like a man?"

"Technically, yes. But you don't understand what you're asking me to do—"

"You'd have his fingerprints?"

"Everything, right down to muscle memory, like signing a document." Cerissa knew where Rolf was going with this, even though she disliked the idea. "All those normal things to prove identity, even retinal scans, I would pass without a moment's hesitation. But it's just not right. He's—he's my mate."

"Is this a Lux rule?" Henry asked, finally entering the conversation. "You cannot morph to become me because of our relationship?"

"No, it's not a rule. It's more basic than that. It's like wearing clothing in public. It's just what you're supposed to do. Or in this case, what I'm not supposed to do."

"It's a social custom?" Karen asked.

"I guess." Cerissa waved her hands, dismissing the idea. "Besides, he weighs at least forty-five pounds more than I do. I can't do a perfect morph of him."

"But you could in all essential ways," Karen said. "We could get padding to make up the difference in the torso, and pants would cover your legs, so no one would notice."

"I..." Cerissa shook her head. Could she really do this?

"*Cariña,*" Henry finally said, "if you did this, would you have to make it anatomically correct? As Karen points out, clothing would cover most of your body."

"True." She wasn't sure if that changed anything. Maybe. "I still don't know."

Henry looked uncertain. "But you would not have my memories, correct? You would be dependent on an earpiece—with me relaying answers to you live—or on your recollection of my retelling. Either of which could fail, and then you'd be exposed."

"Well—if I read your memories of the events involved using the touchstone, then yes, I would have your direct memories, and be able to answer based on those memories. I wouldn't need you in my ear."

She glanced around the table at her friends and fiancée. The looks varied: Karen hopeful, Rolf disgusted, and Henry inscrutable.

Yes, she'd rather not morph into a loved one. But it was only a Lux custom, not a rule set in stone. She wouldn't get into trouble for it. The biggest risk was that someone would guess it was her, which seemed unlikely.

And they were out of ideas. How could she say no?

Remembering back all those years ago—she hadn't been able to save the people in her village who died in the earthquake. The anxiety that blossomed since the quake spurred her to fix things for everyone else…saving Nicholas, helping Seaton, supporting Shayna, and, of course, doing whatever she could for Henry.

Even at the risk of being exposed.

Besides, no one would figure out it was me, right?

Her throat tightened, but she sucked it up and forced the words out: "We could make it work."

Chapter 66

Mirror, Mirror

Rancho Bautista del Murciélago—Moments later

"I suggest we take a break." Henry stood, concerned about the troubled look on his love's face and his own discomfort at seeing it. "Cerissa, walk with me."

He gave a short bow to Karen and Rolf before leaving the dining room and walking Cerissa out the front door.

It was a beautiful early fall night. A few wispy clouds floated overhead. The air was crisp and clean. He slipped an arm around her and walked her toward the garden.

Cerissa let out a sigh. "Karen's idea is a good one."

"I thought you did not want to do this."

"I'm not entirely happy about the idea, but I don't see another way out of our dilemma. I'm at my wits' end to find a solution in the laboratory."

Henry felt her shiver in his arms. It was a warm evening, so he knew it was the thought of becoming him, and not the outdoor temperature, that caused her reaction.

He wasn't entirely happy with the idea either.

"Is it that repugnant?" he asked. If it was, that made their debate easier. He'd never ask her to do it.

"It's not that it's repugnant." Cerissa looked away, her eyes unfocused. "It's the exposure—it feels embarrassing, like walking onto a beach naked when everyone else is in swimsuits. But I said I'd do it to help you, and I meant that."

He should feel like a drowning man who'd finally seen a lifesaver. This was their solution, wasn't it? And yet a strong feeling of unease remained. He glanced at Cerissa. He hated the idea of causing her any discomfort on his account.

Perhaps there was a different way to do this—a way that made them both feel comfortable about it. "Is there another Lux who could help out instead?"

"We could get Ari. But you're going to need him anyway. He can morph into Rolf with little effort. And given this charade, we may need to have Henry and Rolf in the same room at the same time."

"Would it be better for you to become Rolf, and Ari transform into me?"

"No." She shook her head adamantly. "Call me possessive, but I don't want Ari mapping your body. You're mine. And I'm not even sure he could with the crystal in your wrist. The crystal would perceive mapping by another Lux as an attack."

"Then getting someone else from the Enclave to help doesn't solve the problem?" Henry asked.

"I don't think it would. I wouldn't call my brother. We aren't close. And I can't think of another Lux I'd trust to do this." She stared at the night sky. "I, ah, we shouldn't tell any other Lux. Like I said, it's not a formal rule, but I don't know how the Protectors would react. It's…irregular."

That didn't sound good. "Cerissa, I don't want to make you miserable or get you in trouble for my sake."

She shrugged. "I doubt I'll get in trouble, and I'll get over the squirm factor. We should probably go inside and give it a try."

Guilt tightened his throat. As desperate as they were, something about this struck him as wrong. "Now?"

"If not now, when? We have to make sure I can do this. The weight difference is going to be tough to get right—figuring out where to cut the weight to make up the height difference between us. It's not like when I morphed into a smaller-to-scale tiger. With you, I have to rearrange fat and maybe muscle without looking odd. Karen and Rolf will judge whether I succeeded."

He was beginning to hate the idea more than she did. But a solution was necessary, and so far, this seemed the only viable one.

They walked back inside together, and Cerissa went upstairs.

Henry stuck his head into the dining room. "She is going to try. When she is ready, we will come in together. Let us know if you can tell us apart."

He ducked back out and went upstairs. Cerissa wasn't in her bedroom. "Cerissa?" he called out.

Then he felt for her presence. She was in his private space. He went through his office, past his lounging area, and into the walk-in closet that was more a room than a closet.

"No, no, no," she said as she slid his shirts along the rod. From the look of it, she was trying to figure out what to put on for the morph.

"Try this," he said, taking a suit and dress shirt down. "You'll have to wear a suit to go into court."

She took in a deep breath and let it out. "Fine."

She put his clothes on first and looked like a child trying on her father's clothing. Then she morphed, her body reconfiguring itself like a character in a Claymation film.

Now it was his turn to feel a frisson run down his back. He stared at a very, very skinny copy of himself.

She pointed a finger at him. "If you touch me, so help me, I *will* hit you. This feels just too weird as it is."

He held up both hands in surrender. She wasn't the only one feeling weird about the situation.

"I will not try to touch you," he said, as he moved in for a closer look. "Amazing." He circled her and, despite his misgivings, knew it would be difficult to tell them apart. "Is this what I really look like?"

She started to squirm. "Jeez."

"What?"

"They really itch," she said, fidgeting again.

Was she all right? "Cerissa, what—"

"My balls, Henry," she said, exasperated. "My balls itch."

A laugh shot out of him, and he couldn't help giving a bit of advice. "If you scratch them, be gentle."

With a chuckle, she adjusted her pants, and Henry studied her for a moment. How could they make her look right? His pants were threatening to fall off her too-narrow hips. "Let me grab some pillows to see if we can pad you enough for the clothing to fit properly."

When he came back, he shook his head in amazement. She had slipped both hands into her pockets and assumed a pose he had adopted on occasion.

"Here." He handed her the pillows.

She stuffed them in under the shirt and waistband, adjusting the pants over them.

"Turn around. I want to see you from all sides."

She did as he requested.

"I'm going to reposition the rear pillow. May I touch you to do so?"

"Fine."

He made the adjustment and stepped back. "I am quite good looking."

"Don't fall in love with yourself. You're arrogant enough as it is."

"Me, arrogant?" he asked, smiling as he continued to walk until he faced her. "How could you say such a thing?"

"Easily," she said with a smirk. "Now, let's go downstairs and see what they think. Karen and I can arrange to get real body padding at the local lingerie shop." He watched her pause and look over her shoulder, studying her backside in the full-length mirror. "They carry fake butts and other kinds of padding. We should be able to make it work. For now, the suit coat is long enough to cover your butt—I mean, my butt."

He stopped her from leaving. "Let me change into a suit first. If I go back down wearing casual clothes, they will know immediately which Henry is which."

When the two Henrys entered the dining room, they walked around the table on opposite sides, crossed at the head of the table, and walked around to meet at the door.

"Wow," Karen said.

Rolf stood and stalked closer. "I can't tell you apart. Which is the real Henry?"

"I am," they responded in unison, and looked at each other. "No, I am," they each said together with the same Castilian accent.

Karen laughed. "I wouldn't believe it if I hadn't seen it with my own eyes. But it won't work. She can't go out in the daylight if she's a vampire."

Cerissa chuckled and covered her mouth—a very Cerissa gesture—giving away which one of them was not the real Henry. She'd been so focused on becoming an exact copy of Henry that she'd morphed into him as a vampire. "Give me a minute to concentrate. This is not going to be easy. I have to figure out what human Henry was like."

She looked at him, and then thought about what she'd had to do to morph from Cerissa into vampire form. This shouldn't be any more difficult.

Karen was the first to spot the change. "Okay, we have a solution."

"And I have to call Ari," Cerissa said. "He'll become you, Rolf, if you're agreeable with the plan."

Rolf scoffed and returned to his seat. "As long as you aren't becoming me, I'm fine with it."

"Let me run upstairs first and change, literally." The initial discomfort over morphing into Henry had passed, and she'd grown accustomed to being him while distracted by her friends, but it'd be much easier to continue working as herself. Cerissa headed to the dining room door. "I'll also get my laptop. I need to order a hooded coat in the right size, along with gloves and a face covering. We'll need to keep up the charade that Henry must be fully covered during the day."

As she started to leave, Henry reached for her arm. "We should—"

"No," she said, pointing a finger in his face. "Hands to yourself until I change."

That feeling hadn't shifted. She didn't want Henry touching her in this form.

"Kind of sensitive, isn't she?" Rolf asked.

Enough was enough. Rolf's incessant teasing had gone too far. She took one of the throw pillows out from under the shirt and hurled it at him, catching him in the side of the head. He started to get up.

"Sit." Karen put a hand on Rolf's shoulder and pushed down. "We don't have time for this."

"My apologies," Henry said to Cerissa with a bow. "I forgot myself, but we need to talk."

"After I change." Cerissa headed upstairs.

She held on to the suit pants so they wouldn't fall and beelined to her room. Locking her bathroom door, she stripped and was about to morph, but something made her pause. She studied herself in the mirror. What could she learn about Henry if she spent some private time in his form?

She touched her penis, feeling it respond to a firm squeeze, before shaking her head.

No, now was not the time. Her friends were waiting. She'd have to investigate this later.

She carefully scratched her balls—he was right, they were rather sensitive—and then morphed back to herself.

Henry followed Cerissa upstairs, but at the speed of an old mare, one plodding foot after another, his body heavy as if weighted under a great load, his conscience troubling him.

At first, he was concerned over Cerissa's discomfort. But when she pressed forward and seemed fine, the uneasiness remained. In fact, it grew. Now it had finally materialized into a clear idea.

He could not allow them to commit perjury.

The use of *any* imposter was unethical. The fact Cerissa could create a perfect duplicate that could defy inspection changed nothing. Perpetuating a fraud on the court, even one justified because of their situation, no matter how tempting, was wrong. He couldn't use *necessity* as an excuse.

Yes, they desperately needed the water for their vineyards to survive.

Yes, Jackson had cheated him.

Yes, at some level, he felt cheating Jackson right back was justified.

But Jackson wasn't the only one who'd be cheated by the impersonation.

The justice system itself would be.

His moral compass sometimes wavered off true north, but his friends—particularly Yacov—would push when necessary to point him in the right direction.

When he faltered last night, Tig and Rolf had pulled him back from the abyss. They'd prevented him from committing acts he would have regretted today.

Now, faced with this dilemma, he longed to speak to Yacov, to go over the implications with him. But he could not. Tonight, he had to find the courage on his own to do the right thing.

Because it was easier to listen to one's beliefs when all was well. But when things went bad, well, he knew from experience that was when his determination to do the right thing was really tested.

And he wouldn't let all the good counsel Yacov gave him over the years disappear. His friend had believed in him, believed he could do better.

Henry knocked on the door, and Cerissa called out, "Come in."

She was almost dressed. He swept her into his arms.

"Thank you, *mi amor*," he said, kissing her. "For being willing to do this. But I have considered it, and I must turn down your selfless offer."

"Seriously? Why? I'm willing to—it wasn't as bad as I thought it would be."

He stroked her hair. "And for that, I thank you. But I cannot ask you to swear under oath that you are me. It wouldn't be right."

"I don't understand—"

"You would have to swear on the Bible to tell the truth and then lie."

He would not allow that sin—that blasphemy—to taint Cerissa's soul.

"But it would be my choice."

He stared into her emerald eyes, grateful for her willingness to sacrifice so much for him. "I love you too much to ask you to take that sin on your soul."

Cerissa said nothing, only kissed him gently in response.

Ten minutes later, Henry returned to the dining room, took his seat at the table, and explained why he refused to agree to the fraud. "We must find another way."

Rolf crossed his arms and scowled. "When I told Tig you always do the right thing, I didn't expect you to turn around and do the stupid thing. Now is not the time to grow a conscience."

The way Karen twirled a lock of her hair said she wasn't happy, either. Cerissa joined them and took her place next to him.

"Let us hope that the hearing is held at night," Henry replied.

"But what if the judge denies the motion?" Cerissa asked. "I still have two more days to come up with a Plan B. There must be something I can figure out that will work. So morphing has become Plan C, then?"

Henry shook his head. "It is not Plan C, either."

"Henry, be reasonable—" Rolf began.

"I have made up my mind. And before anyone gets any ideas, Cerissa cannot masquerade as me without my help. She won't have my thumbprint."

Cerissa cocked her head at him. "When I morphed into you, I had your thumbprint."

"I used an overlay when I obtained my most current driver's license. Without my help, you can't map it. If they insist on an identity check, you will fail."

"Henry—"

"*Cariña*, I appreciate how you are so willing to help, willing to do this thing that is against your culture. As tempting as it is, we will not cheat. It is better to lose honestly than to defraud the court. I will not let us become as immoral as our opponents."

Chapter 67

Battle Royal

Rancho Bautista del Murciélago—The Next Night

Prior to falling asleep, Henry tried drinking another stimulant Cerissa formulated, but it was all for naught. The dark wine failed to keep him from passing out at sunrise. At dusk on Tuesday, he woke in his basement crypt and his phone instantly lit up in the darkness. Just what he needed. Anne-Louise.

"Yes?" he answered.

"Well, you seem less than pleased to hear from me."

"I don't have time. I have to prep for the trial." He opened the crypt door and went upstairs to the kitchen. He could feed as they talked.

"Oh that. For you, it is always business this, business that."

"Anne-Louise, you must have had a reason for calling other than to harangue me."

"Yes. I want to come for another visit. You owe me two a year. December would be good."

"You were just here for the circus—"

"That doesn't count. You didn't let me take your blood."

He groaned. He didn't have time for this. He didn't even have time to stand still and feed. He grabbed a self-warming pouch from the pantry. "This is not the night to discuss our next visit."

"It is never the right time for you. Every time we talk, you are rude and hostile."

He struggled to restrain his temper and focused on lowering his voice. "Anne-Louise, if I recall correctly, we ended our last phone call with you calling me a series of nasty names. I do not have to stand for that."

"You deserved it. You are always thinking of yourself first, business second, and me last."

"You are wrong on all accounts, and I never deserve your abuse. In fact, it is time your rants ended."

Anne-Louise had a way of making him feel like a child. If he ever turned anyone vampire, he would never treat them like that.

He stopped in his tracks.

Why was he still thinking in those terms? With Cerissa in his life, he'd never have the chance to find out what it was like to be a maker. Cerissa was everything he needed in a mate, and he'd never betray her by turning someone else.

Yet his desire to mentor a vampire was strong, as strong as it had been when he brought Rolf to the Hill.

With his business partner finding his own feet and becoming his equal, was the desire rearing its head again—a symptom of fang fever, as Rolf had suggested?

He kept pushing the thought away, and yet the longing kept resurrecting. The longing to bring someone into the vampire life, to guide them, mentor them, care for them—even if the relationship wasn't based on sexual love.

But how would Cerissa feel if he bonded another person to himself? She wouldn't even let Ari morph into Henry's form. Had she not said, "You're mine"? How could he ask her to ignore her possessiveness, when he, himself, knew it so well?

If his body was telling him it was time to reproduce, he'd resist the urge. He wouldn't allow the desire to ever interfere with his love for Cerissa.

Just as he wouldn't allow his maker's abuse to continue. "We have known each other too long for you to speak to me that way, Anne-Louise." He resumed walking and returned to the basement bathroom to shave and get ready. "You will keep a civil tongue in your mouth when you call me, or you can just not call at all."

"See? You are being mean and nasty for no reason."

"No reason? You have no idea the pressures I'm under right now. Speaking of which, the house I'm building for you will have to be delayed."

If he could get out of that, it would give him some breathing room.

"You promised. Are you reneging on your word?"

"No, I just need extra time to get the winery into shape. You should respect my request."

"Well, if you want my respect, you should show me some."

"Goodbye, Anne-Louise." He stabbed the disconnect button and punched a few commands to change her ringtone to "silent" for the next twelve hours. No more calls from her would disturb him this evening.

Then he checked his email. Another margin call for a stock he'd shorted. He would have to use more of his limited cash reserve to increase the amount deposited against the short sale.

What had he been thinking? He'd been throwing away money left, right, and center. It made him vulnerable and left him with too little cash on hand. He should have increased his reserves when he increased his spending.

How had he been so foolish?

Cerissa spent the whole day in the basement lab, trying to find a stimulant that vampire blood didn't instantly neutralize. Her first attempt with medicating a clone resulted in a fatal heart attack—and though she swore she wouldn't waste any more donor clones, she tried again with a different drug. That clone's heart had also given out.

Henry had drunk down the pouch minutes before dawn. His eyes closed at sunrise, and she could do nothing to rouse him.

Failure.

Last night, Karen came up with a solution. While Cerissa hadn't liked the idea of morphing into Henry at first, she quickly saw it was the best option, but then Henry ripped it away from them. It now fell to her to fix the problem, and she'd flown into another research frenzy.

Why was he being so pigheaded? They were only in this mess because of MWC's own fraud. No matter how squirmy it initially made her feel to impersonate him—and still did, when she focused on the idea—under the circumstances, it was the right thing to do.

At least, it felt that way to her.

And something else was going on with him. Was he hiding other bad news? She thought being engaged meant they shared everything—the good and the bad.

She clenched her jaw, her frustration growing until she felt ready explode.

Then a new idea hit her.

She set up test tubes in a rack on the island lab bench, adding a mix of clone blood and a stimulant to each. Rather than process the stimulant through a clone first, maybe using twice the amount of stimulant she administered to the clones would be enough to overpower vampire blood's neutralizing qualities. She picked up the beaker containing Henry's blood and started to pour it into the last tube.

"I'm leaving for my meeting—"

She squeaked and dropped the beaker on the tray of test tubes, which tipped over, merging the samples together in one big blob on the lab table, drenching her lab notebook. The paper sopped up the liquid, becoming one wrinkled red blob, the blue ink bleeding until her experiment notes were illegible. Why hadn't she thought to use a waterproof pen?

"Damn it, Quique. That was hours of work." Why hadn't the crystal warned her? She should have sensed his presence. "You know better than to sneak up on me like that, coming into the lab unannounced. We agreed this is my domain."

"It's past seven."

She picked up a shop towel to mop up the mess. "So what if it's past seven?"

"I have to leave. I wanted to say goodbye."

"You couldn't knock? Send a text? Let me know without sneaking up on me?" She threw the rag down on the lab bench. The earthquake had her startle reflex on high, and he *knew* it. "I'm doing this to help you, damn it! I dropped everything else to fix your problem, and I have better ways to spend my time than wasting it re-creating an experiment."

Let alone the lost work, the record of failed experiments in her notebook.

He thumped his chest. "Who said I need you to fix it for me? You offered. You. If you are too busy, I'll find a way to fix it myself."

"I had a fix, and you said no. I can go into court for you. But no, you have to get on your high horse and talk about sin." She grabbed another shop towel and continued to mop up the mess. "You're being unreasonable."

He stepped closer. "Cerissa, stop your harangue. Now."

She was only getting started. How could he be like this after all she'd been doing for him?

"You rejected the one solution guaranteed to work. Sometimes, Henry, you're a self-righteous jerk."

"Do not speak to me that way."

"I will if it's true!"

"You are starting to sound like Anne-Louise."

As soon as the words left his lips, his eyes signaled his regret. But it was too late. To compare her to his maker wasn't fair at all.

She looked at the spoiled experiments. Hours of work down the drain. She swept her arm across all of it, sending the glass crashing to the floor.

"Cerissa! Stop."

"If you're going to compare me to Anne-Louise, I might as well act like her."

She brought her arm back to catch those items she'd missed in the first sweep. The rest of the beakers shattered as they hit the cabinets.

"I. Said. Stop."

She did, but it wasn't because he told her to. It was because she'd yet to feel his anger. The crystal was completely silent. "Why are you blocking me?"

"I—I—" he sputtered.

She cocked her head, trying to remember the last time he'd shared his emotions with her.

"You've been blocking me for the past week. I haven't felt our connection since the earthquake." She locked eyes with him. "Even when we've made love, you've left the bracelet on and kept a wall between our emotions. I didn't notice at the time because becoming vampire overwhelms my senses." At first, she'd been grateful he spared her the details of the earthquake's damage. But as time passed, she'd missed the intimate connection. "I don't understand. Why are you blocking me?"

His face dropped into a mask, mirroring the emotional barrier between them. "Perhaps I have grown tired of having no privacy."

She pulled back, feeling like he'd slapped her. How could he say that? Their emotions had been connected for months now. He'd never objected to the crystal before.

Damn it. She wouldn't rise to the bait again. Something in her psyche felt out of control, but she wouldn't give in. What he said didn't make any sense.

But something else did. "What are you doing that you don't want me to know about?"

Karen had been right a few nights ago when Henry and Rolf rushed off to the winery, and her bestie had suspected the guys were hiding something.

He waved a dismissive hand at her. "Nothing. I just want to be alone in my head sometimes."

Counting to ten, she reined in her temper. "No, I don't believe you, because it's never been the case before. You're hiding something from me. What is it?"

"I won't stand here and be interrogated. I'm leaving to meet with Christine. She's prepping my testimony tonight."

Damn. With her experiments foremost on her mind, she'd forgotten the prep was tonight. "It won't take me any time to change."

"Why? You are not going."

"I need to be there. If I replace you on the stand, I need to know what Christine prepped."

"I already told you I will not allow you to swear an oath and then lie for me."

"You don't get to decide what I will and won't do. And you know it's a backup plan."

"No." He sliced his hand in the air. "It is no plan at all. I'm leaving, and you are not coming with me."

Like hell. "You have no right—"

"I have every right. This is my decision to make, and I've made it. I will see you when I return."

VASQUEZ MÜLLER WINERY—LATER THAT EVENING

It was after midnight when Henry finished with Christine and left for his office at the winery. He couldn't face Cerissa, and huddled at his desk to be alone.

He buried his face in his hands. After he testified at the trial, then he'd sit down and talk with her. He couldn't deal with both her feelings and his fears at the same time.

He returned home shortly before sunrise on Wednesday and retired to his crypt. Minutes or hours later—he had no sense of time when he slept—he felt someone in the crypt with him. Something was wrong. The crystal sent him a strong pulse of Cerissa's distress, and a paper rattled near his shoulder.

He sprang to his feet, gripped the intruder's arms, *whooshed* them across the room, and plowed their back into the brick wall.

Cerissa.

He'd moved so fast that the gasp she made sounded as if it was uttered behind him. What was she doing here if she was in trouble?

"I warned you," he said with a growl. "I warned you not to come in here when I slept."

Tears swam in her eyes. "I wanted to leave you that note."

"Why?"

"I may not be here when you wake."

"Are you leaving me? Is that how you solve your problems? Running away?"

She'd left him once before because of what he'd done. Would she do it again?

"No—not willingly. I've been summoned to a meeting with Agathe. I think they figured out that I snuck into a confidential library and read the original research creating vampires. I don't know what they'll do."

"Then I'm coming with you."

"It's still daytime. No early moonrise. Won't you pass out soon?"

"My fear will keep me going."

"Seriously?" Her eyes got big. "But you—you can't come with me. You can't solve this problem for me. I have to deal with this myself."

"But we're engaged." He gently brushed her hair out of her eyes. "What happens to you is my business."

Saying those words peeled the blinders off his eyes, and he saw the one-sided nature of his assertion. He had been treating her like he was responsible for taking care of her and protecting her because it was his duty as a man, not their duty to one another as partners. He'd been refusing to let her share his troubles. He'd excluded her—the same exclusion he was now resisting.

He'd been a fool.

He slanted his lips over hers and parted them with his tongue. As they kissed, he slipped off the tungsten bracelet and opened the crystal to the max. It was an apology and a revelation. How could he ever stay closed off from her? The sweet taste of her mouth, the salt of her tears, the love—and fear—he felt flowing from her melted the icy crust of his shame.

"I'm sorry, *cariña*. You're right. I've been…hiding. But you don't have to face Agathe alone."

"But I must, Quique. This time, it must be me alone." She sniffed and swiped a hand at her eyes. "I have to leave now. I'm sorry. I can't be late."

She kissed him and then flashed, disappearing from his arms.

He stumbled back to the cot. His limbs grew heavy again, the lethargy returning, his hand opening until the bracelet slipped from his fingers and dropped to the floor.

His heart ached—he should be there with her, to face whatever Agathe threw at them. He could use the crystal to flash to Cerissa. The Enclave was inside an extinct volcano, with no windows. Sunlight wouldn't be a problem.

But Cerissa had asked him to hold off. She wanted to resolve this herself.

He'd failed to listen to her before, but as difficult as it was, he wouldn't ignore her wishes this time. If she really needed his help, the crystal would tell him.

For now, he closed his eyes and was soon dead to the world.

Chapter 68

The Truth

The Lux Enclave—Ten in the morning on Wednesday

The flash device built into her watch was programmed to take her to her bedroom at the Enclave. Morphing into her native form, Cerissa donned a backless navy-blue sarong and tied it at the neck above her wings. She chose the muted color to show respect to Agathe, and it also complemented her pale blue skin.

Now, to remove her lenses. They didn't fit her large Lux eyes and created double-vision shadows. Peeling them off, she placed them in a case to wait for her return to the human world. Hopefully.

She spread her wings and shook out her feathers, ruffling them until they all stood at attention, then forced them to relax in neat overlapping patterns.

Agathe hadn't said what the meeting was about.

It could be nothing.

It could be everything.

But the location of the meeting was what made Cerissa so nervous. Weeks ago, she had broken into the Enclave's sacred history library. A room that was off-limits without special permission.

It was in that room that she'd discovered the truth about vampires.

She kissed her engagement ring and left it by her bed, her Lux fingers too thin to hold it on, and then hurried down the obsidian corridor carved from millennia-old lava. She stepped into the shaft and, flapping her wings against the warm breeze blowing underneath her, descended to the lower levels. She landed on the ledge and rushed into the hallway leading to the library, bumping into Ari at the door.

"What are you doing here?" she sang.

"Command performance."

She leaned close to his ear and, in *pianissimo*, sang, "Damn. They know."

"Just play it cool, Ciss. Don't give it all away. Let's see what they have first."

The soft sound of footsteps came from the opposite end of the shiny black hallway, lit by dim bulbs that cast a reddish tone. She turned toward Agathe and gave a respectful bow. "Excellency."

Just Agathe. No one else. Not even the librarian who usually guarded her territory like a mama hummingbird guarded its nest.

But most important of all—no Guardians. Cerissa sighed her relief.

"Don't relax too soon," Agathe sang as she slid a key crystal across the library's door pad. "Follow me."

With a gesture and a flap of her wings, Agathe indicated they should gather around the glass reading table. A book already lay there. A book Cerissa remembered from her clandestine visit. A book that revealed everything the Lux knew about the creation of vampires.

Ninevah's Journal.

"In your report about Seaton and Rolf, you expressed how you wished you had access to the original vampire genome. I thought this book might help your research."

Agathe reached for the twenty-six-hundred-year-old book, her six fingers grasping the edge to rotate the journal to face Cerissa. "Although this journal has been restricted, I decided you should have access, since you already noted a similar structure to the Lux morphing strand in vampire DNA."

Cerissa stared at the cover. The hand-tooled leather. The gold-painted wings. The binding slightly cracked. She couldn't touch it.

Agathe opened the book. On the title page, *Journal of Experiment XIX* was handwritten, and underneath it, *Ninevah Sargon, reproductive researcher.* "Here, you wanted to learn about the first vampire. This will tell you."

Cerissa fluttered her wingtips nervously. She already knew what was inside and couldn't keep up the charade. Her eyes met Agathe's, her lips pressed together, her guilt welling up her throat to add a vibrato, a trembling sound in her song. "I've already read it."

Agathe nodded. "Thank you for admitting that. I discerned that you knew more than you were letting on in your report."

"When I started researching the vampire genome, I hit a dead end in our electronic records and tracked the missing information to this library."

"We will discuss later how you broke in."

Cerissa gulped. Yeah, that wouldn't be a pleasant conversation. "But why are we here? Ninevah's journal doesn't include the original genome."

"We are here so I could confirm my suspicions. And I won't even ask if Ari knew. Either he did and kept silent, or he didn't and is more incompetent than I took him for."

"Hey," Ari sang, fanning his wings indignantly, his silver eyes swirling with anger. "I'm not incompetent."

"Then you knew? Or do you expect Cerissa to cover for you?"

Ari shrugged his wings. "Yeah, I knew."

Agathe swung her gaze to meet Cerissa's. "Do you still want access to the genome?"

"Yes—please."

"Leave the book. You now have access to it whenever you want. But there is a second one you should see if you want to solve Henry's problem with daylight."

Cerissa waggled her wingtips nervously. "How did you know I was working on the sunlight problem?"

Agathe laughed lightly. "Have you forgotten the videos your lenses record?"

Oops. How had she?

The earthquake. The water dispute. Whatever Henry was hiding. Her volunteering to do everything. Too much stress was undermining her otherwise sharp mind.

That meant the Protectors knew of her dilemma, right down to her morphing into Henry's guise. She hadn't planned on letting her supervisors know. In her frenzy to find a solution, she'd forgotten to ask Ari to erase the recordings.

Agathe walked over to the section of the library marked 4000 BCE—books written over six thousand years ago. She gripped a volume in her long blue fingers, slipped it from the shelf, and brought it over to the glass table. "The earliest recorded journal of our history."

Reverently, Cerissa touched the cover. The title was etched in leather: *Journal of Nissaba.*

"You may come here and read at your leisure," Agathe said, before opening the book to a page marked by a very thin—and very old—woven thread. "What you don't know, what many of our living brethren aren't aware of, is that we are not well adapted to this world. Have you ever noticed how your Lux skin has no protection from this sun?"

"That's a well-known problem."

"Over time, with genetic surgery and the introduction of human DNA, we have developed more resistance to the light of this world. But as you'll read in Nissaba's journal, the first Lux who came here slept in caves like this one"—she motioned at the obsidian walls surrounding them—"and only came out at night."

Cerissa inhaled sharply. "You mean—"

"Precisely. Much like your vampires, our ancestors had the same problem. And Ninevah's DNA was much closer to our original ancestors' DNA than yours or mine. She was over eight hundred years old when she created the first of their kind—"

"Using the DNA from her own morphing strand, which hadn't been modified." The insight hit Cerissa like a falling boulder, and her wings sagged.

"You already see the ramifications. I suspect that, with the gene surgery she performed, she may have enhanced the aversion to this sun's light, and the vampire day sleep was born from that."

"But why don't we sleep like that anymore?"

"Have you ever noticed that sunrise and sunset have a certain pull on you?"

Yes, she had. "If I try to wake before sunrise, I find it difficult, and after sunset, I feel, well, better. But I don't sleep during the day."

"What you experience, what many Lux experience with the changes in the sun and the moon, well, those are residual effects after over three thousand years of genetic surgery to correct the problem. There are other books in this library that track the early attempts to solve the issue. You are welcome to read them."

Cerissa rubbed both temples, a headache forming. "Do we know where we came from?"

Agathe raised the top of her wings and fluffed them, signaling her annoyance at the question. "Not even these books record that."

"Oh." Cerissa wasn't sure whether to believe that or not. Too much had been kept hidden in this library.

"You have enough for now to work on your problem for Henry"—which she butchered as "Un-ray"—"so now, come with me."

Cerissa exchanged looks with Ari. She had a hard time believing they were getting off this easy. She followed Agathe and stepped into the shaft, flapping her wings to ascend. Her heart began pounding harder, and not from the exercise.

Were they headed for the Assembly of Protectors, about to face their wrath?

They flew behind Agathe, trepidation building. When the head of the Assembly stopped at the floor housing the clone lab, relief bubbled up in Cerissa.

Agathe led the way in and walked directly to the lab's refrigerator, taking out a small glass petri dish, which she set on the lab bench. "This sample should be about thawed. Use it wisely."

"Absolutely." The small blob of tissue didn't look like much. Cerissa glanced at her watch, the black band of which always looked strange on her thin Lux wrist. Not even noon in Sierra Escondida. Enough time to start a full genome mapping and still make it back by the next day for trial.

She sliced off a thin sample, placed it on a glass slide, laying the tissue in the slide's dimple, and slid the slide into the DNA sequencer. Would the results provide the answer to waking Henry for the day?

Then she glanced up. She'd almost missed what Agathe said. With a respectful bow, Cerissa sang, "Pardon?"

"Do not consider this a reward for bad behavior. I want you to make progress with helping the vampire communities to ensure their antisocial members have an opportunity to become better adjusted living side by side with mortals."

Cerissa stared at the tissue sample containing the original vampire genome—the prototype for all vampires. "Then the Protectors don't know I have this?"

"Correct. If I told them, I would have to reveal what you and Ari did. I didn't think you'd want that."

No, she did not. "Thank you."

"Don't thank me yet." Agathe raised her wings at the shoulders, the equivalent of a frown. "I'm concerned about your new habit of keeping secrets. So you will stay here for now and report directly to me."

"But I have to get back to the Hill in twenty-four hours. I'm due to testify in court for Henry."

Agathe spread her wings. "You're not going anywhere."

"But—"

"No argument. You'll stay until I decide what to do with you. And I haven't yet decided."

Chapter 69

Allies or Enemies?

Rancho Bautista del Murciélago—That night

The pounding on the front door had to be Rolf. It was seven o'clock in the evening on Wednesday, and Henry had yet to speak with Cerissa, although she'd sent a brief text explaining the situation. He checked the video monitor and then opened the door.

Rolf strode into the foyer, his fists clenched and anger on his face. "Where is that mate of yours?"

"At the Lux Enclave."

"Then would you phone Ari? He's not answering—"

Henry shrugged. "I'm not surprised. He's at the Enclave too."

"Well, he's needed here."

"I'm sorry, but that's not possible right now."

"Then how is Christine supposed to prepare Ari to testify for me?"

Henry crossed his arms. "I told you already, that will not happen."

Normally, he would have invited Rolf to the drawing room, but given the disrespect his partner was demonstrating, they'd stay standing in the foyer.

Rolf swept his bangs back and then *harrumphed*. "I can't believe how selfish you're being. This isn't just about you and your morality. This is about the survival of the Hill. Without water, our crops will die. How are all the other vintners supposed to continue growing grapes? Or Zeke and his free-range cattle? If everyone goes bankrupt, it will kill the Hill."

"You're overstating the problem."

"Am I? Water is life. Without water, our vineyards die."

"Then they die. We will find another way to make money. I won't permit a fraud on the court."

Not when it meant Cerissa had to carry the burden, the sin of bearing false witness. Given a choice between his beloved and the Hill, she would win each time.

Rolf poked a finger at Henry's chest. "You defrauded the court the minute you gave your name. *Hölle*, the documents Christine has submitted to the court are full of those lies. You're on your fifth—or is it your sixth?—identity. When you give your birth date, you're lying. When you testify that you inherited the winery from your uncle in the 1980s, you lie. When you fill out your tax forms, you're lying."

Henry slapped the offending finger aside. "I know. I cannot avoid those lies and survive. That sin is on me. But putting Cerissa in my place and Ari in your place, I cannot ask them to take an oath and then lie. That far exceeds—"

"No, it doesn't. They are not going to lie about what happened in 1987 when the water contract was signed. The most important part of their testimony will be the truth."

"But the judge is determining the credibility of the person testifying. Watching an imposter testify subverts the very nature of the tribunal system."

"But MWC defrauded the Hill. They subverted the system first."

"Two wrongs do not make a right." Henry turned away and stormed toward the drawing room. "Let yourself out."

Rolf's footsteps followed him. "No. You don't get to hand me platitudes and walk away. You live in a real world—you couldn't have created our community without being realistic about the compromises you'd have to make. You are a politician, even if you don't like thinking of yourself as one. And everything isn't always black and white. You don't always get to make the perfect ethical choice. Sometimes you have to choose the lesser of two evils. And in this case, if you do nothing, if you let MWC get away with this fraud, that would be the greater evil."

Henry collapsed onto his chair. He couldn't do this anymore. If only Yacov were here. He'd give anything to discuss this with Yacov. Except he couldn't, not now and not even if Yacov was still alive. His friend could never have been told about Cerissa's Lux origins. Rolf only knew because it'd been necessary to save Karen's life.

Then it occurred to him. Another reason Rolf's plan wouldn't work: *Cerissa's secret identity.*

Why hadn't he thought through the ramifications before?

Henry gestured angrily. "If we do what you suggest, how will you explain it to the rest of the Hill? There is no magic medicine, no secret formula to keep us awake and protect us from daylight. The lie becomes impossible to maintain without outing Cerissa."

"Not necessarily. We may figure out a way to explain this. But right now, we have to prep Ari to replace me. Without that, there is nothing to explain. So we do that first."

"Ari can't be here right now."

"Henry—"

"It is not my doing, Rolf. Both Ari and Cerissa are currently confined to the Enclave."

"What?" Rolf screeched. "You might have led with that."

"Her superior is giving her access to the original vampire genome. So she may be able to figure out something to help." Henry rubbed his eyes, wishing Rolf would leave. "But she and Ari are not coming back tonight."

Rolf stood there, staring down at him. "Then I'll record my session with Christine. I know you recorded yours. I want you to promise that you'll send the audio files to Cerissa so she and Ari can prepare. Just in case we lose the motion."

"I don't agree—"

"You don't have to agree this minute, but if you don't send her the recordings, she'll have no time to prepare if you change your mind. Trial starts tomorrow. Send the damn things and decide later."

Henry closed his eyes. As much as he hated admitting it, Rolf was right. "As you say. I'll send the audio recordings, but I'm not giving the plan my blessings. Christine heard us arguing two nights ago in Marcus's office. And if she catches wind of what you propose—bringing in an imposter—she will refuse to conduct the examination and let the witness give their own presentation without her help. She told me so during our prep. If she does that, the court will know it's to prevent her client from putting on false testimony, even if the judge doesn't realize what the specific lie is."

<hr />

THE LUX ENCLAVE—FOUR HOURS LATER

"I'm a bit busy," Cerissa said, skimming the DNA sequencer's results as she answered Henry's call.

"I know. I understand. I'm sending you the audio recordings."

That piqued her interest. She moved away from the lab bench to give him her undivided attention.

"I do not think it's the right thing, but I'll leave my fingerprint overlays in the basement bathroom. If we lose the motion and you decide to testify in my stead, they will be there. But don't do it if it would cause more people to learn what you are. The water isn't worth it, but the choice is yours to make. Use your best judgment." He paused. "And Cerissa, I'm sorry. You're right. I have been keeping things from you. After the trial, I'll explain everything."

She breathed a sigh of relief. The recording wasn't as good as using the touchstone, yet under the circumstances, it was the best option they had. She could listen to it as she worked.

But he was right—how would they explain Henry's appearance in court to everyone on the Hill? Surely she could come up with an idea to cover the situation without exposing herself.

"Thank you, Quique. And I'm sorry. I think the earthquake has me more on edge than I realized before. I shouldn't have taken out my frustration on you. Now I better get back to my research. I don't know if it will make any difference, but I'm trying to drill down on what it is about the sun and the moon that controls your sleep."

"I love you."

"And I love you too. Talk to you later."

Feeling better, she hung up and returned to the lab bench. The genome was the sum of all an organism's DNA—which she now had for the original vampire. Her test so far revealed that the vampire components of the original genome, in particular the Lux-like morphing strand, closely matched Henry and Matt. There was a small deviation with Rolf. Could that gene be the one that controlled his need for adrenaline-enhanced blood?

But when compared to Seaton's DNA, it was clear Seaton was different from the original. Henry, Matt, and Rolf each had the same pattern in one area of the morphing strand DNA that matched the original genome—but it was different in Seaton.

This confirmed her working theory: Seaton's inability to produce fang serum was definitely a genetic mutation. While it didn't help her with a solution, it did identify what that section of the genome controlled.

If only the mutation had allowed Seaton to stay awake and go out in sunlight, she'd have a better idea as to what in the morphing strand controlled day sleep.

Then she thought of something she hadn't before. What if she compared the DNA of her own morphing strand to Henry's?

An hour later, she had her answer. The tiny differences were clear—the Lux had flipped some alleles normally present in the morphing strand, so they turned off. Which was why she didn't have Henry's sleep and daylight problems. But that meant the fix had to be made at a genetic level, and damn it, she refused to do anything in haste that might hurt Henry.

Still, if it were possible...

As the night wore on, and midnight came and went, she plodded through a few more dead ends. The next time she checked the clock, it was three in the morning.

Court would start at eight. She had five more hours to come up with a solution and didn't even feel sleepy. Nothing like fear to keep her awake.

She scrubbed six fingers across her face and redoubled her determination to keep trying. Something had to work. But what?

CHAPTER 70

A ROSE IS A ROSE

MORDIDA COUNTY SUPERIOR COURT—THURSDAY AT SEVEN FIFTY-FIVE IN THE MORNING

Christine removed a yellow legal pad, her evidence notebook, and five pens from her briefcase, organizing them all for easy reach. It was the ritual she did at the start of every trial. Nicholas sat next to her at the table, doing the same.

The plain wooden table had been built by inmates who worked for California's Prison Industries. She'd spent enough time in California courtrooms to rub elbows with bailiffs and learn the ins and outs of the buildings and their furnishings.

The earthquake had damaged the newer wing of the courthouse, so they'd been moved to an older courtroom that had managed to survive with just a few cracks. A throwback to yesteryear, it had blonde wood paneling on the walls and hanging fluorescent lights. Unfortunately, because it was located on the building's corner, the room also had a bank of windows on one wall, the blinds partway open, letting in sunlight.

She was old school enough to feel unprofessional unless she wore a skirt suit. When she first started out, some judges would berate any female attorney who didn't wear a skirt, hose, and heels, and she had no intention of starting out on the wrong foot.

The bailiff announced Judge Susan Aslan, who strode in wearing the familiar black robe and sat down at the bench. Everyone Christine spoke to about the judge had the same opinion—Aslan was smart and fair, and theatrics in her courtroom rarely paid off.

"Before we start with witnesses, I want to hear argument on plaintiff's motion to take Mr. Bautista's and Mr. Müller's testimony at night," Judge Aslan said.

Christine rose to her feet. "Your honor, as you read in our motion, Mr. Bautista and Mr. Müller both suffer from a rare skin ailment. Dr. Clarke, their treating physician, has diagnosed it as porphyria cutanea tarda."

She was skating close to the ethical line, but who was she to say that vampirism wasn't a form of porphyria? A rose by any other name... So in essence, she spoke the truth.

"Bottom line: they cannot be exposed to sunlight. If they are, it will cause life-threatening burns. We ask the court's indulgence to convene the trial after dark so that they may testify then."

Nicholas had spent most of the week writing the motion and had crafted a compelling argument under the Americans with Disabilities Act. Considering he had no trial experience and had only handled transactional matters before, Christine was surprised by his work. His motion was well-written and required very little editing on her part.

Dick Peters, the defense counsel, shot to his feet. "Your honor, this is ridiculous. We've submitted into evidence expert reports on the type of skin ailment plaintiffs claim to have. Porphyria should not prevent them from attending court during the daytime. All they need to do is cover their skin completely. The courtroom itself is on the shady side of the building, and if we draw the blinds, there should be insufficient sunlight to harm them."

Christine schooled her face. Dick had no business interrupting her argument. Why wasn't the judge making him wait his turn?

When Dick ran down, the judge looked at him sternly. "Mr. Peters, this is your one and only warning. I don't care that we aren't in front of a jury. You will wait your turn. You won't interrupt counsel when she is speaking. Do it again, and the fine will be stiff."

He slumped into his seat, looking sheepish. "Understood, your honor."

"Ms. Dunne, you may continue."

"Thank you, your honor. What defense counsel fails to consider is that the Americans with Disabilities Act requires this court to make reasonable accommodations for a physical impairment that substantially limits one or more life activities. The condition that Mr. Bautista and Mr. Müller suffer from meets that definition. Any exposure to sunlight could be life-threatening. They should not have to take that risk in order to have their day in court."

Christine sat back down, signaling her argument was finished.

"Now, Mr. Peters, I'll hear from you. Don't waste my time repeating what you've already said."

Dick stood. "Plaintiff's counsel overstates the risk of harm to her clients. I'm prepared to bring in medical doctors to address the so-called risk that any exposure would be life-threatening. As you've no doubt read in our brief, limited exposure to the sun by a person with plaintiff's condition is not life-threatening."

"Bringing in witnesses won't be necessary." The judge took off her glasses and looked at Christine. "I'm ready to rule. While this court is sensitive to its obligations under the Americans with Disabilities Act, sufficient accommodations can be made to limit the amount of sunlight that comes into the courtroom. The expense of holding the courtroom open at night is not inconsiderable. From what I've read about porphyria, I am not convinced exposure to light is all that life-threatening. Motion denied. Be prepared to have your witnesses here in the afternoon. We will take a fifteen-minute recess so you may notify your clients, and then we'll begin with the witnesses who are here." And with that, the judge stood and left the bench.

Christine looked over at Nicholas. Now what would they do? If she understood Marcus correctly, there would be no way to rouse the two men from their daytime slumber.

"Don't worry," Nicholas whispered.

"Nicholas, I can't be a party to defrauding the court."

She'd overheard Rolf arguing with Henry about the idea. She'd told Henry during their prep that she ethically couldn't put an imposter on the stand. He'd agreed with her, adding he also considered it a sin.

Christine kept her focus on Nicholas. "If they try to bring in an imposter, I can't go along with it."

"You'll do what you have to do, but think of the harm it will cause." Nicholas tapped his pen for emphasis. "The Mordida Water Company cheated. We should be in front of an arbitrator at night, competing on a level playing field, and would be if they hadn't substituted pages in the contract. Why should they benefit from cheating?"

"I don't like it any more than you do, but I can't let Henry and Rolf send in imposters."

"I understand how you feel, but I think you're wrong. Look, do you want me to call Cerissa and let her know that we lost the motion, or do you want to make the call?"

"I'll do it. I'm lead counsel. It goes with the job." She stood up and walked into the hallway. The call went to voicemail. "Cerissa? This is Christine. We lost the motion. Text me. We're going back into court to put on the witness we have."

Then she hit Marcus's number. He had flown to Prague to be awake when it was daytime in Mordida, so he could answer any questions Christine had during the trial.

She told him the same thing.

"I know Cerissa and Henry were working on something," Marcus said. "I just don't know what."

"You must understand, I cannot be a party to fraud. I can't ethically lie to the court, not even with my silence."

"And you couldn't reach Cerissa? What time is the court expecting them?"

"One o'clock. Right after lunch. Can you try Henry's phone? I have to get back into court."

"I'll work on it." And Marcus clicked off.

Christine didn't like it. Why didn't Cerissa answer? Something had to be wrong.

She returned to the courtroom and put on her first witness. It was the records clerk for the SEWC, who established that the file had been in storage and not removed from storage until Mr. Bautista requested it right after the earthquake. It was a minor matter establishing the chain of custody of the transmittal letter copy that had the true contract attached to it and was quickly dispensed with.

Christine and Nicholas ate lunch in the courthouse cafeteria. There was a choice between two types of prepackaged sandwich: chicken salad or turkey, each cut diagonally. She went with turkey. The lesser of two evils.

When she bit into it, she momentarily wished she'd gone with the chicken salad. The bread was slightly soggy from the tomato, and the cheese tasted like paste. She took two bites and gave up.

Normally, she'd use this time to conduct a final preparation of her client before he took the witness stand, but Henry had yet to respond to her texts and phone messages.

She ate the bag of corn chips, her eyes aimed at her trial notes but not really reading them.

I can't be a party to fraud.

In all her years, attorney ethics had been important to her. She'd served on the trial lawyers' ethics committee, and never knowingly breached her duty to the court.

If anyone did, she knew better than to let her client bring in an imposter.

But Nicholas made a good point. They'd be in arbitration at night if it wasn't for MWC's fraudulent conduct.

Her stomach churned. She wasn't sure what to do if an imposter appeared. Which was more sacrosanct? Her duty to her client or her duty to the court?

Mordida County Superior Court—A Short Time Earlier

Jackson Aldridge grabbed his lawyer by the arm. "We'll eat outside under the shade trees. I have someone bringing our lunch."

As soon as he cleared the courtroom door, he ripped the wrapper off a lollipop and stuck it in his mouth. What he wouldn't give for a cigarette, but he'd promised the wife he'd quit.

Once they were settled at one of the lunch tables outside, Jackson texted his clerk with the location and then drew the sucker from between his lips. "I wanted to talk while we wait. I suspect they are running in circles, trying to figure out what to do now that they've lost the motion."

Dick shook his head. "Don't get too ahead of yourself. Bautista could still show up."

Jackson returned the lollipop to his mouth and sucked it against his inner cheek so he could talk with the white stick poking out the corner of his mouth. He leaned in close. "Look, I couldn't shake the feeling that there was something to all this—that it wasn't just Bautista being a whack job. I checked the old records, as far back as I could go. For the last hundred and twenty years or so, there has been a male of Bautista's description going by a variation of this name living at his current address."

Dick shrugged. "So his kinfolk have a long history in Sierra Escondida and they like to keep the property in their family. That's not so unusual."

"But the few photos that exist of these men show the same male, same ponytail, same everything."

"Again, so what? They are related, after all."

How could Dick be so pigheaded with the evidence staring right at them. "And then there's the video my nephew saw—the bite, the blood."

"But *you* never saw it."

"No, but I don't need to. You add all this to Bautista's so-called illness, and come on. Something is definitely fishy here."

"Are you really suggesting that Henry Bautista is an *actual* vampire? If you are, maybe you should see a doctor."

"Dick, I know it sounds strange. But if Bautista shows up, you have to stick with the plan." Jackson crunched on his sucker. He couldn't let that rich SOB take away Mordida's water—or threaten his position. Another two years and he'd have a full pension. "We do it my way. Regardless of whether he thinks he is a vampire or actually is one, we have to throw him off his game."

Dick *harrumphed*. "I don't like it. I'll do it as we planned, but this is on you. If your plan goes south—the MWC board has been warned, and the responsibility will fall squarely on your shoulders."

Chapter 71

Truth or Dare

Mordida County Superior Court—That afternoon

When they returned to the courtroom, Christine still hadn't decided what to do. Then she noticed that there were two new people at the defense counsel's table, a man and a woman. They probably had something to do with the fact Henry would testify soon.

Better to be prepared than caught off guard. She walked over to the table. "So, Dick, who are your new attorneys?"

"They aren't attorneys. This is Dr. Lucille Westin, a handwriting expert. And this is Daniel Harkwood, a fingerprint analyst. We just want to be prepared."

Dick did not say what they were prepared for, but it was pretty clear they expected an imposter to show up and testify in place of Henry and Rolf.

"I hate to see you waste your money on unnecessary experts, Dick," Christine said, and returned to the plaintiff's table.

When she sat down, she leaned over and told Nicholas what she'd learned. "Can you get a message to Henry and Cerissa, let them know what to expect?"

"I'll send a text right now. That will be the fastest way." Nicholas's thumbs began moving at lightning speed.

"All rise for Judge Aslan," the clerk of the court intoned.

Nicholas slipped his phone away before the judge could see him. Using a phone in court was a serious no-no and would get him fined.

The judge took her seat on the bench. "Please sit down. Ms. Dunne, call your next witness."

Christine had no other choice. "Plaintiffs call Mr. Henry Bautista." No one in the courtroom stood up. "He may be waiting in the hall. Could we draw the blinds first?"

The bailiff took care of shutting out the sunlight and then went to the courtroom door and out into the hall. When the door opened again, the bailiff escorted a tall, thin person into the courtroom wearing a black hooded coat with black leather gloves on his hands.

"Mr. Bautista?" the judge asked.

"Yes."

Christine cocked her head, furrowing her brow. It sounded like Henry.

"Please come forward and take the stand. We have darkened the room. Would you please remove your hood so we may see your face?"

"Of course, your honor." Henry walked slowly as he lifted the hood back, smoothing his hair with his gloved hands.

Christine stared bug-eyed. If they had found an imposter, he was an exact match for Henry. Whoever it was walked down the aisle and approached the witness stand. The bailiff seemed to guide—or support—the man.

When they stopped, the bailiff helped Henry to raise his right hand, which hovered about halfway up. "Do you promise to tell the truth, the whole truth, and nothing but the truth?"

"I do."

"Please be seated."

Henry shrugged off his coat and, with some effort, laid it across the witness chair, then removed his gloves, and took the stand.

Christine hadn't moved. She didn't know what to do. Her mind kept saying this couldn't be Henry, yet the match was perfect. She had no basis to claim this wasn't him.

For a moment, the magical ball Cerissa had shown her—the touchstone—flashed through her mind.

Could this be magic? An imposter posing as Henry under an illusion spell?

"Your witness, counselor," the judge said, prodding things along.

Before Christine could stand, the defense interrupted.

"We'd like to make a 402 motion, your honor. We don't believe this is Henry Bautista."

Evidence Code section 402 allowed a challenge for authenticity of evidence, including a witness.

Christine was on her feet in a flash. "Your honor, this is highly prejudicial. Counsel should have included this in his pretrial motions."

"You are right, Ms. Dunne. Mr. Peters, I do not appreciate theatrics in my courtroom."

Fortunately, this was a bench trial and not a jury trial. A last-minute motion like that in front of the jury would have been highly prejudicial.

The judge stared at the defense table. "You had better have a good-faith belief for your claim."

"I have it from a reliable witness that this cannot be Mr. Bautista. Mr. Bautista never left his home today. I have people watching the gate to his community."

"I object on the grounds of lack of foundation and undue prejudice, and call for a mistrial," Christine said.

"Ms. Dunne, I understand why you are objecting. As I said, I don't condone defense counsel's actions. But since the cat is already out of the bag, I suggest we allow him to proceed with a very limited exam of the witness to establish the foundation for his motion or lack thereof. Quite frankly, if he is unable to prove his point, it will only hurt his case."

"Thank you, your honor," Dick said.

Christine returned to her seat.

Dick approached the witness to begin his exam. "For the record, please state your name."

Henry did not miss a beat. "I was born Enrique Bautista Vasquez. I shortened my name to Henry Bautista after I immigrated from Mexico."

"So you're now known as Henry Bautista?"

"My friends call me Henry. You may call me Mr. Bautista." That got a laugh from the audience—a few of the Hill's mortals had shown up to watch, along with some of the MWC's staff who wouldn't be called as witnesses.

"And in what year were you born?"

"I do not believe I can testify to that, as I was but a baby and have no direct knowledge of the year."

Again, laughter arose from the audience. Even though it would be hearsay, a witness was allowed to testify to the year of their birth. But Christine had gone over this with Henry. She wouldn't let him lie.

As planned, he took out his driver's license and handed it to Dick Peters.

"Your driver's license indicates that you were born in 1965."

"Yes, it does," Henry agreed.

Christine let out a breath. Dick had fallen for the maneuver. So far, so good. Henry had only told the truth.

"You recall getting your driver's license?"

"Yes."

"And you know they take a thumbprint when you apply for a driver's license?"

"Yes."

"And were you thumb-printed when you applied for your driver's license?"

"Yes."

"And you signed the application form?"

"Yes."

"Your honor," Dick said, picking up a paper from the defense table, "I have here a copy of Mr. Bautista's driver's license application, with his thumbprint and signature. It is authenticated as a public record by the clerk of the Department of Motor Vehicles."

"Show it to plaintiff's counsel," the judge directed him.

Christine looked at it. The document looked authentic, but she had no way of knowing. "Your honor, we'd like a standing objection to any evidence introduced by Mr. Peters at this time. He has not exchanged this evidence with us, so we have not been in a position to authenticate it."

"If it turns out to be falsified, counselor, Mr. Peters knows that the sanctions will be severe," the judge responded. "But I will enter your continuing objection into the record. Proceed, Mr. Peters."

"I would like to ask the witness to sign a blank piece of paper, and to give us his right thumbprint. I have experts at the defense table who are ready to examine them and determine whether this is indeed Mr. Henry Bautista, or an imposter."

"Your honor, I must object again," Christine said. "These so-called experts were not on defense's witness list. They have not been qualified as expert witnesses. We should have the right to call our own experts."

"We've gone this far, Ms. Dunne," the judge said. "I'll let him take the samples, but if he insists on qualifying his 'experts' to testify, I will give you time to find and retain similar experts to testify on plaintiff's behalf."

"Delay only serves the defense. MWC continues to steal water from Sierra Escondida. Your honor, this is unheard of."

The warning look the judge shot her said it all. Christine knew she was pushing the judge's patience, but Dick had started this fight.

"I understand, counselor. But we will proceed as I've described." The judge turned to Henry. "Please provide a sample of your signature and your thumbprint to the court."

Dick brought over blank paper to the witness stand, smirking. He had an inkless thumbprint kit, similar to what a notary used.

"May I use my own pen?" Henry reached into his suit coat, pulled out a pen, and unscrewed it. "I'm accustomed to signing with a fountain pen."

"Go ahead," the judge said.

He signed his name without hesitation and started to hand it back to Dick.

Christine shot to her feet. "Your honor, I ask that the bailiff take possession of the paper Mr. Bautista just signed. Our current case rests on our belief that there was fraud. We want to make sure there is no opportunity for another paper to be substituted for this one."

"I'll grant the request. And you may approach to look at it."

Christine did. The signature had all the flourishes and curlicues that were part of Henry's old-fashioned signature.

But before offering his thumbprint on another blank sheet, Henry asked, "Your honor, may I see the fingerprint card for a moment?"

Mr. Peters looked like he was about to have a fit. "Your honor, I object. If he sees it, he—"

"Mr. Peters," the judge interrupted, "you're not about to suggest that he could somehow falsify his thumbprint. Show him the card."

"Thank you, your honor." Henry took the card and looked at it intently, and then at his own thumb. He handed the card back to the attorney. He then placed his thumb on the inkless pad he was offered and pressed it on the paper. His thumbprint appeared. Dick started to pick it up.

"Not quite so fast, Mr. Peters," the judge said. "The bailiff will hand the samples to me. Have your experts approach the bench so Ms. Dunne and I may watch them work. The clerk will swear them in so any comments they make will be under oath. Understood?"

"Yes, your honor."

The experts moved with some hesitancy from their seats at the defense table and were sworn in. Henry continued to sit on the witness stand, looking fatigued but otherwise not bothered by the whole thing.

The experts, loupes in hand, closely examined the samples. Dick Peters walked over to where the wall met the windows. Christine scrunched her eyebrows. That was a bit on the extreme end of "giving them space." He must really trust his experts.

The experts continued to compare the samples. The signature was spot-on, but the thumbprint...if it didn't match, would this whole thing get her disbarred?

No matter what she said, the judge would think she'd put the imposter on the witness stand knowingly. And the judge would be right.

Finally, the experts, puzzled, glanced over at the man who had hired them, who now stood near the blinds.

"Don't look at defense counsel—look at me and tell me what you see," the judge instructed them.

"The signature is authentic," Dr. Westin stammered out.

"The thumbprint is authentic too," Mr. Harkwood reported.

"Mr. Peters, your challenge to this witness is denied."

Christine returned to her seat and leaned over to Nicholas. "How is that possible?"

Before Nicholas could answer, Dick pulled on the blinds, and the afternoon sun flooded the room.

"No," Henry moaned, and turned away, crouching down in the witness box and scrambling to pull his hooded coat over himself.

"Mr. Peters!" the judge shouted. "Close that immediately. You are in contempt of court. I will decide your fine after this hearing is over. Be prepared to write a check. A very large check."

Christine ran to the witness box as the bailiff rushed to close the blinds. Henry's eyes were fluttering, like they wanted to close. "Henry, are you okay? Wake up! You can't fall asleep now."

Blisters had formed on one side of his face, and his eyes were solid black.

"Back up," he lisped between his fangs.

"Henry—" She touched her mouth, trying to tell him the problem.

He mirrored her, covering his mouth with his hand. "Get away from me. Now."

She took a good step backward. It *was* Henry. As much as she wanted to ask how, she couldn't in front of the judge. She watched as Henry's eyes returned to normal and he lowered his hand from his mouth.

His eyelids started to flutter, his head nodding as if falling asleep. She rushed back to him. "Henry, wake up."

Henry shook his head once, twice, and then gripped her arm and pulled himself upright. "Medicine. Jacket pocket. Flask."

She reached inside his jacket and took out a gold brandy flask, unscrewed the lid, and held the liquid to his lips.

After his first sip, he gulped it down, and seemed to recover enough to sit up again. He screwed on the lid and, with much effort, returned the flask to his pocket, then wiped his mouth with the back of his hand.

Blood. He had blood in the flask.

Christine grabbed a tissue from the box near the witness stand. It was customary to have a box there in case the witness cried. She wiped his mouth, and then blotted his hand, which was covered with angry red blisters.

The judge looked at the witness with concern. "Mr. Bautista, your hand is bleeding. Do you want to take a recess, or are you all right to continue?"

"I have been better, your honor. But I do not want to stop. I want this over with."

"Objection, your honor," Dick said from his place at the defense table. "The court should be informed what Mr. Bautista just drank. If it is medication, it could—"

"Mr. Peters, your objection is overruled. You created this situation. You will not benefit from it. Mr. Bautista has already said he is able to continue." The judge looked over at Henry. "For the record, will the medication you took impair your ability to testify fully and honestly?"

"No, your honor," he said with a chuckle.

The judge turned her focus to the two experts. "You are dismissed. As for the issue of identity, Mr. Peters, I have ruled. Do you have any further motions?"

Dick looked stunned. "Ah, no. Defense withdraws its objections to this witness."

"Good. Now sit down." The judge cut her gaze to Christine. "Ms. Dunne, the witness is yours."

Thanks to Dick's failed attempt, she had every confidence Henry sat on the stand. She could examine the witness without violating her ethical obligations to the court.

"Thank you, your honor. Now that we have it firmly established that this is Mr. Bautista, I have a few questions that I think you'll find enlightening."

Chapter 72

Game, Set, Match

Mordida County Superior Court—Moments Later

"If your honor would direct her attention to plaintiff's exhibits 103 and 104," Christine said, returning to the table to bring them to the witness.

Both the defense and the judge had an identical binder to the one she had, with all the numbered exhibits that had been submitted by both sides prior to the trial.

"Mr. Bautista, I'm going to show you the contract from 1987 that you located in your files. And one with original signatures from the files of the Mordida Water Company. Do you recognize these two documents?"

"Yes. They are the original and one of the carbon copies that I signed when we entered into an agreement with MWC, except for one page."

Christine walked them over to the judge and showed her the original and carbon copy. "Mr. Bautista, is there something special about this paper?"

"Yes, it is what was called onionskin. It has a watermark on it. If you hold up the paper to the light, you will see the watermark."

Christine waited as the judge did that. "And was the original that you signed on onionskin?"

"Yes, it was typed with an old-fashioned IBM Selectric typewriter."

"How do you know that?" Christine asked. She took the originals back from the judge, walked up to the overhead projector, and placed the contract underneath it so it would be projected onto a screen in the courtroom for everyone to see, including the witness.

"I was at my attorney's office when it was being typed. We were finalizing the terms, and I wanted to make sure all the essential deal points were covered by the document."

"And when you signed, you initialed each page?" she asked, using the overhead projector to display the initials at the bottom of each page.

"Yes."

"When you looked at the contract after the earthquake, did you see something you had not expected to see?"

"Yes. One of the pages I had initialed was missing and had been replaced with a forgery."

"Objection," Dick said, rising to his feet. "Witness lacks the expertise to determine whether it was a forgery."

"Your honor," Christine said, "Mr. Bautista is not here as an expert. He is here because he has direct knowledge of what he signed, and how he initialed the documents."

The judge looked at her sternly. "Then that is what he should testify to, Ms. Dunne. I'll leave the answer in the record, but you are treading close to the edge."

"Of course, your honor." Christine flipped to page eight and projected the faked initials. "Mr. Bautista, are these your initials?"

"They are the initials for my name, but I did not sign that page. Do you see how the initials are in the wrong place? All the others are signed at the lower right-hand corner. Whoever signed this one, they signed my initials more toward the center, and they aren't smoothly drawn. Instead, they are jittery, uncertain—not at all like the way I sign my initials. Also, the watermark is upside down. All the other pages were the same direction. My attorney's secretary was very careful about that sort of thing. Finally, since I use a fountain pen, the ink bleeds through—small dots are on the next page. There are dots on page nine that do not align with the initials on page eight."

"Anything else?"

"On closer examination, you'll see that while the onionskin is by the same manufacturer, it was from a different date than my attorney's secretary used. The watermark is slightly different. I believe we will be calling an expert to explain the significance."

"So you concluded that this is not the page you signed? Were those the only reasons?"

"No. Once we reviewed the document more closely, it became obvious that the text on the page had been changed. We had proposed and they had agreed to an arbitration clause, which specified arbitration at night because of my skin condition. Someone retyped the page with a different provision, calling for a jury trial."

"Your honor, I'd like to show the witness plaintiff's exhibit number 105."

"Our standing objection, your honor," Dick said.

He had argued during pretrial motions that any attempt to introduce an alternate page was in violation of the merger clause. The judge had almost laughed him out of the courtroom when he made that argument.

"Noted. Ms. Dunne, you may show the witness the document."

"Mr. Bautista," Christine said, "looking at this page, labeled page eight at the bottom. What is this?"

"That is a photocopy of the original page that was sent to MWC that the town attorney retained in his files."

Dick stood. "Objection, foundation."

"Your honor, the town clerk already testified as to the provenance of the files."

"Agreed," the judge said. "Objection overruled. You may continue, Mr. Bautista."

Henry gave a bow-like nod in the judge's direction, his movement more restricted than usual. "On the original contract, my initials—in the right place—appear at the bottom. The shading shows a hint of the watermark, which is in the correct orientation. And it has the arbitration clause. This is what we sent to them to have them sign. We did not realize until a month ago that they had substituted a different page for this one and forged my initials."

"Objection. Witness does not have any foundation for his conclusion."

Henry glared at the MWC attorney. "Your client is the only one who had it. Are you suggesting the post office replaced the page?"

Christine turned away to squelch her smirk. Henry would have made a good attorney.

"Mr. Bautista," the judge interrupted, "you will only speak when a question is directed to you. Your attorney will argue the case for you."

"Of course, your honor. My apologies."

"Mr. Peters, your objection is overruled," the judge said. "Ms. Dunne, you may continue."

"Just to make sure I understand," Christine said, "you signed the agreement before you sent it to the Mordida Water Company?"

"Yes," Henry replied. "We signed first, and then mailed the signed original and three signed carbon copies to MWC. The manager and attorney for MWC signed them and mailed two back to us."

"And the initials that appear on page eight of both plaintiff's exhibit 103 and 104, the original and copy signed by Jackson Aldridge on behalf of Mordida Water Company, those initials were not placed there by you?"

"That is correct. I did not initial page eight on those two documents. If you lay the photocopy of page eight, the page I did initial, over page nine of the version with the fake page, the initials line up perfectly with the ink bleed-through."

Christine did just what Henry suggested and showed the judge on the overhead projector how the initials and the ink bleed lined up.

"I have no further questions at this time," Christine said.

"Your witness, Mr. Peters," the judge said.

"I have no questions at this time for this witness," Dick said. "Reserve the right to recall when we get to the estoppel issue."

The trial had been bifurcated. If the judge found in favor of SEWC on the fraud claim, they wouldn't need to deal with MWC's claim there had been waiver of SEWC's right to cancel the contract, and the judge would then decide whether to void the contract and enjoin MWC from taking any further water from SEWC.

"Mr. Peters," Judge Aslan said, "if you recall Mr. Bautista to the stand, it will be at night, as he originally requested."

Dick stood. "Your honor, I object."

"If you wish to argue it, we will do so after we are done with testimony for the day. When we discuss the *sanctions* against you, you may argue your motion." The judge looked over at the witness. "Thank you, Mr. Bautista. You may leave the courtroom."

Christine watched Henry slowly walk from the room, leaning on the audience bench-backs to support himself every few steps. "Plaintiff calls Mr. Rolf Müller."

When the door opened, Henry walked out, and Rolf walked in. Rolf took off his hat and scarf as he walked down the courtroom aisle. Defense counsel looked ready to kill whoever had given him the bad information that Henry and Rolf were being replaced with imposters.

Dick rose to his feet and said, "May we approach the bench?" The judge signaled them to come forward. "I want to make a suggestion, if Ms. Dunne is agreeable. I would like to recess early today and meet with plaintiff's representatives and their attorney and see if we can't work out a compromise."

"That is a most unusual suggestion, counselor," the judge said. "We cannot just hold the courtroom for you at your convenience. You should have considered making your best settlement offer before we began this trial."

"Your honor, tomorrow is Friday—the courtroom is dark. If we stop early today, we can begin our discussions and, if necessary, carry them on over the weekend, and hopefully have a settlement by Monday morning."

"My clients have been stressed by this unnecessary imposition of holding the trial during the day," Christine said. "They may not be up to negotiations until tomorrow night."

"We will agree to meeting at night with them."

"Ms. Dunne, I suggest you consider defense counsel's offer," the judge said. "The case is going your way right now, but we know how easily that can change."

"Of course, your honor. We agree to enter into negotiations tomorrow night. However, I'd like to take Mr. Müller's testimony now. He has taken the risk of coming out in daylight, and if negotiations aren't successful, I don't want to make him return on Monday if he doesn't have to."

"Agreed. We'll take the next witness."

After Rolf's testimony, the court adjourned for the afternoon. Christine lifted a surprised eyebrow when Cerissa appeared and helped Rolf to a nearby bathroom, purportedly to get him fully covered before taking him out in the daylight.

"Go on," Cerissa said. "I have a lightproof van to take him home. Return to the Hill, and we'll meet you there."

Christine took her time packing away the trial documents, and then she and Nicholas left the courthouse.

"That went well," she said.

Nicholas grinned at her. "I really don't know how they did that. But let's order a pizza to celebrate."

"And beer," she said with a laugh. "I need one. Badly."

When they arrived at her temporary office, Henry and Rolf were already there, and on speakerphone with Marcus, who was in Prague.

Christine collapsed into her cushy desk chair, rolled it over to the table, and kicked off her high-heeled shoes from her aching feet. "Okay, you have to tell me how you did it."

"Did what, Christine?" Henry asked.

"It *was* you, wasn't it?"

"Think about what you are asking. Is it not better that you don't know?"

"You even sound like him."

"That is because it is him." Cerissa entered the room looking as tired as Henry and *tsked*. "Don't let him tell you otherwise."

Sitting down next to him, Cerissa kissed his cheek and added, "Quique, you shouldn't tease your attorney."

CHAPTER 73

BEHIND THE CURTAIN

THE LUX ENCLAVE—FLASHBACK TO EIGHT HOURS EARLIER

Cerissa checked her watch—it was almost nine in the morning on Thursday. Christine would already be in the courtroom, arguing the motion to let Henry and Rolf testify after dark. If the court didn't grant the motion, Cerissa had four hours to come up with a solution for how to wake and protect Henry.

Yesterday afternoon, she'd sent Ari back to the sacred history library to read through the *Journal of Nissaba*, the one that documented the Lux attempt to deal with the harsh sun of this planet. So far, he hadn't reported in.

Her head drooped onto the lab bench.

She'd been awake more than twenty-four hours, working on both prongs of the problem.

For Henry's sleep problem, she'd re-created the experiment she'd started that he interrupted. She'd completed it before sunrise and, if it had worked, could have transported it to him. But once more, failure.

For the sun protection prong, she'd whipped up another batch of sunscreen to try it on the real deal—the sample grown from unmodified stem cells. Ari had been pissy about being a test subject again.

She also performed a delicate gene surgery on the stem cell of the original prototype. Two containers, one with the modified stem cell, and the other an unmodified original, sat inside the replicator machine, which would accelerate their growth. Once both had replicated and were large enough, she'd test the new sunscreen on the original, and expose them both to sunlight.

But even if her gene surgery worked, it made little difference to the current problem. She couldn't do gene surgery on Henry right now. She'd done the surgery more for the prospect of future research into a cure. She had no idea if Agathe would give her access to another sample of the original prototype ever again, and she couldn't forgo the opportunity.

I'll rest my eyes while I wait for the cells to replicate...

A sharp pain woke her, jolting her upright. Her wing throbbed. What the—

Ari stood there, twirling a long feather between his fingers.

"Hey, give that back!"

"Whatever will I ask for?"

It was a childish game. Whoever stole a feather from a Lux could have whatever they wished for—provided it was within the power of a Lux to grant it.

She stomped across the room to where he stood. "What, are you thirteen again?"

"You snooze, you lose." The phrase sounded so strange sung in their language.

She stopped in front of him and grabbed for the feather. "Give it back!"

He held it out of reach. "Who knows what future favor I might need?"

She jumped and fluttered her wings, trying to get high enough to grab it.

Just as quick, he lowered the feather and slid it inside his sarong. "Try to get it back now."

She couldn't go there. The rules about body autonomy were too ingrained in her—despite his misbehavior, she couldn't overcome the rule to reach inside his clothing.

"Fine. Be that way—"

Her phone *dinged*, cutting her off. She looked at the screen. A new voicemail had come in from Christine, and the speech-to-text program translated it for her to read.

She sang out a frustrated note.

"What happened, Ciss?"

Her wings drooped. "Henry has to be in court by one in the afternoon."

Ari's swirling silver eyes gleamed. "Then you may be glad I got our production engineers to assist me in manufacturing this."

Ari held out a solid bracelet with a large white jewel in the center.

She accepted it, the metal heavy in her hand. "What is it?"

"A prototype Nissaba had been working on. If I had to guess, it throws up a protection screen around the wearer, bending light away and juicing the parts of our brains that are affected by sunlight, so we'd stay awake."

"It's a crystal?"

"Yup. The integrated circuit pattern was in Nissaba's journal—we nano-etched it onto a more modern crystal. The bracelet's material uses sunlight to power itself, a solar battery of sorts. Real cutting edge for their day."

"Have you tested it?"

"Not yet."

She suddenly recalled the report about magic stones in *Living from Dusk to Dawn* magazine. Had such a bracelet been gifted to a vampire by the Lux centuries ago? Was the white crystal what started the rumor about bewitched stones?

"We have an hour. Either the bracelet works, or I replace Henry in court." She strode to the lab's door. "We have to test it now."

"No way. I'm not going outside the Enclave to test it on myself."

"You don't have to. If the assembly room isn't in use, we can test it there."

A hole in the cavern let in sunlight. Anyone accused of wrongdoing was forced to stand right under it. She'd never understood the significance. Now she did.

Ten minutes later, she snuck into the cavernous room, pulling Ari with her. "Okay, morph to vampire."

He gave a disgruntled frown. "Why me? Why not you this time?"

"I have to observe." She shoved him closer to the light in the center of the room. "Come on. If you manufactured the bracelet correctly, then you shouldn't be harmed."

"Yeah, famous last words." Ari ruffled his feathers, closed his eyes, morphed, and yawned. "All I want to do is sleep."

She shoved the bracelet into his hand. "Here, put it on."

He slipped the bracelet onto his wrist. "I don't think it's working. I still feel like passing out."

"Go on." She gave him a push, but he didn't move. "Step into the light."

He looked at her like he was crazy. Instead, he thrust his hand, the one wearing the bracelet, into the sun's rays.

"Yow," he cried, and snatched back his arm, cradling it.

"Let me see." The skin was bright red but not blistered. She took a photo with her phone. "We're on the right track. You had less of a reaction this time. How long did it take to make the bracelet? If we tweak the light frequencies it bends, it might just work."

Ari morphed back to Lux. "It took me two hours to translate the schematic, and another couple to create it."

She shook her head. There wasn't enough time left to take a second shot at manufacturing a bracelet that worked. Would Agathe approve a team of engineers to keep working on it? If they could perfect it, the breakthrough would be life-changing for the Hill.

For now, she had no choice. She'd have to impersonate Henry.

Except he didn't want her to. How could she ignore his feelings and go ahead with Plan C? The question churned her stomach.

She thought back to where they'd left things. Her heart ached to hold him. He'd looked so apologetic—both about the secret he'd been keeping, and for slamming her against the wall. She'd forgiven him for his mistake, for confusing her for an intruder. After all, she'd disturbed his sleep.

Then it hit her. She *had* disturbed his sleep.

"Ari, come on. I've got the answer."

She flew back to her lab, Ari hurrying to keep up with her.

She didn't need to fool the court.

She needed to fool Henry.

Chapter 74

Behind the Curtain – Part 2

The Lux Enclave—Five minutes later

Cerissa was ready to drop on her feet from exhaustion when she returned to the lab. The samples she'd been growing, both original genome and modified cells, had finished in the replicator while she was in the assembly room.

Unlike with Ari, she didn't have to worry whether the samples survived the test, and to save time, she flashed outside with them—both the naked modified sample and the unmodified sample lathered in her latest sunscreen.

The unmodified one went up with a puff of smoke. The sunscreen was useless.

But the naked modified sample sat there looking unharmed.

What good it did her, she couldn't say yet. Moving from the petri dish to a living subject took a lot of research.

She sighed a musical note. With the sunscreen failure, her only option was to keep Henry out of the sun.

Now, to wake him.

With Ari's help, she gathered the necessary supplies to carry out her plan, retrieved her engagement ring, and then phoned Agathe. "You can pick up the remainder of your sample. I didn't think you'd want me to leave it unguarded in the lab. I have to return to Sierra Escondida."

"I don't recall giving you permission—"

"Look, Henry did everything he could to help us eliminate the VDM. He put his life on the line. You can't abandon him now. He—actually, the entire Hill—needs my help. We have to help them save their water."

Agathe made a whistling sound, the Lux version of a sigh. "Very well. You may leave. But you must wait for me to come collect the sample first."

Agathe arrived minutes later at the lab. After handing Agathe the petri dish holding the remainder of the original sample, and saying goodbye to Ari, Cerissa flashed back to her home bedroom, toting the supplies. She morphed, changed clothes, and raced downstairs. The seconds were ticking, the time to get everything done short.

She flew off the last stair and, hanging on to the banister, spun to her right and stopped in the foyer, thinking.

She didn't have time to drive to the courthouse, go through security, and make sure there was a lightproof way to bring Henry inside. So she dropped the bag of supplies she held, flashed to the courthouse, and figured out the best way to deliver Henry safely. She then returned home, found a box waiting for her on the front porch, and brought it inside.

Thank you, Jayden.

The box had everything else she might need if her first attempt to wake Henry didn't work. She carried her supplies to the basement, set them down, and wadded newspaper into a metal waste can. Hopefully, Henry wouldn't mind sacrificing one of his *Wall Street Journals* for the cause. She added a small amount of kindling wood on top and a spritz of ethanol for good measure.

Flicking the trigger on a portable barbecue lighter, she touched the flame to the paper, and the fire lit with a *whumpf* and then settled into a smokey mess. She touched her watch and flashed into Henry's crypt with the waste can, which triggered the smoke alarm. She dropped the can in the corner, far enough away from both him and the door. Flashing back out to the hallway, she hammered her fists on the steel door, yelling, "Henry, the house is on fire!"

She stopped to listen for movement.

Nothing.

All she heard was the shrill sound of the alarm. "Henry, wake up, the house is on fire!"

No answer.

How is Henry sleeping through this when the rustle of paper woke him before? Or was it my heightened anxiety that forced him awake?

Well, she was definitely anxious now. But maybe a loud noise would work. She grabbed the flash-bang Jayden had left for her. He'd done so with much reluctance and words of warning on his part.

Well, no choice now.

Holding the flash-bang, which looked like a skinny grenade, she transported back into the crypt, pulled the trigger, dropped the device by the waste can, and flashed out.

She could hear the loud noise through the concrete block walls, the walls themselves vibrating with the concussion.

If that didn't wake him, nothing would.

"Henry!" she yelled.

She felt the door rattle and the lock turn. He stumbled out and worked his way forward with one hand feeling along the wall, pulling her with him, until he reached the stairs. "Go. I'll follow."

He spoke very loudly, rubbing at his ears. The flash-bang must have hurt his sensitive hearing.

She shoved a vial of Rolf's blood into his hand.

"First, drink this, to heal your ears," she yelled, and then grabbed the fire extinguisher she'd left outside his crypt and ran inside to put out the waste can fire.

When she returned to him, he looked puzzled. "How did a fire start in there?"

She shoved him toward the small basement bathroom. "No time for that now. We have to get you ready to testify. Here, drink this."

She handed him a pouch of adrenaline-enhanced blood. He focused on it. "Why are you giving me this? It didn't work before."

"Just a theory, one we don't have time to discuss. Now drink!"

The stimulant wasn't strong enough to keep him from *falling* asleep at sunrise. But because his own internal adrenaline had woken him—a survival response—her theory was that the adrenaline-enhanced blood would be enough to *keep* him awake.

"Shave. Turn your hair gray. Get dressed. Your bulletproof suit is hanging there. It's the most lightproof clothing you have. I tested. Leather gloves are on the counter."

"I don't understand."

"I'm going to get you into that courtroom."

He blinked slowly, like he was trying to get bleary eyes to focus. The stimulant seemed to barely keep him awake. She figured he'd need another after aging himself. And possibly a third for good measure.

"But what if I fall asleep again?" he asked.

"Then the court will have no choice but to take your testimony at night. Come on. Less than an hour. Let's go."

"But I can't go out into the daylight."

"You won't have to. And you'll be fully covered in any case." She pushed on his shoulder, turning him, aiming him at the bathroom. "Just get ready. You'll see."

Twenty minutes and two more pouches later, he was fully dressed, and she helped him into the hooded wool coat.

Adding the black ski mask made him look like the bad guy in a horror movie.

She slipped welder's goggles onto his face and then stepped back as he held on to the bathroom doorframe. "Perfect." She slid a gold flask into his inner suit pocket. "And take this. If you need a boost, it contains more adrenaline-enhanced blood."

He sighed. "I don't know if I can climb the stairs."

"You don't have to." She adjusted her watch to flash two people. "Ready?"

Seconds later, they were inside the handicapped-accessible restroom just down the hall from the courtroom. She opened the door and peered out. Still standing in the hallway was the "out of order" A-frame sign she'd stolen from a nearby janitorial supply cabinet and placed by the door during her quick visit to reconnoiter. She felt guilty depriving a disabled person of using their dedicated restroom, but under the circumstances, Henry qualified, even if the judge disagreed.

"Okay, let's get you to those chairs." The sitting area was just outside the courtroom door. She held his arm as she guided him over. He sat down heavily, and she handed him another pouch. "Drink this now."

"I am already buzzed enough."

"I know. But your movement is still freezing up. You have to make it to the witness stand without me." She helped him take off the goggles and mask so he could hold the blood to his lips. Their end of the court hallway had no windows, so he didn't need the face protection any longer. "I'm going back to help Karen wake Rolf. When you finish testifying, I'll be waiting here for you. If you get done before I get back, then wait here for me. It won't matter if you fall asleep. I'll get you out. Trust me."

"Thank you, *cariña*. I'm sorry again for—"

"Don't worry about that now. Focus on this."

She took the empty blood pouch from him and went to the courtroom door to peek in the little rectangular window. The judge had taken the bench. When Cerissa looked over, Henry had dozed off.

She grabbed his bicep and shook him. "Henry! Wake up!"

His eyes suddenly sprang open. "What is the danger? I feel your fear."

"I'm afraid of you falling asleep." She let out a long breath. "No—don't close your eyes again. Drink this."

Another pouch. He chugged it down.

The bailiff stepped into the hallway. "Mr. Bautista?"

"Yes."

"You're being called as a witness. Please come with me."

Cerissa helped Henry to stand. "You can do this, tiger." She glanced over at the bailiff. "He's not used to being awake during the day because of his condition. If he needs assistance making it to the stand, would you please help him?"

"Sure. This way," the bailiff said, holding the door open. "We'll stop by the judge, and I'll swear you in once you're inside. Then you can sit down again."

Cerissa watched through the door window until Henry made it all the way to his seat. Now, to go and wake Rolf.

She just hoped waking Rolf would work without triggering his vampire instincts. There was no crystal in his wrist to protect her from his attack, and despite the way he teased her, she had no desire to hurt him. But she would if she had to.

Chapter 75

No Trick

Christine's temporary office—Five hours later

Christine still couldn't believe Henry and Rolf were sitting at the conference table. When she'd returned from court, the sun hadn't set yet, though the sky had started to take on the purple glow of early dusk. Her mind kept saying the vampires couldn't be awake. It must be some trick.

But when Henry kissed Cerissa in greeting, she had to accept the truth—from what she'd learned about Cerissa, the young scientist wouldn't have let anyone else kiss her like that.

"Indeed," Henry said, when he broke from the kiss. "Now that we are all here, we should discuss the next steps. Marcus is on speakerphone."

Christine scooted her chair closer to the microphone. "Hi, Marcus, it's Christine. Today couldn't have gone better. They are waving the white flag. How soon can you be back in California?"

"By tomorrow night. Arrangements have already been made."

"You need to start thinking about your settlement position. What do you want in order to settle this?"

"Everything," Henry said. "They tried to cheat us. We give them nothing."

Christine shook her head. "Henry, you have to be willing to give something if you want to settle this. We can't guarantee that the judge will see it your way. There is always the risk that she will be sympathetic to MWC—she lives in Mordida."

Henry *harrumphed*. "I will consider it."

"*We* will consider it." Rolf's forehead rested on the table. "I never want to be forced awake in the day again," he grumbled, and sat up, brushing his blonde bangs to the side.

"How's your jaw?" Cerissa asked, leaning around Henry to look at Rolf.

"Ack. It's healed already. How's your fist?"

She flexed her fingers. "I'll survive."

Christine raised a brow at the exchange. If she was following the two, Cerissa had punched Rolf in the jaw. "Why—"

Henry raised his hand, cutting her off before she could ask. "Where are we meeting with MWC tomorrow evening?"

"I'll send you an email with the location once it's set," Christine said, glancing down at her phone to see if Dick Peters had emailed her yet. "I assume you don't want to hold it on the Hill."

"That is correct," Henry said. "See if you can get a conference room at the local hotel complex. I do not want to meet at MWC headquarters. The negotiations should be on neutral territory."

"Understood. Now tell me how you did it."

Because after seeing Cerissa work the touchstone, Christine couldn't resist her curiosity. Had the scientist used something just as magical to wake the men?

Henry shrugged and glanced at his mate. "Cerissa figured out how to wake me and keep me awake. It wasn't pleasant—it involved a very loud flash-bang and stimulants, if you can imagine—but it worked."

"Intriguing." An exception to day sleep. She tucked that thought away for later. "But there's more to the story than that—how did she convince security to let you through fully covered—"

The scientist shook her head and mouthed, "Privileged."

Christine furrowed her brow. What did it have to do with the touchstone? Or was Cerissa going to use that one word to roadblock all future inquiries? She hoped not.

"Can I at least ask why Henry had to look at the DMV thumbprint?"

"Ah, that is nothing so interesting." Henry laughed with a shrug. "I had to make sure I'd glued the correct overlay to my thumb. When the DMV started taking thumbprints, vampires started using latex fakes. I have a set of ten with all identical prints. Whenever I have to renew my driver's license in person, I wear the current fake."

"Brilliant." It truly was.

The idea of becoming a vampire continued to churn in Christine's mind. The more she learned about their world, the more certain she became about her desire to join them. She didn't feel an ounce of doubt over bringing it up to Marcus. It was a whole world—an entire life—for her to explore. A beginning, rather than a beginning of an end.

But joining them had a lot of drawbacks. She'd never be able to go out in the daylight—not that she did that a lot now, since most of her work was inside an office. Still, to have the choice eliminated...

Then there were all the workarounds—like the fake birth certificates and driver's licenses. And she'd never be able to go into the courtroom again. Not that she'd miss it. The stress of trial was beginning to outweigh the excitement. After today's victory, she'd be going out on a win.

So there were downsides, sacrifices, certainly, but given that she'd just seen Cerissa figure out a way to overcome the day-sleep problem, she wondered what else the young scientist—or should she say, the young witch—might be about to change for vampires.

In fact, she wondered quite a lot of things about Dr. Cerissa Patel, including what sort of magic she really wielded.

"Christine?" Henry said. "Do you want to discuss the settlement now, while we have Marcus on the phone?"

"Sorry, I was woolgathering. Fatigue caught up with me. Of course you're right." She took out a pristine yellow pad. "Now"—she glanced at Henry and Rolf—"do you plan on letting them retain any water?"

Nicholas's phone rang, interrupting her.

"I'll be right there," he said, and jogged out of the room, returning shortly with a wonderfully fragrant box and a six-pack of microbrew. By consensus, they paused the settlement discussion while the mortals ate.

"Pizza and beer," Nicholas said. "I feel like I'm back in law school."

"How does it feel to pop your trial cherry?" Christine asked.

Nicholas laughed. "You did all the work."

"No, I didn't. I could never have gotten the motions written in time without you." Christine unscrewed the bottle cap and raised it in toast. "To a great team. I've never had a better one."

And with any luck, she might even become part of this team for the long term.

Of course, the vampire council had to agree. And she had to make sure it was what she really wanted. Because if she took that step, there was no turning back.

CHAPTER 76

CONFESSION

CHRISTINE'S TEMPORARY OFFICE—TWO HOURS LATER

By the time they wrapped up their proposed terms, the sun had fully set, and Henry was more than ready to leave. He pulled Cerissa to her feet. She looked a little out of it, having not slept in well over a day.

"Good night," they said in unison, then left and headed to where the Viper was parked out front.

"Let's..." Cerissa began. "Let's drive up to Look Out Point."

Confusion filled Henry. "Shouldn't we go home so you may sleep?"

"Sleep can wait, Quique. I need some time with you. And I've been stuck in the lab for what feels like forever. I need fresh air."

He helped her into the car, then fell silent to consider her suggestion. She'd shared pizza and beer with the lawyers, so she'd been fed. Maybe she'd caught her second wind.

He started the Viper and headed out to Robles Road. After everything that had happened, they needed to talk, to reconnect. Perhaps her idea was a good one.

"As you wish, *mi amor*."

"And while I'm not hungry, are you?"

"Thank you, yes." He glanced over as she fished a silvery-blue pouch from her purse—the color indicating it contained regular clone blood. "You would think I drank enough today, but I could use some refreshment."

She pierced the self-heating pouch with the sharp end of the straw that came affixed to the packaging. She held it out, and he leaned over to take a long swig as he continued to drive, and afterward smiled at her, flashing a little fang.

She smiled back at him. Since he needed both hands to drive—one on the wheel and one on the stick—she continued to hold the pouch and feed him sips.

"I'm glad I didn't have to become you and testify. But I still think you were wrong about that."

He had stood his ground on what he thought was right. "Yes, it must be disappointing that your man toy is not a pushover."

She took a deep breath. "On the contrary, Henry," she said, becoming quite serious, "I wouldn't want you any other way."

He took another sip, and they fell silent together.

So why had he cut her out of his problems? If he was going to talk with her about everything, he needed to understand his own motives.

Except he wasn't sure of the *why*. But he knew where to start.

They arrived at the area closest to Look Out Point that a car could reach. He parked, turned off the engine, and faced her.

"Cerissa, I want to apologize. I've been under a lot of stress, yes, but the stress does not excuse my behavior. I should never have cut off our connection for so long. I should not have hidden my troubles from you. Once you hear the reason I stopped sharing my feelings, I hope you can forgive my poor decisions."

She took his hand. "Whatever it is, we can get through it together."

Where should he even begin? He thought for a moment how to unpeel the onion.

"I—I am not in a good place financially. The damage to the winery was more than the business can afford to fix, and we need a capital infusion. I don't have the cash to pay my share. My money is tied up in fixed assets. And with the drop in both the stock and real estate markets, now is not the time to sell those assets or take a loan against them."

When Cerissa's gaze dropped to her engagement ring, he quickly covered it with his hand. "No, we are not selling your ring or your necklace."

"But—"

"Never. I will find another way out."

"If we're to be married, shouldn't that be 'we'? We will find a way together?"

His trial testimony had only been possible because they worked together as a team. So much of what they'd overcome was only possible as partners, as mates. They were always better together than apart.

His heart warmed, and he felt lighter. "Yes, *mi amor*. You are right. It is our life now, not only mine."

She raised her hand, brushing her fingers along his jaw line. "When we get home later, perhaps you can show me the problem on paper. Together, we might be able to economize. And Biologics Research Lab will reimburse you for the equipment and materials charged to your credit cards."

"You don't have to do that."

"I want to," Cerissa replied. "And it makes perfect sense to do so."

Why was it so hard for him to accept the money from her? She was right: those purchases were properly an expense of her business. Still, the fact he couldn't pay for them right now made him feel less than a man.

Do I really equate my manhood with having money?

He'd wondered before whether that might be a factor, but it seemed almost too clear to him now. He was indeed equating the two.

Nicholas had pointed out that the Hill put too much emphasis on money, and Henry's personal beliefs likely drove the community in that direction.

Henry's father had married a woman he didn't love—a woman he resented for her mixed race—because all he desired was money. From a young age, Henry's father had drilled into his head that a man without money was nothing.

He'd heard it said that when two people married, they came to the relationship with the examples and expectations they'd seen in their parents' marriage. But was that truly the best way?

Because the last thing he wanted was to be like his father, to marry for money. But in distancing himself from his *papá*, had he swung too far the other way, believing that his hard work, his ability to make money, was what made him a good husband for Cerissa?

Given his history, his past belief that he couldn't be trusted with a mate, he'd never planned on marrying, and thus hadn't thought through how the insight might apply to his behavior. But now? It suddenly all made sense.

In his parents' marriage, his *mamá* never had anything to do with the family finances—his *papá* made sure of that, even though it was her money that gave them their start.

With his childhood role models driving his subconscious, Henry hadn't been able to untangle his conflicted feelings and share his situation with Cerissa. He struggled between fighting the image of marriage his parents presented and feeling emasculated by his own financial woes.

As he initially suspected, his refusal to share his financial crisis with Cerissa was more of the toxic masculinity he'd tried to battle on multiple fronts.

Would he continue to stumble over such mistaken beliefs one at a time? Maybe he needed to be proactive and take a closer look at everything toxic masculinity encompassed. Perhaps he was overdue for some time with Father Matt.

Because his father was wrong. Money didn't define him.

Love did.

He raised Cerissa's fingers to his lips. "Thank you. You're right. It is time I show you my finances. Together, we may find a solution I could not find working alone."

The adoration in her eyes warmed his soul.

"And I should apologize too," she said. "The earthquake stirred up more feelings than I was willing to face. I kept trying to fix everything, rescue you, even when my vision of a fix wasn't yours. I'm sorry."

It was a difficult balance—sharing their problems without forcing a solution on the other person. "We both need to work on communicating."

Which brought him to the other thing he needed to confess—he'd withheld the blackmail video from her. But why? The answer whispered through his mind.

Shame.

He felt ashamed. It was his fault they'd made love in the owner's tasting room. He'd failed to protect her.

Madre de Dios, he'd fallen victim to the sin of pride. He didn't want her to think less of him for his failure.

But now, he'd put his trust in Cerissa and take the risk. "I'm sorry to say I also concealed another problem. Though it has been solved, you should know about it. I should've told you from the start, I think, but I told myself at the time that I was protecting you."

She sighed. "Tell me."

"The night of our engagement party, an ex-employee hid a camera in the owner's tasting room." He explained the blackmail scheme, and how Tig and Jayden helped catch Bruce.

She sat there, looking stunned. "How bad is the video?"

"Very. He caught us making love, as well as the bite."

Her eyes opened wide. "On no, did I morph that night? I can't recall if I morphed to kitty to sleep—"

He stroked her jaw. "No. You didn't. You stayed human the entire time."

Her feelings were difficult to resolve through the crystal. A mixture of embarrassment, relief, and…something he'd never experienced from her before.

"*Cariña*, are you all right?" He wrapped her in his arms and pulled her as close as they could get across the Viper's center console. "Please tell me. Your feelings are…confusing."

She leaned away, breaking the hug. "I feel"—she cocked her head and ran her hands over her arms—"I don't know, violated?"

"I'm sorry."

"It's not your fault." She glanced at her lap. "Does Father Matt know?"

"I have not seen him for confession since the earthquake, so no, he doesn't."

She raised her eyes to meet his. "Do you mind if I tell him? I may want to process this with someone, and Ari would just laugh."

"Perhaps Ari's sister, the therapist who helped Karen, could help you?"

If that was satisfactory with Cerissa, he'd prefer it. The fewer people on the Hill who knew about the blackmail scheme, the better.

"Fidelia. Maybe." She breathed out a sigh and turned to look out the windshield at the night sky. "I'm relieved my cover wasn't blown, but the video, the bite—"

"I understand." He knew the rage and the helplessness it inspired. "It will not change the feeling, but I want you to know that the blackmailer's memory was wiped, and we have the original video and the copy. He claimed there were no other copies out there, but it is difficult to be entirely certain."

He watched her stare at the stars through the windshield.

She abruptly swung her gaze back to him. "I wish you'd told me, Henry. There was no need for you to go through this alone. Next time, let me help you carry the burden, okay?"

With any luck, there wouldn't be a next time. But if there was, he'd not hide it from her. "Of course, *mi amor*."

She was quiet for a moment. "Is there anything else?"

"No, thankfully." He laughed. "No—well, perhaps there is. I may be showing symptoms of what some call 'fang fever'—similar to what mortals call baby fever, but in this case, the desire to reproduce by turning someone vampire. Normally, it would be my mate—"

"But that's not possible, even if the Hill's laws allowed it."

"Precisely. The symptoms will pass with time. But if I seem a little more…overprotective, or solicitous, or—"

"Controlling?"

He huffed out a breath and wagged a finger at her. "Do not take advantage of my good nature by calling me that."

"Fine. I will try to be patient if I see any *strange* symptoms appear. But you—you have to tell me when you recognize you're doing something that might be related to your reproductive drive."

"I promise." He looked down at the center console. There was one thing that might help. "Making love to your vampire form did seem to calm the desire for a few nights."

She smiled, her eyes shining brighter, her expression light. "When it's your night to choose, I'm more than willing to oblige."

"Thank you, *mi amor*."

"*Da nada*." She squeezed his hand. "Anything else?"

He thought for a moment. "No."

"Good." She reached into the backseat storage compartment and pulled out a bag.

"What's in there?" he asked.

"You'll see," she said with a catlike grin. "We still need to celebrate tonight's win—two wins, really, now that you've recovered the video."

They got out of the car and hiked to the place with the stone bench. She set the bag down, took out a blanket, and spread it on the ground, followed by a bottle of wine. Two glasses appeared as well.

"Allow me," Henry offered, using the corkscrew to open the bottle. He poured her a full glass, but only an inch for himself, and took a quick sip to clear the taste of clone blood from his mouth, then took another look at the bottle. "One of our reserve wines, I see."

"I figured I was worth it after today's success."

"On that I must agree."

"After this one bottle, I'll go back to drinking one of our less expensive wines—after all, we need to economize."

As she sipped her wine, he stared into her beautiful emerald eyes, which shone with the moonlight. How had he gotten so fortunate to find her? Her patience, her understanding, her love—he was one lucky vampire.

CHAPTER 77

THE KEY

RANCHO BAUTISTA DEL MURCIÉLAGO—THE NEXT NIGHT

Henry pulled a guest chair from against the wall and placed it in front of his home office desk. With a sweep of his hand, he offered the chair to Cerissa. Then he set the laptop, with windows already open to his various investments and balance statements, in front of her.

Not the most romantic way to spend a Friday night.

Last night, when they'd arrived home from Look Out Point, Cerissa's fatigue caught up with her. She was too tired to go over his finances and instead caught up on her sleep. He'd spent hours cuddled next to her as she softly snored, which he found quite endearing.

Tonight, after negotiating with MWC's team for five hours, he wanted to spend time with her, even if all they did was review his finances. She agreed, although it was after midnight—they usually used the hours after midnight to relax together, and money issues were rarely relaxing.

"I'm going to explain my holdings and answer any questions you have." He then took the seat behind the desk, so he had the same information on the screen to his right. "If you have questions I can't answer, I'll put you in touch with my accountant and my financial advisor."

"I don't think that will be necessary."

"You should meet them. Get to know them, particularly my accountant. Once married, we'll have to deal with tax returns."

"But if he or she is *Henry's* accountant, how will he deal with *Enrique's* finances without revealing what you are?"

"He's the husband of one of our community members. He's in on the ruse. It makes it much easier for him to do tax planning surrounding the transition."

She laughed. "That's good to know. On another night, I can walk you through mine. The Lux aren't into acquisition, but I'm not poor, either."

He suspected as much from his visit to the Enclave. "And, with your permission, I want to tell the mayor and Tig that you will no longer work for free. When there is a need for your professional services—DNA testing, creating encapsulated blood, whatever it is—the town will have to pay you at the going rate for your time and supplies."

"Henry, that's not necessary, I'm happy to have Biologics Research Lab absorb it—"

"No. The town pays Ari for his services. It isn't right that they expect you to work for free, just because we are mated."

She sat back in her chair. "I see your point. But let me approach Tig. I'd rather do it myself than have you do it for me."

"Understood. And I do have some encouraging news. I was able to sell some of my stock investments without a loss. That will free up much-needed cash."

The day after the earthquake, once he knew he needed greater liquidity, he'd placed the sell limit order at a price he could live with and waited the nail-biting two weeks. Today, the trade executed.

"But the stock market tanked the day after the earthquake—"

He gave a nod. "I sold on the dead cat bounce."

"You what?"

"While we've been in a bear market, and the decline got steeper due to the earthquake, there was a momentary upward surge—a bounce in prices—and my trade executed then."

"But 'dead cat'? What does a dead cat have to do with it?"

"Even a dead cat will bounce if it falls far enough and fast enough."

"Henry, that's terrible."

"*Cariña*, I'm not making fun of you. It's a term used in investing."

"Seriously?"

"Truly." He sighed. Cerissa was extremely intelligent, and knew a lot about science, but so very little about investing. Could he influence her to take an interest? It would be fun, something they could do together.

"Was the cash from the sale enough for the winery expenses?" she asked.

"Although the deductible for the policy is large, I now have enough to cover my share. And the insurance company hasn't gone bankrupt yet. They agreed to cover our losses—we've received a check for their part subject to final audit. We start repairs this week, and then I'll be able to finish mixing and bottling the remaining half of our Cabernet."

"That is good news."

"I also told Anne-Louise that her house would have to be put on hold."

"Oh my. How did she take it?"

"Not well. But I promised to visit her in December." Once the trial was over, he'd called Anne-Louise and tried to make amends. His peace offering included the December visit.

"Can I go? I love New York at Christmastime. The decorations, the ice skating at Rockefeller Center—ooh, we could have so much fun at night."

"Let's not get ahead of ourselves."

"We can do it on the cheap. Leopold would give us an apartment to use, I'm sure. And if we take your plane, two is the same expense to travel as one."

He wasn't sure he wanted her spending more time with Anne-Louise. But he also had a hard time telling her no. "We will see."

"Wonderful."

Her eyes lit up when she was happy. He loved seeing that light in them again.

"And I have some good news, too," she continued. "My family will cover the wedding expenses. I spoke with my mother, and while she isn't in favor of me getting married so young—"

He raised an eyebrow. Cerissa was over two hundred and thirty years old.

She shrugged. "*Amma* thought I should wait another century at least. Despite that, she agreed to fund the wedding."

Although tradition called for the bride's family to pay for the wedding, his throat tightened at the idea. He had planned on giving her a lavish wedding, one fit for *his* bride.

But no. He had to stop equating money with being a man. He had to learn to think in a different currency. He had to start measuring his worth differently.

"Thank you, *cariña*," he said as graciously as he could. "Even so, what would you say to a small wedding here? We could pick an early moonrise night, and then hold it outdoors thirty minutes after dusk. The ceremony could overlook the vineyard, with the orange and pink glow of sunset in the background."

"That sounds lovely!"

He took her hand across the desk, the three diamonds in her ring reminding him of the family they'd have someday. Even if the winds of fortune changed in the next one hundred years, and they didn't have every material luxury then, he'd make sure Cerissa and her children would be surrounded by love. Because that was what really counted.

Chapter 78

Scotch and Sorrows

Mordida Water Company office—The next afternoon

Jackson sat alone behind his large hardwood desk, waiting for the MWC board to finish deciding his fate. After last night's settlement discussion with SEWC, which felt like being gutted with a dull blade, he'd met all day Saturday with the board to review the proposal.

Then they'd kicked him out of the closed session so they could discuss his employment.

Of all the ungrateful things they could do. Didn't they understand the sacrifices he'd made to protect them?

When Dick Peters walked into his office carrying two envelopes, he knew it was over.

"Are those what I think they are?" Jackson asked.

Dick didn't answer. He strode over to the sidebar and poured two generous glasses of scotch. Returning to the desk, Dick placed the tumbler in front of Jackson and laid the envelope next to the glass.

Jackson ignored the envelope, picked up the whiskey, and shot it down. Once the alcohol's heat subsided, he asked, "What did those losers have to say for themselves?"

"About what you'd expect. They blame you for the bad press, and me for not stopping you. When they heard about what you ordered me to do with the shades—exposing Bautista to sunlight—they became worried that he'd sue the MWC for personal damages, infliction of emotional distress, yada, yada, yada. They're offering him ten thousand to settle his personal injury claim."

"Sniveling assholes."

"You can't blame them, Jackson. We played our hand and lost. They're bringing in interim agency counsel—one of the big firms that represents public entities and has a spotless reputation. They are cleaning house."

Jackson had heard enough. He got up and grabbed the bottle of scotch, returning to his executive chair to pour another tall one. If they were going to fire him, he'd get drunk on their dime.

Dick reached over to the bottle and refreshed his glass too. "What I can't figure out is why you substituted the forged page. It's such a stupid provision to take a chance on. Of all the things you could have changed, why something as unimportant as an arbitration clause?"

Jackson took another big swallow. "You really want to know the answer?"

"Yeah."

"Bautista was such a prick when he was a twenty-something. You know how he wound up in Sierra Escondida? He inherited his uncle's house and winery. I had to work my way through college, starve myself eating mac and cheese out of a box three times a week while getting my master's degree in public administration, and for what? To get told I could suck eggs by a fucking entitled prick who was younger than me."

"Go on. I'm sure there's more to the story."

"You bet there is." Jackson poured another shot and downed it. "So he comes in all swagger and bullshit and wet behind the ears, and insists on that one-sided deal. Yeah, we got some of their water. But the price we paid? The escalator clause? He insisted on a formula that guaranteed SEWC a higher payout when water got scarce, which it was sure to do."

Dick frowned. "So why didn't you forge *that* section? You know, go big or go home?"

"Because I was sure they'd catch it if I did. Besides, I was playing the long game. I knew at some point we'd have to sue them to keep the water coming. And when I did, I wanted MWC to be in front of a Mordida jury. A jury that got their water from MWC and would pay a higher bill if Bautista prevailed."

"You're not making any sense. When dealing with another public entity, arbitration is a fair option. Sure, when a big company insists the consumers of their product arbitrate any disputes, well, that consumer has little ability to influence the situation." Dick waved his half-full glass in the air. "I mean, arbitrators make their living by being hired to arbitrate, and since the big company will hire twenty arbitrators a year, well, that will have more impact—even if it's unconscious—on how the arbitrator decides the case. The arbitrator knows who hires them and which side the bread is buttered. The little guy loses. But when it's two big guys like us? The playing field is pretty level, then."

"That's what you think?"

"That's what I know. I've tried hundreds of matters before arbitrators. They see through the bullshit."

"But that's my point. I didn't want a fair professional. I wanted a jury who'd see it our way because of the impact the case would have on their pocketbooks."

"Are you serious?"

"I am. And I wanted to stick it to that young prick, too." Jackson polished off his glass. Yeah, he was feeling the alcohol but couldn't care less. "Bautista kept insisting on the nighttime arbitration clause. I figured he'd never check to see if I substituted the page, and I was right. By the time we had to use it, he'd be long gone, and no one would know the difference. The only thing I hadn't counted on was him staying on the SEWC board as long as he has."

"That wasn't the only thing you miscalculated."

"What does that mean?"

"Open the envelope."

Jackson grabbed his letter opener and sliced the top. He unfolded the document. A simple notice of employment termination. No buyout incentive, no severance. Behind it, a release. If he signed the release, agreeing not to challenge the termination, and agreeing to cooperate in the event Bautista didn't take the settlement and sued, Jackson would be able to keep his pension.

Otherwise, the board would prosecute him for his part in the fraud, and he'd be lucky not to serve jail time—plus a felony conviction would mean he'd forfeit his pension.

He tossed the paperwork back on the desk. "Assholes."

"They want you to clean out your office now. I've been instructed to give you an hour to pack your personal belongings, and then escort you out. It's my last official duty."

"Fuck you."

"You already did that." Dick looked at his wristwatch. "Start packing. Your hour begins now."

Chapter 79
A Surprising Offer

Rancho Bautista del Murciélago—Later that night

"Please come in, Marcus," Henry said, when he answered the door. "You brought the settlement agreement?"

"Yes. We just need your approval."

Henry walked Marcus to the drawing room. "We can talk in here."

Cerissa bounded down the stairs and joined them. "Can I get you anything, Marcus?"

"No, I'm fine, thank you for offering."

"You don't mind if I have some wine while we talk?"

"Not at all."

"Let me get that for you." Henry retrieved an open bottle from the small refrigerator hidden in a cabinet underneath the small, polished granite-topped bar. The last of the bottle they opened on Look Out Point. He smiled at the memory. They'd sat on the blanket, cuddling, watching the stars come out and enjoying their time together, talking and decompressing.

He poured and handed her the glass. She thanked him with a smile.

Marcus sat on the rustic leather couch and took the blue-backed drafts from his briefcase. "There really is not much to talk about. Christine wrote an excellent settlement agreement. It puts into effect all the deal points we agreed to."

Henry pulled over the two heavy armchairs, one for him and one for Cerissa, and then read the papers that Marcus handed him. Once everyone got realistic about the situation, the bottom line was easier to reach.

Mordida already recycled sewer water, using it for landscape irrigation. But to install special recycled water pipes throughout Sierra Escondida for irrigation was cost prohibitive.

And using it to replace fresh water didn't appeal to consumers, even when faced with extreme water shortages. The engineers had suggested the phrase "from toilet to tap," but it was roundly voted down as a public relations nightmare.

Henry had asked for Cerissa's help with reading the water quality reports for Mordida's recycled water. She explained to him that the process they used for recycling produced clean water, except for microscopic particles of some pharmaceuticals—like birth control hormones. The molecules of those were so tiny that they even survived the most stringent purifying methods. Still, the amounts were so small, the risk was low.

That said, Mother Nature had a solution for them on both scores. A much less expensive capital investment would be made to pipe the recycled water to the spreading grounds that fed Sierra Escondida's underground aquifer. Percolating through the dirt and rocks to reach the aquifer would add an additional purification step and further dilute the residual pharmaceuticals. The project would cost MWC around eighty million dollars.

Additionally, SEWC would invest in inflatable rubber dams along the creek running through the Hill. The creek, a dry riverbed during summer, only filled with water when the winter storms hit. Inflating the dams would hold the stormwater in place, keep it from flowing out to the ocean, and give the usually raging water time to stand still and seep through to the aquifer below, at an estimated cost of twenty-five million dollars.

The SEWC board members collectively choked when they heard the number, but a multi-pronged approach was required to solve the problem. If they jumped on it fast enough, they'd likely qualify for partial funding through a recent federal infrastructure bill.

In exchange for the recycled water recharging the aquifer, SEWC would continue to sell a reduced amount of fresh water from the aquifer to Mordida Water Company, while leaving enough for watering the vineyards if everyone on the Hill switched to drip irrigation.

A bond would be sold by MWC to pay for the recycled water pumps and piping—a bond that SEWC would buy and forgive the annual payment for each year a specified quantity of recycled water was delivered to the spreading ground. The aquifer levels would be monitored to ensure the recycled water was sufficiently recharging their reserve.

Of course, ornamental landscaping in Mordida, which had relied on recycled water, would likely be left to die or converted to drought tolerant. Large swaths of grass would be things of the past. Golf courses and parks would suffer—or have to convert to a low-water alternative. Of all the water uses, landscaping and grass were the least favored.

Everyone gave something. Everyone got something. It was the best they could do under the circumstances. The destruction of the levees meant water throughout California would be at a premium for many years to come.

"The document looks fine. Thank you for bringing it by."

"We will wait to sign, and only after MWC does. I've learned my lesson." Marcus stood. "I want to get these back to Christine. She'll take them over tomorrow, during the day, and stay with the originals until they're executed."

"That is a very good idea."

Marcus put the agreement in his briefcase and latched it closed. "Oh, there is one other thing. Christine approached me again after we met with MWC. She wanted to know if we'd come to any conclusions."

"Conclusions?" Cerissa asked before Henry could reply. "About what?"

"Her request. She still wants to become a vampire."

Cerissa had been taking sip of her wine and coughed, choking out, "Are you serious?"

Henry patted her back. He'd forgotten to tell her that bit of news. It had escaped his mind entirely with everything else they'd been going through.

Marcus sat back down again and leaned forward. "Yes, I'm serious. And so is she. She's going to be sixty in two months. She's starting to feel her impending mortality."

"But she has never been a vampire's mate. How can she even begin to understand what it's like?" Cerissa asked.

"She's talked to a lot of us. She's met the SEWC board, which means she knows most of the powerful vampires on the Hill—at least, in terms of the current political structure. She's served as a city attorney before, so she's current on the law—I spent two hours grilling her. Her answers were not much different from the advice I've given the council in the past.

And she's had a couple of long talks with Father Matt. Believe it or not, he thinks she's a good candidate."

Henry agreed. She did seem a good candidate. Maybe this was the solution Marcus had been seeking. And his friend had already assured him it wasn't about permanently leaving the Hill, but simply about having someone to tag-team with for all the responsibility he carried. "And you support this?"

Marcus nodded. "We could use another good lawyer on the Hill. Nicholas and I are working too hard. I need a break—the idea is to enjoy life, isn't it?"

"Indeed."

"So, if the council were to ask my opinion, yes, I support it," Marcus said. "We can spare one of the open slots to add a critical skill set. I know it may upset some of the Hill mortals…"

"True, but the subcommittee has already discussed the proposal to hold three slots open for such skills, particularly if we can find a compatible doctor. And Nicholas expressed your desire to find a backup town attorney."

"Precisely. Which is why I'm prepared to find her a sponsor."

"A sponsor?" Henry repeated.

"Yes. I'm still too young to turn her, and I'd like to work with her, bring her into my law practice. It wouldn't work well if she were my child."

Henry nodded. "So what patsy were you thinking of getting to turn her?"

Marcus tugged at his mustache. "Ah, well, I wouldn't use that word for it, as I was hoping you might do the honors."

"Me?"

Him?

Without warning, his fangs deployed. It was clear what his body wanted.

But Cerissa…

"Yes, you," Marcus continued. You're old enough now—two hundred years a vampire, and stable. You would probably do a good job of socializing her."

"I—"

"Think about it, Henry," Marcus said. "You have no interest in her as a paramour, so it actually makes you a good candidate. And you did a good job raising Rolf."

"I would not put it that way." Rolf would certainly take offense at Marcus's appraisal of their relationship. "I may have mentored him in business, but I was not his maker."

"No, you were more of a foster father. But that doesn't matter. You'll do a good job with Christine."

Cerissa started laughing. Through the crystal, Henry felt joy from her, but also, oddly, relief. The latter was curious, but he opted to tackle her humor first.

"And just what is so funny?" Henry asked.

"This is perfect. You like being bossy. Just wait until you have a child—you'll see how far that attitude gets you. Oh, this is going to be so much fun." She laughed again.

"I am not *bossy.*"

"Call it what you like—but you do like to give directions. And Christine is more headstrong than I am. This is going to be great fun to watch."

"It'd be a good kind of challenge," Marcus added.

"Yes, well, I would have to talk it over with Cerissa," Henry said, knowing he was intentionally stalling.

Marcus's lips twitched and curled into a grin. "She seems in favor of it."

"We will discuss this if the town council approves Christine's petition."

"Very good." Marcus picked up his briefcase. "I'll call as soon as there is any news on that front. Until then, think about it."

Chapter 80
Self-Determination

FATHER MATT'S OFFICE—LATER THAT EVENING

With all the research Cerissa had performed, she hadn't discovered an answer to Seaton's problem, short of genetic surgery. And that was no easy avenue. It'd mean developing an edited virus—or injectable nanobot, something the Lux were on the verge of perfecting—that would modify the genetic code of every cell in his body and flip the switch in his morphing strand to create fang canals and modify the gland to produce the serum.

She had no way to test the process and was concerned about creating a bigger problem. She explained to both Seaton and Matt how a virus could be used to do genetic surgery. Of course, she simplified the explanation, keeping it in line with mortal technology to minimize their questions—questions that could lead to exposure of her Lux origins. She'd taken enough risks with Christine. She needed to think of the ramifications before leaping to help.

"So given the difficulties, genetic editing is on the back burner." Opening her medical bag, she took out a jar. "Instead, I wanted to test a different theory."

"Nuh uh." Seaton backed up on the couch, getting as far away from her as he could. "I'm not your guinea pig."

Cerissa stayed where she was, the jar of clear yellow liquid in one hand, an eye dropper in the other. Her theory was to give him a drop of fang serum and see whether that stirred something for him.

Father Matt frowned. "Seaton, Dr. Patel is just trying to help."

"But I told you already. I don't want her kind of help."

Cerissa sat back and glanced to Father Matt. Seaton had expressed this in their last interaction, but when Matt called her again, she thought perhaps the young vampire had changed his mind in one of his sessions with Matt.

"Why?" Matt asked.

Seaton scratched his head, running his fingers through his red hair. "I know I'm not like you, and I don't want to be."

Cerissa considered his response. Perhaps they were approaching this the wrong way. "Father Matt, may I ask a question?"

"Certainly."

"Seaton, just to confirm once more: before becoming vampire, you experienced sexual attraction toward women, but since becoming a vampire, you've had absolutely no sexual feelings, correct?"

"I told you this already. Yeah, I liked women before. It's how I ended up with Jane." He shrugged. "Now, there's nothing. And I don't care. Why do I have to keep saying it?"

Cerissa carefully phrased her next words. "Yes, well, the key here is whether you see the lack of sex in your life as a problem."

"I don't. It's not a problem for me. I'm not missing anything. Call me what you want—asexual or whatever—but I don't want a mortal pet at all."

Father Matt cleared his throat. "Seaton, we will respect your sexual orientation, but I must ask that you talk about mortals with respect."

"Yeah, yeah. Whatever. I don't want a mortal *lover*. Is that better?"

"Yes, thank you."

Cerissa returned the fang serum container to her medical kit. Dosing him with fang serum wasn't the solution.

With Father Matt's encouragement, she'd continued to search for a medical solution. In their desperation to socialize Seaton—and save him from the council's threat to destroy him if he didn't improve—they'd plowed ahead, ignoring Seaton's feelings. They knew sex was one sure way that vampires bonded with mortals.

But pushing him in that direction would stop now. If he was comfortable with his sexuality, she had no business trying to change it.

And surely sex wasn't the only way to get him to connect better with mortals, to respect them. She'd leave that to the trained psychologist. The Protectors would understand—she couldn't force treatment on Seaton, and she'd keep an eye on the situation, make sure the community was upholding their obligation to protect humans from Seaton's appetite.

"Matt, I don't think there is anything more medically to discuss at this point. I think it's up to you and Seaton to work through the other issues."

Seaton crossed his arms. "I don't have any issues. I can't see why you people don't leave me alone."

"You don't have any respect for mortals, Seaton. That's an issue," Father Matt replied. "You also don't contribute to the community, and everyone who is a part of our community contributes. We need to find something you like doing that contributes."

"Whatever. Fine." Seaton threw his hands in the air. "But we don't need her here for that."

True. And if she was honest with herself, Cerissa felt a little relieved at spending less time with Seaton. Somehow, he knew she was different. While no one else had picked up on his comments—and likely wouldn't, given his feelings toward mortals—she didn't want to be the focus of his attention.

Moreover, she had to honor his wishes. "Of course. I was just leaving."

"I'll be right back," Matt said to Seaton before escorting her outside. He closed the door behind them. "Thank you for trying. I should have listened more carefully to what he was saying."

"I never told you what he said in our last interaction when you left the room. It was similar, but I thought he'd changed his mind—that his words were in reaction to the moment. It seems that he may be on the ace spectrum now, and we will respect that."

"Thank you for understanding. I'm glad I didn't have to deal with Dr. Clarke over these issues."

"I know he can be heavy-handed." Then an idea occurred to her. "You know, Henry mentioned that the mortal rights subcommittee discussed key positions the Hill needed to fill, and that Haley put Seaton forward for the computer programmer position."

Matt seemed to consider the idea. "Do you think Seaton has the aptitude for that?"

"He loves playing video games." She knew that from her time staying at Gaea's house. "He may want to design one."

Matt raised an eyebrow. "If he can get his attitude about mortals under control, he could go to night school to learn. Our local community college is pretty good."

"That's what Gaea said as well, from my understanding." She paused.

"How do you plan on doing that—changing his attitude so he can be trusted around mortals?"

"I've been working on a treatment plan while you were doing your medical research, a combination of cognitive behavioral therapy and social skills training. I don't know whether he'll ever be able to develop empathy toward them. Part of the training will be to make sure he understands the system of rewards on the Hill for those who acclimate to our way of life—and the punishment, if he hurts a mortal."

"I hope it works."

In reality, she'd do more than hope. She planned on talking further with her Lux superiors about Seaton's problem. They couldn't risk him going off like a time bomb on mortals. Still, Matt's plan was a good one. And if the Lux thought of anything that might help, something short of gene surgery and the risks attendant to that, she'd pass it on to Matt.

She started to say goodbye, then realized there was one suggestion she could make now that would allow the Lux to keep an eye on Seaton as well as potentially help him.

"You may have heard that my cousin Ari is dating Gaea. If Seaton shows an interest in learning about computer programming, he can talk to Ari about what the work entails, and since he's hanging out at Gaea's house…"

"Ari is in a perfect position to answer those questions." Matt nodded. "But please don't say anything to Ari yet. I want to work with Seaton some more before broaching the idea. I'll contact you if I need anything further. I better get back in there. He'll be defensive, knowing we've been out here talking about him."

"Understood. Call me anytime. Good night."

Cerissa sighed as she strolled back to her car. Night-blooming jasmine lined the sidewalk and perfumed the cool night air. She inhaled a deep, relaxing breath of the sweet scent.

With Seaton's problem off her plate, when she got home she'd work on the replies for Shayna. Guilt over ignoring the stack of correspondence had been bothering her. Now she had time to take care of that important task and let the vampires who'd written know that Shayna needed more time.

But before Cerissa picked up that task, there was one thing she needed to do for herself. Her own anxiety had been masked by the frenzy of helping everyone else, and now, with Henry's revelations, she had even more to process.

She took out her phone and made an appointment with Fidelia. Taking that step made her feel better than she had since the night of the earthquake.

Chapter 81

An Unexpected Request

Rancho Bautista del Murciélago—The next evening

Another sleep, and Henry woke on Sunday at dusk. He raised an eyebrow when Cerissa greeted him in the kitchen with a mug of dark wine already heated and a coy smile. He kissed her before accepting the offering.

Despite the eagerness in her eyes, she didn't say anything until he was halfway through his drink.

"Henry, may I see the video?"

He swallowed hard. "Cerissa, I do not think that is a good idea."

"Why not? You've seen it."

Would she feel worse after seeing it? They'd talked about her feelings of betrayal, of being exposed. He could not come up with a good reason to say no that wouldn't insult her—she knew her own mind, and if she wanted to see the video fully aware that it might resurrect those feelings, he had to trust her choice.

"All right. After I am done, we will go upstairs and watch it together." His phone vibrated. A text message had arrived from Marcus, asking to meet at nine. "Ah, and Marcus will be coming by later. He has paperwork for me to sign."

"That's okay," she said. "I just want to see the video. It's early; we have time."

"If you insist."

She never ceased to surprise him. That was the last thing he thought she'd want to do, given how shy she'd been when they first became lovers. "Let me check my email, and I will meet you in the media room in twenty minutes."

When he entered with the laptop, she was lounging back on the couch and sipping from a glass of red wine. One of their less pricey Cabernets, from the scent wafting his way. Tig had returned the flash drive to him after she wiped Tyler's memory. With both Bruce and Tyler taken care of, the case was closed.

Henry connected the laptop to the large television and started the video from the beginning. Cerissa sat there, intensely watching the two of them on-screen.

What was she thinking? The crystal gave him no sense of her emotions—she must have blocked it using her phone app—and he didn't have any hint until his on-screen self presented the necklace to her and she squeezed his hand, her lips curling happily.

The video continued with them in bed, and he squirmed, feeling uncomfortable watching the video with her.

But she didn't blush once.

Strange.

Her reaction—or lack of one, really—struck him as unexpected.

When it was over, she asked, "May I have a copy?"

He blinked in surprise. He thought she would want it destroyed. "Why do you want a copy?"

"Are you kidding? I would love to have a video of us. And it's from our engagement celebration—a beautiful keepsake of that night. I'll hide it in my room at the Enclave, where it'll be safe." She cocked her head and gave a little smirk. "And, well, I never get to see that side of you when we are making love. You look good from behind."

He started laughing. He had worked so hard to keep this from her, and now she wanted a copy.

Women. He would never understand them.

"What's so funny?" she asked.

He laughed until tears ran from the corners of his eyes. "I do not know if I can explain it. Suffice it to say, that was the last request I expected you to make."

"But I like looking at you."

"You can have the real thing any time you want. Why would you want the video?"

"Why do people keep pictures of their loved ones on the wall? To look at when they aren't around? I don't know, I just want it."

"Then it is yours, *cariña*," he said, kissing her hand.

"Have I told you tonight that I love you?"

"Not yet."

"Well, I do." She cocked an eyebrow at him. "And I'd love to show you how much, if you're interested?"

He felt his eyes widen. Had watching the video excited her?

She set her glass of wine on the end table and started unbuttoning his shirt. When she reached the last button, she rested her hand on the bulge in his pants. "And I do believe your interest is showing, too."

"When I watch a beautiful woman make love to me, I cannot help my reaction."

"Good looking and smart," Cerissa said, not able to resist teasing him. "Who would have thought?"

She lifted her phone from the end table where she'd left it and punched the app that allowed the crystal in his wrist to communicate with her.

Following her lead, he unfastened the tungsten bracelet he wore, the one that he used to mute their exchange, and laid it on the end table.

His emotions hit her strongly, and she sat there for a moment, her fingers poised to unzip his pants, letting the reconnection flow through her, caressing every fiber of her being with his love. She welcomed the feelings and spun out hers: the deep love she held in her heart and the excitement of anticipation. She wanted him between her legs, now.

He closed his eyes and moaned. "*Gracias a Dios*."

She muted the television but started the video running again, then pulled him to his feet, slid her hands inside his pants, and deftly lowered his Dockers and silk boxers to his knees. His interest was immediately apparent, poking out from the hem of his shirt.

She dropped to her knees, angled his hips so she faced him and could still see the television screen, and took him into her mouth.

He stroked her hair, resting his hands gently on her head as she moved. "That feels good."

She could tell. The powerful surge from the crystal's connection made it feel like his erection was between her legs, instead of her lips. She gently smoothed back his foreskin and ran her tongue along the underside of his shaft.

To her left, she could see the TV silently playing the video of them making love. Seeing his naked butt on-screen sent another sizzle through her.

Henry gripped her hair as he guided her faster. The moans coming from him told her that he was very close.

She had no fear that bringing him this quick would end the tryst, and tightened her lips, sucking him hard, taking him deep into her throat. The little jerk his erection made told her what was imminent, and he came in a magnificent explosion of ecstasy that washed through their bond, and she rode it with him to the end, her eyes focused on the video as he bit her on-screen.

The combination about sent her over the edge, her sheath clenching, clutching at air, wanting to be filled by him.

When he was fully spent, she released him. She rose to her feet and picked up the glass of wine, taking a sip before moving into his arms and kissing him. After a very long kiss, she started the video again from the point they'd begun making love and dimmed the ceiling lights. Taking the throw blanket from the back of the couch, she spread it on the floor and suggested, "Why don't we lie down?"

He kicked off his shoes and stepped out of his pants. She'd been in such a hurry that his ankles were still hobbled by them.

He swept her into his arms and onto the blanket. "It does appear that you are wearing too much for what I have in mind."

She smirked at him. This was her turn, and no way was she letting him take over.

But he was right about one thing: the clothing had to go.

She let him unfasten the single button at the back of her neck and slipped her blouse off over her head. He took his time undressing her the rest of the way, slanting his mouth over hers while he unfastened her bra, and then stripped off her jeans.

The video's light flickered on their skin, and she caught glimpses of him making love to her on-screen. She was so wet that her thong was plastered against her skin, riding up between her legs. When he broke from the kiss, he had to use his finger to hook around the soaked scrap of fabric to pull it away from her skin before rolling the waistband the rest of the way down her thighs.

Normally, he'd think nothing of popping the elastic and tearing them off her. But if they were being economical, his restraint made sense.

He propped himself on an elbow, looking at her like he wanted to eat her—in more ways than one. But his erection had yet to recover.

"Roll onto your back," she said with a little push. Well, maybe more than just a push.

Her fingertips brushed his shaft, and instantly, he was hard again. The pupils of his eyes expanded, wiping out his irises. "What did you just do?" he asked incredulously.

"A little of my aura strategically directed." She threw a leg over his hard abs and rose to straddle him. "You just lie back and enjoy."

Satisfaction at being able to surprise him warmed her. By experimenting when in his form, she'd learned how his body reacted to her aura.

"You are so beautiful," he said, lifting her breasts and tweaking her nipples. The sensations he created rushed directly to her core.

His gorgeous eyes had returned to their bourbon-brown color, and his erection pressed against her inner thigh.

She leaned forward and captured his lips, diving in, licking his fangs, which had already descended. Catching a drop of fang serum with her tongue, she shivered as the stimulant coursed through her, and then he did the same.

"I have missed this so much," he said. "Feeling what you feel."

"Me too." She kissed his cheek, and then planted a series of little kisses on his neck. Pressing her hips down, she took his erection inside and paused, basking in the fullness of him, the pressure filling her up, and then pumped up and down. Their shared emotions, entwined by the crystal, magnified the excitement.

As her release grew closer, she offered him her wrist, and he bit, his fangs gently piercing her. When he came, he cried out in pleasure, his mouth crimson with her blood, echoing what she saw on the video.

His orgasm pushed her over the edge. She couldn't tell the difference between them as they merged into one sexual peak together.

Afterward, they lay together on the blanket, her head on his shoulder, their legs intertwined, his arms firmly wrapped around her.

"*Mi amor*," he finally said. "Usually, I want no secrets between us. But in this case, I do not want to know how you knew your aura would prepare me so quickly."

Was he afraid she'd discussed their sex life with Ari? Or that she'd learned the technique with another man? Neither were true.

She had always been the shy one. But she could feel he was a little uncomfortable talking about it, so she let it go. It felt good knowing that he had his bashful moments as well. She had learned so much about his physical being by becoming him and experimenting.

"I'm just glad I can make you happy." She snuggled up against him.

He rolled onto his side and looked into her eyes. "You make me happy just by being you."

Chapter 82

Cigars

Rancho Bautista del Murciélago—Thirty minutes later

The doorbell rang. Henry released Cerissa with a kiss and dressed at vampire speed. "That must be Marcus."

"Damn." She picked up her jeans and blouse just as fast and morphed her hair into order. "Is it already nine o'clock?"

"I'm afraid so, *mi amor*."

"I have to stop in my room for clean underwear. I'll join you in a moment."

He ran downstairs to the front door. Five minutes later, all of them were in the drawing room, and Marcus had piled a stack of papers with blue backs on the coffee table. "MWC caved. They accepted our written proposal without any amendments. I have the settlement agreements for your signature."

Henry took out his fountain pen, unscrewed the cap, and, using the coffee table, initialed each page before adding his distinctive signature.

Hmm. He'd have to change it when he started signing as Enrique Vasquez.

But then he noticed the signatures for MWC.

"What happened to Jackson Aldridge? Why didn't he sign?"

"The MWC board fired both him and Dick Peters. Dick's performance in the courtroom was an embarrassment to them. Speaking of which, they are offering you ten thousand dollars to release all claims based on Dick's opening the blinds."

Marcus held out a check.

Henry stared at the amount. It was a drop in the bucket considering the personal pain and suffering that Jackson had caused him. He waved it off, declining to accept the pittance. "Tell them no."

"Do you want me to tell them anything else?"

"If they want a full release, tell them one hundred thousand."

Yes, it felt fitting for MWC to compensate him. If they paid that sum, he'd save the money until he'd rebuilt his cash reserve. Then he and Cerissa could spend it together on something for themselves—perhaps their honeymoon. And, if all went well, it would give him a cushion to pay for the other celebrations leading up to their wedding—even if he couldn't make them as lavish as he wanted.

Marcus laughed. "I'll tell them two hundred thousand and settle for one. All I have to do is threaten to subpoena Judge Aslan to testify. That will have them quaking in their boots."

Once all the copies of the settlement agreement were signed, Marcus shuffled them into a neat stack. "One other thing. Nicholas spoke with Haley, and Haley reached out to Gaea. If you're in agreement, the council will approve my request to turn Christine based on the subcommittee's recommendation."

That was quick. "And you still want me to turn her?"

"As I said before, you're the best choice."

True, the desire to make a child had been growing in him. He wanted to mentor someone again. He could help Christine grow into being a strong and independent vampire.

He'd discussed it with Cerissa last night, and she was in favor of it. She'd been a little worried over the use of her touchstone, concerned Christine might suspect something, and thought having Christine under his control would ameliorate the risk.

Cerissa even wanted to be present for the turn. She wanted to witness it as part of her study of his kind, not out of jealousy. He smiled to himself. Ever the scientist, his mate.

"I certainly don't want the mayor to do it," Marcus added.

Henry laughed. "Neither of us wants that."

He took Cerissa's hand, and she nodded her encouragement, bolstering his confidence.

"In that case, we agree." Henry couldn't stop the giant grin that spread across his face.

"Shall I break out the cigars?" Cerissa asked with an enthusiastic smile in her voice. "We're going to be parents."

A Note from Jenna

Thank you for reading *Dark Wine at Disaster*. I hope you enjoyed it!

Cerissa and Henry's journey continues, along with the adventures of Tig and Jayden and all their friends, in book 7 of the Hill Vampire series, *Dark Wine at the Grave*.

Here's a quick tease:

> Henry never thought he'd turn someone vampire. Especially someone who wasn't his mate.
>
> But when everything goes wrong, it puts Cerissa in Tig's crosshairs.
>
> Henry is desperate to protect his mate. Because if he doesn't, Cerissa might have to leave the Hill—and Henry—forever.

Grave is a stand-alone mystery and continues the ongoing romances of the couples you've come to love. Pre-order now, and *Grave* will be delivered to your Kindle on April 19, 2022. As of this writing, Amazon doesn't make print versions available for pre-order. The print version should be released April 19, 2022, along with the ebook.

Want to be among the first to receive updates about *Grave*'s release, along with special announcements, exclusive excerpts, and other free fun stuff? Join Jenna Barwin's VIP Readers at jennabarwin.com and receive Jenna Barwin's Newsletter.

Hate newsletters? Then follow me on BookBub to receive a notice when *Grave* is released.

Happy reading!
Jenna Barwin

P.S. To an author, reviews are better than dark wine!

Acknowledgements and Dedications

To my husband Eric—thank you for all you do. I couldn't write as much as I do without you. Love you!

To Sharon Bonin Pratt for your generous assistance with Jewish traditions. Thank you so much for your insights that helped me craft Shayna. Any mistake in interpreting those traditions is my own.

To Ellen Keigh and Ophelia Bell—thank you for your gentle suggestions and encouragement. Always appreciated!

To all the public works engineers in California who are doing their best to protect the Sacramento-San Joaquin Delta and our water supply—thank you for your hard work.

To my editing team—it takes a team to polish a story and ready it for readers. Katrina, Trenda, and Arran—you are all fantastic! You push me to make the story better, and I sincerely appreciate it. Any errors in grammar, clarity, or plot are mine, not theirs. Their full names are:

- Katrina Diaz-Arnold, Refine Editing, LLC
- Trenda K. Lundin, It's Your Story Content Editing
- Arran McNicol, Editing 720

And thank you to my cover designer, Christian Bentulan with Covers by Christian, who took my rough draft ideas and picked a winner. As always, he did an outstanding job on the cover design.

There are many other wonderful people who have helped me improve my writing, and also advised me on tackling the business of being a writer. The generosity of other writers, who have freely shared their expertise, is greatly appreciated. Thank you everyone, for your support and guidance!

Printed in Great Britain
by Amazon